MW00654103

This is a work of fiction. Names, characters, places, and incidents either are the product of the author's imagination or are used fictitiously. Any resemblances to actual persons, living or dead, events, or locations is entirely coincidental.



Library of Congress Cataloging-in-Publication Data
Name: Beishline, Nicholas, author.
Title: No Evidence But Himself / Nicholas Beishline.
Location: Boalsburg, Pennsylvania.

Identifiers: Library of Congress Control Number: 2022907261 | ISBN 978-0-578-35326-5 (paperback) | ISBN 978-0-578-35327-2 (ebook)

First edition

# Dedication

This book would not have been possible without the help of my wife, who sacrificed countless afternoons for me to sit alone in a room and write. Thanks for listening to me complain about the process and for never letting me quit, Liz.

For my son, Cormac. Always be who you are.

I also have to thank my parents and my brother, who were my earliest champions and always reminded me that I was born to write. I know the stories and poems weren't all gold, but you made me feel like they were.

Thanks also to Adriene, who offered quite a bit of wisdom about interior book design.

Finally, to all of the people who encouraged me along the way, and to everyone who reads this book and finds something meaningful in it: thank you.

# A Note About The Text

This book contains depictions of mental illness, trauma, and suicidal thoughts. If you or someone you know is struggling with these issues, please reach out to the National Suicide Prevention Lifeline at suicidepreventionlifeline.org or 800-273-8255.

# No Evidence But Himself

A novel

By Nicholas Beishline

# I

*"'If it is your intention,' said the magistrate, 'to confess the crime with which you stand charged, you may, upon producing sufficient evidence, criminate whom you please.'*

*'Evidence!—I have no evidence but myself,' said the woman."*

—from Joseph Sheridan Le Fanu, *A Chapter in the History of the Tyrone Family*

*"All my life I've dangled over everybody else's malice Everything explodes in my head; only you can make things better"*

—from War Dogma, "Intentional Entrapment"

*From the journals of Leonard Kellison:*

Sept. 22

We discussed bullying and violence in schools today in sociology class, and the teacher called on me to give the class a fresh viewpoint to go off of. Figures. I think she had good intentions, but really?

I wasn't quite sure what she wanted to hear but I went out on a limb anyway. It quickly sprouted into a recollection of the past few years, which have been increasingly depressing for me. One girl sided with me so fiercely that she broke down in tears. Another approached me outside of class and told me how much respect she has for me, that I'm strong and she knows people "like me" and that we're the sweetest clique in the school. I don't know whether to be insulted or soothed by this.

I was deeply touched by this display of unexpected caring, but things culminated anyway during the next period, English. I left soc and spent the next twenty minutes locked in a bathroom stall, on the cold floor, silently crying my eyes out and praying to God to make everything stop so this wouldn't go on any longer.

2

You people are destroying me. I have no escape anymore. It's because of all of you out there that I was crying in the bathroom stall and that I'm sitting here in the school library rather than in history where I belong.

If I were truly strong, would I really be sitting alone at night, crying and hoping I might get a chance to somehow validate myself? I need a break.

# Chapter One

Leonard sat back and watched dispassionately as the little man paced behind his desk and ran a hand across his prematurely balding head. He could no longer count the number of afternoons he'd spent in the cramped office, sitting in the same thin-cushioned chair he was now certain was not meant to be comfortable in any way. MR. MANFRED, PRINCIPAL, read the small brass plaque perched along the front edge of the little man's desk. Leonard scoffed inwardly for what he suspected must by then have been dozens of times, unwilling to play the principal's game.

"Tell me again what happened in the halls this afternoon, Mr. Kellison," the older man demanded, and Leonard had to smirk at that self-important tone of voice. He glanced behind Manfred's desk to his own vague reflection in the window there: a tall boy of sixteen, lanky, a thin trace of eyeliner still visible under his eyes even now, at the end of another long day.

"I already told you," he pointed out, picking at what remained of the black nail polish on his fingers. He leaned forward a bit in his chair, necklaces clinking together as he did so, creating a series of small chimes that seemed inappropriately cheerful in the close air of the office.

He took a deep breath, let it out. "*He* attacked *me*. He dared me to hit him and I said no; he called me…queer, and when I looked away, he just launched himself at me. I hit him once, and he dropped."

Manfred removed his glasses and pinched the bridge of his nose, the way he always did when he was pissed off. "He gave me quite a different story, Leonard."

"I'm sorry." The words sound anything but apologetic, he knew, but he was tired of playing these cat-and-mouse games. Manfred asked; Leonard dodged. Manfred asked again and again, and eventually Leonard, resistance worn down, gave in and answered. The final bell was due to ring in less than a minute, and he refused to be late to the bus because some authority figure with an ongoing crisis of ego had suddenly decided to exercise his right to make him so.

When the bell did ring, a series of short, sharp tones, neither figure moved. Leonard wondered if Manfred was trying to be patient, maybe trying to wait him out, and indeed, the man was taking his time. He adjusted his tie, played with his watch, and slicked back his thinning hair, all the while keeping one eye on the boy to see whether he would cave.

He didn't.

At last, he waved Leonard away. "Get out of my office, please," he sighed, "and don't ever let me see you in here again." He paused, then repeated, "Please." Leonard wondered briefly if that meant he could get away with just going home the next time he was sent down to the office (which he was sure he eventually would be), but he decided not to push his luck, which was normally tenuous at best anyway.

Anyway, that was the way things normally went. Other people could get away with a lot more than him, because he was *different*. He was scary. He was the boy who emulated The Crow every Halloween, powdering his face white and smudging kohl around his eyes and on his lips. He was the boy who owned only black clothing, who wore band shirts every day and sporadically painted his fingernails and shaved his eyebrows. He was a junior in high school, nearly seventeen now, but he felt he was regarded as nothing more than a troubled child.

The trek back to Leonard's locker seemed impossibly long. Despite his teenage angst/rebellion front, he felt every labored step of it, unable to stop his shoulders from hunching in anticipation of the inevitable taunts and one-liners every five feet, little jeers like “hey homo” or “look out, here comes Satan.” Just last week, a boy had actually crossed himself as Leonard passed him. The little shit had actually crossed himself. Was it odd that he almost felt a twisted sense of power, of influence, for this? For being recognized for his audacity?

*It doesn’t matter*, he decided. It was the weekend now, and all he wanted to do was crawl into bed and sleep for days.

The sun was trying to peek out when he stepped outside, a vain attempt to melt the unseasonably early snow that had recently fallen, and he slipped on his black sunglasses without really thinking about it. He pulled his long coat tighter around himself, noting with distaste as he did so that he needed to fix some of the buttons again.

A short kid, probably a freshman, came tearing down the sidewalk, and when Leonard turned in surprise he caught sight of Glenn and Jez. Glenn was wearing torn jeans and an old band shirt, as usual; Jez was wearing a plain back T-shirt under his bomber jacket. His neon camo pants were startlingly bright, even through the shades, and despite his rough afternoon, Leonard shouted to them, smiling, and raised a hand in greeting. Jez nudged Glenn, waved back, and pantomimed sending a text message.

Leonard nodded, waved again, and climbed the steps onto the waiting bus. Glenn and Jez were odd, no way around that, but they’d always been a source of support and friendship for Leonard, and it lent him some comfort to see them and remember that not everybody was just waiting for him to come to school with heavy weaponry one day. They, more than anyone else, understood that the only person Leonard would ever pose a danger to was himself.

The bus began its slow movements as Leonard dug his phone out of his pocket, only to have it nearly knocked to the floor a moment later by a quickly melting snowball launched from somewhere behind him. It was followed by a shout of "Take that, Dracula!"

Threads of nervous laughter issued from the students around Leonard as he turned in his seat, located the assailant, and gave him a deliberate middle finger. "This phone probably cost more than your bail money, asshole," he said loudly, and the other boy, a much larger, bulkier student with cold eyes, stood angrily and took a step forward.

"What are you going to do, *faggot*?" Unlike Leonard's own response, the larger student's aggression was clearly unwavering and self-assured, and Leonard felt himself shrinking back a bit despite his bravado.

But before Leonard could respond, a heavyset girl in a loose blue blouse intercepted the confrontation and planted her feet firmly in the aisle. "You're not going to fight, Leonard," she said sternly. "And you won't, either, Louis. Both of you just sit the hell down and let it go."

Louis looked past her and raised his fist. "What are you going to do, freak?" he demanded. "Let *her* take charge?" He cut his eyes to the girl, as if to challenge her, too, but if she felt any intimidation, she didn't let it show. His insinuation—that a woman being in charge was somehow shameful—did not bother her.

Just then, the bus slowed to a stop; it was time for Leonard to leave. "Wouldn't you like to find out?" he retorted, and with a long glance at the girl who had interfered, he exited the bus and headed for his house.

Nobody was home when Leonard arrived, which suited him just fine. He grabbed a can of soda from the small refrigerator in the garage and ascended the stairs to his room. Somewhere along the line he had taken to counting the stairs as he mounted them; there were seventeen, and the third and fourteenth steps always creaked under his weight.

In his bedroom he dropped his bag on the floor behind the door and sprawled out on his bed, flipping on the small electric heater against the wall and turning on the black light as he passed them. He chose a song from his laptop and closed his eyes, finally releasing some of the stress that the day had brought. From the corner of his consciousness the music seeped into his thoughts, and he tried to let the Nightshade Illusions song take him out of himself. The urgent bass line of "Roadmap Wrists" brought him back to himself, however, and he couldn't help but replay the confrontation in the halls earlier that day.

"*I am the detour of all lost scars,*" the singer crooned. "*Phantoms of sages wander my heart.*"

Leonard said nothing throughout the song. Normally he took pride in his deep voice and would sing along to any song playing on his laptop, but he felt no joy from the idea today. As the next track started, he cast his mind back to the events that had led him here, to this dark room and this particular frame of mind.

He hadn't always been this way ("this way," that was how he'd overheard his teachers and peers refer to it, a polite euphemism for their confusion and unease). A quick flip through his journals would confirm this, although that same flip would also illustrate what had changed. (Or, he thought now, moodily, what had changed *him*.) His parents divorced when he was six, and his mother was granted sole custody. His father accepted weekend visitation for a while but had steadily lost enthusiasm for the visits, eventually disappearing altogether for several years. Upon returning, he would demand to see Leonard with no warning whatsoever. Leonard would refuse, reminding him that the court order was outdated and he had no reason or desire to go with the man, and once, his father had left with an angry promise: *I'll be back.*

Nobody paid it any mind at the time, but within the hour his father returned with three police cars and a particularly poignant threat: come along, or your mother could face legal trouble. The threat was meant to imply that his mother might be arrested, and the thought terrified him and filled him with preemptive guilt. Driven out of his own house by strangers in uniform and taken out of state by his father, Leonard had spent that entire weekend crying, hiding behind the locked doors of the bedroom and bathroom. That sense of helplessness had followed him throughout the years, sometimes giving him the sense that he was shadowboxing in a darkened room: assailants just out of reach, waiting to close in the moment he let his guard down.

"I'm just trying to give you the chance I didn't have," his father would say. "I want you to have a father. Mine was never around for me." Leonard wondered if it ran in the family, and if he would turn into a man unwilling to accept his responsibilities as well.

And so the saga continued. Middle school assailed him with an onslaught of new trials and emotions. Perhaps it was a subconscious retaliation towards his absent father, as his guidance counselor had suggested; it may also have simply been a case of adolescent hormones gone awry. No matter the origin of his anger and depression, Leonard entered high school with a collection of several earrings and, briefly, a lip ring, and his music collection of blues and psychedelia had expanded to include heavy metal and hard rock acts, everything from older Marilyn Manson albums to Swedish and Norwegian black metal to hybrids of styles that defied easy categorization.

During his freshman year he'd discovered nail polish and eyeliner. His mother tolerated the former but the latter had to be smuggled out and applied at school, only to be taken off before anyone came home from work in the evening. He'd begun growing his hair out, and sometimes when he ran his hand through its length he remembered how he'd let his friends convince him to shave the sides and back at one point. His private reaction to the look the first time he'd seen it in the mirror had been unexpected: head half shaved, looking like a prison inmate, he had felt a sense of recognition, even at fourteen, as if here at last was a representation of how he felt every day. It felt like bad luck to look the part of the inmate, even if he felt that way most days in school, and he'd let it grow back out shortly afterwards. No reason to tempt fate.

His mother had remarried after being single for two years, and his stepfather, Roland, was an overweight, short-tempered bear of a man with a strong taste for control and the drink. He seemed to associate one with the other.

When Leonard first met Roland, Roland had said, "This is your son? He's going to grow up to be queer. Look at him; he's all puny." His mother was too meek to intervene, already too used to having somebody else dictate her life. Leonard's eventual interest in makeup and androgynous men would cause the big man to say "I told you so" out of nowhere, a drunken allusion to his first words to the boy. Roland may have been the patriarch of the family in name and deed, but Leonard had long ago decided not to adopt his mother's new married surname.

All of this led to Leonard's regular visits to a certified psychologist's office, and his subsequent prescription for antidepressants had at least led to a more stable kind of depression, rather than a low baseline with frequent dips into suicidal behavior. It was harrowing, but less harrowing than the unpredictable mood swings he'd long endured.

The song ended, and Leonard found himself gazing with detached interest at the fishnets tacked to the ceiling of his room. It had started as an act of genuine friendship in his sophomore year, back when his friends had first noticed the angry red welts along his wrists and inner arms. Concerned that an overreaching teacher might report the injuries to the school nurse, who would in turn be obligated to make a report to the principal, Jez had torn the fishnets from his own arms and forced Leonard to wear them for the rest of the day. Since then, Leonard had begun collecting his friends' worn-out fishnets, connecting them into a vast, multi-colored blanket of sorts. He hung them with the private resolution that when they covered his entire ceiling, he would disappear. It would be his sign that he had done enough, suffered enough in the circumstances of this particular life, and that it was finally time to start a new life somewhere else. He had contacts online; he could disappear to Boston, or Seattle, or St. Louis.

He now reached listlessly for the fishnets on his ceiling, unable to reach them from his supine position on the bed but satisfied by the proximity anyway. It grounded him, helped to keep the sadness at bay, especially on days like this: Friday night, no plans, limited options. Nothing too exciting really existed in such a shithole town.

*When I get away*, he thought distantly to himself, *I'm going to find something better than life; I'm not going to stop until I've found the meaning of* my *life.* It was a familiar refrain, and one that comforted him.

He closed his eyes and sighed. His playlist, set to random, skipped ahead to The Cure, and to Robert Smith's crooning voice he drifted off to a restless sleep.

*From the journals of Leonard Kellison:*

<u>Sept. 24:</u>

"My Lunar Veil"

My heart can break, my heart can ache,
My heart repeats its same mistakes.
My hopes can fall, my hopes can stall,
My hopes are murdered overall.
I'm burning down; my broken crown
Lies buried in this frozen ground.
If love is blind, why can't I find
The will to leave it all behind?

"Untitled"

I bleed the sky like it's my vein
Erase the world like I am God
Avoid the fact that I'm insane
Escape the shame that makes me crawl

# Chapter Two

Leonard was awakened by a sharp pain in his ribs.

"Get up."

He slowly recognized the pain to be from Roland's boot. The man stood over him, prodding him with one foot as if he were loathe to touch him with his bare hand. "Your mother says it's time for dinner."

"Good for her," Leonard mumbled, but he rolled out of the way of another hard nudge anyway.

"Get this gothic shit out of your room, too," the burly man added. "I didn't fight for this country so my wife's dumbass kid could dress like a girl and grow his hair long and keep his room looking like a morgue." He paused. "But eat your dinner first so I don't get bitched out. If I do, you're next in line. Remember that, boy."

"Yes *sir*." His stepfather didn't move. "Get out of here so I can get changed first!" he shouted. "I'm going out afterwards."

Roland scoffed. "Yeah? Where?"

Leonard looked away. "Anywhere."

The night was cool against his face, and light snowflakes blew down the streets and danced where they crossed under the dim streetlights. It wasn't sticking, but it was a bleak reminder that colder months were coming. Leonard pulled his trench coat more tightly around his body and pulled the hood of his Cradle of Filth sweatshirt down over his ears. Joy Division blasted through his headphones, and he found himself humming along to "Day of the Lords."

Most of the stores were closed at such a late hour; the streets were all but empty. The dollar store on the corner of Maple and Heather was open 24/7, but Leonard and his friends usually avoided it because it was boring in there and it always smelled like rotten eggs.

Instead, Leonard pulled open the door to Lino's Pizzeria, stamping his feet on the floor and unbuttoning his coat once he was out of the chilly night air. The place was far from warm, but it was a marked improvement from the unpleasant night outside. He pulled a cigarette from a pack with his lips without really thinking about it, then put it back when he saw the cashier's warning look. He had to stare at the stained tiled floor for several moments while his eyes adjusted to the fluorescent lights of the place.

"Hey, Leonard—get the hell over here!" a deep voice shouted from a booth in the back. Still blinking, he wandered down through the place and found Jez and Glenn sprawled out across the cheap plastic bench seats of the last booth. They were balancing sugar packets in an apparent contest to see who could build the taller tower.

"Oh hey. This is Susan," Jez said in his distant way, stretching the syllables until they all but lost their meaning. He wasn't slow; he just never felt the urge to hurry to whatever point he was trying to make. His mode of speech had always been one of his most defining characteristics.

For the first time, Leonard saw the slim girl sitting next to Jez, leaning against the wall. Waves of her long, straight hair, which was dyed a deep blue, fell haphazardly across her shoulders and down her back. Her eyes were painted to match. Her lips were a deep scarlet, her nails long and perfectly tapered. They were the same raven black as Leonard's hair. She wore vinyl pants, shiny black shoes, and a blue baby-doll tee that said PUNK in metal studs. She looked young, deprived of the curves many other high school girls had already acquired, but she looked comfortable in her own skin, not like she worried that she might be lacking something that other girls had.

No: not *comfortable*, Leonard amended silently.

*Unconcerned.*

Leonard stopped himself from studying her too closely. It felt invasive. She was probably fifteen, like Jez and Glenn, but she looked like a young fifteen. Despite her bold look, she somehow appeared to be less jaded than he considered the two boys to be.

"Hey," he ventured, a beat too late to sound natural. "I'm Leonard."

Soft blue eyes flickered across his face, then back down to her half-empty glass of soda. "Hey," she said quietly. Her voice had a slightly fuzzy cigarette smoke quality to it that seemed oddly personal, as if she and Leonard were the only two patrons in the pizzeria. It reminded him of the more crooning Tom Waits songs.

An awkward silence ensued. "Can I sit?" Leonard finally asked.

Glenn shrugged, slid down the bench a little. "I thought you'd never ask, big boy."

Glenn was a head taller than Jez but still shorter than Leonard. He sported a shaved head that served to enhance his rosy-cheeked, cherubic appearance, but Glenn was anything but innocent. Jez was the shortest of them all, and he kept his head shaved, too, except for his bangs. They hung in his eyes and shined purplish-black under the hazy fluorescent lights.

Glenn tapped his feet to an unheard rhythm. "Now that you're here, we should figure out what's next for the band. Any ideas?" he asked. His sugar tower toppled when his knee hit the underside of the table; Jez's wobbled, but stood firm. Leonard thought he could detect a faint trace of marijuana on someone's clothes.

"What about it?" Jez shrugged. "We kinda suck."

"Yeah, but we could get better," Leonard volunteered. "All we need is about…five grand for better equipment, a singer who can sing—"

"You *can* sing," Jez interrupted.

"Yeah, whatever. The point is, we almost kind of rock now."

Jez shook his head. "Practice is tomorrow, don't forget. Let's work on that new song you wrote the other day." He smirked. "You talented motherfucker."

The band was Glenn's, for all intents and purposes. The equipment was in his basement, and he refused to bring his drum set anywhere else to rehearse, probably due more to laziness than concern for his set. The agreed-upon name had simply been Trash for a while, but the trio had eventually dropped it in favor of War Dogma. It was Jez's suggestion, and it had stuck. Glenn drummed, Jez played guitar, and Leonard played the bass and provided lead vocals.

The girl in the PUNK shirt—Susan—lifted her eyes and for the first time they settled squarely on Leonard's face. "I've heard your demo," she said in that ashen voice. "You have a pretty beautiful voice."

Very few things left Leonard fumbling for a reply, but those two statements effectively cleared his head of any responses. Somewhat stupidly, he found himself wondering whether she had meant his voice was pretty *and* beautiful, or "pretty beautiful" as one phrase. He cleared his throat and replied, "Thanks. I'm glad you like us."

Jez smirked. He often seemed like he was barely aware of what was going on, but he was observant. "What are you listening to?" he inquired suddenly, reaching for Leonard's headphones as he spoke. Leonard realized his music was still playing.

"Joy Division."

The shorter boy started to bang his head violently up and down while moving his hands across an invisible guitar. "'Day of the Lords,' right? I mean, it's one of their only songs that I know."

"That's actually what was on when I walked in," Leonard said, marveling—and not for the first time—at how in sync he and his friends seemed to be.

"Yeah, well." Jez shrugged. "It's one of, like, three songs of theirs I actually know. I'm not *actually* psychic."

Their conversation was cut short when a server approached them and asked for their order. "Let's do the usual," Leonard suggested. The rest of the group nodded; Susan merely shrugged with a *whatever-you-want* expression on her face. She seemed only minimally concerned with what was going on at their table. Jez started muttering the lyrics to another song under his breath and tapped Susan's glass with his fork while Leonard ordered.

Glenn gave Leonard some of Susan's background over the sausage-and-pepper pizza; she clearly wasn't going to offer any information herself, but neither was she interested in preventing Glenn from doing it for her. She'd briefly dated one of Glenn's friends the year before and had kept in touch with Glenn after the breakup. She was into The Cure (and more importantly, War Dogma), some form of witchcraft or spiritualism—Glenn wasn't sure—and any literature she could get her hands on. Most of her time, at least according to her (for here she felt compelled to chime in), was spent avoiding the depressing, small-town experience she called Life, although she conceded Jez's point that, at least musically, post-Zappa anything was bound to be unfulfilling. Glenn just mumbled something about Dylan and offered the group his pack of cigarettes as they stood to leave.

"Got my own," Jez proclaimed. "I only like menthol anyway, and—no, Leonard, you can't have any! No! You'll kill your voice by smoking, dumbass." He mimed squirting a spray bottle at Leonard, as if he were a misbehaving cat.

"That's the plan," Leonard replied, pulling one out from his own pack. "It would only improve things. Where are we going?"

"Let's go back to your place," Jez said. "Where'd you park? 'Cause we walked here, and hey, snow."

"Right down the street, but we have to be quiet, dude. Roland was already drinking when I left."

It wasn't hard to sneak the group past Roland, who was passed out on the couch with a beer cupped loosely in his hand. "Look at good ol' Rolaids over there," Jez whispered as they passed him, and the rest of the group had to stifle nervous laughter. Other than Susan, who was new to Leonard's house, they had all witnessed Roland's angry outbursts more than once.

Maybe it was only the addition of Susan to the group, or maybe it was the late hour (Leonard noticed as he checked his phone for messages that it was already nearly one in the morning), but nobody seemed to have much to say. They lounged in his room—on his bed, on the floor—in comfortable silence.

"Where'd you get the nets?" Susan asked at one point.

"On the ceiling? From here and there…mostly from my friends when they got too many holes in them to wear anymore."

Jez was already sleeping on the carpet at the foot of the queen-sized bed; Glenn stepped around him to slip out of the window and onto the roof to smoke. Stabbing Westward played quietly from the far corner of the room, and Leonard skipped ahead to the next song before sitting on the bed to brush the knots out of his hair.

"So, what do you like to do?" he asked Susan now. He glanced at her where she lay, oriented sideways across the bed, apparently still staring at the fishnets on the ceiling.

"Do? I don't know. Read, mostly. Try to design clothes. I don't have much of a life."

"Yeah, join the club. Making clothes, though—that's unique." Another silence followed.

"You fall into a rhythm the more you do it. Hey, I like your bracelets," she ventured.

"Want to take one?" he asked. She nodded, and he slipped off two of the thin black jelly bracelets and handed them to her. They looked much larger on her wrist when she put them on.

Both jumped when Glenn slipped in through the window. "Cool if we go?" he whispered, motioning to Susan and Jez.

"Yeah man, definitely. Just lock the door again."

"Sure. Jez." He nudged the sleeping form on the floor. "Hey, dildo! Wake up, it's time to go." This time he kicked him, somewhat gently, in the shin.

"Go? Like for breakfast? Hey, can we get bacon? *Canadian* bacon?" He grunted and rolled over.

"No, special child, we're leaving. C'mon, let's go to your house and watch your dad's porn."

Jez sat up at that and looked around. "*Again*? Um…sure, let's go."

Leonard watched through the window until he saw his friends cross the driveway and head off for home. He would have offered to drive them, but he knew better than to ask. They knew him well enough to ask if they didn't feel like walking.

He considered grabbing a smoke break of his own, but ultimately decided against it. He was too tired. He turned off the lights and sat alone in the dark, thinking about the next band practice and mouthing the words to his own songs as he reviewed them.

*From the journals of Leonard Kellison:*

Sept. 25:

"Nitro Sanctuary"

How can something lead to nothing
How can lies be simple bluffing
Why can nothing promise everything?
What's the point of sitting lonely
Thinking life is one chance only
Why do angels point to where you sing?

Never will I bring myself to
Practice lasting gratitude
Just because somebody said they cared
Psychos wander down the alleys
Back from death beyond dark valleys
No one's hiding just because they're scared

Break away from those around you
You don't need them; they've been untrue
Your meds just serve to ease their troubled minds
They think you're a totaled psycho
They're too blind to see you might go
Crazy, sending nitro down their spines

(NOTE—still needs chorus. Work out chords, bring to band practice.)

# Chapter Three

*"I watch the night fall/ I am its only son/ It nurtures me/ It tortures me/ It takes me as I am...Nothing whatsoever/ And nothing to you/ Nightshade on your lips/ Let it be/ It nurtures me/ Let me be/ It tortures me still..."*

The song ended, but Leonard held the final word longer than usual, so long that he felt his throat restrict and his chest lock. Following along, Glenn played around on the high hats until the singer's voice faded away.

Silence. Leonard didn't realize his eyes were closed until he opened them. "That's an older one," he said into the mic. "I just really wanted to use 'nightshade' in a song." He paused. "So, we've got one more song to play." He felt strange, speaking as if to a large crowd when this was a rehearsal and not an actual gig.

Susan, the only witness in the basement tonight, shook her head and stretched out farther across the couch. "Don't worry, you're great!" she called, blowing an exaggerated kiss to the band.

Glenn's basement was a mess, and his friends preferred it that way. Old candy wrappers, condom wrappers, and cigarette packs littered the floor; a few old porn DVDs were stacked against the side of the television, interspersed here and there with some adult videos on VHS that were probably too worn out to play anymore. Evidently, Glenn's mother either never ventured down to the basement or never looked too closely when she did.

Standing lamps with red and blue bulbs cast ugly lights across the instruments and their players, and amps were stacked in two different places, to the left and the right of the drums. Apparently Glenn was on a mission to ruin his hearing by graduation. Insulation and soundproofing were held to the ceiling in uneven folds thanks to Jez's recent frenzy with a nail gun. The entire band had spray-painted crude sayings and band logos on the cement block walls:

*Jez fucks midgets. Glenn is a transvestite. Leonard likes blind chicks. Glenn's sister is easy. Make war not kids. If I had a mind left I'd be wasting it. For a terrible time, call Jez.* The sayings decorated the cement blocks like the ugly tiled walls of the school's bathrooms.

Glenn was in his boxers; Jez stood in his pink stockings. Leonard alone was wearing pants, his favorite old Levi's that had long ago lost most of their color. None of them wore shirts; the heat was cranked up full blast to warm the basement, and the exertion of playing their music had worn them out.

"Here's our last song," Leonard announced. "It's called 'Too Much to Handle.'"

From his place between singer and drummer, Jez loosed a nonsensical scream: *RRAAAAAAAAAAAAGGGHHHHHHHH!* He was prone to such outbursts, though nobody knew whether they were deliberate or merely impulses.

As he sang, Leonard allowed his gaze to linger on Susan's legs, covered in fishnets, and her face, painted with kohl and lipstick. Jez often wore makeup, but he'd always done so ironically; here, Leonard found himself responding to Susan in a way he hadn't responded for a while.

*Not since—*

But he didn't want to remember her name. Not tonight, and not here. He pushed the half-finished thought from his mind as he watched Susan's face under the odd-colored lights in the basement.

Working at the local grocery store was sometimes more than Leonard could take. The customers complained about his jewelry; the employees commented on how quiet he was. The specifics of his job often necessitated distractions from the shelves he stocked, and these random tasks—cleaning a spill, directing a customer to a specific item—were welcome changes to his routine.

He knew that a better job existed for him somewhere down the line, and he was usually confident that he would eventually happen across one of them. It was never the working that bothered him; it was only *where* he worked, and for whom. Besides, it earned him enough money to pay for gas, guitar and bass strings, and the occasional impulse buy, and for that reason alone he showed up for every shift and gritted his teeth to get through the bad days. Plus college was fast approaching, and he knew he would need more money than he could even conceptualize to survive there.

The last hour of his shift was dragging; he usually volunteered to work early mornings so he could finish most of his stocking before too many customers came in, and he'd been up late again with Jez and Glenn the previous night. He found himself yawning helplessly until he caught sight of a slim figure in black jeans and a matching Bauhaus shirt.

*Is that Susan*?

Any uncertainty was washed away when the girl caught his eye and waved to him, pushing through shoppers as she approached him. She rocked back on her heels and examined a package of edamame while she waited for him to speak; she seemed too have lost her confidence once she'd actually reached him.

"What's up?" Leonard asked, and immediately cursed himself for sounding so disinterested.

"Nothing much. Glenn told me you were here, so I decided to pay you a visit."

"That's cool. Work sucks more than usual today."

Another awkward silence, seemingly weighted with things unsaid, passed between them.

"I'm off in forty-five minutes," he added at last. "How long will you be around?"

Susan seemed to think for a minute. She chewed on one black-painted nail; then she shrugged and looked around. "I'll find somewhere to sit up front," she said, and Leonard was struck again by her hazy, oddly detached voice. It reminded him of old actresses and singers, of Marlene Dietrich and Julie London. He briefly pictured her as one of the burlesque performers he'd seen old pictures of online, in black-and-white and sepia, and he felt heat in his cheeks. She smiled. "I wanted to take a walk with you," she admitted.

"It's like thirty degrees out."

"Then make it a drive."

Leonard didn't consider himself a desirable partner by any stretch of the imagination. In fact, he generally couldn't care less about romancing except for the sake of sex. He'd been linked to both genders in the past—occasionally at the same time, if the rumors could be believed—but he felt strongly that affection and attachment were dangerous. It always left someone hurt. Lately, whenever he thought of romance, it was always accompanied by unwelcome flashes: dusky red hair, a white smile, an old Neil Young song about a cinnamon girl. It made him angry and left him upset for hours, so he simply turned away from such thoughts.

None of this, however, prevented the unfamiliar giddiness that filled his limbs as he clocked out of work and led Susan to his old Caravan. When she reached over to slam the door behind her, he found himself gazing at the way her hair fell in her eyes and rippled with each new movement.

"Where are we going?" he asked, checking behind

him and then backing out of his parking spot.

"Just out. Around. I don't have any money anyway."

"Want a pizza or anything?"

"Hmm." She gazed at the parked cars through her passenger window, lost in the contemplative mood Leonard was beginning to expect from her. She crossed her legs and uncrossed them; she pulled down the visor and used the mirror there as a guide to smoothing out her hair, which had caught a few stray snowflakes in the walk to the van.

"If not, it's okay—"

"No. Yes. I'd like a hot chocolate or something, actually."

"Really?" She nodded. "That sounds good, then. Let me just run home on the way and grab another shirt." He detested wearing his work uniform when he wasn't on the clock.

"I doubt your father wants company, so I'll wait in the van."

"Step." She wrinkled her nose, a childish but surprisingly cute gesture, and he chuckled. "He's my stepfather," he reiterated. "I hate to acknowledge even that connection to him, the way he his."

"Oh."

"Anyway, you're probably right about the company thing, but it's not anything to do with you. He's just…how he is."

He handed her the leather binder he kept in his van and asked her to find a good CD to listen to while she waited. She flipped through the pages rapidly before slipping in a Depeche Mode album.

"Be right back," he said as he unbuckled his seatbelt. "Just don't, like, steal the van or anything."

"You know, I just might."

* * *

Roland was waiting for him, already visibly drunk, and when Leonard tried to slip by him he grabbed his arm and threw him against the wall. “Six feet tall and still a pussy,” he sneered, wiping some spilled beer from his shirt.

“Fifty years old and still a bum,” Leonard countered without thinking.

He saw the stars before he realized that he’d been hit again. They erupted somewhere behind his eyes and exploded time and time again.

Both Leonard and Roland shouted as each tried to gain some advantage over the other, and when Roland finally tripped over his own shoes Leonard darted upstairs, grabbed a shirt without looking at it, and checked himself in the mirror. A bruise was already beginning to rise under his left eye, and he could feel a welt growing where the back of his skull had hit the wall.

*Fucking asshole.*

That same old mantra flew through his mind again, summoned by more pain and remorse: *Why me?* He couldn’t think of what he might have done wrong, perhaps even in another life, to deserve the trouble facing him now.

With a groan, he slid through his window, dropped to the lowered deck roof, and then ran full force for the van.

Susan’s breath caught sharply at the sight of Leonard’s wounded face. “What happened?” she demanded.

“That drunk asshole,” he spat angrily, shifting the van into reverse and speeding down the driveway. By the time he had hit the road his stepfather was running down the driveway. Susan’s face showed fear, but something else, as well: recognition. She seemed to be familiar herself with domestic problems, or at least problems that hit close to home. Leonard noted this distractedly and filed it away for examination at some later date, preferably when his head didn't hurt so badly. It was throbbing, and he was sure that his bruise would look horrible tomorrow.

"Where were we going again?" he asked at length. He had to make a conscious effort to detach himself from what had just happened in favor of returning his attention to his present company.

"For hot chocolate." She seemed unwilling to say more, at least for the time being, and Leonard considered thanking her for not bailing altogether, but he remained silent as well.

Susan twisted her many silver rings uneasily around her fingers in the ensuing silence, and Leonard eventually queued up a Coal Chamber album. He sensed the silence between them slowly growing more comfortable, more companionable. The snow had picked up without warning; the road was slick with it and he had to take the turns much more slowly than he would have liked to. He wanted to put as much distance as possible between himself and the angry figure at home. The windshield wipers slid furiously across glass, but more often than not the snow just stuck to them.

Not for the first time, Leonard pondered the angst spread throughout the past several years. He was vaguely aware that he was still in his work uniform, and that the shirt he had grabbed was the first Marilyn Manson shirt he'd ever bought. His first band shirt ever, really. This in turn brought his mind back to the fight he and his mother had had when he'd first worn it. She had cried and tried to get him to take it back, but he had refused. He'd been grounded and when he bought another shirt (this one from The Cure), his mother had opted to use silence as a weapon. It had hurt.

Oftentimes throughout his teen years, Leonard had felt like one of Leonard Cohen's "Bunch of Lonesome Heroes" (and he had always appreciated the first name he shared with the singer), desperate to find someone who could identify with his story but increasingly aware that he would eventually turn to ash and he would be forgotten. Cohen's idea that such a person could turn into gold had always seemed too optimistic to him.

Then there was his old pocketknife, which for quite a while had basically been his only constant friend; later, razor blades had taken its place. It all seemed like a black spiral leading only to more black, and Leonard thought perhaps he had recognized that from the first cut, but it got him through most of the nights and that was really all that mattered when he was cutting. He had recently learned a German phrase in his German language class: *die Qual der Wahl*, meaning that one had the pain of choice. It resonated with him, because here was something he could finally control—not *whether* he would suffer, but *how*. It shouldn't have been comforting, but it was.

Whatever peace he wanted to believe he could find, though, was always out of his reach, somewhere—

"On the right."

He started at the sound of Susan's voice.

The coffee shop stood on the corner of two nameless streets, its presence meekly advertised by the dim neon signs casting their lonely glow against the windows. Its name, *The Better Bean*, was emblazoned on a small sign over the door, difficult to see in the bad weather and poor light. Some nights there was live music, performed on a small stage near the rear exit of the building; today, however, the stage was vacant, and only a few customers sat huddled over their hot chocolates or coffees. The quiet music pumping through the speakers only made the interior seem more drab, like it was a living thing desperate to provide evidence of its worth.

Nobody looked up as Leonard and Susan entered. Everyone seemed eager to keep to themselves today, and for one crazy moment Leonard pictured it as a saloon in one of the old Westerns he'd enjoyed watching with his grandfather as a child. It crossed his mind now that today was the perfect afternoon to be robbed, or maybe even killed. Certainly most people experienced their own private violent thoughts, tucked them safely away in the backs of their minds, permitted to escape only in fantasy or dreams. He wondered, not for the first time, how many murderers or violent offenders he had crossed paths with throughout his life. It was a numbers game; surely he'd walked by at least one without knowing it.

Curiously, though, Leonard felt his spirits lifting again as they chose a table facing the window to watch the snow, lighter now and falling less urgently, as it pirouetted lazily to the ground. Nothing new had happened today, after all; with the exception of this sit-down with Susan, it was basically the same old shit, just on a different day of the week. Nothing could be done to change things right now, so he'd might as well ride it out.

Susan caught his eye and noted the change in his expression. She raised an eyebrow.

"It's nothing," he said. "Or nothing I can explain. I just realized that since my life isn't going anywhere, I should try to make the best of it when I can. How's that for corny?"

"Like now? Are you enjoying life?"

"To an extent, I guess."

"Oh, thanks!" she said with mock offense. "I'm glad I'm such good company."

Leonard rolled his eyes, and he felt a smile begin to grow across his face.

Once their drinks had arrived, Susan asked if he had ever played here, nodding vaguely towards the stage. He grinned.

"They wouldn't like me here."

"Then play something they *would* like."

He pursed his lips. "I don't think so."

She shrugged. "Maybe you'd be surprised." Her phone buzzed, and she checked the message before setting it facedown on the table.

"Nothing urgent, just my dad checking in," she explained. "I should probably get home after this," she said, and Leonard noted the change in her attitude. He filed it away for later consideration, unwilling to add even more to the list of things troubling him that day.

He finished his drink and dropped a few dollar bills into the tip jar on the way out, feeling both chagrined and relieved that their outing had been so short. They left the shop and ventured into the snowy world yet again, and it wasn't until later that he realized she'd never thanked him for the drink.

*From the journals of Leonard Kellison:*

Sept. 27:

"Haiku"

New hardcover book
In it: ninety ways to die
Which have I not tried?

Fuck the dreams away
Why is the sun burning black?
I can't help myself

When you disappeared
Atmosphere collapsed on me
"Ha! Ha!" screams the train

"Holiday Celebration In Finality"

Later, spent, you slept in my arms.
The demons of my depression
Set the tree alight
In a conflagration of hungry emotion.
We felt no pain in this,
My secret celebration.

# Chapter Four

"What are these for?"

Leonard sat up a little from his place on the floor of his room and found Wesley sitting at the desk in the corner of the room. He dangled a cheap pair of handcuffs from his fingers.

Leonard studied his friend for a moment. They had met in elementary school, before social cliques had become so divisive, and their friendship had lasted despite their different paths leading up to high school. Much had been made of their long friendship, the *prep* and the *Goth*, but the simple truth was that they got along well.

His friend's current appearance typified the "prep" look, Leonard knew: short blonde hair gelled up in the front; blue jeans; sports jersey. He looked so *nineties.* Even if they both dressed casually, not really typifying their cliques, their differences were apparent.

"I don't know," he finally answered, looking away. "One of my old girlfriends…" He trailed off, catching the look on Wes's face. Leonard might pretend that he simply didn't want to kiss and tell, but he trusted that Wes knew him well enough to know that it would be painful to relive certain memories—to relive memories of happiness and pleasure so pure that looking back on them felt like looking back on dreams. Similar experiences simply did not exist after that break-up. Somehow, it all paled in comparison. "It's not that weird, you know," he said instead. "Plenty of weird people out there."

Wes laughed, but not judgmentally, Leonard thought. He seemed genuinely amused. "People like you, right?"

"I don't know, I guess so. I was never cuffed. Just her."

Leonard found himself wondering, not for the first time that week or even that day, what *she* was up to. He found that it hurt less to avoid identifying his ex by name. Right on the heels of that thought came another: he shouldn't have kept everything from that relationship. Despite repeated admonishments from his therapist, he had a habit of making himself feel even worse on his bad days by digging through the old notes and artifacts from that relationship. He kept them out of sight otherwise, in a shoebox in the back of his closet.

Wes's words broke into his thoughts, delivered in a dramatic falsetto: "*Ooh*, I've been *bad!* I hope I don't get *arrested* and sent to *bad girlfriend jail*." His impression devolved into giggles, and he tossed the cuffs aside. "I'm sorry, man, it just sounds awkward to do that stuff with a straight face."

"What?" Leonard couldn't formulate a response at first—not until he was able to pull himself out of his thoughts and back into the present. He felt his face burning, though he didn't know why. Wasn't this the stuff of bragging rights? "I don't know…it wasn't like that. It was just fun." The words sounded lame, even to his own ears, but he wasn't willing to get into the details, with Wes or anyone else: how his ex had stolen the cuffs from a store in the mall; how, rather than roleplaying, they'd experimented with blindfolds, feathers and restrained limbs; how smoking beforehand had made it even better. These were experiences he was too protective of to let them out into the world.

"Where'd you find those, anyway?" he asked instead.

"They were peeking out from under the bed. You should hide things better, man."

Leonard grunted in response and made himself busy by organizing his CDs. They were spread out all across his room, most of them in the wrong cases or no cases at all, and he knew that the task was monumental and nothing more than a distraction. Nevertheless, he had to distract himself somehow or Wes would know what he was thinking.

"Anyway, I was just wondering," his friend said softly, but the words rang false and both of them knew it.

"No, it's cool." And he felt that, if he pretended to ignore the possible implications of this conversation, it *would* be cool. Nothing would have to change.

He bent farther over the CDs spread out around him, and he was suddenly glad that his hair was down and the room was dim. Both factors helped to conceal his burning cheeks. That, and the way his body was reacting in his jeans.

"Sorry, man, but I have to ask," Wes ventured, and Leonard braced himself for what he knew was coming. He waited for his friend to finish his sentence, and it was almost a relief when he finally did: "Is it true, what they say at school? Is it only girls with you, or…?" The question hung in the air as Leonard calculated the merit of different responses.

"No. I mean, not exactly."

"What does that mean?"

"It means that I've only been with women. Once, a guy was there, too, but we never touched."

It seemed like the most delicate way to frame that one exception, but it still hurt him to remember it. It hadn't been his idea, but he'd gone along with it to make the relationship last a little longer. At that point, he'd known that it was dead, but he was desperate for anything that might revive it.

Wes took the hint in stride, and Leonard appreciated his tact. "Were you not into it?" he asked gently, and Leonard appreciated this, too.

"I was…not into *him*, specifically." This much, at least, was the direct truth.

"If you *were* into, uh, something like that, who would be your type? Surely not popular guys like *me?"* He laughed, but it sounded forced, and in that moment, Leonard understood that they were sharing the same thoughts and hesitation. For some reason, that made him more nervous.

"I really don't know," he answered, and he winced at how defensive it sounded.

Wes's gaze bit through Leonard's attempt at dissemblance like a bomb through a papier-mâché village. A million thoughts tumbled through Leonard's head at once. He wanted to pursue this; he no longer doubted that. But what would happen from there? Who would find out, and how? Could a secret this big be kept? And, finally, what would it mean for who he was? He knew, knew beyond the shadow of a doubt, that he enjoyed sex with women. So how did this new information factor in? The weight of his questions dizzied him, left him feeling unmoored.

As if on cue, he heard his friend say, "No one will know."

Yes, no; yes, no. The words began to lose meaning in his head. *What do I do?* He felt that it would be wrong, but was it? And according to whose rules? What would it matter if—

"All right," he heard himself say. He wondered if he looked at scared as he felt, or as determined.

Wes slid down to the floor and sat, cross-legged, across from Leonard. The tableau vaguely reminded Leonard of the setup in some teen romcom, but one of the players had been a girl in that movie. It felt like the typical coming-of-age scene where the shy teenagers finally shared their first kiss, and he found it exciting and scary to remember that this was about to be exactly that, but under very different circumstances.

And, finally, he remembered something a playwright had said a long time ago, some rule in drama that if a gun is introduced in the first act, it must be fired by the third. Chekhov, he was sure it was Chekhov. He wondered, wildly, if the same were true of the handcuffs. Was this scene unfolding specifically because Wes had found them under the bed? Did that act as the catalyst for whatever *this* was?

*No*, he decided, and he found comfort in employing the analytical side of his brain. It was familiar, and it gave him some distance from which to evaluate the situation. *No, because the gun would have to be used. And that particular "gun" isn't in play here.*

Neither said anything for a long moment. Leonard didn't know what to do, so he simply sat there, eyeing his friend's form and appreciating what he saw.

Leonard found himself leaning forward a bit.

"So." Wes coughed. Both laughed uneasily.

"So," Leonard echoed. Then something inside of him broke free, and he felt his cheeks relax from their burning. He was suddenly unafraid.

Susan Ingram was nothing.

At least, that was the conviction that her therapist had been trying to break her of for the past year or so. Once in a while Susan would leave her weekly session feeling marginally better about things, almost believing that things would improve and she would find a way out of her depression. That feeling usually lasted about twenty-four hours, and then the doubts would begin to creep in. She would be sitting in class, or listening to music or watching a movie, and then the looming suspicion that she was only happy because she was *missing something* would grow near again. *You're only feeling better because Dr. Campbell listens to you*, that doubt would whisper. *It might make you feel like someone cares, but she can't fix you. You're broken.*

It was a maddening cycle Susan had dubbed the "shame spiral," and once it began, she could never reset herself, find her ballast, without Dr. Campbell's help. The weekly reminders that medication would only address the symptoms, and not the core of the problem, did nothing to motivate her to look within or to practice the coping skills the doctor was always trying to impart to her.

Susan had read somewhere that taking antidepressants could actually increase the risk of suicidal thoughts or behavior, and that seemed endlessly amusing to her. "Feeling sad? Take these and you'll finally feel motivated enough to actually get up and do something *final* about it" was her tagline for such commercials. She'd been better able to get out of bed and function since beginning the medication, sure, but she felt neither cured nor suicidal. She often just felt like she was in a void, like she was nothing.

*Stupid bitch*, she thought now, crouching lower under the huge tree in her back yard and taking the final drag of a cigarette that, like every other one she'd ever smoked, seemed too short for its own good. She found herself wondering why they didn't just make them longer, like the gum they rolled up and sold as one big piece. It would be a much more efficient form of self-destruction.

Susan's yard was moderately large, but not huge the way that some of her parents' friends' yards were, like having big-time wealth didn't count if you didn't flaunt it. Her parents, both religious and extremely conservative, were shocked nearly to death when they realized that their daughter shunned organized religion and spent her time hanging out with the Goth kids, or "deathers," as her mother had called them once.

How many times had her parents confiscated her black makeup? How often had they tried to take away her laptop or her CDs, afraid that her taste in music would invite the devil in? It was wasted effort, she knew, and she suspected that most of their fear about such a risk extended only to herself, since her parents undoubtedly considered themselves too virtuous to be at risk of such unwanted personal attention from the devil. And how many relatives had lectured her and kept at it even after she told them in no uncertain terms (much to their disappointment and aggravation) that she didn't give two shits about their opinion?

Only Matt, her older brother, didn't seem concerned with her outlook or appearance. *People hate other people for no real reason*, he'd told her last year, during a visit home from college. *So you may as well give them a good reason.* Matt wasn't overly religious, either, but he'd always had the good grace to play nice with their parents. Despite his rough-around-the-edges reputation in high school, and now in college (or so he told her, anyway), she'd always felt safer around him than around her parents. She never felt threatened around her parents, exactly, but she trusted Matt more for protection. He acted like a good guy, but he didn't always live up to the label. She knew he could be fiercely protective where his younger siblings were concerned. Sometimes she admired his respect for their elders; other times, she thought it was his weak point. And sometimes, respect and weakness bled together for her, and she would simply give up trying to measure herself against her brother.

Sighing, she brushed a stray leaf off of her long black raincoat and shoveled a few breath mints into her mouth. If her parents complained, she could always tell them that her friends were the smokers; they usually seemed eager to buy into the easy out. Denial was a powerful tool, she supposed.

"Honey?" Susan imagined that her mom's voice, always worried, had the power to send the entire street into a state of relative unease. She pictured dogs cowering, babies waking up crying. *There goes that Ingram girl again*, her neighbors probably commented, *sending her parents straight to the grave. Such a shame. Now, where's that bourbon? I can still feel emotions, and that's not good for my happiness.* Fuckers. Stupid fuckers, all of them.

Her mom called again, and she stood up and shouted back, "What do you want?" She winced immediately; she hadn't meant to sound so short, but her attention was claimed elsewhere. Her mind was heavy with her visit with Leonard to the café, endlessly analyzing his curt response to her suggestion that he play there sometime, returning time again to his smile directly beforehand. She wanted to brood over their conversation, not socialize with her family.

"Honey, it's time for dinner! Come eat."

"I'm coming, I'm coming. I'm not five years old anymore," she mumbled as she passed her mother and stepped into the welcome heat of the house.

"Oh, hush." Her mother tried to brush off the comment, but the pain of that realization was evident in the way the muscles around her eyes tightened into a wince. Susan wondered whether she had actually seen her mother's eyes flit to the framed photograph of Susan as a child, proudly hoisting up her backpack on the first day of school, or if it had just been her imagination. Either way, the truth was undeniable: Susan was no longer a child, and hadn't been for a long time.

"What's for dinner?" Her father, seated in his study, leaned back in his expensive leather chair and peered through the doorway into the living room, where mother and daughter still stood. "It smells delicious."

"Oh, thank you, dear. We're having pork chops tonight."

*My God. We're the fucking Brady Bunch.* But Susan bit her tongue.

Dinner *was* delicious, like always, but there wasn't much to talk about, and Susan was too lost in her thoughts to contribute to the halting conversation. *This silence*, she thought, *shows the cracks in the fantasy of the perfect family.* The thought depressed her even further.

In the background, the television related the story of the conviction of a sex offender. The story was jarringly incongruous against the peaceful dinner they were having. She vaguely remembered the original story, something about a family friend who had grown overly attached to a younger member of the family, and she grew chilled at how harmless some people could seem when they wanted to.

*Sometimes you don't have to look much farther than your own family to see how well some people can play that game, and how easily they can fool people who want to trust them.*

The knowledge stiffened her, and it was suddenly difficult to continue eating. She had more or less blocked all memory of the painful nights, but it still came back in dreams sometimes. It had been short-lived, but she'd been young, far too young to experience such things, or even to attempt to understand them. *Forget age, nobody should have to live through that, you godless, hypocritical, asshole fucking PERVERT! I HATE YOU! Die and rot alone in your own—*

"May I be excused, Mom?" Her own voice felt foreign to her ears.

"Of course, Susan. Are you feeling well? You look a little sick."

*Yeah, sick of hiding this from you.* But again, she said nothing.

She half-ran up the stars and into her bedroom on the second story of the house. There were two additional rooms upstairs, all connected—a small bedroom and a large storage room—and she had it all to herself. Matt had claimed the finished basement as his own long before he'd left for college two years earlier.

None of the familiar possessions lent her any comfort tonight, though. Band posters, concert tickets, piles of CDs—they all littered the three rooms. The large room to the right housed her expensive sound system, which was complemented by speakers around the room that effectively turned her television into a surround-sound experience.

She sat on the bed and brooded, but she did not turn on the TV or any music. Instead, she turned her thoughts to the news story and her reaction to it. According to Dr. Campbell, the underlying issue was compounded by Susan's refusal to address it in any capacity. Several times the doctor had tried to coax Susan into talking about her *violations*, as she called the experiences, but never successfully. Hypnosis had not worked; neither had free association writing or anger therapy. Once, in a particularly embarrassing attempt, the therapist had extended her first two fingers and moved them slowly to the left and right, then up and down and back again. Susan was instructed to follow the fingers as the hand moved and allow the repetition to unlock her mind, unloading it of the trauma stored there. It was no less futile than the other attempts.

Now, overcome with disgust and hatred directed at both herself and her abuser, she was no freer than she had been the day after it had happened. No—days, plural. It had happened three or four times that she could remember, and possibly more than that. She'd gotten good at blocking the memories when they resurfaced.

The real killer was, when she was in the fifth grade, her babysitter's boyfriend had also made advances toward her, although she had successfully kept him at bay. She couldn't even compare the two aggressors; they were equally terrible as people and equally deeply traumatizing as experiences.

She feared she would be sick.

Needing to find some sort of emotional ballast, she scrolled through the music on her phone before settling on Silverchair. The music played through wireless speakers, something from *Neon Ballroom*, and she turned the volume up until she could no longer hear the sounds of her own sobs and curses over the song. She badly wanted to be somebody else; she longed to know that she wasn't the only one who suffered this way. She wanted to disappear.

"Emotion Sickness" played on, and she listened wistfully to Daniel Johns singing about the sickness in his heart.

No matter what, at the end of the day, she was still only Susan Ingram.

*From the journals of Leonard Kellison:*

<u>Sept. 3o:</u>

I've found myself thinking a lot about the past lately. This isn't anything new, I guess, but it's something that's difficult to leave alone when life is still swirling around me. I see traces of my past everywhere, and even though it's overdramatic to say that the past is haunting me, I do think it's accurate.

I see her around school sometimes, and it's scary even though it shouldn't be. We dated and we broke up, and it was ugly but I know these things happen. Still, I can't help but feel sick when I see that dusky red hair. One of the last times we slept together, we both knew we were nearing the end. She'd just dyed her hair that color, and since she was on top I remember thinking as it fell down her shoulders that it was just a little bit darker than the skin around her nipples. (I know it's the areola but that doesn't sound very poetic.) We both refused to admit that things weren't working, but that was the saddest I've ever felt during sex, and it's the saddest I can remember her ever looking, even more than the day we broke up.

The point is, my therapist might be right. I might just associate the sight of her hair with that day and the devastation it signaled. She always says that one day I'll be able to look back fondly, rather than looking back with gut-wrenching emotion. But I can't seem to shut the door to make that happen.

Meanwhile, I still don't know what to think about everything that happened with Wesley. I saw that red hair in school shortly afterwards and immediately thought, *what would she say? Does she even care?* And then I was angry with myself, because I shouldn't fucking care. I wonder when I'll move out of this reaction, and how it will happen, because right now I just want to disappear most of the time. This isn't living.

# Chapter Five

Leonard was restless for the short remainder of the weekend. He couldn't sleep, but he couldn't quite wake up, either. He would have preferred to think of it as some form of heightened consciousness, but he knew that in reality it was probably just a mixture of stale cigarette smoke and the sugar in the Trix yogurt his mother kept buying and stocking in the fridge.

Whatever the reason, Leonard felt drained, like he was a walking zombie running low on batteries. When Sunday night finally came around, he collapsed into bed before nine o'clock, rolled around, and slept straight through until six the next morning, when his mother shook him awake and told him to get his ass to school before he wound up like his father, a good-for-nothing dropout who couldn't even take care of himself.

He wanted to ask if she'd meant to say "stepfather" instead.

He dressed quickly, in the dark, pulling on yesterday's jeans, his well-worn combat boots, and what he assumed to be an old band shirt. Every shirt he owned was black, anyway, so it was a safe bet.

Even dressed, however, he felt stiff and more than a bit scuzzy from having slept for so long the previous night, so he spent a little extra time in the bathroom, lingering on the act of brushing his teeth and brushing his hair for longer than usual. He decided to leave it down for once. He checked his nails; they were beginning to look like they needed to be repainted, but that could wait. (After a vicious battle of words where he worked, Leonard had been permitted to wear nail polish as long as the color wasn't dark. He currently wore a subdued teal color.)

Breakfast was the same as always: two waffles from the freezer, a glass of milk, a sip of orange juice, and his medication. It felt like too many pills sometimes, antidepressants and antianxieties and, for a while, even an antipsychotic. Once he had tried downing all of the pills at once with a shaken, stale can of root beer—courtesy of Jez, of course—and his stomach had felt like a fireworks show all afternoon.

"You're wearing that shirt to school?" his mother asked, sitting at the table with her usual morning cigarette and toast.

He didn't bother looking down; this was their usual song and dance. "I guess so. Let me have a drag."

"You shouldn't smoke," she said sharply, but she handed him the cigarette anyway.

He inhaled, released the smoke, and smirked. "I don't." He shrugged on his coat and grabbed his bag. The coat felt good to him, familiar and warm, even after being out in the cold for so many days while he was waiting for the bus. Once, months ago, he'd had an embarrassing dream that he was a vampire, gliding down the halls at school, his arms outstretched and his mouth open, fangs gleaming, and to Hell with the fact that school was held during daylight hours. He'd worn the coat in that dream. He'd never shared the dream with anyone, not wanting to be a vampire fanboy cliché, but it had felt good.

"Be a good boy in school!" his mom called after him as he headed for the door. That was her way, insulting in one breath and caring in the next. "And for God's sake, don't get in trouble for your clothes again."

Students who drove to school had to pay for either daily passes or an expensive monthly pass, so he trudged through the snow to the bottom of his driveway, where the bus picked him up. He thought again of his dream as he walked, and from there to his seat on the bus. He boarded without bothering to look at anyone; he heard the huge guy from last week say something to him as he passed, but he ignored it. There was no reason to instigate anymore. He settled into his usual seat and turned up his music, grateful for the twenty or so minutes of relaxation before the school day officially began.

Gradually, he came to realize that somebody was watching him.

She was seated across the aisle and one seat up from him, and she had probably been staring from the first moment his booted feet had touched the two steps by the metal door. When he looked over, she looked away; when he looked again she was looking in his direction again. All he could see from his seat was that she had brown hair with some highlights, and her face was possibly the most delicate he'd ever seen. Elegant cheekbones, set just a little higher than normal, curved down to meet thin lips touched with a red that should have been tacky, but somehow looked perfect against her tanned skin. *Still tanned, in early fall.* He didn't catch the color of her eyes, but they looked intelligent and warm. And, perhaps most notably, they didn't look weathered like he'd been told his own were; they didn't reflect a fading zeal for life.

She caught him looking again, managed a half-smile, and then shifted in her seat so she could look out the window.

*She's definitely new. I'll have to meet her.*

Frowning a little, painfully aware that the floodgate of his emotions seemed to have been released since his recent conversations with Susan, he flipped through his music until he found something more fitting to his mood. He wanted something introspective, not angry.

Then he sighed. He wanted to just get to school and get the day over with, and who was he kidding, anyway? He couldn't believe that someone might actually be interested in him, not really. Not someone like her. He was the quiet freak boy in the back of the bus hoping that the pretty new girl would be his friend. It made him feel desperate, and more than a little like a loser. It was only just after seven in the morning, and already he was frustrated and a bit depressed.

Jez was wearing pink tights. To school.

Leonard looked again and again, as if the sight would disappear like the disturbing hallucination it had to be, but no such luck. The pink tights were still there, still stubbornly presenting their offensive image to his eyes. Everybody entering the school turned, pointed, laughed, and Jez loved the attention. He flexed his arms and struck ironic poses until his tousled hair covered his face.

The outcasts of Lincoln Memorial High had been given an ultimatum last year: either stop harassing the students congregating in the cafeteria in the mornings, or they would be forcibly separated from one another and forbidden to associate in groups of three or more during school hours. The group had unanimously decided to find a new hideout before homeroom began. Scaring freshmen was only amusing for so long, anyway, and eventually consciously defying expectations became more work than it was worth.

Then Hank, who was now a junior, had somehow seized possession of the alcove beneath the stairs in the main lobby from the football players and upperclassmen. Those students' days of trying to roll coins across the floor without being hit by people's feet were suddenly just over, and nobody knew how Hank had done it. A few in Hank's circle of friends had suggested that Hank might have blown the star quarterback or something, and that may have been true, but for whatever reason, the Space Under the Stairs was now exclusively Goth oriented.

This was where Leonard found his friends this morning and every other school morning for the past year, in the Space Under the Stairs of the lobby—the Cave, for short. Susan had occasionally hung out against the far wall, all the way under the stairs; Leonard suddenly remembered having seen her under there a few times without ever thinking twice about it. Now he saw her sprawled under the stairs, her trench coat beneath her on the dirty floor, her eyes closed and her head in her hands. She appeared to be sleeping or dying, or both. Hank and a few of his friends hung out in chairs in front of her, partially obscuring her from view. Glenn leaned against the wall near the inner set of doors, one leg bent to place the foot flat against the wall, picking at his fishnet sleeves and gazing down at his knee-high boots. Jez…well, Jez was his own person. He routinely defied the assertion that no man was an island.

He had forsaken flexing for making up lyrics to "Iron Man" and lifting up his shirt, showing his exaggerated gut to anybody who walked by. He was currently screeching, "I'm just a Jez girl/ I'm ugly enough to make you hurl" in a very off-key, falsetto voice.

Leonard caught the new girl's eye once again as she passed him; she actually stopped and stared at Jez, her mouth open a little, eyes wide. Then she hurried off very quickly.

Shaking his head, Leonard approached his friend. "Did you take your medicine today?" he asked quietly.

"Yeah, I took something. I dunno, I think it might have been my mom's, actually." He shrugged. "Guess we'll know something's wrong if I die. And remember, *never operate heavy machinery while under the influence of fruit snacks!*"

"Good advice. So tell me: are the tights just a random impulse today, or are you going for the *Rocky Horror* look? Because Halloween isn't for—"

"*Rocky Horror*? Hey, everyone, it's *TIME WARP* time!*"*

"Um, no."

"Oh well. I just threw them on this morning, anyway. I have shorts in my backpack for when I get yelled at, though." It was, Leonard thought, typical Jez logic.

"What about your blue ones?" Leonard asked.

"Oh, those are reserved for *Mega Man* days," Jez explained in an exaggeratedly patient, *where have you been?* tone.

Hank crept up behind Jez as he was talking and when there was a break in his conversation he shouted "BOOGIE BOOGIE BOOGIE" and waved his arms in Jez's face. The whole group laughed, because little was more amusing than Jez's dramatic reactions to anything unexpected, and a passing teacher scowled and shook her head at the noise.

"You know what would be cool?" Hank asked. Without waiting for a response, he continued, "I think we should all come in one day in gangster clothes."

Murmurs of assent and derision rose from the group.

"You know what would be even cooler, though?" Glenn asked. "We should all draw a pentagram on the floor in chalk and come in with like black robes on or something, and then we can form a circle around the pentagram and join hands and chant and shit. Then when a teacher comes up and yells at us, we can be like, 'Shit! We almost had him that time, too!'" There was scattered laughter at this.

"We could even get a plastic chicken and cut off its head," Hank cut in.

Glenn turned to him. "Why are you so fucked up?"

Hank shrugged. “Probably because when I was about four or five, my dad aimed a gun at my head and pulled the trigger but it was just one of those fake ones that shoot out a sign saying BANG. Then another time, he took me to a bar and he didn’t have any money to bet when he was playing pool, so he bet me instead.”

“That’s pretty nuts, dude.”

“Yeah, but it sure explains a lot,” Susan muttered from beneath the stairs. Hank tossed his plastic soda bottle in her general direction; the same teacher from before walked by right as it hit the floor and she shook her finger at them. It was a ridiculously anachronistic gesture of disapproval, and several of the group laughed again.

Leonard straightened. “Let’s get out of here,” he said to the group. “The bell’s going to ring and that teacher looks ready to write us up.”

“Rock on!” Jez screeched. “Let’s…go…*learn*!”

The five or six friends, plus a few others who sat around with them just for the company and a place to hang, said their good-byes and went their separate ways. One of the hangers-on, a sophomore named Jason, caught up with Leonard at his locker.

“What’s up?” he asked.

Leonard looked up, surprised. To the best of his knowledge, Jason rarely spoke to anybody. He was shorter than Leonard, maybe five and a half feet, and very slim; his arms and legs stuck out at sudden angles and were thin enough that Leonard could probably grab both wrists with one hand. His hair was tangled and fell only to his ears and his eyes were the uninteresting shade of coffee beans.

“Nothing…Jason, right?”

“Yeah. I just wanted to ask if you have the new Nick Cave album already.”

“Definitely, man. It’s good.”

Jason nodded quickly. “Yeah it is. I was just going

to offer to make you a copy if you still needed it. By the way, nice shirt. Don't get in trouble for it."

For the first time, Leonard glanced down at his shirt. *Shit*. It was the old one with the Stabbing Westward logo on the front…and some lyrics that included the word FUCK written in large red letters and flipped upside down and backwards on the back.

"I might want to change this," Leonard agreed, speaking mostly for his own benefit.

"Nah, let it slide."

"Can't. If I keep getting detention for shit like this I'll probably get my ass kicked at home." In all probability, Roland would do nothing but sit there on his lazy ass and call him worthless, but Leonard didn't want to push his luck.

The late bell rang.

"Hey, listen, I've gotta get going, Jason. Talk to you later?"

"Sure."

Leonard watched the kid shamble off. He walked kind of crookedly, a hyper-aware kind of gait that made him look extremely vulnerable. Leonard wondered if Jason knew this.

Sighing, he hung his trench coat in his locker and pulled off the FUCK shirt, as Jez called it, and tossed it onto the top shelf. He was glad he'd been lucky enough to have thrown it on over a long-sleeved shirt that morning. There was a mess of random junk at the bottom of his locker—old homework; notes; plans Glenn had drawn (presumably accurate) of how to get to various areas of the school undetected through the ductwork (this last, Glenn assured him, was strictly for planning pranks); new lyrics for his band; old textbook covers made from paper bags that had ripped when they were thrown into the locker; his gym uniform—and it took him a moment to find the old Nine

Inch Nails shirt he was looking for. It was plain but for "nothing" printed in dark green letters and boxed in on the front. More boring, but unquestionably safer to wear.

Grabbing what he guessed were the books he would need for his morning classes, Leonard locked his locker and picked up his bag and the shirt.

The hallway seemed longer than he remembered it, but weirder things had happened when he was half-asleep and in a hurry. He rushed past the hall monitor posted near the bathrooms and entered his homeroom with scant minutes to spare. It seemed he'd missed the pledge to the flag, which was only recited on the first school day of the week.

Mr. Miller, the homeroom teacher, looked up from his massive desk, where he was taking roll. "Nice of you to drop in, Leonard," he muttered, marking the tardiness on the little green sheet he would soon have to forward to the attendance office.

"Thanks, I was busy doing *homework*," Leonard muttered, dropping into his seat and shaking out the non-FUCK shirt. Nobody laughed; nobody seemed to be paying him any attention at all.

Putting his head into his arms, Leonard gave himself over to the exhaustion already plaguing him and followed the snatch of a song circling through his head. It was catchy, but he couldn't remember where he'd heard it. It probably wasn't very important, anyway. He stretched his legs and fought the sleep that had been chasing him all morning.

The day dragged by until English, by which point Leonard had already skipped gym in favor of lunch with some of his friends, fumbled his way through a chemistry quiz he'd entirely forgotten about, and grabbed a snack during his designated lunch period to be eaten later.

By the time English started, he was in the middle of

formulating a story that would allow him to go home sick when he noticed a very pretty girl sitting beside him in the next row of desks. He glanced over, looked back, glanced over again; her brown hair and elegant cheekbones made her instantly recognizable as the girl from the bus. It seemed nothing short of a minor miracle that she'd shown up in his class—in the very next seat, no less—and he allowed himself a longer sidelong look, emboldened by something he could not readily identify.

She caught him looking and her eyebrows lifted a little in recognition. Flustered, he looked away and began tapping a tune on his desk. *This is crazy*, he thought, but he found himself unable to verbalize what made it crazy. Up until just recently, he hadn't felt the need for companionship, often even on a sexual level. He'd taken partners, sure, but those were nearly always matters of convenience: he was there, she was there, and a few minutes or an hour of stress relief seemed desirable. But it was always detached, almost mechanical. He flashed back to the other night, to Wes, and he felt his cheeks flush. *That* had been memorable, but he couldn't decide if that was due to the novelty of the experience or to something deeper.

In fact, when he thought about it, this reawakening of libido had started around the time he'd first met Susan in the pizzeria that night. Something about her—maybe her tiny stature, maybe the shyness that manifested as apathy—had sparked something within him. It was a vague description, but it seemed to fit.

He realized that she was still looking at him, and he looked up again and offered a faint wave: *Welcome to our hell.* She returned a smile that seemed to say *I already hate it here.*

"Hey," he ventured, and it came out more softly than he'd intended. He was aware of several guys leering in her direction, licking their lips with animal attention (intention? Both seemed apt). It put things into perspective for him, reminded him that he was basically a nothing, a nobody, but needing to reach out anyway.

She returned the greeting and looked away. Several of the guys seated around her turned red, having been caught in their objectifying gazes, and Leonard watched her roll her eyes. She rested her chin in her palm, waiting for another new class to start.

Mrs. Kearns walked into the room in the middle of the tardy bell, as was her custom, and Leonard forced himself to pay attention. He liked her; she was hard, a bit severe, but fair, and she seemed to be blind to clique boundaries. A young, somewhat short woman with dramatic makeup and hair the dirty-blonde shade of nothing, Mrs. Kearns held an unbridled enthusiasm for all sorts of literature that often made Leonard feel bad for the books she held. She routinely cracked their spines, scribbled notes in the margins, crossed them out, folded pages, and used sticky tabs to mark so many passages that Leonard wondered how she could always find just the right marker. On a couple of occasions, he'd also seen her sniff the pages of whatever book she had in her hand.

"Hello, everyone; good afternoon," she offered as she took her place at the front of the room. It was her usual ritual, a call-and-response greeting that you could time like clockwork. A scattered "hello" rose from the class; then she was on her toes—literally—and ready to teach. She was a little ball of bouncing energy.

"Today I'd like to start sharing your projects with the class, which we'll do on a volunteer basis until we reach a standstill. At which point—" Here she held up her slim green gradebook— "we'll start calling names randomly." The week before, she had assigned some creative writing to the class, a song or poem about something meaningful in her students' lives. "It can be something good or bad," she'd said, "but it must have personal meaning to you. If you write a song, you won't have to sing it, but if you do, you'll get extra credit whether you sing well or not."

Now, she waited expectantly, perched on her desk like a bird of prey, but nobody volunteered. "My sister ate mine," somebody shouted, and few people laughed.

Mrs. Kearns did not miss a beat. "Eric! Thank you for speaking up. Why don't you sing yours?" Leonard understood that this was her way of punishing the other boy for the comment.

"Okay, I guess I will!" he shouted, and bounded up to the teacher's desk. What followed was a brief ode to winning football games through sheer domination and superior strategy. A few people snickered, but Mrs. Kearns pursed her lips at a few of the more graphic moments and merely waited for him to finish.

Eric grinned like a maniac and waited for applause that never came. Instead, Mrs. Kearns asked him to redo it for tomorrow, and to be serious this time. "If football is that important to you," she said coolly, "you might think about presenting it in some other context than as a violent joke." He looked like he wanted to cry, and Leonard pictured him as an infant who'd just been dropped on his head.

"*But*," the teacher continued, "since nobody wanted to volunteer earlier, Eric may now choose the next person to go. Those are the rules."

*Dammit*.

Eric must have seen Leonard smirking because there was no hesitation before he declared, "I choose Charles Manson there in the back of the room." Nobody had to turn to see whom he'd pointed out. Everybody knew Eric's distaste for the "freaks."

*Son of a bitch.*

Leonard let his English folder drop to the floor and

rummaged in his bag for his band folder instead. It was black, and in bright yellow gel pen Jez had written *MIDNIGHT SCARE CHOIRS OF WAR DOGMA.* He was scrambling, but he thought he might get lucky.

Mrs. Kearns was unruffled. “Is our future bestseller ready to dazzle and amaze us?” she asked. Leonard liked her and he appreciated the compliment, but her enthusiasm wasn’t helping today, and he momentarily wished that he’d never shown her his creative writing outside of class.

Trying to look only mildly concerned, he searched through the fat stack of half-finished songs and notes jammed into the folder, looking for one appropriate enough to pass for the project he’d forgotten to do. Among the first few he flipped past were “Satan’s Playground,” “Too Much to Handle,” and “Cerebral Slaughter.” Finally he found the wrinkled piece of paper he’d hoped might still be in there somewhere, closed the folder, and smoothed the song out on the desk.

“Are we reaching desperately into last year’s homework for credit, Mr. Kellison?” the teacher asked, but there was no malice in her voice. If anything, she seemed surprised by the possibility that he might have come to class unprepared. Leonard may not have been a model student across the board, but he’d always excelled in English class.

“No, I just misplaced it,” he lied, not looking her in the eye. “After I wrote this I thought it might be a good change of pace for my band.” This last was only a half-lie: he’d written the song independently, intending to develop it acoustically, but it was an old song.

The downside was that the song was extremely personal, written during the breakup he’d suffered through two years earlier. Well, he’d been dumped. Putting it any other way trivialized the soul-crushing despair and confusion he had waded through as the endless swampland it had felt like. He'd always heard that you never forgot your first love, but that saying fell far short from the reality of his experience.

*Candles burning.*

*Desperate words whispered against damp hair.*

*Stomach-wrenching release.*

"Today, please, Leonard," came the teacher's voice, cutting through his reverie, and he nodded and started to the front of the room. He was hyper-aware of everyone around him, their expectation, and he felt the new girl's eyes on him as he bypassed the stool and remained standing.

"This one is called 'A Hymn For Zero.'" He cleared his throat, ran a hand through his hear, and began:

*In a life such as hers if you rest it gets worse*
*'Cause the pain is so prevalent here.*
*She won't her herself cry out for help; can't*
*ask why*
*It still seems like nobody would care.*
*Through all of her rages she's dying in*
*stages*
*And burning the pages of thought.*
*Destruction and anger increase with the*
*danger*
*To herself as she grows more distraught.*

*Such a rapid decline to her past left her*
*blind*
*And she never accepted my pain.*
*It's my fault, she thought, that this torment*
*was brought*
*To my love; it's as if I'm a stain.*
*I died when she cried yet I stood by her side*
*When she wanted no more than to hide.*

*She never slowed down; in her pain she was crowned*
*As an angel from lowering skies.*

*I can still hear her weep; I never could keep*
*From my dreams how I tasted her tears.*
*My angel, so tragic, is slipping like magic*
*And I cannot even be there.*

Silence followed. Nobody spoke; when he looked up, no one would meet his eyes, and Mrs. Kearns tried to be discrete as she wiped at her eye. Leonard felt simultaneously relieved and guilty: guilty of sharing such secrets, particularly since everybody could probably guess who the "angel" in the song was, but guilty also for creating the somber atmosphere in the class. It had happened before, and he had been mocked for it afterwards.

Unable to bear the silence any longer and impatient for the teacher to formulate a response, Leonard finally said, "It's pretty self-explanatory, I think. I don't want to talk about it." He returned to his seat.

Mrs. Kearns chewed on her lip for a moment before commenting. "Interesting. And heartbreaking. I think you've outdone yourself, Leonard." She said nothing more, but she looked like she wanted to. Leonard thanked her, called on somebody else to present next, and looked down at his desk.

A folded piece of paper sat there, although he had no idea how it had gotten there or when it had arrived. Eager but nervous, he unfolded paper and smoothed it out on top of his open band folder, hoping as he did so that the act would go unnoticed. As the other kid started reading a poem about a pet bird or something, Leonard glanced down to read the note.

*Scary Boy:*
*My name's Ariel. If you want to talk, wait for me after class.*
*I liked your song, too. I moved here from Virginia...guys there are pigs,*
*but you seem decent.*
*Peace*
*~*~Ariel~*~*

Leonard read it once, twice, and then again. He was still trying to wrap his head around those three short sentences—realizing as he did that it was from the girl on the bus, the girl who currently sat next to him—when he noticed something else written beneath her name: *P.S. Write back.*

More excited than shocked now, he dug around in his bag for a clean sheet of paper and a pen. He never used pencils, and his bag was littered with black ballpoints pens. It didn't take him long to find one.

It was dead. He checked his watch: two minutes to the bell.

*I need a damn organizer or something.*

He found another pen, scribbled on the song he'd written to make sure it worked, and after a moment's hesitation he wrote: *I'm Leonard. Girls here aren't great either, no offense. Where in Virginia?*

He packed up all of his shit, ran a hand through his ponytail to smooth it back a bit, used the back of a CD to check his eyeliner, and was just starting to wonder if his watch was fast when the bell rang. Everyone got up to leave but Ariel (what a name!); she glanced at Leonard and they rose together.

Mrs. Kearns asked Ariel how she liked the class so far; she asked if she was finding her classes okay. Leonard figured that was as good a reason as any to be hanging around a complete stranger after the bell, so he stepped in and announced that she'd asked him to show her to her classes.

"Oh…how nice," the teacher said without conviction. "Leonard is an interesting boy."

"I've gathered that." It was the first time Leonard had actually heard her speak, and he was taken aback by how smooth it was. Soft and flowing, it lingered on each word and careened slowly into the next. What was the passage from the Song of Solomon? He wasn't particularly religious, but he'd heard it in a movie once and thought it was beautiful. It took him a minute, but he got it: *Thy lips drip honeycomb; honey and milk are under thy tongue.* It wasn't exact, but he thought it was pretty close, and it fit. He'd never heard a voice quite like it before.

"Well, I'd better go," she continued, and Mrs. Kearns smiled and waved them out into the busy hallway.

*From the journals of Leonard Kellison:*

Oct. 01:

Faggot written on the locker
Outcast written on my face
You sadistic motherfucker
Tell me now where is your grace?
Where the fuck is all the good you said would finally come to me?
Murder, mayhem, nothing but humility you gave to me

[Chorus] 'Cause of you my life's a living hell and I don't think I'm sane
'Cause of you I'm choking on the pain, don't act like it's a game
Fuck this shit, I'm sick of it, and I don't want to see it through
Now there's no escape for you!

Just to sit and think on this
Still brings a fucking rage
Go to hell, you need to see
That life is not a stage
I refuse to wait on something good that might not come to me
While you strip away the final shreds of my humanity

[Chorus X2]

62

One day you'll be just like me
Lost within your own mind
Locked up by your own kind
This is what it feels like
When nothing turns out right

# Chapter Six

"I'm actually from Richmond," Ariel said to Leonard, staring unabashedly at his eyeliner and fingernails. Her eyes kept straying from his eyes to his hands and then back again.

"Cool. So you really liked my song?"

"Yeah, I'm actually kind of into stuff like that. I'm teaching myself bass."

"Really? That's cool. I could show you what I know, but it's nothing impressive or anything. I play bass right now in my band, but I sing too, and I screw up a lot because I can't concentrate on both." He shrugged. "Sorry, I'm just rambling."

"No, it's okay. I saw you watching me." He started, unprepared for the sudden change in topic, utterly confused for a moment. "On the bus?" she added.

"Yeah, about that…sorry. New student and all." It wasn't the whole reason, not by a long shot, but it would have to do.

"Don't be—I'm used to it."

"You must be." He realized what he'd just said, and he found himself backpedaling in clumsy haste. "I didn't mean it like that, sorry."

"Yeah." This time it was she who shrugged. They dodged an underclassman on a skateboard who was leaning forward and flying through the halls, the principal hot on his trail. Leonard tipped an imaginary hat in his direction, a nod to their recent meeting. The older man ignored him. The late bell had already rung, but Leonard figured their excuse was valid. He was being noble, after all, showing her to her next class, which was *all the way* on the other side of the school.

* * *

Unable to concentrate on any of his afternoon classes after his short conversation with the new girl, Leonard turned instead to scribbling half-formed song lyrics in his notebooks and pondering again his newly awakened awareness of the opposite sex.

He understood that he liked Ariel, but he couldn't quite get his mind around *why* he liked her, or even *how* he knew that he liked her. Aside from her stunning looks and the kindness she had demonstrated toward him, he really knew very little about her. *Or is that enough? Is that all it takes?*

And then there was his recent encounter with Wes, which also bore heavily on his mind. He'd always considered himself straight, give or take the occasional lingering gaze he'd cast at a particularly feminine musician on TV or at a drag show in the city. But, really, Wes was none of the above—not feminine, not in drag, and certainly not overtly interested in same-sex relationships. At least, not before that night. He hadn't seen him since then, had only exchanged the occasional bland text with him, but suddenly he found himself fervently wishing that he knew how Wes felt, or what the experience had meant to him. Had Wes's sexual paradigm shifted as curiously and as suddenly as his own?

At his locker at the end of the day, Leonard stuffed his FUCK shirt into his bag along with a few books he thought he'd need for homework. *Time to buck up*, he thought, unconsciously borrowing the phrase from Roland. *I can't fucking fail this quarter. That would be a shitty after-Christmas present for that asshole*. At that last thought, he looked over his shoulder without realizing he was doing so, instinctively looking for his stepfather as if he had somehow heard Leonard's thoughts and was out to beat his ass.

Nobody out of the ordinary was in the halls.

Sighing, Leonard pulled on his trench coat and plugged his headphones into his phone, noticing as he did so that he had missed a new text from Susan earlier that day: *Want to take an extra lunch period today? I eat during period five.* He texted her back, apologizing for missing the invitation, and started in the direction of the exit, mouthing lyrics as a thousand thoughts collided in his brain and created new anxieties for him to deal with once he got off the bus and into his house.

The weight of Leonard's bass across his shoulders comforted him. He adjusted the strap and was tuning up for another War Dogma practice session when he realized just how welcome and familiar the feel of it was; he ran his fingers of the glossy instrument, recalling the day several months ago when he had bought it and an amplifier after deciding that he could no longer continue to commandeer Glenn's for every practice and whim. He remembered teaching himself how to install new hardware, customizing the instrument to his liking; remembered the first time he'd tuned it, how right it had felt. It felt like he was doing himself a world of good to be playing his own instrument for a change, and when he wasn't using it, it looked good next to his acoustic and electric guitars in his room.

When he was in the fifth grade, Leonard's mother had somehow convinced him to join the school band. He had eventually relented, seeing how much she liked the idea, and in a moment of inspiration, he'd chosen the saxophone, recalling as he did so a sax solo in an old Ray Charles song and thinking that maybe his father would be impressed by his selection. (This inspiration, as it turned out, would be misguided, because the next time he saw his father—two years later—he had already forsaken the saxophone and moved on to writing.)

A couple of years later, Leonard had met

*(smell of cinnamon)*

*(skin like milk)*

*(the new sensation of fingers laced with his)*

*(that halting first kiss)*

a girl. She'd been teaching herself the electric guitar, able to pick up simple tuning changes and chord progressions by ear. She had no distortion pedal and only a ten-watt amp, but she'd been decent, and he had admired how quick her fingers were on the strings, how certain. Seeing the instrument in her hands, he had become motivated to learn the guitar for the first time.

Last he had heard, she'd been recruited into a local college band called Nailheart, with whom she played regular gigs at local clubs every month or so. He'd never actually gone to see her play, but he heard about the shows through some of his older friends. He often found himself wondering what it would be like to watch her play, preferably from a dark corner where she wouldn't see him and they couldn't make awkward eye contact, but he'd never worked up the nerve to actually go.

Remembering now her self-conscious display of her musical knowledge, how she'd hunched over the guitar and kept her eyes on the frets and her hair covering most of her face, Leonard tried unsuccessfully to picture her onstage, confident, sexy, a more adult version of the girl he'd dated a couple of years ago. He'd seen her around school, of course; knew how she looked now, how thin she was and how she was always surrounded by her new circle of friends, but for some reason he couldn't translate those stolen glances into her presence on the stage.

Now, stepping up to the microphone on another nameless practice day, he wondered when *his* band was going to get its big break. He couldn't help but think of it as a living, breathing thing, and he sometimes felt like he was the only damned member of the band willing to keep it alive and kicking. How many times had Glenn gone off and fucked some random girl on the couch, one or both of them too high or wasted to remember what had happened the next morning? When did Jez ever turn off his newest video game or porn DVD to play the guitar like he was supposed to? They were his two closest friends and he loved them dearly, but they got on his nerves with stupid shit like that. Sometimes he imagined himself playing in a different band, but his heart was with War Dogma, and he didn't want to give it up just because his fellow band members were as horny as he was and couldn't always prevent themselves from showing it.

"Turn off the lights!" Glenn shouted, breaking Leonard's train of thought. "I'm getting naked!"

Jez appeared at the top of the stairs and closed the basement door behind him, trying to balance in his arms a few cups of yogurt (a children's cereal mascot adorned the sides, Leonard noticed), a new package of cookies, and two cans of soda in his arms. He managed to hit the switch without dropping anything.

"I thought you weren't supposed to have too much caffeine while you're taking that new drug," Leonard observed, switching the amps on.

"The antipsychotic?" Jez asked, and Leonard shrugged. Who could keep track? "I'm not." His grin was reminiscent of pure childhood bliss. "That's the fun in it!"

"Rock on," Glenn said between giggles, pounding his drums in the infamous bad joke rimshot: *badum-TSS*. He laughed again after the rimshot, and Leonard wondered, not for the first time that night, if he were already high.

Jez stuffed two cookies into his mouth and opened the first can of soda before tuning his guitar. He was good enough to tune it by ear, and Leonard too had played in drop D often enough to recognize when the strings were sharp or flat.

"Are we ready?" Glenn asked, and for the first time Leonard realized that his friend was already nearly naked, sitting on his drum stool and masturbating in an exaggerated fashion to a nudie pin-up he'd taped to his drums at some point. He wore an oversized sock over his genitals, an ironic gesture of modesty that Leonard thought summed up their camaraderie pretty well.

"Um?" Leonard couldn't fully stifle his laughter.

"I'm killing time, dude!" Glenn retorted with a mock-defensive tone, and Jez began rubbing his own nipples through his netting shirt.

"I feel sexy, too!" he declared, and he nearly knocked over his guitar and his can of soda as he started singing: "I'm…too sexy for my drugs…too sexy for…um, me. But not Glenn. Sorry, Leonard. I'm…too sexy for myself! I'm the All-American Superqueer! *I'M SO GAY!!!*"

*These are my friends*, Leonard thought, but without malice. He'd met Glenn first, had in fact been invited into the band guerilla-style, just a random guy who'd stopped him in the hall and asked if he played an instrument, because he "looked like someone who did." From there, he'd been introduced to Jez and Hank and the others, and the rest was history.

What was most important to Leonard, though, was his friends' loyalty. Glenn had taken the pair of scissors from Leonard's hand moments before he'd been about to cut into himself, half-drunk and depressed over the most recent painful run-in with his father; Jez had let him unleash his fury, standing by while Leonard punched walls and kicked over furniture because he couldn't bring himself to hit Roland himself, and then holding him on the floor afterwards. They weren't blood, but they were family, both of them his brothers, and like family—*real* family—they'd remained by his side, weathered the worst with him and abstained from judging.

Looking at them now, Leonard felt a deep appreciation for their friendship, but he refused to get weepy. Not at band practice. In order to return to the comfortable heathenry of the moment before, he pictured the first time he'd seen the basement: Glenn behind him on the stairs, Jez looking up from his phone to ask if he was okay with male nudity ("It's a must for this sacred man cave," Jez had recited very seriously).

"Let's rock!" he shouted instead, and as he spoke, he felt the blanket of depression lift a little. When he played, especially for a crowd (which had admittedly only happened a couple of times, both at birthday parties), he could just *be*. He didn't have to worry about anything; his mind focused only on his bass and his own voice. *The voice of a golden god*, Glenn had once called it, likening it to the vocals from Cannibal Corpse or Napalm Death, but Glenn had been drunk at the time, so Leonard didn't take it seriously. That was when they'd taken some time to write some particularly heavy songs, Leonard pulling the deep growls from within and allowing them to tear their way out of his throat.

"Which song?" Jez called out, his mouth now full of yogurt and another cookie. Bits of food sprayed onto the carpet.

"Satan's Playground," Glenn suggested, and Leonard nodded. It was the first song he'd written for the band, and it was one of the heaviest. "Too Much to Handle" had followed: Glenn's creation, the heaviest of the heavy, somewhere between grindcore and deathcore. A short while later, they'd unanimously decided to tone down their screams a little so they could get more gigs.

Glenn kicked off the song with a short drum solo;

the sudden blast of Jez's guitar followed. Leonard came in last, and within seconds he'd lost himself to the song.

"*Kill, maim/ A slave to fascist games/ Hurt, cry/ Too young; you can't decide/ Life, death/ The outcasts summon threats/ Scream, die/ We'll massacre your lies,"* he started. Then he again noticed the sock Glenn had thrown over his dick, and he lost control and started laughing in the middle of the chorus.

Glenn, a look of innocent confusion plastered on his face, looked at Jez, who just shrugged. The music continued.

*"Blood flies/ Stains walls and burns your eyes/ Life ends/ You're much too weak to fend/ Heads explode/ Won't stop till I reload/ Guts fall/ Our playground slaughters all."*

Leonard had regained control after his initial outburst, and he had put all of his energy into the second verse. Now, after Jez's unbelievable guitar solo (his mind was gone, all right, but he could play better than anyone else they'd let set in on a practice), Leonard launched himself into the bridge:

"*Suffer, torture/ Killed in a cannibal war/ Genocide, hate crimes/ Self-hate through blood...shot...eyes."*

Then the chorus again, and finally the song was over. Leonard plucked the last few notes on his bass, and then he allowed himself to breathe again. He looked at Glenn and Jez, and they both nodded and grinned. The song was too violent to play often, its content outweighing its satire of other, more serious violent bands, its nod to iconic thrash metal bands lost in the face of its evident aggression.

"We're getting better," Leonard ventured.

"Damn fucking hot patootie straight," Jez agreed. Glenn said nothing but gave a thumbs-up, then twisted to turn on a few of the colored light bulbs on the lamp nearby.

The basement was suddenly bathed in a crimson glow.

"Gothic song next?" Leonard guessed.

"Love in Vein," Jez suggested, and without waiting for a response, he began the song, pulling long, mournful notes from his guitar. Glenn and Leonard followed suit. The song, written by Leonard, always managed to mellow out the entire band. When it was over, Leonard found himself considering his own wrists, the crisscrossing scars, scabs, and words he had carved there over the past several months converging into something like a roadmap. Indeed, he could look at each one in turn and follow it back in time to its origin, to the event that had triggered its creation.

At the same time, he was thinking of his conversation with Ariel. He was replaying their short conversation in his head; he wondered what she was doing at that exact moment. Rather than picturing her naked or showering, he envisioned her sitting in a soft chair beneath a window, half-emptied boxes stacked around her, reading a book or listening to music.

The rest of the rehearsal went like that: Leonard distracted, Jez and Glenn coming up with different ways to show how irreplaceable they were as friends, band members, and human beings in general. When at last nine o'clock rolled around, Leonard packed up his bass perhaps a bit too eagerly and said farewell to his friends. He knew that he had homework to do; he also knew that he would have to write the note he had wanted to write to Ariel in English class. He prayed his stepfather would be asleep when he got home.

* * *

Susan loved school. Everything about it bugged her—from the short-tempered teachers to the stuck-up popular kids to the hours of homework assigned to her—but she figured she could have it worse. She could have been a damn cheerleader.

No, Susan didn't love school because of the education. It was just that there was really no other way to avoid being at her house for so many hours each day. Every morning she resented her parents a little bit more, and every night she went to bed wondering when it would all end. She was terrified to tell anybody of what she had experienced because of the threats of what would happen if she ever tried to. Her personal devil had left town, at least. It didn't help much, certainly didn't erase the pain she felt, but it had lessened the threat level she perceived on a daily basis, anyway.

It all killed her; when Dr. Campbell asked her why she felt like a nobody, she found the answer so easy to acknowledge but so hard to convey. It was what made her cut herself; it was what had made her take up smoking last year. She kept a butterfly knife under her pillow at night and some part of her was praying for a reason to use it. She couldn't remember the last time she had felt safe in her own room.

The nightmares kept her up at night, and sometimes she couldn't even go to sleep. She had taken to "borrowing" her friend's sleeping pills, and once she had taken a few too many and wound up half-asleep in all that she did for two days straight. That was how she nearly always felt, though, and sometimes preferred to feel: half-dead and half-numb, unconcerned that she was unable to maintain any balance or equilibrium in her own damn life. It would be easier to be completely fucking comatose.

Now, sitting alone in her room while she knew War Dogma was practicing at Glenn's house, she was writing in her journal—or, as she called it, the suicide book. In it, she logged every experience she had with self-mutilation, drug use, or thoughts of suicide—"suicidal ideation," Dr. Campbell had called it. It was another of the doctor's projects, and she knew that if she didn't cooperate she would probably be threatened with a mental hospital again.

Running one hand through her sleek, navy blue hair, she pondered how to write what she was feeling. Her notebook was made for gel pens; it had black pages with white lines. USE YOUR IMAGINATION! the cover shouted. So she did.

She wrote about how she had just smuggled a long-bladed hunting knife from her father's cabinet, just taken it out and carried it upstairs, and explored how the ease of her theft felt *wrong*, like maybe her father had intentionally left the cabinet unlocked so she could steal herself a new weapon and maybe use it on herself. She wrote about how she felt both thankful and horrified at such a possibility.

She also wrote about how she was really beginning to like an older boy named Leonard whom she knew would never like her back. She wrote about the self-destructive thoughts cycloning around in her head, and about the balls of light she liked to imagine floated around her room, trying to get her to put the knife back. Angels, she called them, although they were just headlights passing outside.

She liked to imagine that they were really there, had been sent by some higher power to balance out the demons in her life and in her mind. Some days she wanted to banish the fantasy, just carve pentagrams into her walls and doorframe to keep them out, but she knew she'd never bring herself to do that. They were often the only good things she could identify in her life, even if they weren't real. Everything else was black; everything else was death.

I HATE MYSELF, she wrote in the notebook. I BLEED TO HEAL. Although that last wasn't really true; she didn't bleed to heal. No, she bled to bleed. The only reason she still bled so much (so said the illustrious Dr. Campbell) was because she needed a way to feel the pain she wasn't allowing herself to acknowledge. It was the only way for her to make real what she was feeling, day in and day out.

Closing the notebook and returning it to its place amid the other journals and binders full of poems, she turned off her overhead light and flicked on her blacklight. By its light, the blade looked funereal; it looked like the weapon of an angel, not a tool a fucked-up girl would use to bleed for shit.

She rolled up her shirtsleeves and tested the knife's weight in her hands.

It wasn't until both of her wrists were bleeding that she realized she had cut too deep, way too deep. The blood flowed thick and rich; it was thicker than congealing oil, darker than grape jelly. She fumbled for her light switch, leaving trails of blood on the walls, the panic rising up in her and one phrase racing over and over in her head, stumbling over itself in its urgency to make her aware of what was happening, what was—

—HAPPENING IT'S HAPPENING IT'S HAPPENING I'M GOING TO DIE IT'S HAPPENING OH SHIT, SHIT SHIT SHIT IT'S HAPPENING IT'S HAPPENING I'M GOING TO DIE—

Her shaking hands finally found the light switch, and in the new light she finally saw what she had done. The blood stained the carpet now. She screamed to nobody in particular; she screamed and screamed and the sound of her voice was small, so small in her own ears. She felt dizzy but still she screamed. When her mother crashed through the door she too started screaming, and crying as well, and she just fell to the floor next to her daughter and sat there screaming. By the time her father got to her room her mother had pulled the covers off of the bed and wrapped one sky-blue sheet around Susan's wrists and between them, trying to stop the bleeding but immobilizing Susan's arms in the process.

Her father dialed 911 and cried a little, but he seemed more bewildered than panicked, as if he weren't sure that this could actually happen in his house. He acted the part of the good father, but it often felt mechanical, and in that moment she hated him for it, felt sure that it was somehow his fault and her mother's fucking fault that she was so fucked up and dammit, somehow they were going to pay, even if it was with her own life—

He tried to put his arms around her and she screamed something that may have been FUCK YOU. She pulled off the bedsheet and slipped in her own blood as she ran down the stairs and out onto the deck. Her mother screamed for her to stop; her father threw himself at her at the far end of the deck and she fell, her flayed wrists screaming in agony as they were ground into the gravel and dirt and stones on the ground. All three of them were stained with her blood. Her knees connected with the hard wood of the deck and her breath was momentarily knocked out of her.

And her father, on top of her like somebody else had been many years ago, trying to hold her down; he had her arms pinned so she wouldn't thrash out and she didn't see that and she kicked him right in the fucking balls. He howled and rolled onto his side, and she was trying to run again when the sirens sounded and two young cops ran after her and tackled her. She hit the ground again and now, finally, she felt like she had no blood left to bleed. She lashed out at them, unthinking in her fury and humiliation, her shirt riding up and her legs mostly bare and thrashing, knowing she was exposed but not registering anything but the panic. Finally another squad car arrived and a burly cop helped his comrades to stand her up in the fish-belly moonlight.

She was crying, and when she spit into the burly cop's face he stopped being gentle and tried to handcuff her. Her parents started yelling in protest, both of them, and he relented, settling instead for pinning her with his huge arms, a bear hug she had little hope of breaking.

An ambulance arrived next, and now she was screaming *GET LEONARD, GET LEONARD YOU ASSHOLE LET ME GO, GET LEONARD FOR ME OH GOD GET YOUR FUCKING HANDS* ***OFF OF ME!*** But nobody listened and then she was strapped to a gurney and two nurses were putting something on her arms and it fucking burned, but she couldn't lash out anymore and finally she stiffened, giving up some fight. All of her jewelry was removed except for the two jelly bracelets Leonard had given her; when they had reached for them, her reaction was so sudden and violent that they had let her keep them. She couldn't lose them, those mementos from a friendly face she hardly knew.

Dimly, through oblivion, she heard one of the younger cops explaining to her parents that she technically should have been arrested for assault and a host of other reasons, but because she was still very young and obviously mentally unfit at the moment, she would be given *one chance*. Consider it a privilege, ma'am.

When the ambulance doors were closed, she let herself sink into the exhaustion that reached out with startling suddenness to cradle her, and she found herself unable to follow the urgent words that were spoken to her as blackness spread inward from the edges of the world.

*From the journals of Leonard Kellison:*

Oct. o3:

I noticed that Susan wasn't in school again today, but nobody seemed to know what's up. This is the second or third day, and I don't know her well or anything but I hope she's okay. It sounds terrible to say, but I've been too focused on Ariel to reply to the text she sent the other night.

"Need I'm sorry." That's all it said, and I don't know if there are words missing or what, but I should really see what's up.

Okay, I just texted her. We'll see if I get a response. It's weird, I've been actively pursuing Ariel, but Susan was actually in my dream last night. We met up at a concert but I didn't even know she was going to be there, and we had to go through these separate hallways that ended in what looked like cryogenic sleeping pods from a sci-fi. I got in and it raised up and there was no lid, so I saw that the whole audience was in them and we had monitors in front so we could see the show even if it was too far away to see clearly.

So my pod was raised and I saw the band setting up, and I looked to my right and Susan was there, and the first thing I recognized her by was her eyes. She looked at me and smiled like she was happy to see me, too, and I reached out of my pod to hold her hand even though we probably weren't supposed to. It was sweet like only dreams can be. I wonder if I'll think of it when I see her; that might be interesting.

My phone just buzzed. It's a text from Susan's number but it says it's her mom?

Oh holy shit. Gotta go.

# Chapter Seven

Ariel lay back on her bed and wished she were home. *Home* home, Richmond, not here. Living in this new town was beginning to get interesting—especially in regards to the nightchild, Leonard—but not enough to make her forget her old life.

She sighed. She had only told him part of the truth, she supposed. She *had* been through a bad breakup, but perhaps that had something to do with the fact that he had been abusive, alcoholic, and a chronic liar, and he'd had no interest in changing his ways. She could never fully relive the memories of the horrors he had put her through; she could never bring herself to resurrect the pain, even for someone who seemed to be as kind and sincere as Leonard. Moving had been her parents' suggestion; she had agreed at their insistence. It seemed pointless, even dangerous in some superstitious way, to dredge things up when she was just getting settled. Some of the physical bruises hadn't even fully disappeared yet, and the emotional damage would surely take much, much longer to mend.

Her room was as messy as her past, she reflected moodily as she gazed at the piles of boxes forming shabby columns halfway to the ceiling. She would need to really make a push to unpack everything tomorrow.

With another sigh, she undressed and lay naked against her cool sheets, a practice she had been enjoying with more regularity lately. Being far away from Nathan helped her to feel moderately safe; she took comfort in the distance and in the fact that he had no idea where she was.

Tonight, rolling luxuriously in her bed, she felt both comforted and stimulated by the sheets she sensed more than felt against her bare skin in the darkness. She contemplated digging through the boxes for her *intimate aid* (the term always made her giggle, especially amongst friends, but she'd always found "vibrator" too candid), but she was already comfortable in bed so she decided it wasn't worth the effort. *Tomorrow*, she promised herself.

Nathan had hated the thing.

Which was ironic, she thought now, considering how little he had ever seemed to care about her own gratification. He was single-minded when it came to sex, concerned only with his own pleasure, but even without his help, he expected her to abstain from any outside help. It had made her helplessly, enormously insecure about herself, and even now, as she turned on a lamp and stood in front of the mirror, she found it difficult to appreciate her body.

"What's to like, anyway?" she asked aloud.

The image reflected back to her was that of a sixteen-year-old girl, standing a bit shy of five and a half feet tall, with a sort-of hourglass figure and brown hair streaked with thick burgundy stripes. She supposed her ass was nice enough, but her stomach was getting bigger and she had begun to notice that she was no longer able to dance as well as she used to. Over the past year she had shot up nearly four full pants sizes, a situation she dimly recognized as the old "eating your feelings" defense mechanism, and most of last year's school clothing no longer fit right.

Her breasts, she knew, were what some boys categorized as enormous. They'd certainly never been shy about voicing their opinions. She'd begun noticing some back pain recently, a fact that left her both ashamed and scared, and some days she could barely endure the pain of wearing a bra from morning to night. Cupping them in her hands now, feeling their weight, she wondered—certainly not for the first time—whether a surgical reduction might be in order in the near future.

A knock on the door brought her out of her reverie, and as she tied her bathrobe closed she heard her mother asking from the other side if she could come in. Unlocking the door, Ariel greeted her mother uncomfortably, suddenly very conscious of her nudity.

"I just wanted to tell you to sleep well, dear," her mother said now, kissing her on the cheek and taking in the room around her. "Try to unpack the rest tomorrow so we can get rid of these boxes, would you?"

"Sure thing, Mom." Ariel called her mother back as she was turning to leave. "I'm getting fat," she said bluntly.

"Oh, honey, no you're not, but…well…I'm sure working at the pool, with all of that free food around, didn't help much." Immediately aware of the pain on her daughter's face, she pulled her in for a big hug.

"I know, but I can't even dance right anymore. I just…" She trailed off helplessly, hoping it would all register on her face so she wouldn't have to verbalize what she was feeling.

"You can't help who you are," came the answer, along with the usual reassurances: you are beautiful; you are smart; you are attractive and desirable. Very soon, her mother predicted, Ariel would find someone who would make her feel good about herself (Ariel longed for a moment to yell at her mother that that wasn't the *point*, that she didn't *want* to need outside validation; she wanted to be good enough for *herself*—but in the next instant she knew that it would only hurt her mother, and she didn't want to do that). Besides, high school was an awkward time for everyone. Whoever said they had gotten through it gracefully was either dim or a liar.

Frustrated now, Ariel sat down on the bed and said goodnight to her mother. Looking hurt but unwilling to force further conversation on Ariel, she left her alone and retreated downstairs.

Ariel shut the door tightly.

She had been a dancer since she was four years old. She was experienced in ballet, tap, jazz, and Pointe, focusing on these but dabbling a bit in everything so she could be an instructor at her own dance studio in the future. Whenever she was at friend's house, or her grandparents', she would look for hard wooden floors, admire how they looked, and make a mental note that her own place (she always thought of it this way, as a "place," not a "house" or "apartment") *must* come with hardwood floors. Her grandparents, now so far away, had beautiful wooden floors. Her grandfather had put them down himself after tearing up the ugly beige carpeting that had originally covered the floors.

It was at her grandparents' house that Ariel had first experimented with Pointe. The elegant shoes with the flat wooden toes hurt like hell, but she looked good doing it, and she had improved exponentially since she'd begun. Whenever she would visit their house, she would bring her Pointe shoes and dance on her toes in the middle of the living room after her grandfather had moved the furniture out of the way. Originally, her mother would worry aloud that the shoes would damage that floor, but her grandfather would just wave her away and smile.

Now, tapping one foot on the hard floorboards of her new room, she wondered how much her parents would mind if she asked them to leave out the carpets and just let her dance in the privacy of her own bedroom. The thought excited her and shocked her out of her fantasies. All of a sudden she was back in her own house, naked but for a thin bathrobe, and now she was growing cold as well.

Feeling a little better now with the prospect of a private dancing studio, Ariel pulled on a nightshirt and a pair of running shorts and turned off the light. In the dark of the night, she slipped into bed and started her next few hours of uneasy sleep.

Leonard did not go to school the next morning. He woke up at his normal time, dressed a bit more nicely than usual—black khakis, a black button down over a black tee, and his Docs—and informed his mother that he would be taking a skip day.

"Is that a thing?" she asked when he announced it.

"Sure it is. They're not just for seniors anymore."

He was actually pretty sure that this wasn't the case, at least not officially, but she just laughed at this and handed him a coffee mug.

"Just make up your work, Len," she warned him. She was the only one who called him Len, and the only one he would allow to use the nickname.

After a hurried breakfast, Leonard started his car and drove north, toward the hospital. He knew from his brief talk with Susan's parents that he would find her in the psych ward, and although he still didn't know her that well, he found himself pulled to her. It was a friendly responsibility to visit someone you knew when they were in the hospital; he knew this, but it was something else, too. He was drawn to her company, this quiet, intense girl he'd only just met.

It took several minutes and a heated discussion with a hospital administrator to be permitted to visit Susan—something about observation, group therapy, one-on-one meetings with the good doctor—but in the end he made it through. He knew that he was early for visiting hours, but he didn't care. When he was finally permitted entry he wandered the bland halls, not at all like the psych wards he'd seen in movies and imagined himself being confined to during his darkest moments, before finally seating himself outside of the room where Susan was supposed to be finishing up some session or other.

Several people passed him while he waited, most of them patients and only a couple of them accompanied by a doctor or a nurse. The patients who seemed least aware of their surroundings shuffled along as if nothing really existed, evidently spurred on by neither destination nor any concept of when they needed to be wherever they were going. (Indeed, it occurred to him as he watched their slow progress that time probably had no real meaning for some of them.) Distantly, he heard what might have been pounding on locked doors, and he wondered how many patients were in isolation and what they had done to land there. *This isn't a prison*, he reminded himself. *They're sick, not criminals*.

It seemed alien to him to apply the same reasoning to others that he'd so often used to put his own circumstances into perspective.

When she emerged from the therapy room, Susan looked markedly different from when he'd last seen her in school. Thin to begin with, now she looked positively frail, her cheeks withdrawn and her arms dwarfed by the various hospital bracelets and the too-large shirt she wore. She wore no makeup and her hair looked tangled.

She saw Leonard immediately and rushed over to him, tripping over her own feet as she did so and forcing him to catch her in his arms. She looked up at him, eyes a little unfocused, and apologized several times, her speech a bit unclear so that Leonard was reminded of someone who was just beginning to grow tipsy from drinking too much alcohol. *It's the meds*, he thought. *Whatever they put her on, it's having the zombie effect.* He was no stranger to that feeling, had experienced it himself back when he'd first sought out therapy for his deepening depression. Jez referred to it as the "cocktail festival": try a med out for a few weeks, see if it works; if not, wait a few more weeks (often suffering through side effects and withdrawal at the same time); try again; hope for the best. He found himself hoping for her own sake that whatever cocktail she was on would only be temporary.

"What happened?" Leonard asked. "How long are you in here for?"

Susan sat down next to him and looped her arm through his, as if contact with a friend might be the only thing keeping her in this world. She seemed to think for a moment, and Leonard waited.

"Mandatory three-day observation," she said at last. "After that they'll decide."

"Decide what?" But Leonard thought he knew already. They would decide whether to keep her in there or let her go home.

"I still have these," she muttered, and held up her wrist. For one sick moment he wondered if she was referring to the gauze and medical tape, but then he noticed the black bracelets he'd given her, and he felt an unexpected warmth spread through him.

"That's really great," he told her. He felt deeply touched that she'd taken care to keep them despite the resistance he was sure the hospital had presented. If she were anything like him, those bracelets would come to represent much more than they actually were; he himself had a couple of mementoes from friends who had cared for him in his longer bouts of depression.

An awkward silence passed between them, and Susan eventually broke it by telling him about the night she had been dragged here from her house. She spoke slowly and quietly, and he had to lean in to hear everything properly. Her breath was stale and her lips were noticeably dry, but he found himself tracing them with his gaze anyway.

He had played this role of guardian, of confidante, in the past, had been on the receiving end of it just as often, but had never been part of a support network in quite the same way as he now found himself. Something about her physical *small*ness appealed to the reptile part of his brain, put him into the hunter/gatherer paradigm as he had never been before, and he found himself fiercely protective of her in that moment.

His phone buzzed in his pocket, and Susan withdrew as suddenly as if it had stung her. She replied to his confused look with a nonanswer: "I can't even have my phone here. I thought it might be mine, but that would just be. Well. Crazy."

It took him a moment to realize it was her attempt at a joke, and he chuckled although it had clearly fallen flat. She smiled her appreciation at the gesture anyway.

The text message was from Jez, and it said simply, *Wrap it! Crazy is contagious, brah.* He'd told Jez that he would be visiting Susan, but he hadn't anticipated that anybody might read so much into it. He put his phone back in his pocket and turned back to Susan, noting regretfully as he did so that the spell had been broken. He was no protector, and she was no ward of his. She was a self-destructive girl in a hospital psych ward, and she would probably stay the mandatory seventy-two hours and then return home and nothing would change.

He thought of Ariel, tried to picture her in this setting. He found he couldn't do it. He thought he'd recognized some kind of pain in her eyes the other day, some breed of familiar world-weariness, but he somehow doubted she had experienced the same vile depression that he'd suffered through. *That Susan is suffering through.*

A wave of guilt rushed over him at the thought. He was suddenly ashamed of his wandering mind, and to make up for it, he stood and offered his hand. "Let's go for a walk."

The ward was small, and their aimless path led them back to the same bench a couple of times before their small talk came to an end. They stood there for a long moment, their gazes meeting in a way that no longer seemed so awkward, until a passing patient broke their reverie. The woman was old, bluish hair wiry and unkempt, and she spat at the wall art every couple of feet.

Susan laughed, but cut it short when the woman turned sharply in their direction. "That's my roommate," she whispered. "Only bed they had free, and that woman is *scary.*" She paused. "Not as scary as what they consider art, though."

Leonard shook his head, studied the nearest picture: a hotel room-caliber print of rippling water spreading outward from a dock. "Vat do you see in zis picture, hmm?" he asked, stroking an imaginary beard.

"Death, death everywhere!" came the response, and both smiled. Susan sat down on the bench again, her fatigue apparent. Whatever they had her on, the short walk had taken all of her energy.

"Listen, I'm going to let you get some rest," Leonard said, and she nodded.

"Thank you. Really. And by the way, you look nice."

He acknowledged the compliment with a shrug and smoothed the buttons on his shirt with exaggerated care. Then he drew her in for another awkward hug before turning to locate the exit. He was reluctant to admit it to himself, but the thought of fresh air and some sunlight was suddenly very appealing to him.

*From the journals of Leonard Kellison:*

Oct. 04:

"No Pulse (Sonnet 08)"

Discordant frets are fading from my ears
A little more with every hour I dream,
But nothing truly makes them disappear
When I'm too weak to salvage self-esteem.
Such truths are too well veiled to contemplate,
Locked in a box of webs behind my eyes.
I fear there's nothing left to do but wait
As stars loose desperate grips on twilit skies.
As every vein bleeds dry the world will change,
The language of the dying stars no more.
Such happenings have never seemed less strange;
It's winding down—I'm down to one last door.
The canyon walls within my mind grow steep.
Saint Suicide can sense me as I sleep.

# Chapter Eight

Leonard returned to school the following day but sat in a different bus seat than usual, letting his ear buds dangle around his neck rather than provide a barrier against the world. Both actions had previously seemed like cardinal sins against his very nature, but he wanted to talk to Ariel, and he found it increasingly difficult to maintain his customary defenses against the surrounding world.

He dropped his bag onto the seat beside him with a yawn and turned to Ariel: the girl whose memory had distracted him at the hospital yesterday; the girl about whom he knew next to nothing; and now—he noticed this with a guilty sort of thrill—the girl who was trying to eye him with a subtlety that wasn't quite there.

"Hey," he said clumsily, and immediately made a mental note to kick his own ass when he got home later for sounding so idiotic.

"Hey," she returned, apparently feeling the awkwardness in equal measure.

Leonard broke the ensuing silence by describing the band practice he had so enjoyed earlier that week. "You should have been there," he told her, although he secretly suspected that the parts he had left out—Glenn's nudity, Jez's self-destructive way of life—might have turned her away. "It was really fun."

"Really?" Ariel seemed to relax at the prospect of conversation and leaned forward a bit. "That's cool. I don't know, though; my mom usually doesn't let me do too much on school nights." That was a bit of a lie, but she didn't want him to know that she was just making up excuses to hide her growing interest in him.

If Leonard noticed, he didn't comment on it. "Yeah, that makes sense. Anyway, listen, I know it's none of my business, but you seemed kind of bummed yesterday talking about that breakup and everything. If you ever need someone to talk to, will you get in touch with me?"

"Yeah, I guess." She felt herself blushing furiously. "I don't want you to think that I need someone to save me on a daily basis, but if it comes up, I could use a friend."

As everyone unloaded onto the sidewalk at the school, Leonard waited for Ariel to leave and followed her into the cool autumn air. She had gone quiet again, and he wasn't sure how to break the silence but he felt the need to get a conversation going again.

"Want to meet Jez and them?" he asked, and she shrugged.

"I don't know, he seems kind of…a little weird. Scary."

"You called *me* the scary kid, remember?"

She laughed at this. "That's true." She studied him for a moment, and he could see that a thought had struck her. "Why don't you have your eyeliner on today?"

Despite himself, Leonard felt his cheeks burning. It wasn't often that anyone commented on his fashion sense anymore, and when someone did, it was usually with derision. "I don't know. I guess I didn't get around to it yet. Usually Jez lets me borrow his."

This was true. The year before, Jez had started wearing eye shadow and eyeliner to school again; apparently he had been threatened with a Saturday detention for it during his last year of intermediate school, and if there was one thing Jez hated, it was the idea of more school. He remembered the day that Jez had put the stuff under his eyes for him that day, telling him softly that the trick was to get it as close to the eyeball as possible without actually touching it. "That burns like my mom when she tried to piss," he had said earnestly, and Leonard decided that such an event sounded painful indeed. From there,

Leonard had stolen one of Jez's pencils and begun applying it himself.

Now, Leonard entered the school and introduced Ariel to Hank, Glenn, Jez, and the rest of the group. Glenn and Hank simply nodded; Jez offered to give her a complimentary "Welcome To the Hellhole" striptease, but she politely declined.

"Leonard, remember that time at that one party when I put you in a dress—"

Leonard cut Jez off before the sentence could be completed. "No, but I remember the time when you said you wanted to screw Glenn's sister." That party had been fun, just dicking around with friends on an uneventful Saturday night, but Leonard loathed the thought that something might jeopardize Ariel's perception of him, especially this soon after meeting her.

Immediately on its heels came a sense of anger. He felt indignant at the desire to hide parts of himself from her, but he pushed it away. *Baby steps for now*, he admonished silently.

But Ariel just laughed, and Leonard felt something unclench in his gut. "I'm glad you're so fun-loving," she joked.

At one point Leonard placed his hands on Ariel's arm in an effort to show her how he had grabbed a standing lamp the day he had tripped over a cord in Glenn's basement. The event itself had been ridiculously humorous at the time, one of those you-had-to-be-there moments, the entire band drunk and trying to burn off too much energy all at once, and in the end the lamp had fallen with Leonard. Ariel reacted strongly to his touch when his fingers made contact, and he pulled away as casually as possible, trying and failing to read her body language. She could have felt aroused or violated by his touch; he wasn't sure that he could tell which.

The conversation continued easily, however, and when they left for their various homerooms and Hank wondered aloud whether Susan had decided to skip school again, nobody but Leonard winced or reacted with any concern at all. It made him feel like he was protecting her secret, and he found that he didn't mind.

Friday arrived at its customary unhurried pace, and that evening found Leonard sitting on the floor of his bedroom with his acoustic guitar. He'd woken that morning with a single lyric in his head, some holdover from the dreams he could not remember: *Saint Suicide can sense me as I sleep.* He'd worked on it during his downtime all afternoon, and the music he was currently composing was something of a departure for him, nothing based in metal or the standard acoustic three-chord progression but almost Eastern in influence. The finished lyrics fit together like a sonnet, iambic pentameter and all, and the final couplet served as the chorus to his song.

> *The canyon walls within my mind grow steep—*
> *Saint Suicide can sense me as I sleep.*
> *Saint Suicide can sense me as I sleep.*

Satisfied for the time being, he switched to his electric guitar, grabbing the expensive headphones and the jack to connect them to a small amp. It wasn't late yet, but Roland had come home in a black mood, and Leonard wanted nothing more than to avoid the man altogether.

He was in the middle of tuning up when his phone buzzed, and he set the instrument flat across his lap to check the incoming message. He'd stopped by the hospital very briefly that afternoon to visit Susan, where he had been notified that she'd already been released. She hadn't returned his texts, so his mind immediately jumped to her face when he opened his messages, but it was Ariel's name that appeared on the screen.

*Shitty day* was all it said, and then, a moment later: *What's up?*

Leonard tapped out a reply and returned to tuning his guitar. *What happened? I'm just doing guitar stuff.* "Playing guitar" always seemed too impressive a phrase for the way he liked to hammer on the strings.

The conversation continued: *Someone started a rumor that I switched schools b/c of slutty behavior. Said I got myself into trouble. No idea who even started it!!* A series of emoticons followed.

*People are full of shit*, Leonard replied. He refused to ask if the rumors were grounded in truth. *Doing okay, though?*

*I guess so. I don't know why I thought this school would be any different. I just want to disappear for a while.*

Leonard thought of Susan, who *had* disappeared from the real world for a few days, and he felt himself bristle at the offhanded nature of Ariel's text. He understood the desire to escape, but escapism was different from trying to disappear completely.

*That's hard to do*, he replied, following up with emoticons of an airplane, a beach, and some books. *Do you have any plans this weekend? Distractions might work, since you can't really disappear.*

A long pause followed, during which Leonard began fiddling with the settings on his distortion pedal. The dials each had a cryptic name next to it: Death, Fury, Crunch, and Howl. Manipulating the dials changed the sound of the output, and he was in the mood for the most crunching, guts-resonating rumble possible tonight.

*Maybe*, came the reply, halfway through the first song. Then: *Let me see your guitar.*

He briefly toyed with the idea of asking whether that might be a euphemism, but shrugged off the urge. Instead, he snapped a couple of pictures of his guitar, his other instruments, and the musical equipment against one wall. He carefully kept his face out of the pictures, not wanting to seem too eager to share anything other than what she had actually asked for.

*You're for real, aren't you?* she asked a moment later.

*In what sense?*

*You don't just wear that stuff to school, it's inside you. Those posters and the tone of your room...I can tell that it's not just an act, you carry a lot inside. I think it shows in your eyes sometimes. I'm sorry if that's too forward or insulting, I just mean that you present yourself true to who you are.*

Leonard looked around his room, trying to see it through a stranger's eyes. He'd grown accustomed to it, even preferred those dreary surroundings, but he'd never thought of his space as a true reflection of himself. It was easy to see it now, though. Anyone would have been able to glean certain things about him.

He realized that several minutes had passed since Ariel's last text, and he fumbled for a reply that would sound soothing and nonconfrontational. *That's just me*, he typed at last. *I'm not offended. I just figure, why pretend?*

*From the journals of Leonard Kellison:*

<u>Oct. 08:</u>

I feel truly alone.

I really wish I had therapy tonight, I can't help it. I can't even function right now. I used to come home from school, sleep, eat dinner, sleep more, and then get up the next morning and do it again. I wish I could do that again now, but I don't even know if *that* would be enough distance from the world.

I might not even wait until I have enough fishnets to cover the ceiling; I might just disappear tomorrow.

Need a smoke.

# Chapter Nine

Despite the tumultuous nature of his past and the fine line he navigated daily between spiraling depression and tenuous stability, Leonard was a boy with dreams. He wanted to teach, maybe even give guitar lessons; he wanted to rock out on stage; he wanted to write. What he wanted most, however—possibly more than the combined ambition of his other dreams—was somebody to protect him, somebody to love him. He always carried with him the dream of meeting a wonderful girl, one whom he could love and depend on, a beautiful girl from some unnamed transcendent place who might even have younger siblings who looked up to him and some pets to sleep in his lap.

He thought he'd found that person—*Anna*, he told himself now, flipping through old poetry he'd written, *you can't move forward if you can't even say her name, and you clearly need to move forward*—a couple of years ago, but apparently that hadn't been the case. Despite the fact that her only sibling was on probation and she herself had a separate, if not entirely unrelated, host of problems, the dream had survived, at least for a while. A dream under reform, but a dream nonetheless.

Unfortunately, the weeks before the breakup had shattered any hope he may have had left of him living out the dream he'd harbored for so long. In the early days, of course, they had both harbored the same dreams, and had accordingly crafted a future of possibilities that featured both of them in a naively perfect apartment, with naively incredible jobs and more happiness than they knew what to do with. In response to the pain and the increasingly difficult reality that followed the breakup, or perhaps simply as a defense mechanism, he'd simply packed it all away in the deepest recesses of his mind, only to be looked at from a distance and always to be put away before the pain could slip through the cracks in his resolve to never love again. Like the toxic material he imagined it to be, however, its effects always found ways to seep into him, tainting his conscious mind with memories and dreams of candlelit dinners, of Christmases spent laughing and rejoicing, of whispering secrets into a lover's ear while she laughed, eyes bright with the bounty of providence, and twirled his hair through her fingers.

Nothing so good had come to pass.

Leonard had spent the months following the breakup alternately spreading himself around and isolating himself as completely as he could, freely giving and receiving sexual satisfaction where and when he could without finding the peace and the presence of the sacrosanct that had once come with it—and then cutting himself off from everyone, leaving his room only for school, and sometimes not even then. At times he still felt himself retreating into that unfathomable hole, and it didn't always seem possible to avoid the descent, even now.

So he was a bit surprised that he had found himself relating some of this private history to Ariel over the phone later that Friday night, when texting had become a chore and the conversation had begun to get deeper.

Putting his old writing away in favor of plucking at his bass, he remembered the odd security he had felt in her silence as she'd listened to him speak, and it had not felt strange or contradictory at all to divulge the details of his failed past relationship to the woman he felt himself drawn to now. *Well, one of them.* His mind flashed to Susan, and he checked her online profile to see if she had uploaded anything new since she'd returned from the hospital. Just one post, a couple of lines from an old Cream song he wasn't familiar with: something about a tree and the pain of the world.

He left a comment on the post with the next couple of lines, asked how she was doing, and then returned to his bass. He could barely parse the situation he found himself in: two women, both of whom showed interest in him and both of whom he was in turn interested in (although for very different reasons), but neither of whom had made any real advance on him. All he knew for certain was that, despite his brief period of sleeping around post-Anna, he still believed himself to be, if not a *good* person (and he wasn't entirely sure how to define that), then at least someone who would not willingly hurt anyone else. Reflecting on this understanding of himself, he finally determined that the moment something definitive happened, whether at his own instigation or not, he would stop his waffling.

It was confusing, of course, but at the same time, the validation he felt at being wanted again—and not only that, but wanted for something more than an hour with his rumored talents in bed—was something new enough that he found himself unable to do little more than simply to enjoy it.

This feeling lasted until Monday morning, when his world began falling apart from the outside in.

On the bus going to school, Ariel was more reserved than usual, and though she refused to talk about what was on her mind, Leonard immediately ran the past couple of days through his mind in search of something he might have done to offend her. It was mostly a narcissistic response, he knew that, but at the same time he couldn't help himself. For too long, he'd suffered from a knee-jerk "what did I do now?" response. Was she annoyed that he'd asked about her weekend plans and then failed to follow up? Her behavior seemed to indicate that it was more than that, but he supposed it was possible.

When they got to school Ariel quickly excused herself and disappeared into one of the bathrooms near the front doors. She wouldn't meet his eyes, and her own looked red, as if she were going to cry. Leonard waited for her in the hall for nearly ten minutes before leaving for the Place Under the Stairs, his stomach in knots and depression rising to blanket him in a fresh wave of despair.

Everyone under the stairs sat or stood in a loose semi-circle around Susan, and when he pushed past Jez, Hank, and the rest of the gang, he saw why. Her wrists were covered in thick gauze pads held in place by clear medical tape; as he watched, she pulled up a sleeve of her sweater to scratch at one of them. She still looked pale, but her eyes were clearer than they'd been at the hospital, and Leonard took that to be a good sign.

When she caught Leonard's eye, she pushed herself off of the wall and rushed over to him, clinging to his trench coat like he was her only lifeline. Whatever demons hounded and haunted her and drove her into situations that required wrist bandages, they seemed to lessen their grip as she strengthened her own around the coat's fabric.

She didn't cry, but her breathing grew ragged as if she were fighting back the urge to start. Feeling the others' curious eyes on him but unable to provide them with any explanation at the moment, Leonard suddenly found himself feeling alien in a territory that was supposed to be familiar to him: someone gets hurt, he helps them through it. It was the give-and-take dynamic that at least partially defined his relationship with most of his friends. Sometimes he was the victim; sometimes, the comforter. But today, with Ariel in the bathroom and most likely crying, and everybody but Jez looking at him with questions in their gazes, he simply couldn't figure out how to react.

As the group gathered more closely around the two figures, Susan recounted the tale of her most recent cutting, describing in her quiet voice the hospital and the tubes in her arms and the blood she had lost. Leonard noticed that she left out the hardest details, including the police presence at her house that night, and despite everything else he appreciated the trust she'd placed only in him.

"I ended up hooked up to all these machines," she told them, her voice choked with emotion. Her cheeks burned. "I just wanted to die. At first I was scared, but then…I don't know. It started to feel right, and peaceful. To just accept it. But of course then I remembered people like you, who actually care what happens to me, and I tried to stop just accepting thoughts like that. That's what got me out of there. There was this one doctor who headed group sessions and he. Well. He helped me realize that not everyone would want me to die. That maybe some people would actually be sad if I did." She left it there, and Leonard sensed that she would refuse to elaborate on that last if anyone should ask.

The conversation continued with words of thanks and promises of support, and when Leonard looked over her head he saw Ariel walking past the stairs. She froze when she saw him looking, standing there stupidly with Susan in his arms, and whether or not she had been crying before, she now began to cry in earnest. She ran off with one hand covering her face, and Leonard, pained and torn between the two women who cared for him, was too numb with indecision to break free and follow Ariel.

Committed to supporting Susan but desperate to explain the situation to Ariel nonetheless, he found himself grateful when the bell rang after a minute or two. He wished his friends well, promised Susan to text her when he got a minute, and hurried through the crowded halls in the direction Ariel had run. He searched the hallways, eyes tearing from face to face, feeling every pained step of his search, and when at last he ran out of time and was forced to backtrack to his homeroom, he was tired and out of breath and felt utterly helpless.

There were snickers and catcalls when he entered the room, but he didn't pay any attention to it.

Twice he passed Jason in the hall, once going to his first class and again before lunch, and both times the normally shy boy shot him belligerent looks and muttered under his breath. Papers were thrown at Leonard and food was aimed at him during lunch, and when somebody attempted to knock his tray out of his hands he'd finally had enough.

"What the fuck is going on?" he asked Hank as he sat down at their usual lunch table. As he sat, the boy sitting nearest them stood and moved to another table with a look of disgust on his face.

"What do you mean?" Hank edged away from his friend as he spoke, eating lunch a little farther down the bench than he normally would.

"I mean that everyone is fucking with me today, dude. Like…people are throwing shit at me and calling me fag." He paused. "A lot more than usual. What the hell happened that I don't know about?"

Hank was silent. He picked the cheese off of his slice of pizza and ate it separately. He tightened the laces on his faded black combat boots. Finally, when he could avoid Leonard's gaze no longer, he muttered, "You fucked Wes, didn't you?"

"*What?* What the fuck? Who told you that?"

"Just answer the question, dude. Everyone's talking about it."

He remembered how upset Ariel had been that morning, and things started falling into place. All at once, his time with Wes returned to him: the CDs he'd tried to organize; the drug-like, heightened self-awareness; the rush of new experiences; the whispers; even the comfortable silence afterwards as they'd both lain there, spent but fulfilled.

The promise to keep it a secret.

*That motherfucker. He made a promise to me.*

Out loud, he said, "I want names." When Hank tried to interrupt him, he leaped out of his seat, and when he spoke he found himself unable to keep the emotion out of his voice. It was nearly a scream; it presaged violence or tears or both, and everyone seated nearby turned to watch. "I want names, Hank! Who the fuck said that?"

"Calm down, Leonard—"

"*WHO?*"

Hank pushed his tray away, defeated. "First it was that Jason kid. You know, the quiet one. He's friends with Wes, you know. I guess Wes told him. From there, who knows? Maybe Jason told, or someone overheard them talking." He gave Leonard a long look as he chose his next words with care. "Look, I don't really care if you did it, dude. I just don't want lies between us, because according to Wes, you kept badgering him and he only finally said yes because you were both really drunk. He says he regrets it. I don't know what really happened, but I can't defend you when I don't even know what's going on with you."

Wes's side of the story was so far from the truth that Leonard couldn't even articulate a response to it at that moment. Maybe Wes was ashamed, but to make up outright lies? To duck any responsibility for his part in the night and to blame it on alcohol and peer pressure?

The insult inherent in that was astounding. Avoiding the lie completely, Leonard focused on Hank's reaction instead. "You do care, though. Obviously you care." He sat back down and held his face in his hands. "You know how I was getting along well with Ariel?

That's probably over now. I don't know what people are saying but that's just—that didn't happen. I didn't *fuck anyone*."

"But something did happen." It wasn't a question.

Leonard leaned back in his chair. "Yeah." He said it defiantly, but with less indignance than he felt. Inside, he was crumbling.

Hank returned to his original seat, not so far away from Leonard anymore. "Look, maybe she hasn't heard yet."

"She has. I'm sure she has. She was upset about something this morning. And besides, even if she hasn't yet, she will. It doesn't even matter that it was with—that specific person. It's that I was with someone right around the time we first started talking. It just looks shitty.

"And look, was it really that bad of a thing to happen? It was just…I don't know. *I don't know!* It was experimental. It never happened before—it was *one time*." Leonard experienced a strange knot of emotions as he spoke, a confusion of shame for what he'd done and gratefulness for Hank's compassion, or at least for his willingness to listen. The effect was overwhelming, and he railed violently against the first pinpricks of tears that he felt in the corners of his eyes.

"I believe you," Hank said. "Not that I would care anyway; I was just surprised that you wouldn't want to talk about something so huge. We're all friends. Anyway, Jez is throwing a shit fit over it."

"*What?* Why? He's openly bisexual, for fuck's sake."

"I think he's changed it to pansexual now. But I don't know, man, I think he just wanted to get to you first."

"Bullshit."

An apple core went sailing through the air and into Leonard's bowl of soup before Hank could respond. His untouched grilled cheese sandwiches were doused with the stuff, and it splashed onto the table and in Leonard's lap. Angry as well as humiliated now, Leonard turned around very slowly, very carefully. With one hand he wiped at his crotch with napkins.

Nobody would meet his gaze. Nobody would say anything. In fact, he realized distantly, the entire cafeteria had gone silent. Shaking his head disgustedly, he rose to throw out his ruined lunch. As he did, somebody shouted, "Watch out, here comes the homo! Cover your ass!"

The lunch attendants were instantly combing the tables, trying to find out who had said it, but Leonard didn't care to stick around to see. He was already moving toward the bathroom, determined to hold back his tears and his frustration until he was safely locked away in a stall. He finally let the tears come after he had locked himself in. They were tears of frustration, anger, and betrayal, and they burned like vitriol or cheap whiskey. How the hell could this happen to him? Wesley had promised not to tell! Leonard punched the blue metal wall dividing the stalls once, twice, rapid hits that echoed against the impassive tiled walls and faded rapidly into nothing.

Just as hurtful as the fallout was the betrayal. They had participated in this thing together, this uncharted sexual landscape, and now everything was ruined.

The tears ran hot for another minute or two, and then he steeled himself and willed them to stop. Under the pain were the anger and indignity and he thought those might be more helpful to embrace. He took a couple of deep breaths and assessed the damage to his jeans. Luckily, most of the soup had only hit his sandwiches, and the stains on his lap were minimal.

Grateful that he was alone in the bathroom, he wet some paper towels, wiped at the denim until he was satisfied that it was as clean as it would get without a thorough washing, and then scrubbed away what remained of his ruined eyeliner. He didn't bother reapplying it.

Feeling more composed now, and with ten minutes remaining before his next class began, Leonard dug in his pockets for some extra change and headed for the vending machines to get something to eat. He texted Susan as he walked, not knowing where she was but suddenly needing to be in the company of somebody else who had lived through recent pain. Later, when he was calmer, he would try to infer meaning from his choice to text Susan rather than Ariel, but for now he operated in a purely reactive manner.

*Already here*, came the reply moments later. *Come back in, I'm with Hank.*

Package of cookies in one hand and a bottle of diet soda in the other, he imagined that he could feel everybody's eyes on him as he retraced his steps to the lunch table. Hank and Susan were waiting for him, and Jason, Jez, and Glenn had appeared out of nowhere, too.

"How'd you guys get in here?" Leonard asked, trying to sound natural but hearing the guarded edge in his voice anyway. He fought the urge to rub at his eyes.

Jez shrugged. "The usual, man. Making up excuses, slipping past teachers, lying to the principals. You know, undercover ninja work." He said it like it was the most natural thing in the world.

"Oh. Cool."

There was another uncomfortable silence as Leonard opened his pack of cookies and sipped his soda. The cafeteria was too silent to his ears; everything seemed abnormal, off just a bit. Not everybody could know already, could they?

He forced himself to consider the possibility. He could still feel the weight of everybody's stares on him, but when he turned to meet them his watchers would drop their eyes, maybe hoping they had not been caught, maybe simply wondering what was going on in the mind of a gay freak.

Except he wasn't gay.

He was just about to say something about the unusual quiet when Glenn sighed loudly and shifted in his seat. After a moment's thought, he said, "Should I give any credit to the shit that's been flying around about you?" He said the words slowly, as if unsure how appropriate they were to convey his meaning.

"Dude, just drop it," Leonard responded, feeling his stomach rise. He felt sick; he was already sick of it and it was just the first day. He was sick of Wes and his betrayal and sick of the knowledge he held of his own actions, but just as powerful was the sickness he felt when he considered how Susan might react. It was different with her, somehow, possibly because he was interested in her or possibly simply because she was about his only close female friend.

"Is it true, though?"

Leonard looked to Jason for help, a desperate attempt at best, but Jason just looked down, and Leonard realized that he was on his own. At that moment he could have punched the kid, torn his quiet vocal cords right out from his fickle throat. *I thought we were friends.*

But he just sighed. "I guess so." It sounded lame even to him, and he could feel his face burning again as he spoke. "But just the one time, man, seriously, and I don't know, I was just curious and stuff and…fuck! Jez, you've screwed around before! How can you be against it? Can't *you* understand at all?"

Jez shook his head vehemently. "No, Leonard, I wasn't saying that it's wrong." There was an urgency in his voice that Leonard had rarely heard before. "I was just curious, too, that's all. I offer to give head a lot because…well, I'm just damn fricking good at it and all. And, you know, I lost my virginity when I was nine, but that's another story. It's cool with me. We all get naked during practice anyway; look at Glenn, he's always aroused."

"And proud of it!" Glenn climbed onto his chair and struck a bodybuilder pose. It looked ridiculous on his thin frame. "I…am…*SO AROUSED*!" he shouted, and it reminded Leonard of the time they'd all watched *Blue Velvet* together. Glenn was no Dennis Hopper, but in this case, at least the energy was identical.

If people weren't looking before, they were now, and they had abandoned any pretense at subtlety. Leonard buried his head in his hands, trying to sink into the table, but thankful all the same that his friends were willing to embarrass themselves for his own sake.

"Look, dude," Glenn said, dropping back into his chair and sitting normally again. "We don't care, seriously. You're our friend. You kick ass as a singer, we want you as a bassist no matter what, and we just don't give a shit. Who the fuck cares if you're half gay or bisexual or some shit?"

Leonard looked up sharply. "*I'm not.*" But even as he said it, he wondered if that were true.

Glenn held his hands up defensively. "That's fine too, I'm just saying."

"So. Are we cool?"

Glenn nodded. "Fa sho, man. When Hank texted me what happened, I got these fuckers to skip their classes to come hang out, didn't I?"

As the topic of conversation shifted to their next band practice, Leonard felt himself loosening up by degrees, and while he knew the calm wouldn't last, he embraced it while it was there. Susan joined in, too, asking about their new songs, trying to keep the conversation alive, and Leonard texted her a few words of thanks from the phone he held under the table. He knew the situation wouldn't, *couldn't*, just blow over, but knowing he could find the eye of the storm, where things were calmer, helped tremendously.

Then the bell rang, and Hank rose swiftly from his chair, a scowl on his face, and departed without so much as a farewell. Leonard thought he heard Hank mutter something under his breath as he left, but he couldn't be sure.

"What's his problem?" he asked, more to himself than to anyone else. "He seemed okay before."

Jason shrugged apologetically, pointed to his watch, and followed Hank out. Jez headed over to the doors at the far end of the cafeteria. Leonard knew that Jez's lunch period was next, and that Jez would probably leave the cafeteria, wait thirty seconds, and then waltz back in as if he'd just arrived and grab something to eat. He envied his friend's brazenness.

Now it was just Glenn, Leonard, and Susan. The three of them walked through the halls mostly in silence; Jez joined them and playfully tried to twist Glenn's nipples through his shirt before saluting and looping back toward the cafeteria. Leonard walked a bit apart from them, and when he was only a few rooms way from his next class, Ariel caught sight of the group and cut her way through the crowd to intercept them.

"Leonard, I need to talk to you."

"Ariel, listen, I'm not—" The bell rang. "Shit, Ariel, I can't be late to class—"

But the look in her eyes cut him short. She wouldn't be brushed aside so easily. "I have a question for you, but I'm afraid to ask. It's just something that people have been saying."

*Wes.* Fucking traitor! Anger flared inside of him again, but he fought it back down.

"What's the question?" he asked, choking back the fear that Ariel might never speak to him again. Someone yelled something that sounded too much like *faggot!* to be anything else, and the anger returned. With it came sudden defiance. He knew that his reaction to Ariel's homophobia, if that's what this was about, should be a "fuck you" and a proud march in the opposite direction, but he wasn't there yet. The defiance felt more like a defense mechanism than a genuine response. It was premature.

Ariel hesitated for so long that the late bell rang. He grew aware of the rest of the world again, the world beyond Ariel's concerned face, and when he looked, he found the hall magically empty. At last, she spoke.

"I heard a rumor," she said at last.

"I know." He was unable to form anything longer, so he simply waited.

"I can tell from your face that it's true. It is, isn't it?" When he didn't reply, she pushed on: "You're *real*, Leonard; I said that the other night. You embody the whole Goth thing, or tortured soul…whatever this whole thing is. For some reason, that made me *more* attracted to you, probably because I've never known anyone so honest about himself and—living true to the heart, not a lie for the sake of being what other people expect—"

She lost her train of thought, sighed, started again. "This won't work. We've been getting closer—or I think so, anyway—but even as much as I like you, I can't. I couldn't kiss you knowing you kissed a guy." She was suddenly angry, and he watched with growing dismay as her tears returned and her words grew choked. "Dammit, Leonard! Fucking—ruined—" But whatever else she might have said got lost as she turned and hurried away.

Leonard stood where he was, dumbfounded. Of all of the scenarios he'd played in his head, he'd never anticipated this one. This was not just rejection, but outright denial of the person he was. Without separating his actions—which he assumed she only knew one version of—from his personality, his mind, the kindness they'd shared, she'd damned the entirety of his existence, not only rejected him but degraded him as well, voiding everything good or redeeming about him.

*I couldn't kiss you knowing you kissed a guy.*

He slunk into his class and tried to disappear. How could he be so damn stupid? None of this made any sense; it was crazy. When he had spent all of those lonely nights wishing for some fantasy-world perfect love, praying for somebody who could drag him out of his darkness, even for just a little while, he'd had no idea that it could be fucked up so quickly while still in its nascence by something so completely unrelated, something he'd done out of idle curiosity and basic *need.* He had *needed* to be close to somebody that night; he had *needed* to expend his energy on something that felt good for a change. It already seemed like a lifetime ago, something far detached from who he was or who he believed himself to be.

"I'll talk to you later, I guess," he'd muttered to her back as she'd walked away.

He tried now to pay attention to the teacher, if for no other reason than to get out of his own head for a while, but everything he heard was overpowered by the echo of Ariel's parting words: *I couldn't kiss you knowing you kissed a guy.*

# II

*"A man of blunted possibilities he seemed to me,—of defeated aims, and thwarted will."*

—from Marie Corelli, *The Sorrows of Satan*

*"I'm scared to stay here, I'm scared to leave this town*
*But a feeling just tells me to burn this house on down"*

—from Bessie Smith, "Haunted House Blues"

## Oct. 14:

*From the journals of Susan Ingram:*

Sometimes I'm glad I'm out of the psych ward, and sometimes I'm not. Leonard came to visit me, which is definitely on the positive side of things—or maybe it's not, or at least not completely positive. The fact that he visited me means he knows I've got a lot of shit going wrong inside me, which does suck. But he seems to genuinely care, which doesn't suck so much. I keep seeing him around school with the new girl, though, so I really can't decide how much of myself to invest in this line of thinking.

I'd like to see Dr. Campbell sooner rather than later, because she usually helps me make sense of things. She drives me crazy (ha, ha), but she has this annoying habit of being helpful. Other than Matt, who still does text me a couple times a week from college, she's my only real sounding board.

Did I mention Leonard? I don't want this to become a one-track journal, but he has this cute way of just looking so intense when he plays with the band. Maybe he'll miraculously start liking me and write songs for me, but if that doesn't happen I wish he'd cover one of the more romantic Type O Negative songs and I could pretend he's singing them to me. Even though that sounds creepy even to me.

# Chapter Ten

A specific brand of pain exists where the end of a relationship is concerned. It is different from the bereavement that follows the death of a loved one; it is more exquisite than the realization that nothing lasts forever and that one day you, too, will die. For Leonard, the only way to survive the pain of losing Anna's affection was by redirecting it, which he found he could do—to some minor extent, anyway—by turning it into an intellectual exercise. He remembered a lesson in English class where the teacher had described the etymology of several English words; nostalgia, he'd told them, came from the Greek words for "return or homecoming" (nostos) and "suffering" (algos). The Greek roots hadn't interested Leonard very much at the time, but the feeling—*that* he understood well. He *lived* it.

In the immediate aftermath of the breakup, both he and Anna had taken measures to avoid one another in the halls of their high school. The building wasn't large enough to house both of their struggles to return to the normalcy of single life, however, and they would invariably cross paths several times a week in a series of increasingly awkward meetings. For too long, the turning of every blind corner was the flip of a coin for Leonard: either he would intercept Anna's path, or they would miss one another and he could resume his day relatively unscathed.

This masochistic dance had continued for several months, until the spring quarter had ended, and by the time the ensuing summer had ended Leonard was more prepared for the possibility that he would run into Anna at some point.

And although he did, they never spoke, and they still averted their eyes. For Anna, it was probably a way to avoid confrontation. For Leonard, it was an attempt to avoid pain.

The year and a half between their breakup and Ariel's parting words to Leonard seemed both impossibly short and interminably long, but the time that separated the two events folded in on itself before the day had even ended. Having passed Ariel once more in the hall near the end of the day after she changed seats in English class to be farther away from him, Leonard found himself awash in alternating waves of anger (how dare she invalidate everything he was by judging one experience?) and shame (was she in the right? Did his time with Wes come with more consequences than he'd been aware of?).

Lost in these thoughts, Leonard had just shut his locker and begun to shrug on his coat when his eye was caught by a quick form with a shock of red hair weaving lithely down the hall in precisely his direction. *Shit.*

It was Anna, and she was clearly angry.

Not knowing what had pissed her off or why she was heading in his direction, he had no choice but to give up on any early defense or opening argument. Instead, he waited, the sight of her twisting him up inside as it always did (*nostos* and *algos*, *nostos* and *algos*, he thought dimly), and when she used one hand to push against his shoulder, the contact threatened to shut him down completely.

*Not only is this the first physical contact since we broke up; it's just as negative and emotional as it was at the end of our relationship.*

"I don't know that new girl, but whatever you did to her, she deserves an apology," she hissed. There was more than just concern for Ariel in her words; her tone reminded him (as once everything did) that he'd never actually apologized to Anna for his animosity in their breakup, and he registered the phantom pain in her eyes and in her voice. She identified with Ariel because they'd both been hurt by him, but clearly Anna either hadn't yet heard the rumors about him and Wes, or she hadn't connected the dots.

"Anna—" he tried, but she cut him off.

"Whatever. Man up. We're done here."

And just like that, she turned away and left with a deliberate stride. He watched her go—tight black top, long blue skirt, tall black boots, cinnamon-red hair—and the twisting in his guts became an ache that threatened to collapse him where he stood. He watched her go, and his shoulder still burned at her touch. He watched her go, and—

Nothing.

He watched her go.

At home later, Leonard retrieved the pilfered whiskey bottle from its place in the back of his closet. It was usually easy to repurpose a modest supply of alcohol from Roland's supply; the man was largely unaware of his surroundings when he came home from a night of drinking, and he always assumed he'd just polished off more at home than he actually had.

This whiskey was pretty decent, not top-shelf but not cheap gasoline, either, and it sloshed at just below the halfway mark as Leonard pulled off the top. It would do.

He never drank heavily, his periodic urges to dim all awareness tempered by his knowledge of the generations of alcoholics that preceded him and their slow self-destruction always heavy in his mind, but he seldom shied away from a sense-dulling buzz when he needed one, either.

He connected his phone to the Bluetooth speakers and navigated to the play list he wanted, and Tom Waits's graveled voice filled the room: "Watch Her Disappear." It was an appropriate song for his mood, and he played it a second time when it had ended. Midway through the second playing, he picked his phone back up and scrolled through his contacts, suddenly desperate for unaggressive company. After a moment's hesitation he sent a text to Susan:

*I'm going crazy here, just stuck in my head. Want to get coffee or something?*

The reply came through almost immediately: *God, yes. I've been playing the same game on my phone for a solid hour.*

Susan's house was picturesque in a Norman Rockwell aesthetic, Leonard thought as he pulled up an hour later and parked on the curb, but the heavy blackout curtains blocking the upstairs windows saved it from being sickeningly quaint. Those dark curtains seemed to announce that here secrets were hidden, an *I know something that you would just love to know* smugness that, if houses had personalities, this one would surely embody.

He pursued this line of thought for moment, wondering distractedly what personality his own house might exhibit to strangers, then shrugged off the thought. The ugly scene Susan had described to him of the events leading up to her admittance into the hospital, and nothing more, was responsible for his sense of this particular house's secrecy. If houses had souls, surely they were provided and sustained by those who lived within the walls.

Along with directions to her house, Susan had texted Leonard earlier that her house was empty for the evening. Her parents were at her younger brother's soccer meet and would then be out for dinner, so they would not be interrupted. *There isn't any subtext here,* she'd written, *I just enjoy your company and I trust you. And I have something to ask you, too.*

This last line caused Leonard's insides to run cold and shut down. He knew it would have something to do with Wes, and he didn't think he could handle a third confrontation that day. Nevertheless, he'd showered, changed, and driven over, spurred on by a tenuous faith in a universe that surely couldn't *always* punish him.

Now they sat together in her room, or what seemed to be one of three. He tried to imagine having the entire second floor of his own house to himself, but that would encompass two bedrooms, a full bathroom, a couple of closets, and access to the attic, and he couldn't even imagine himself *wanting* that much space, let alone enjoying it. When he voiced this comparison to Susan, she laughed and stopping picking at the label on her diet soda bottle long enough to jerk a thumb behind her.

"That sounds like something Dagny would say, if she could talk."

"Who's Dagny?" They were seated on a couch against the back wall of the middle of the three rooms, a small office-type area to the right and the bedroom proper to the left. He followed the direction in which she'd pointed, but could see little in the light cast by the single lit table lamp whose shade was shrouded in a shawl or scarf.

"Dagny's my python!" she exclaimed, surprised. "I didn't mention her to you? She has a good amount of space but usually hides in her cave. You're not afraid of snakes, are you?"

He shook his head in answer to both questions. "I'm not afraid of them, but I've never seen one up close before, other than at zoos or wildlife exhibits." If he expected her to invite him into her inner sanctum to view the creature, however, he was disappointed, or at least subverted.

"She just ate, or I'd take her out," she said, "but only after you've proved yourself."

"Proved myself in what sense?"

She smirked. "Proved yourself worthy."

He eyed her as she reached up to brush her hair out of her face, trying to think of a witty response, but he found himself distracted instead by the contours of her face. She was a slight girl, but something in her face, maybe the way she set her jaw, suggested real strength. Her cheekbones were distinct without being physically sharp, her eyes observant: alert, he thought; poised. He suspected that very little escaped her attention.

Indeed, she had noticed his gaze, but apparently mistaken the spirit behind it, for she quickly lowered her sleeves where they had fallen back and refolded her hands around her drink. Leonard realized, perhaps a beat too late, that she probably thought he'd been eyeing the angry red lines, fresh enough to still be raised, on her wrist. She returned his gaze, and although it seemed defiant, it was also warier now, more cautious.

"How have you been doing?" Leonard asked quietly.

She replied with a question of her own. "You know what it's like, don't you? We don't know each other that well yet, but I feel like I can recognize the same sadness in you."

He leaned back, carefully considering his words before committing them to the air between them. His first instinct was to protect this part of himself, but he'd already seen her at her most vulnerable, and to deny her this part of himself seemed willfully cruel.

"I call it the void," he said at last. "Not in the sense that something is missing, but that there's something that can actively suck in everything else and make it disappear."

She leaned forward a little, clearly interested in the concept. "Like a black hole?"

"Or a vacuum, yeah. You know that feeling you get when you're at the beach and you're just hanging out there in the water, and then people start pointing and you realize there's a big wave cresting behind you? It's like that moment, but it lasts and lasts. It's that knowledge that you can try to dive through it or just let it take you, but either way you're going to get water up your nose, and afterwards you'll still be in the same water."

He smiled when she laughed at the image he'd evoked. "I'm sorry," she said quickly. "I know what you mean. It's just the water-up-the-nose part that I wasn't expecting. God, that's so true." She smiled again, but more soberly this time. "For me it's like that moment in a horror movie that you know is leading up to a jump scare, but you don't turn off the movie. You have to just endure it to get to the other side. You're tensing for it, ready to fight or flee or just freeze up completely, and even if it doesn't happen at that exact moment, you know it will happen eventually, and even if you prepare yourself for it, it still gets you."

"I do like horror movies," he admitted.

"Yeah, well, horror movies are enjoyable. Depression isn't. It complicates everything—I had to tell my parents I'd be at a friend's house tonight because they don't trust me on my own after…you know." She smiled a bit when she said it, and even though it looked a little sad, Leonard knew she wasn't criticizing his reply.

They sat in silence for a while, listening to whatever play list Susan had started before he'd arrived, and Leonard allowed himself to take in his surroundings. Across from the couch was a large television with an impressive speaker setup on either side; the only other furniture were a secondhand coffee table and a bookcase crammed to overflowing with a disparate array of authors: Anne Rice, Edgar Rice Burroughs, even a collection of old Ian Fleming spy mysteries. Situated atop the bookcase were several movie and video game figurines, most of which Leonard recognized and also enjoyed.

"Why Dagny?" Leonard asked impulsively. "I've never heard of that name before."

Susan rose, crossed to the bookcase, and withdrew a thick tome from the bottom shelf. She tossed it to him. "Character from an Ayn Rand book," she explained. "I take it you haven't read it?"

He read the back cover, flipped to the first page. "No, but I've read some old books nearly this long. Mostly classic Gothic novels. I thought they'd have more to do with, you know, Goths, but I actually enjoyed them anyway." He rose to his feet and handed her the book, but she shook her head.

"Keep it, at least for a while. Let me know what you think. By the way, if you see a cat running around, that's Sasha. I didn't name that one." As he flipped through the pages of the book, warming inside at the sight of her copious handwritten marginalia, she added, "I feel like we're the overly literate characters in one of those pretentious nineties teenage dramas, discussing cosmic-scale issues and existential literature and sharing our angst. Do you ever get that feeling?"

Leonard reached behind him to place the book on the coffee table, where he would see it and remember to take it when he left. "I haven't really watched much of those. Why, are we?"

"Pretentious or angsty?"

He laughed. "Both."

She shrugged in answer and flipped on the light switch to the small office area beside them. He followed her in and admired the numerous ongoing projects inside.

The room seemed to be divided down the middle; one side was overcrowded with sewing and tailoring equipment, scraps of material, and a mute mannequin that he thought must look particularly creepy at night, while the other was furnished with a small desk and chair, an easel, and neatly organized painting and drawing materials. The walls were hidden by evidence of the two crafts: designs and patterns on one side and drawings and paintings on the other.

"Riley—that's my younger brother—he likes to be artistic up here. I told him he's welcome to it; I like the company. That's his artwork, so don't judge it too harshly. He's only ten."

Leonard fingered the edges of some of the drawings on the wall with appreciation. "He likes fantasy and dragons, huh? And what about the clothing, can I judge that harshly?"

She placed one hand on his shoulder and shoved. "You'd better not. It's the biggest passion I have."

He'd swayed on his feet at her push, but hadn't really moved; he looked now at her hand, still flat against his shoulder, and raised his own to cover it. He moved slowly, not wanting her to feel ambushed, giving her time to move or object.

She did neither.

"What did you need to ask me about in your text?" he asked, his voice low. He was loath to bring it up, but he needed to know.

*I couldn't kiss you knowing you kissed a guy.* Would she too reject him with that sentiment? He hated the idea. If she felt the same way as Ariel, he'd be wasting his time, expending energy both emotional and mental on a moot possibility. He knew he would be worse off than before, knowing that Ariel's distaste wasn't just an outlier in the spectrum of responses.

*And why would it be a waste of time?* came his

immediate reaction to that idea. *Isn't her friendship worth something?* He knew it was, but the embarrassment would be too much to endure. It would be another rejection of a part of himself that he'd only recently begun to acknowledge. He felt himself putting too much weight on whatever her opinion might be, but he found himself unable to change his thinking. So entrenched was he in his thought process that her response took him a moment to comprehend.

"I heard you were seeing that new girl," she said, looking away. "And I have to know if that's true because…I just do."

His relief was so powerful that he actually laughed. "No! Of course not. Believe me, we aren't compatible." And by finally saying it, he felt a little better. It seemed to clear a path through his mind, allowing more space to think about something else, *anything* else. It was freeing.

"How do you know?"

He sobered at the question. "Wes." He said nothing more.

She nodded slowly. "So that's true." It wasn't a question.

He sighed and dropped his hand from hers, putting both of his own in his pockets. "Yes."

"And that immediately disqualifies you for her."

"Basically."

"Well, shit. But you know what? Fuck her."

He studied her face, sure he'd misheard, but she nodded with unmistakable certainty when his gaze met hers. "Seriously. Fuck her if she thinks that." Her hand moved to touch his wrist, and when he removed it from his pocket she held it in both of hers. He raised his other hand to touch her cheek, brushing her hair back as she had done earlier before resting his palm against it, lightly, almost reverently. He felt her eyelashes dance against his thumb as she blinked. Her cheek was warm, almost hot, against his palm. Her hair was smooth against the back of his hand, and he imagined that he could feel every individual strand brushing his skin. She looked up at him, and her eyelashes stood in stark contrast against her pale skin and green eye shadow. Her lips, bare but for gloss, parted slightly, and he imagined that he felt her breath warm the air between them.

He leaned in closer, more certain of this than of anything in recent memory. *"Fuck her,"* she whispered once more, and then he kissed her, and her lips tasted sweet in a way that had nothing to do with lip gloss or diet soda.

*From the journals of Susan Ingram:*

Oct. 23:

My mom was complaining today that she's already sick of Halloween, even though it's still a week away, and then she was complaining that as soon as Halloween is over they'll be pushing Thanksgiving and Christmas shit at every store we go to. It's true, they do start putting things out earlier and earlier every year, but I absolutely fucking love the Halloween season. I've been making little shopping trips off and on for weeks, a cheap skull candle here, a skeleton chalice there. And of course, lots of that cheap dollar store vampire makeup. Halloween should be year-round, really. At least my mom still makes a big deal out of it for Riley, and now that he's a little older she's even letting him make some of his own decorations (but still won't spring for a haunted house). God, how is he in fourth grade already?

Dad is completely different with Riley than he ever was with me when I was younger. I envy it, but I also still wish he'd just disappear most days. It's fucking tragic that Riley gets to feel so involved with his dad when I grew up just wishing he would do something with me. Even way, way back in the past, I wished he'd been more involved with me. It would have been nice to be his friend. But most of the time, he just looked…dispassionate. Like he couldn't care less, or like he wished I could have been a boy instead.

Leonard doesn't get along with his dad, either. Or step-dad, I don't know. It was so scary that day in the van, when he basically chased Leonard out of the house and into the street. I don't know the whole story, but he's told me bits and pieces. I feel so bad for him.

# Chapter Eleven

Dr. Campbell's office was tastefully decorated, though still a bit too clinical for Susan's tastes. The doctor shared an office suite with several other therapists, and in the beginning she'd gone to great lengths to keep Susan comfortable and get her talking. "Do you hear that?" she would ask if Susan faltered, and Susan would listen and admit that, no, she couldn't hear anything at all. "That's right," the doctor would reply. "These rooms are basically soundproofed, so nobody can hear what we talk about and we can't overhear anyone else, either." That had been two years ago, and it wasn't lost on Susan that a white noise machine had been added to the office after one particularly difficult visit. It looked a bit like a small air conditioner or large radio, and the noise it emitted when it was turned on was something like the static between radio stations.

In retrospect, it had been the appearance of the small machine that had convinced Susan that she could trust the doctor, and although they didn't always get along—in fact, there were some appointments when Susan barely opened her mouth—Susan believed that Dr. Campbell really did want her to get better. She wasn't just a meal ticket, another messed up kid who had to be endured to get a stack of money in the end.

Susan also took some small comfort in the generally unchanging appearance of the office. It was something she could rely on. In one corner sat a large potted bamboo plant; against the wall to the left of Dr. Campbell's desk were an impressively overstuffed bookcase and a standing lamp with adjustable levels of brightness. Wireless Bluetooth speakers hidden somewhere around the room often played relaxing music that she would somehow turn off as Susan walked in. Once, she thought she recognized an old Nick Drake song, but she couldn't be sure.

The desk itself was rarely used when Susan was there. Instead, she and the doctor occupied the twin wingback chairs stationed at an angle from one another, and there they would go back and forth for an hour of difficult conversation: one, a teenager in dark clothing whose sharp features were made more dramatic by bold makeup; the other, a professional-looking woman on the younger side of middle age in subtle makeup, a neat ponytail, and a casual business suit or skirt. A small table positioned between the two chairs held a box of tissues and Susan's small plastic cup of water. A water dispenser stood in the corner. The blinds were drawn partway to block the worst of the late afternoon sunlight.

"You look like you want to say something," Dr. Campbell said now, and Susan jerked out of her reverie and looked up. She hadn't realized that she'd been chewing on her nail until she came back to herself.

"I was just thinking about the white noise machine," she answered after a moment, more as misdirection than an honest answer.

The doctor chuckled. "What about it?"

"It's been two years, basically, that I've been coming here, and I didn't stop feeling like I was being spied on until that machine showed up one day. And then I was thinking about the time I sat sideways on that big chair that used to be in here with my legs dangling off the side. You knew I was just trying to get a rise out of you."

"And do you remember what I told you?"

She did. "I said I wasn't allowed to sit like that at home because it was bad for the chair, and you said the chair was stronger than it looked. It wouldn't break." She paused, and she felt her face grow hot. "Like me," she finished.

The doctor nodded. "Like you," she agreed. "And look, neither has broken."

The warmth in Susan's cheeks spread upwards, and she felt the tears rise a moment before they spilled over and down her cheeks. "What if I am?"

If her doctor was surprised or taken aback by the sudden change in demeanor, she didn't show it. She calmly reached for a tissue and handed it to Susan. She took a breath. "Susan, you're one of my favorite young patients, and do you know why that is? It's because you're so insightful. You're self-aware to the point that it maddens you. I have a cousin who studies comparative literature and teaches graduate seminars on the intricacies of these complicated books, he's presented at conferences in a half-dozen different countries, and I don't think he's as analytical as you are. You're very aware of yourself, and maybe sometimes you don't know what to do with everything you see. It overloads you." She smiled sadly. "It's a gift, but it's a painful one. You see things more clearly than most people your age."

Susan ran one hand through her hair and clutched the tissue tightly with the other. She used it to wipe at her tears and allowed her hair to fall back into her face. The doctor waited patiently; she knew from experience that asking too many questions or pushing too hard would cause Susan to shut down.

When she felt ready, she took a sip of water from the plastic cup and reminded herself that she was in a safe place with one of the very few adults she actually trusted. There were no microphones, no two-way mirrors, not even a pen and notepad in the doctor's hands. She willed herself to speak, knowing that if she said even the bare minimum, she could trust her doctor to keep the ball rolling.

"Remember Leonard?" she asked softly. They were only two words, just a verb and a name, but they carried the weight of fragile hope and a crushing expectation of disaster.

"The boy who visited you when you were away?" They always referred to the psych ward as "being away," a euphemism that made it easier to talk about. "Yes, I do; how is he? Do you still talk to him?"

Susan recalled the way he had kissed her that night and again blushed fiercely, this time through the tail end of her crying spell. "We've been talking more lately, yeah. Well, he came over one night and we were talking and listening to music and—he kissed me."

Dr. Campbell didn't even attempt to keep her face neutral. "That's great news, right?" Her happiness for Susan was unmistakably genuine, and Susan found herself wishing, for the hundredth time that week, that she could have spoken with her mother like this.

"No, it is. But, I mean, I'm…you know." After an expectant silence, she finished, "I'm just so fucked up. Why doesn't he see that?"

"Do you mean, why doesn't he see that you're struggling with very real issues? What makes you think he doesn't see that?"

"He has to see it! He must associate me as a person with how I was when he saw me when I was *away*, and if that's how he sees me, then how can he see anything else?"

"What kind of person do you consider Leonard to be?" Answering a question with a question: the classic therapy cliché.

"I don't know, he's nice to me. But I think he's also, um. I hate the word *depressed*, but he has this look to him sometimes that makes me think that I'm not the only one on a tightrope." It was a continuing metaphor in their sessions together: walking a tightrope over the deep chasm of depression, danger all around, just struggling to stay balanced.

"So then, something in you might call to him, don't you think? Maybe he does see it, but he also sees more. How does that make you feel?"

Earlier in their sessions, these stereotypes—answering questions with questions, the *how do you feel about that* spiel—bothered Susan to no end. They made her feel like she was in a movie, playing the part of the head case but not knowing her lines. Over time, however, they had become a source of normalcy; they constituted a script that she could anticipate and consider without any detriment or surprise. She considered the question now, and she found herself answering without even having been consciously aware of the truth of the words beforehand: "Not so alone. But vulnerable. I feel like he already knows more about me than anyone else, but he still keeps in touch. We even eat lunch together at school sometimes. I think he likes me for real, and that's scary but I also think maybe it wouldn't be the worst thing in the world."

Dr. Campbell nodded sagely. "That's good, Susan. This is that hyperawareness I was talking about earlier. It's interesting to me, the way you phrased that, though. 'It wouldn't be the worst thing in the world.' Not 'it might be good,' but 'it might not be bad.' Why is that?"

Susan opened her mouth to answer and found that she had no response.

*From the journals of Leonard Kellison:*

<u>Oct. 25:</u>

Mom's birthday party is later today, and I'm happy and nervous. I don't know if that's a normal way to feel, but it's what's going on, so I guess all I can do is try to ignore it.

I'm happy for her, because she's going to have some friends over, and it's been a long time since I can remember her being social. I don't know if it's because she's tired after work or because Roland is just a controlling asshole, but she usually doesn't do the hanging out thing. I hope he just lets her have her day.

And I'm nervous because it'll be the first time my mom will meet Susan. Or vice-versa; I can't decide which I'm more nervous about. It's only been a week since I was at her house and we kissed. Or, scratch that, it's been eleven days. Since then, we've hung out at school and there's been some more-than-friendly contact, like a lingering hug or a hand on her shoulder, but we haven't been going at it like animals, either. And I want to. And we talk about the progression of things sometimes, and I think she'd like to, too, but we've been kind of dancing around each other. It's not a bad thing, and I don't mind letting things take their time.

I admit that two depressed people being in a relationship sounds like a difficult situation, but I can also ignore that expectation most of the time. I'm just not sure how today will go; I guess we'll see.

# Chapter Twelve

The birthday event wasn't really much of a party; compared to even the smaller gatherings Leonard had attended in Glenn's basement, it was barely even a get-together. Nobody had hung any streamers or prepared a play list of raucous music to be played through unseen speakers, and the only guests his mother had invited were a couple of people from work, probably other secretaries or assistants from the doctor's office where she worked. Leonard had met one of them a couple of times before, a heavyset woman somewhere in her fifties with a haircut better suited for someone twenty years younger. She was nice enough, though, and Leonard appreciated that she didn't patronize him over his style of dress like some of the other guests had. He remembered that her name was Joan.

Roland was conspicuously absent from the event, which Leonard appreciated even more than Joan's tact. He'd excused himself when the first of the ladies had arrived, mumbling something about things to do, apparently on his best behavior for his wife's birthday. Secretly, Leonard suspected that Roland's benevolence was a cover for his disdain for the event, and that in reality he'd simply wanted to avoid it altogether. Had Roland worn hearing aids, he probably would have gladly just turned them off and sequestered himself somewhere alone for the afternoon. Leonard's own grandfather had often done that during his grandmother's biweekly poker nights, parking himself under a lamp in the living room and becoming absorbed in whatever book he was reading at the time.

Roland's absence was preferable to any affected obliviousness, of course, and Leonard watched from the kitchen for a moment as his mother gossiped with her friends in the dining room.

She seemed different when her husband was away; she laughed more freely and moved more easily, and she owned her space more fully and confidently. She seemed larger; her *presence* seemed larger. Briefly, Leonard wondered whether she was the same way at work, and he decided she probably was. Her friends probably knew a different woman than he did when she was away from the stresses of the home.

He rarely thought like this, but he was glad to see her resemble once more the strong, self-reliant woman he remembered from his childhood. It was nostalgic, like seeing a photograph from better times in a photo album. He hoped it would last.

"Don't bother, Mare; I'll get it," he heard one of the other women say now, and a moment later she was heading for the kitchen with an empty soda can in her hand. Leonard excused himself as he passed her, making note of the familiarity of terms. Not Mary to her friends, but Mare.

He retreated to his room and picked up his guitar, but then thought better of it and grabbed *Atlas Shrugged* again. He propped some pillows behind his head and read for a while, almost more interested in Susan's notes and underlines than in the plot itself. It was dense stuff, layered with enough meaning that he was sure he was missing some of it, but it was enjoyable, too. He hadn't expected the type of commentary or dystopia that powered its storyline.

Susan had promised to arrive around three; it was just after two now, and there seemed to be no immediate reason to move. He put the book down and texted Glenn—*What's up on your end of town today?*—and a minute later, the response came through:

*Jez and Hank are here, just chillin in the basement and watching cartoons. They say hey and Jez just called you Professor Sexybottom.* The text was accompanied by a picture of Glenn giving the devil horns, Jez sticking his tongue between the fingers. In the background, Leonard could just see Hank sprawled out on the couch in the background, a can of soda in one hand and the remote resting on his chest. He seemed uninterested in being in the picture, and Leonard tried not to read too much into his reticence.

Leonard had enjoyed countless similar afternoons and evenings in Glenn's basement, listening to music or concocting ridiculous musical covers on unlikely instruments (Leonard's favorites were Jez's ukelele versions of early-nineties rap music) or simply watching television. He had seen many of his favorite movies for the first time at Glenn's house: *A Clockwork Orange; Night of the Living Dead; Hedwig and the Angry Inch; The Rocky Horror Picture Show*.

Similarly, their endless late-night discussions about women, social anxieties, personal neuroses, and future plans had created a deep bond between them that Leonard imagined must be comparable to what actual siblings experienced.

His phone buzzed again, this time with a text message from Jez. *Lenny Lenny Leonard! Olly Olly oxen free! Do you know anyone who can get us something drinky and tasty tonight? What are you doing right now? Why aren't you here? Don't you love us anymore? Is your hand down your pants AT THIS VERY MOMENT?*

Although he generally enjoyed being inebriated around his friends, Leonard didn't consider himself much of a steady drinker. In fact, he drank far less, and far less often, than his best friends did. His immediate mental response to Jez's question was one of derision, and he bristled at the hypocrisy of it. His therapist often reminded him that his relationship with alcohol was bound to be complicated and contradictory, given the associations with it that had developed as a result of living with his father and stepfather. It was dangerous; it was fun. It was a trap; it was freeing. It incited violence; it encouraged laughter. It usually wasn't until the beginnings of the buzz that he was able to get past the "why am I doing this" phase and into the "everything is fine" mentality.

Finally, he texted Jez back.

*Probably not a go for tonight but of course I love you, brother! You're my sunshine! But I'm at home waiting for Susan to get here. Hopefully my mom's birthday thing will be done by then. I hate socializing.*

Jez replied almost immediately:

*Shit where's the cake I'm supposed to jump out of?? I love me some Mary! Does she ask about me? xoxoxoxo*

This banter was nothing new from Jez; for the most part, anybody with a pulse was at risk of receiving his affection. He regularly hit on women his own age, women twice his age, and, on one memorable occasion at a family restaurant, women old enough to have already seen their grandchildren grow into adulthood. He was a nice enough guy, but people were often put off by his eccentricities and blatant disregard for the general rules of appropriate social behavior.

He shot back a smartass reply and returned to his book, but he hadn't read more than a page or two before he heard a car pull up outside. A quick glance out the window confirmed that Susan had just pulled in. He took a moment to appreciate the jolt of nerves he felt while watching her get out of the car, an older sedan in need of a paint job, and then forced them down and told himself to ignore them. Anna had been the last person to elicit such a response from him, but also the first, so somewhere along the line he'd begun to associate those damn butterflies with her alone. To feel them again now, after a stolen glimpse of Susan sliding out of the car, was both unfamiliar and jarring, and he didn't have the time to deconstruct the pleasure/pain response of such a response.

They'd spoken a bit about the drawn-out kissing they had done a week earlier, but it was mostly in the context of each making sure the other was okay with the progression. They hadn't been alone since then, and Leonard found himself wondering if the desire would still be present when they were alone again. He had to admit that watching her from his window was voyeuristic, almost deliciously shameful in the joy he took from it, but he worried that the interest was one-sided.

Leonard had hoped for an emptier house when Susan arrived, but his wishes were dashed when he went downstairs to greet her on the porch. He nodded awkwardly to his mother's friends as he passed through the living room and slipped outside, closing the door behind him. Susan was just walking up the drive when he appeared.

"Am I okay parked there?" she asked, and Leonard was grateful to her for finding a way to bypass any initial awkwardness. She hadn't been to his house since the night with Jez and Glenn, which already seemed months ago instead of just weeks, and that was a clandestine visit all around. He remembered with a smile how his friends had snuck around to avoid getting him in trouble.

"Looks good," he said, and then, just a beat too late to sound natural, added: "So does where you parked. I mean, you know, you look good." She laughed at that, and he shrugged. "My mom still has people over, but we don't have to be a part of that or anything. And I have to give her her present, but that'll be later."

He paused, not knowing whether to take her hand, put his arm around her, or maintain his awkward six-inch distance from her. He was on the verge of acknowledging the awkwardness with a joke when she slipped an arm through his. He pulled her into a hug and murmured against her ear, against her hair, that it was good to see her. She nuzzled, catlike, against his shoulder, and kissed his cheek; it was a strangely affectionate and exotic gesture, and he smiled again. He considered that answer enough.

Mary Kellison leaned back in her seat at the dining room table and watched her son and the strange new girl converse on the couch in the other room. It was like there was an invisible bubble around them; for the most part, they seemed to have forgotten that the world at large still existed, so intently were they focused on their conversation.

Susan had seemed well mannered enough when Leonard had introduced her; they'd shaken hands and exchanged the typical pleasantries. It had never struck her as odd before, but looking back now, she could think of very few female friends brought around by her son.

There had been Anna, of course, and privately, Mary thought that the break-up had been as hard on her as it had been on Leonard. She had felt sure, early in her pregnancy, that her first child would be a girl, and she'd been willing to see what the universe might deal her after Leonard had been born, but the timing had never been right and Leonard's father had left too soon. During the time Leonard spent with Anna, Mary had grown to regard her as a daughter of sorts. They'd grown close and Anna was never too shy to come to her with big life questions that she was too embarrassed to bring to her own mother.

Mary had watched the two grow closer and closer, codependent to what she considered an unhealthy degree. She remembered her own first boyfriend, and seeing Leonard and Anna together evoked memories of her own maelstrom of emotions as a teenager in love, so any cautions beyond a particularly awkward and abbreviated safe sex talk had been limited on her end.

When they finally separated, she found it exceedingly difficult to keep her own grief at bay in order to help Leonard with his. For a very frightening couple of months, he'd kept himself to himself, completely shutting her out and rarely leaving his room except to go to school or to eat. He slept too much and started looking sallow and unhealthy. This was when she'd started getting to know Jez and Glenn. One or both of them would come over nearly every afternoon, and often spend the night. She still sometimes worried that she'd never appropriately thanked them for their part in her son's recovery.

Since then, Leonard's friends, or at least the ones he invited over, were nearly all boys, and the girls who did come by were always part of a group. She rarely remembered any of their names or saw them twice; she assumed they were friends of friends, not constants in Leonard's life.

No, the only friends she saw with any regularity were Jez and Glenn and, to a lesser extent, Hank and Wes. She knew very little about this Susan, other than that Leonard had gone to visit her on the "skip day" he'd recently taken, and even that was an incomplete story. "She's just a friend who's out sick," she remembered him telling her, but she suspected that he wouldn't go running after just any friend who had a cold. She may not have even been sick; Mary didn't know, and she didn't ask. She worried about her son, but other than his persistent melancholy—which, she often reminded herself, he seemed to finally have some kind of handle on—he seemed okay. She would monitor him more closely if the need arose.

At the moment, however, she was happy just to see Leonard with some company. The girl was small and seemed to use her long blue hair, so dark it was almost indigo, to hide her face, but there was also a certain strength to her. It wasn't so much in the way she held herself, but it was there in her eyes; Mary had often seen the same look of determination in Leonard. It was there if you knew to look for it; it seemed to say, "I'll power through this like I've powered through everything else." Mary wondered what weight Susan might be carrying that would give her such a look.

She watched as Leonard leaned forward to retrieve a book from the bottom shelf of the coffee table. It was a fat paperback that she thought she recognized, though she couldn't immediately place it. He said something to Susan as he flipped absently through the pages, then handed it to her. She flipped it over to read the back, tucking her hair behind her ear as she did so. Mary noticed that she had her eyebrow and one nostril pierced, and the overall aesthetic—oversized black top, black pants, tall black boots with silver buckles—reminded her of something between the Goths of the eighties and the metalheads of today.

"Are those two, like, *together*?" Kathleen asked, leaning in from Mary's right and waggling her eyebrows meaningfully. "They certainly make a pair."

Mary shrugged. "They do, don't they? But this is the first time I've met her," she answered. "I honestly have no idea."

Joan rose to refill her drink. "I think it's cute!" she said with a nearly maternal smile. "I'm glad. I remember when you used to come into work so worried about him, after that big breakup."

"They certainly make a pair, don't they?" Kathleen said again, and they all laughed obligingly. Kathleen had a habit of repeating jokes she thought were funny until they'd received sufficient laughter.

Mary leaned forward again in her chair. "They certainly do," she repeated, wondering as she spoke the words whether she would be seeing more of Susan in the near future.

* * *

"I read this last year," Leonard explained, handing over the book. "It's not as deep as the one you let me borrow, but it's pretty creepy, and since you said you were into horror, I thought you'd like it. I dug it out this morning."

Susan studied the cover—*Summer of Night*, by Dan Simmons—and turned it over to read the back. It *did* look good, and she'd burned through everything by her favorite horror authors, so she was excited to start something new, and told him so.

"Anyway, I think I'm probably missing some of the bigger points of your book so far," Leonard admitted, vocalizing for the first time his earlier suspicions, "but I actually really like how the whole thing started with a question. It's cool that a thousand-plus pages can come from a single question."

Susan nodded . "I never thought of it that way, but you're right. Come to think of it, that might be the only book I've read that started with a question."

"I can only think of one other," Leonard agreed. "There was an author around the turn of the century—last century, I mean—named Marie Corelli. She wrote a book called *The Sorrows of Satan* and in the first sentence she asks you directly if you know what it's like to be poor."

"Where do you even find this stuff?" Susan asked, but Leonard sensed no judgment hiding behind her smirk. He felt a great surge of gratitude at that moment, not least because he'd never really discussed books with anyone before. He enjoyed the easy, back-and-forth flow of the conversation.

"I got this one at a used bookstore downtown. I've kind of gotten to know the staff there over the years—one guy in particular, who's read basically everything in the world. I actually picked up *The Sorrows of Satan* on my own, just because the title seemed ironic, but when I told him I liked it he started recommending other weird stuff to me." He shrugged "I just like variety."

By this point, many of his mother's guests had already left, and the stragglers were also getting ready to go. When the house had emptied of all guests, Leonard stood and retrieved a wrapped package from the shelf under the coffee table. "I guess I should probably give my mom her present now," he said, and Susan followed him a bit awkwardly into the kitchen, where his mother was cleaning up the last of the snacks.

Leonard had put a lot of thought into what might be a meaningful gift; he didn't work many hours during the school year, and a lot of his paycheck went into his gas tank or his musical equipment. Every year she told him not to get him anything, and every year he disobeyed.

So it was with some trepidation that he watched her open the gift, and when she didn't immediately respond, he felt himself at a loss for words. She held up the jigsaw puzzle, a thousand-piece underwater scene, and thanked him for fueling her hobbies. She often unwound in the evenings with a glass of wine and an ongoing puzzle set up on an end table, but it was clear to Leonard that she didn't immediately grasp the meaning of the gift.

He cleared his throat. "When I was a kid, one year you got me a puzzle for Christmas that had a bunch of hidden objects in it. Dad was still there that year and he just laughed. He said it was a waste of time and there weren't actually all of those things hidden in the scene. I just…felt really bad. I don't even remember if I ever did the puzzle." He felt very awkward, but he forced a smile. "I already checked this one out. They're all there," he finished, pointing to the list of objects on the back of the box. "Happy birthday, Mom."

Mary's smile went from bemused to touched, and she hugged Leonard with a warmth they didn't often share. Leonard knew then that she remembered, and that she understood the significance of the fact that *he* remembered, too.

At that moment, the house phone rang in the other room, interrupting the pleasant moment with an insistence both jarring and unwelcome. With an apologetic smile, Mary disengaged from the embrace and walked off to answer it. Leonard stayed behind, accepting Susan's hand when it sought his and the encouraging squeeze that accompanied it. He was about to say something when he glanced after his mother and noticed a marked change in her demeanor.

She gripped the phone tightly, fingers white with tension, her face the sickly gray of old chalk. She didn't look scared, exactly, so much as angry, possibly even enraged. She removed the receiver from her ear and gave it a harsh glance, as if it might wither under the force of her gaze, and then slammed it back into its cradle. Her exhale came a moment later in a heated rush. Leonard watched her visibly compose herself before she turned to him and said simply, "That was your father, calling to say happy birthday."

*From the journals of Susan Ingram:*

Oct. 26:

Seeing Leonard's mom's face change from happy to something much worse when she answered the phone this afternoon should have been a signal that something was wrong, but I guess I wasn't paying close enough attention to catch it. Neither was he. If I'd noticed, maybe I could have warned him, even if just a minute before she tried to hand him the phone. After all, if it was upsetting to her, it probably would be for him, too. But I doubt we would have been able to predict the turn the day took anyway.

I'm probably not the best person to help, anyway. I have my own issues with family; maybe the details are different, but the hurt is the same. This is hard.

# Chapter Thirteen

Later, Leonard looked out across the street from his vantage point on the second floor. He and Susan sat on the roof, much as Glenn had done several weeks ago after they'd returned from the pizza place. The air was cool, bringing with it the promise of winter, but it wasn't uncomfortable. He found himself welcoming the cool breeze, feeling it refresh him a bit. It helped him to ground himself, put a little distance between himself and the evening.

"I didn't like what I saw," Leonard said at length, accepting the cigarette Susan was offering and looking at it with something like chagrin before putting it to his lips. He exhaled slowly. "Not whatever feelings about my father the phone call dredged up, just how afraid for me she looked before she slammed down the phone. She always knew how to manage my father; he was a drunk asshole like Roland, but not violent. Just…*absent*. She knew how to get him into the house and into bed without waking me up when he would come home at three in the morning."

"How long ago was this?" Susan held a new cigarette between her fingers but didn't move to light it. She moved her fingers slowly and deliberately, watching it dance, end over end, from between her index and middle fingers to between her ring and pinkie and then back again. It was a nice trick, Leonard thought.

"I was five? Maybe six? I think I was seven when she kicked him out for good. Anyway, I was too young to really *get it*. I knew my dad came home really late, or sometimes not at all, and that's just how it was. My mom wasn't happy, but she wasn't afraid, either—just resigned. Not like how she's, what's the word, *cowed* by Roland."

Susan shivered, and he moved closer to her. “Anyway, my dad did damage, too, but it was mostly by being absent most of the time. One time as a kid I got up for a drink of water or something and I heard my mom crying. It was the middle of the night, but I wanted to keep her company waiting for him to come home. Eventually I fell asleep on the couch, but he didn’t come home that night.” He fell silent, smiling as he half remembered something else about that night. “No, he did come home, but he was sleeping on the porch when I woke up. My mom wouldn’t let him in because he was so drunk he’d thrown up on himself, and she just let him wallow in it.”

This prompted a laugh from Susan, and after it had run its course she turned to study Leonard. “So, what changed? With Roland?”

Leonard felt the humor of the memory fade; he could almost see it losing its color and crumbling around the edges. The dislike he felt at the mention of his stepfather brought him back to himself all at once.

“I don’t know,” he admitted. “She was single for a little while and she was happy and seemed to be thriving, even if I wouldn’t have known to describe it that way at the time. The closest I can get to an answer is something I overheard once.”

She waited, and when he didn’t continue, she put his hand on his arm. “I don’t need to know if it’s too private.”

“No,” he replied immediately, and it came out heated, determined. He saw her eyes widen, just a bit but enough to reveal that he’d alarmed her. He smiled sadly, took a final drag of his cigarette, and ground it out on the shingles. “It’s not something I’ve told anyone about, but you should know,” he amended. “Your opinion of her matters to me.”

As he spoke, his mind rushed back to a summer

night not long after his mother and Roland had married. The two of them, Leonard and his mother, hadn't been living in Roland's house for too long at this point; they were still somewhere in that exciting period after relocating when it was still a thrill to see one's own belongings in new surroundings. Leonard remembered being a child and being able to point to things—a painting, a piece of furniture—and recall precisely where they could be found in the old apartment he'd shared with his mother. Except, of course, they could no longer be found there, because they'd moved in, and they were a new, bigger family now.

It was a warm night, maybe the first truly warm night of the year after the frigid, snowy winter they'd just endured, and Leonard remembered how he'd opened the windows in his bedroom, reveling in his new ability to do so, since at the apartment there were no screens and his mom hated when bugs got in and flew around. "These damn flies can get in through the tiniest crack," she would always complain, "but they can't find their way out of a wide-open window." He thought of this familiar complaint now, in the present, just as he'd thought of it back then, his bedroom light turned off, face bathed in what little illumination reached him from the lights overlooking the back deck, and the memory helped him to relax a bit, although he knew the scene would soon turn sour.

He explained all of this to Susan, trying to get the details right, because it was important to him that she understood that this marked perhaps the exact night that his understanding of their new family changed.

Scooting forward to lie on his back to look at the night sky, hands under his head, Leonard steeled himself for the next part. "They were arguing over something, and I knew I wasn't supposed to hear it because they were trying to be quiet. They were out there that night and I was on the second floor, but I heard it anyway. 'Don't you think you should wait until his bedtime to have a drink?' my mom was asking, and Roland just kind of snorted and said there was nothing to hide. It shouldn't be a secret because it wasn't something evil, just something men did, and he was damn sure a real man. They went back and forth for a while, and finally he said—and I remember this word for word—he said, '*If you want me to raise your kid, I have the right to drink when I want.*'"

Silence fell between them, and in the relative privacy of the darkness under the stars, Leonard felt tears prick the corners of his eyes as he superimposed his mother's face then against it now. He'd always remembered that night, but before finally verbalizing it, he'd never explicitly connected her subsequent submissiveness to the ultimatum Roland had issued that night. And it *was* an ultimatum, not a compromise or a negotiation. He wondered now if she'd ever considered leaving it, leaving the financial stability and promise of a household and family to start over somewhere, just she and her son, escaping the prison of ultimatums and overdrinking and seeing where such a path might lead them.

But he doubted it, and the strength and purpose in her surrender astounded and humbled him.

Later that night, in Glenn's basement, Leonard's thoughts remained stuck on that same question. The earlier conversation had not progressed much beyond it, and more out of frustration than acquiescence, he'd steered it in a new direction and tried to ignore the fresh awareness of his family's situation summoned by recounting his memories to Susan.

For her part, Susan seemed to understand this turmoil, but spared him the further aggravation of trying to parse things out. He would not have placed any of that aggravation on her; she knew that instinctively. Still, she felt that she had little insight to offer, so she welcomed his attempt to move on and let things be. It wasn't in her nature to push, although part of her had wanted to. She wanted to know everything there was to know, the better to understand him and the affection that was growing between them.

Glenn's basement was unusually busy; it seemed that a dozen other friends and acquaintances had gathered there, probably simply for a lack of anything better to do, and Leonard was forced to park several houses away and double back on foot. He felt that entering the basement might be different in light of the recent developments in his love life, though, and he paused before leaving the van. He struggled with the sudden realization that Susan might not be comfortable with airing their business too publicly.

Susan regarded him with surprise when he voiced his question to her. "Please, I'm much more concerned with everybody—strangers, I mean, not our friends—knowing about *this*"—and here she held up one wrist, indicating the scars that Leonard knew were still red and angry—"than who I'm currently *snogging*."

This description of their developing relationship freed Leonard from the heavy implications of his earlier thoughts in a way that nothing else had been able to, and his laugh escaped him in an unsuppressed snort. "*Snogging*? Is that what we're doing? Are we also in a trashy British sitcom?" He paused in contemplation. "Hey, that's just making out, right? Because I wouldn't want to give the wrong impression."

"Yes, Leonard, it's just making out. Although the 'just' is unnecessary at this point, isn't it? It's been a bit more than casual making out. The point is, I'm happy to be with you. People can say what they want to or interpret…other things…in whatever ways they want, but it has no bearing on me or on us. On the other hand, the hospital is embarrassing and extremely personal and I have no answers for that."

Leonard understood "other things" to mean his evening with Wes and the aftermath at school, and he tried to ignore the mortification that acknowledging the event still made him feel. It could wait; it would eventually require more analysis, and he knew that he would inevitably suffer more for it, but it didn't have to be tonight.

"Let's hope no one gets naked tonight," he muttered as they walked up the drive to Glenn's house. "It happens more than you'd think."

"I've heard that only happens when they get bored, so I'm counting on you to keep them entertained. I don't need to see a bunch of horny boys watch porn and masturbate in front of me..."

Again Leonard laughed aloud, and he reached over to take her hand in his. "I have no idea where you get your information."

"Please, then, enlighten me!"

A beat of silence followed. "No, that's pretty much accurate," he admitted.

Glenn's parents were nowhere to be seen, and when nobody answered the door after Leonard's second knock, he shrugged and let himself in. He followed the sounds of laughter and competing conversations to the basement door, paused, and kissed Susan once before he reached for the knob. It was relatively chaste, communicating more tenderness than desire, but Jez opened the door at that moment and caught the end of it. He groaned and gave them both the finger.

"Fuck all you capitalist romantics!" he sneered, but with no real malice. "Fucking keeping candy and card companies in business year-round, not just on mass market-approved, heteronormative romantic occasions!" His sneer abruptly broke into a grin, and he waved his hand in an *ah, gosh* gesture. "Check out what I got, though, guys," he said with real excitement, and pulled a black pirate's eye patch out from his pocket. "Now I can be Captain Cooter Scooter! No dicks headed for *this* eye!" He pulled it on with a feminine squeal and bounded down the hall toward the kitchen.

Leonard and Susan stared after him and followed. He didn't know how often Susan had been to Glenn's house—he'd only noticed her there after they'd been formally introduced—but he was encouraged by Jez's disregard for her unfamiliarity with their rituals. It seemed to indicate acceptance of her presence.

In the kitchen, they both grabbed a soft drink and headed down to the basement.

For once, the large room was lit brightly enough for Leonard to see the opposite wall without having to strain his eyes. He thought it looked better in the dark. Susan was quickly pulled away by a few vaguely familiar girls, and Leonard saluted her with his drink and turned to find Jez mere inches from his face, hunched over dramatically and peering at him with exaggerated interest through the eye that wasn't covered by his pirate's patch.

"Doctor…*Kellison?*" he hissed, his posture and voice a clear reference to their favorite Gene Wilder movie. Leonard pulled on his eye patch and let it snap back against Jez's face. Jez switched it to the other eye and rubbed where it had struck him, then straightened up.

"So! Leonard! How's it going, where've you been, when did this charming development occur and when were you going to tell your best friends about it?" He spoke almost too quickly to follow, the words pushed together and the punctuation nonexistent, so it sounded more like *howsitgoingwhereyoubeenwhendthicharmingdevelopment-occur.*

Leonard opened his mouth to reply, but before he could, Jez slapped his hand over Leonard's mouth and whispered, with mock urgency, "*Don't speak. I can guess, you whore.*" And he blew Leonard a kiss and gave him a thumbs-up and dragged him along to find Glenn. A brief announcement trailed after his retreating body: "Music time!"

This perked Leonard up a bit; he knew that Jez was referring to *live* music, not a playlist set to repeat. He followed eagerly, knowing there was little need for actual preparation or a formal tune-up—the music could begin almost immediately. Leonard's bass was still sitting in his room at home, but he had played on Glenn's often enough, and the guitar and drums were always set up at one end of the basement. They rarely played anywhere else, so there was little need to disassemble their equipment.

Glenn was already sitting at his drums, and Leonard could not help but flash back to the last time they'd played. He was thankful that Glenn was fully dressed this time.

"War Dogma sucks!" somebody shouted, and Leonard wasn't surprised to see that Jez himself was responsible for the invective. *And why not*? He wondered. They weren't professional by any means. They loved the music, but they had no illusions about their talent or their chances.

Leonard glanced around as he slipped the strap of the bass over his head and saw Susan sitting with the girls who had dragged her away earlier. They were deep in conversation, their heads together as they spoke, but Susan seemed to sense his eyes on her and glanced up while he watched. One side of her mouth turned up in a grin, and then she was focused once more on what her friends were saying. She tucked her hair behind one ear and Leonard imagined that he could see the scars on her wrist from this distance, and it hurt him for a moment. He hated to imagine that night.

Then Glenn called his name and tossed him a package of gummy worms, and the moment was over. He sniffed the candy cautiously but couldn't detect any signs of it being soaked in vodka—he'd fallen victim to that particular trick once before—and so he grabbed a few and handed the plastic package to Jez, who had just arrived at the makeshift stage. Jez tuned with one hand and used the other to shovel a handful into his mouth.

Susan was grateful that Natalie and Rachel were also at Glenn's house that night; it saved her the awkwardness of trying to force her way into a conversation with people she hardly knew. She hadn't known Rachel long, just for the year since Rachel had transferred into their school, but Natalie was one of her oldest friends. She felt that their dynamic was strange: it wasn't unusual for them to go weeks or even months without catching up, independent and generally antisocial as they both were, so running into each other in the basement provided the perfect opportunity for them to exchange stories and relive awkward memories.

"One time," Natalie was telling Rachel now, "Susan was just getting over being really sick, like flu sick, and she came over to my house and we were just watching music videos online. She asked if she could have some of the ice cream in the freezer because her throat still hurt, and I told her to just finish it. No need to bother with a bowl."

Susan knew this was one of Natalie's favorite awkward-Susan stories, and she waited patiently for the punch line. Rachel had never heard the story, but she knew something good was coming because Natalie was already laughing.

"So she asks if my mom would mind if she finished it," Natalie continued, trying to catch her breath between laughs, "and I just said, 'Yeah, she'll come up and say, oh hi, girls, what are you doing, watching porn? That's nice—*hey! What are you doing without a bowl?*'" And Natalie laughed with unrestrained glee at the memory.

Susan cut in here. "I said that we weren't even watching porn, and Nat said, 'oh, we are now,' and started looking up all kinds of weird shit. It was pretty gross."

For Susan's part, such things were unbearably taboo. Her history with sexuality was riddled with shameful memories and the unapologetic disregard of boundaries at the hands of boys who should have known better, and as a result, she tended to keep her opinions and feelings to herself. This introverted, repressive behavior, according to Dr. Campbell, directly led to the externalization of stress in the form of cutting. Susan wasn't quite as eager to make those connections yet, but she couldn't deny that she had very few ways of releasing stress when it started to build up.

In any event, she reflected now, her least painful encounters with sexuality had been as a result of Natalie's influence. In one form or another, the topic would come up, either in conversation or, as she'd just told Rachel, in impromptu porn searches, and for a short time, Susan thought she could view sex as others might: a series of sweaty, skin-slapping-against-skin, invoking-the-name-of-God, noisy acts of pleasure and acceptable, passionate aggression. As long as she was able to separate it from her memories and remind herself that she was in safe company, she could manage.

Of course, this complicated things where Leonard was involved—and she *was* involved with Leonard; that much was beyond any debate or argument now. Her boldness during Leonard's visit to her house just weeks ago was uncharacteristic of her, and she'd found herself wondering immediately afterwards whether she wasn't just tempting fate by putting herself in a situation that could easily slip out of her control. But nothing with Leonard felt masochistic. She didn't feel like she was tempting fate, just stepping toward what it seemed to be offering her. She sensed no danger from him, either as the object of his respectful affections or as the counterpart to what she knew must be a maddeningly increasing, hormonal deluge of desire. She knew, because she felt it, too, and she found herself at a loss to interpret or manage the feelings because she'd never had them before. She'd never believed that she could let herself trust a man before, certainly not enough to allow herself to be alone with him.

Now, jerked back to her present surroundings by feedback from Jez's guitar, she experienced a feeling of warmth spreading through her chest as she watched the long-haired figure approach the microphone. Nat, who had been relating yet another story of the past to Rachel, noticed the look of distraction on Susan's face and nudged her with an elbow. She gave Susan a knowing look, and Susan felt the warmth spread in a blush to her face. She didn't mind.

"Time to rock!" Jez shouted into the microphone.

"Or try to," Leonard added with a wry grin.

Glenn counted off on his sticks, but before they could begin the first song, Jez returned to his microphone and began speaking in a surprisingly professional voice that made Leonard think of the fast-talking small print reader in a car commercial: "War Dogma is not intended for children, babies, or animals of any kind that do not walk on four legs and have fur. The views of this band absolutely reflect the views of each of the members and are meant to shock and offend. Stay tuned for more."

Glenn and Leonard exchanged a confused look. Jez

raised his hands in a dramatic *Who, me?* gesture and mimed playing his guitar.

Leonard shrugged. "Right, so this song is called 'Satan's Playground.'"

Glenn counted off the beat with his drumsticks once more, and then the explosion of sound from Jez's instrument took over. The band usually started their sessions with "Satan's Playground," both because it was the first song they had written as a band and because it was extremely heavy and a good way to command the attention of anyone who was around. Most of the people in the basement had heard the song before—some of them, multiple times—but the response was encouraging anyway. People stopped talking and turned to watch while the band played. It was an entertaining, if not very professional, sight.

The band tore through three or four more songs, and Leonard allowed his mind to wander a bit near the end. When he was in the right place mentally, he found himself able to lose himself in the music and reflect on things more clearly than usual; it was almost meditative for him. He saw Susan on the couch, sitting between two of her friends; Hank, talking loudly into the ear of a girl Leonard didn't recognize; and, in the far corner of the basement, a vaguely familiar boy sitting against the wall with his arm around—

Leonard fumbled for a second, almost derailing the song, but he recovered quickly and he didn't think anyone even noticed. His gaze returned to the couple sitting against the wall, and he wondered, with more than a passing streak of anger, what the fuck Ariel was doing in Glenn's basement, of all places. He was angry that she would even bother to show up where she knew he might be; angry that her presence had torn him from his contemplative state;

angry, most of all, that she had spoken to him the way that she had.

A conversation from several weeks ago slowly returned to him as he watched the two of them in the dim corner, an inconsequential exchange about his FUCK shirt, and finally he recognized Ariel's partner as Jason, the quiet guy who walked with an anxious, hurried, slightly harried stride. He recalled with annoyance the disgusted looks Jason had given him in the halls when everyone was talking about Wes's side of the story.

*When did* that *happen?* he wondered, but he pushed the question from his mind in the next instant. Ariel's parting words to him were tied now to Susan's verdict, the oddly sexual refrain of "*fuck her*," and he much preferred the verdict to the confrontation. He thought he might have to deal with this in some fashion eventually, but for the moment, he was playing with his band and felt untouchable. Everything else was just peripheral.

The song ended, and Glenn took hold of Jez's microphone and shouted, "We rock! Yeah! I'm going to be a bum after high school, but at least I'll be in a band!" Scattered laughter and applause followed the announcement.

Jez jerked the mic back and said, "One last song, guys! Check me out!" He began playing "American Woman," or at least something like it. He screeched the lyrics in his highest voice, careening recklessly through the song without the benefit or distraction of Jez's drums or Leonard's bass, and when he was done half of the audience held their ears while the other half hooted and began chanting for more.

"Yeah!" Completely taken by the response of the group in the basement, Glenn left his drums and flung himself at the nearest cluster of people. Unfortunately, nobody was ready to catch him, and he crashed to the ground in a tangle of clothing and limbs, taking two people down with him in the process. They all cursed loudly, probably more out of surprise than any real distress.

"Glenn? You okay?" Leonard said into the microphone.

Glenn groaned from the floor. "Yeah, man, I'm great," came the croaked response. "Just not sure if my legs are still connected to my body, that's all." He paused. "I can't feel my ass, either."

"I got it!" Jez yelled, bounding over and trying to get Glenn back to his feet by pulling upwards on his hips. A moment later, already having lost interest, Jez ran in a streak for the stairs. His voice floated down after him: "I'll be right back!"

When he returned a minute later, it was with a cardboard box with the band's name in marker on the top flap. Glenn shot Leonard a questioning look; Leonard shrugged in answer: *I have no clue.* Jez opened the box and the three of them looked inside. "T-shirts?" Glenn asked.

"Not *just* T-shirts, *ob*viously! *Band* T-shirts!" Jez grabbed one and held it up, and from where he stood Leonard could see a stylized skull and two skeletal hands reaching above it. One hand held a burning candle; the other was giving devil horns. The skull had the words *War Dogma* tattooed across its forehead in jagged letters. "I had them made up for cheap by my cousin who works in…something related to this. I don't know. But look! *That's us!*"

*From the journals of Leonard Kellison:*

<u>Oct. 28:</u>

It's kind of a strange feeling to be so into Susan, so fast. It's disorienting. I jumped all-in with Anna because it was all so new and fantastic, but the break-up was probably a hundred times worse because of that. I don't want to shrink my worldview to just Susan, even if part of me does want to do just that. What are the options? I guess to go all-in or to go into total avoidance mode. I'm trying hard to tread water here in the middle ground.
But I don't want to drive myself crazy with this (crazy, haha, too late, right?). I should try to focus on something else. The band shirts Jez had printed up are pretty cool, but I feel arrogant wearing my own band's advertising too much. Or do I have that right? Shouldn't I be proud?

Not to go back to Susan again, but fuck it, we'll just go "stream of consciousness" today. I'll probably be meeting her parents soon, or anyway, at some point, and I don't want a repeat of Anna's parents. They tolerated me, but they never liked me, and eventually they tried to put all kinds of restrictions in place to limit our time together. I thought the dad was supposed to be the one who didn't trust the boy, but her dad was honestly the more neutral of her parents. Her mom thought she could see right through me, and all she could see was the guy who was sleeping with her daughter. I hope I can handle Susan's parents a little better...

# Chapter Fourteen

Leonard drove to Susan's house that Monday shortly after returning home from school. The days were passing a bit more quickly, and he knew it had little to do with the shortening hours of daylight that came with the season; it felt good to have something to look forward to for a change, to know his incoming texts might be from Susan. Even better, with their arrival came the knowledge that she was thinking of him. He still lived in a state of wariness whenever Roland was home, never knowing what the man's mood might be, but confining himself to his room no longer felt quite so lonely. He could pluck idly at his guitar and remember the peppermint taste of Susan's kiss goodbye at the end of the school day, the gum fresh in her mouth and the taste lingering as the bus took him home. He could nearly feel the thick fullness of her hair as he slipped his hand under its weight to cup her cheek as they kissed. He hadn't felt the need to drag a blade across his skin for several weeks now, and while he was conscious of the dangers of basing such a change on one person in his life, he found it difficult not to surrender to the feeling.

In the fading daylight, he was able to see more of the property on which Susan's house sat. *114 Aspen Drive*, announced a small post rising above the mailbox, and a fence of modest height enclosed what he could see of the back yard. A small above-ground pool, covered for the season by a bright blue tarpaulin, peeked out around the side of the house. Flowerbeds of impressive size flanked the front of the house along either side of the front door. He was reminded again of a Norman Rockwell painting, and he wondered what it would look like in the spring as he made his way up the footpath to the door and knocked.

He heard a shouted conversation from inside the house. A moment later, the door swung open with a creak and Susan stood framed in the doorway. She wore faded black jeans and the same PUNK-studded shirt in which he had first seen her at the pizza place, a long beige cardigan framing the letters and falling nearly to her knees. She gave Leonard a quick hug and made a small nod behind her. "My dad's waiting to meet you," she warned. "Have to behave."

Leonard had known today's visit would be accompanied by her parents, at least for part of it, but he still felt a vague sense of panic twist in his guts. He tried to brush it away. "Your door has a great horror movie squeak," he said instead, trying to sound offhanded and unconcerned. In his own mind, he was unable to make light of the fact that he was about to meet her father, and they still hadn't exactly defined the parameters or terms of their relationship. Although he felt like her boyfriend, he still wasn't sure that he actually was, and he'd been too caught up in things to find the courage to ask outright.

She agreed with his comment in her own offhanded way and stepped aside. He figured the comment had fallen flat, but a moment later he heard a prolonged creaking noise and he turned to see a devilish grin on her face as she closed the door as slowly as she could.

"Welcome to hell," she intoned ominously, and at that moment, her father entered from another room.

"I hope not," he said, rolling his eyes. "Leonard, right? How are you?"

He extended his hand and Leonard shook it in what he hoped was a confident manner. He was painfully aware as he did so that his black-painted fingernails and his abundant jewelry stood in stark contrast to the man's polite but reserved presence. For a moment, he could almost see himself as he imagined Susan's father surely must: a tall kid with long hippie hair who wore too much black, took himself too seriously, and who would, in all likelihood, try at some point to sleep with his daughter and then somehow end up breaking her heart. It was immensely uncomfortable for Leonard, and he tried hard not to show it. He had been nervous about the meeting, but until this moment, he hadn't expected to care quite so much. That part was new.

For his part, Susan's father didn't seem to be particularly concerned with the boy who may or may not have been his daughter's boyfriend, and this annoyed Leonard for reasons he couldn't quite define. Her father was an imposing man, not exactly tall but clearly solidly built. He had the physique of somebody who kept himself in shape for his own reasons, not to play sports or win any competitions. The effect was ruined, however, by the sort of stereotypical cop mustache that reminded Leonard of the thick caterpillars that always signaled the end of spring.

He released Leonard's hand after a moment, and Leonard stuck them in his jeans pockets. He did it in part to hide his nails, by which he was suddenly embarrassed. He felt overshadowed, somehow, and he hoped it wasn't obvious. He wanted to be seen as a man, but his style suddenly felt a bit juvenile.

"I'm glad Susan is making new friends," her father said with a nod. "She hasn't had friends over in a while, anyway, and I was beginning to wonder whether we'd ever see any of them again. It's good that—" He was looking mostly at Susan as he spoke, and he fell silent at her warning look. His gaze returned to Leonard. "Anyway. She could use a few good friends." He invited Leonard to grab whatever he wanted from the kitchen and retreated somewhere deeper into the house.

"Yeah, emphasis on *friends*, right?" Susan muttered. She met Leonard's glance and shrugged. "After the hospital, he started grilling me about *why* that had even happened. Like I needed to name a reason, and that reason had to be because I was upset with him, or lonely or friendless, or, I don't know, godless. Friends are great, but he won't even acknowledge that, God forbid, I might actually *like* someone."

She probably didn't need to look embarrassed after a declaration like that, Leonard thought, considering that they had spent the past couple of weeks kissing in dim rooms or walking through the halls at school holding hands, but color rose to her cheeks anyway. He already knew that his affection for her was reciprocated, of course, but he hadn't yet found a way to verbalize it as clearly as she just had. "I like you" seemed too simplistic for the starburst he felt when she kissed him; "I love you" was too heavy, too fast. There had to be something in between that wasn't *infatuation* or *codependency*. It wasn't about rescuing her or being rescued, either, although he did feel like he was finally heading toward land after a long time adrift. His affection was a hopeless tangle of individual, emotional storylines, and as a result he shied away from saying too much.

For her part, though, she felt like a movie star when he kissed her. It was never cheap or forceful; it was often with a hand against her cheek or in her hair, behind her ear, and it made her feel brand new and very adult at the same time. This new feeling of maturity, unfortunately, made it difficult to act like herself—a teenager in high school—around her family now that Leonard was actually in the same room as her father. It made her acutely aware of the rules of the house, and she didn't like to imagine that Leonard might find them overbearing or childish or even unnecessary.

"Anyway, come on," she said now, taking his hand and tugging him playfully in what he remembered to be the direction of the stairs. For a moment, he became all too aware that, as far as Susan's father knew, this was his first time in their house. He was glad that he hadn't immediately turned in the direction of the kitchen at her father's invitation to grab a drink or a snack.

They grabbed a couple of cans of soda and climbed the stairs to the middle room on the second story, where they'd stood and talked—a bit awkwardly, Leonard thought—before they'd shared their first kiss together. Leonard sat down on the couch, but Susan continued into her bedroom and motioned for him to follow.

"Is that okay?" he asked, reluctant to incur her father's wrath so soon after meeting him.

"I really don't know," Susan admitted, and followed that with a short laugh. "This is kind of a first. We'll just leave the door open."

It was Leonard's first time in her actual bedroom, and if he hadn't been so preoccupied with taking everything in, he might have realized that it was his first time stepping foot into a lover's room in a long time. (This realization would come later, not that night but a couple of nights later, as he lay in his own bed and read *Atlas Shrugged* and allowed his mind to wander, not without a small amount of guilt, to the excitement and terror he'd always felt when he and Anna would sneak off in Anna's house to envelop one another with searching lips and hungry hands).

Susan's room—or her *inner sanctum*, as he'd heard her refer to it once or twice, a moniker that he felt had a decidedly sexual connotation—was smaller than his own, but he thought his perception of its size might be misguided because the walls were lined nearly completely with furniture: a vanity; a desk; a television stand supporting a TV of decent size and stacks of DVDs—and bookcases, a number of them, some overflowing with books and others displaying carefully placed knickknacks, crystals of various colors and sizes, and figures of characters from movies and video games.

A tarot set in its box sat next to a book on divination; several candles stood in clusters atop many of the shelves. The bed was shoved against one wall, presumably to make room for the squat, long desk against the wall next to it, and dark curtains covered the windows on the wall behind it. Rather than posters, which covered much of the wall space in Leonard's on room, sketches and clothing designs covered the walls above the furniture. The overhead light was soft when she flipped the switch.

Susan popped the top of her drink, took a sip, and set the can down beside a large glass aquarium topped with a wire mesh lid and a dim red bulb in a ceramic dome. He remembered their previous conversation about Dagny, the snake with the literary name; curious now, he crossed the room to stand behind Susan and slipped his arms around her slim waist. He did so carefully, aware that the gesture held more weight here, in a room full of possibility, than in the cafeteria or the hallway between classes.

The flowery scent of her deep blue hair surprised him; he'd expected something darker, more secretive, something more akin to cloves or incense. She squirmed in his arms, turned around to kiss him. He got a mouthful of her hair and she brushed it away impatiently to kiss him properly. She was thin in his arms, so slim and seemingly vulnerable, and he felt again that primordial need to protect her that he'd felt in the hospital. *Crazy is contagious*, Jez had warned him that day, but he was hotly aware that, whatever else she might be, she wasn't a carrier of anything that might harm him.

A thump from the glass tank behind them interrupted their kiss, and Susan spun again in his arms. He peered over her shoulder and saw Dagny for the first time as the snake returned to the branch from which she had apparently just maneuvered. She moved with the smoothness of flowing oil, although her lithe body was much more colorful than that; Leonard saw beige-tan and an almost banana-yellow tone alternating along the length of her. When she turned toward them again, he thought her snout looked surprisingly like a puppy's.

The branch clicked against the glass again as she shifted her weight to bask more comfortably beneath the red bulb, and Susan sweetly cooed at her as she removed the lid of the tank. "Look at my pretty girl," she said softly, reaching in and lifting Dagny out of the tank with both hands. The creature moved like nothing Leonard had ever seen before, and he watched with fascination as she curled around Susan's upper arm and rested her head on her shoulder. It was hard to tell, but he thought Dagny might be more than two feet long, and she was surprisingly thick at her widest. A forked tongue flicked out, once, twice, and Susan giggled with unmasked delight. "That tickles, girl!"

They remained like that for a minute, Susan with the python around her arm and Leonard asking questions about her, and then Susan handed her pet to him and he found himself handling a reptile for the first time in his life.

Dagny's body was warmer than he'd expected, and incredibly strong; he allowed her to move from hand to hand in a never-ending bridge, and each time he felt that she would surely fall, she raised herself back up to start her exploration anew.

"She greets me like this every day after school," Susan explained. "She hears my voice and just pokes her head out of wherever she's been hiding, and I'll just keep her on me while I do whatever."

Leonard nodded, fascination still gripping him. "We had a cat when I was a kid," he said distantly. "But he was too independent for anything like that. He would leave the room whenever I came in, even if I had treats in my hand.

He loved my mom, though, just followed her everywhere."

"What was his name?"

"Benjie." He paused, remembering how he'd attempted to bond with the cat. "I don't remember now where the name came from. But that cat was completely spoiled. He knew he was the king. When he passed, I had fish for a while. They're less judgmental."

Susan laughed and raised her hands to reclaim Dagny, who, apparently tiring of her new company, was currently struggling to return to Susan's own hands. Susan lowered her back into her tank and replaced the lid and the lamp.

"No more snake?" Leonard asked.

"Just for now. She was getting antsy."

"So, this means I'm worthy, huh? Last time you said I could meet her if I proved myself worthy."

She chuckled, and it was different from her usual laugh, huskier and weighted with more mischief than levity. "Oh, you're worthy, all right. Dagny has spoken."

She pushed him back toward the bed, and although he could have withstood the gesture, he allowed himself to be guided to its edge. This insistence was new to him—was, in fact, new to Susan's own understanding of herself—and if they had been alone in the house, Leonard would have worried more about how quickly they might end up together on the shores of some as-yet undiscovered milestone of unity, but he trusted her to set the pace. He felt bizarrely thankful for a moment that her father was downstairs; he trusted the threat of the man's presence more than any off switch either of them might be responsible for pushing themselves.

But he knew in the next instant that Susan was in control of herself and her desires, maybe more so than Leonard was of his own, for although she straddled him on the bed, she did not further their contact in any blatantly sexual manner. Instead, she kissed him on the mouth, fully and slowly, and guided his hands to her hips, where he let them rest, warm and sure and firm without being domineering. She knew intuitively that there would be no threat from him, even when he danced his fingers up her sides, not tickling but caressing, until his hands came to rest just below her bra, but still over her shirt, still chaste in a manner more symbolic than literal. *I could*, his hands were saying. *You're so tempting.*

She stopped kissing him long enough to straighten up and tie her hair back to keep it out of their faces, and then she placed her own hands against his chest, not in warning but in affection, delighting in the warmth emanating from beneath his shirt. She leaned forward to kiss him again, bracing herself with one arm, before giving in completely and running her hands under his shirt and up his chest.

It was the first such contact they'd shared, and he felt his body respond with redoubled urgency. His hands found the hem of her shirt and slipped beneath it, gripping her hips now with nothing between his skin and hers, and when he raised both hands a moment later to glide smoothly up her back, his pulse quickened still further in response to the way her hot breath warmed his lips in a forceful exhale—

—and their exploration was cut short a moment later when her father's voice carried up the stairs, telling Susan that her mother was home and, yes, she would love to meet Leonard.

They both froze, Susan going cold and Leonard hot, and a moment later Leonard had fairly launched himself away from her to pretend to examine one of her bookshelves. Back positioned squarely to the doorway, he made sure he was presentable and took a deep breath before turning around again. Now that the immediate danger was over, Susan allowed herself a bemused smile that belied the fear and frustration that accompanied their interruption.

"I guess we should go downstairs, then," she said with a weak laugh, and offered Leonard her hand.

"I…might need a minute," he replied, his breath as shaky as hers.

*From the journals of Leonard Kellison:*

Oct. 29:

Want to know what's really great? Having what feels like a huge, cosmic shift in the tone of your life, to the point that you're actually happy, and then getting to stand around and watch everything go to shit again. Only this time you're even worse off, because you can't forget that happiness was actually possible at one point.

If I'm being cryptic, it's because I can't really verbalize what's been going on. Not yet. It's only Tuesday, and I already need another weekend; at this point a fight seems inevitable. I'm so fucking done with everyone. It's just amazing to me that people were literally throwing food at me a couple of weeks ago when they heard about the Wes thing, and then they seemed to forget about it, and now it's the only thing anyone cares about. Do they not even see me with Susan? Don't they remember when I dated Anna? If I didn't like girls, I sure as hell wouldn't be wasting my time pretending I did.

What's that old song, "God is a Bullet"? Concrete Blonde? I'm guessing the gun is probably pointed at me.

# Chapter Fifteen

Susan watched Leonard pull out of the driveway and begin the short drive home. After his van disappeared into the coming night—which, she noticed with the satisfaction of one who deplores the heat of the summer months, was already growing chilly—she entered the house again and hung her coat in the closet. She thought that she could still smell her boyfriend (she secretly thrilled at the word) on her, and the thought made her want to wear the same clothes forever, until the scent faded and the warmth disappeared and there were no traces of the charming Leonard on it anymore.

She walked into the kitchen and was beginning to set the table (it was her night to do them, according to the chore sheet hanging on the refrigerator door) when her mother and father walked into the kitchen. She continued what she was doing in the ensuing silence, growing increasingly tense all the time, as they regarded her stoically for a moment. They seemed to be trying to communicate volumes of conversation through their eyes. A bit scared now for some reason, she refused to turn until her mother said her name.

Trying to hide the conflicting emotions coursing through her, she closed the silverware drawer and turned to face them. She leaned against the counter, trying not to look like would rather disappear from view than engage in the awkward conversation that was clearly brewing. "What's up?" she asked, her tone one of controlled offhandedness, but her mind was screaming *Just get it over with; say what you need to about Leonard!!!*

"Oh, nothing much," her father answered. His lips came together in a playful grin.

"You like him, don't you?" The question, despite Susan's certainty that it would be asked, came more bluntly than she'd unexpected, and her mother seemed embarrassed to have blurted the words out from nowhere.

"I do! I don't know. He's a nice guy; I'm sure you saw that. Don't you like him?" She fidgeted as she talked, using her thumb to spin a silver ring around and around on her finger. It was in the shape of a serpent eating its tail; as she twisted it, she could feel the distinct edges of its mouth against the pad of her thumb. She thought distractedly about the day she'd bought it a couple of summers ago, when she'd gone to the city's annual Renaissance Festival with a couple of friends. She remembered how uncomfortable she had felt in the bright sun, how her dark clothes had absorbed the heat and left her feeling wilted. It was cute, but she'd mostly bought it because it reminded her of an old Leonard Cohen song that used the same imagery. She'd spent many hours sitting with her father in his home office and listening to records together.

She was beginning to feel wilted again now from her parents' scrutiny, no matter how lighthearted their banter seemed.

Again, it was her mother who spoke. "No, no, he was a very nice boy. Very polite. But just…sometimes you don't choose the best people to get involved with, and I don't want you to get hurt."

"Mom! It's not like I'm sleeping with him or anything!" Susan knew her face was burning, and she very nearly felt like crying—not because her mother might have assumed they were already having sex, but because she knew how dangerously close they might have come to it if they hadn't been interrupted. Later in the night, in privacy, she would return to the trajectory they'd shared in her bedroom; it felt so new to her, and she would relish the memory of his hands beneath her shirt.

Her father edged his way into the conversation now. "I believe you, but that kiss goodbye wasn't just let's-be-friends action." She started to protest, but he held up a hand. "I wasn't spying. But kiddo, you just met him, and if he hadn't acted toward me the way he did—the polite, considerate way—I don't think I would know what to think of him. Hell, I don't even know what to make of him now, either. Other than that you two must shop in the same stores. In truth, if I'd seen him just walking around, I might have kind of wondered whether he was straight or gay."

"Dad! That's horrible! He didn't do anything to you!"

"Well, we know now, don't we? He obviously wants to spend more time with you, but at the same time, you're my daughter, and I need to protect you." He held up a hand when she started to object. "No matter how old you are," he added forcefully.

"I'm confused, Dad. Do you like him?"

"I've only met him once, but right now, yeah, I do, Susan. Let's just keep it that way."

Despite herself, a relieved grin broke out on her face. She tried to force it back in, but she was afraid of looking like she was smirking, so she let it be. Her default mode was to hide her feelings anyway, but all was well, at least for now. She wasn't thrilled about discussing her romantic life with her parents—despised it, in fact; it was uncomfortable and she hated feeling exposed and vulnerable, wondering if they were picturing her in compromising positions—but it seemed necessary, at least for the moment. The smile dimmed on her face at the thought.

"I'm going upstairs," she said, regarding the half-set table wearily. "Right after the table is set."

"All right, Suze," her father said. "We'll call you down for dinner."

Her parents left the room, and Susan began to hum to herself as she continued her chores. It was a relief to be alone again, and she knew she would need some time to isolate herself in her room if she wanted to appear more composed at dinner.

Leonard swept his hair back from his face and lay across his bed, staring at the fishnets tacked to the ceiling of his room in the alien glow of the blacklight. An old Kings of Convenience album played quietly through his earbuds, but he barely heard it. His attention was instead direct toward the litany of thoughts and emotions running through his head and heart; unable to control them or make much sense of them, he could only let them come, and ride them out as best he could.

Susan's parents had retired to the sofas in the living room once her mother had returned from her outing. Leonard, uncomfortably aware of himself and his posture, sat a bit stiffly until Susan leaned into him a bit and slid one arm through his. He saw her parents try to hide the glance they exchanged at this gesture of familiarity, and inwardly, he took a bit of comfort from their reaction. They didn't really trust him yet; that, at least, was familiar territory for him. He indulged himself in the outsider role for a moment longer, settling into it like an old coat, before reminding himself that he actually wanted her parents to eventually accept him.

The conversation, somewhat halting at first, naturally centered on Leonard: what kind of a student he was, what he wanted to do with his life, how he and Susan had met. He tried very hard to emulate the calm, collected individual he'd spent the past several years wishing he could become.

The rest of the evening mostly blurred together in

his mind, and he found it increasingly difficult to separate his present consciousness from the memory of the intense, frenetic coming together they had begun so recently in the dim privacy of Susan's bedroom. Her physical nearness to him complicated the matter; he felt himself responding to her as she secretly stroked the inside of his arm with one finger, and he hoped his parents remained oblivious to their closeness. Several times he caught himself gazing at the curve of her lips, at the deep indigo waves of her hair, and each time he wanted nothing more than to worship at the altar of her paleness and warmth, to complete the rituals they'd so recently begun to explore. She was impossible to ignore completely. When she shifted, he caught the faint scent of vanilla, and he wondered how he'd missed it before.

Now, searching the blackness that spread from behind his closed eyes, he found himself seeking her scent again. It lingered very faintly on his shirt and his fingertips, maddening proof that the evening had been real. He didn't know how long he lay there, but he must have fallen asleep at some point because he remembered waking up to complete silence. The Kings of Convenience album must have ended sometime recently, and he supposed that the sudden lack of music had jerked him awake.

With a little moan—a minor vocalization of the waterfall of emotions and sensations he'd so recently experienced, perhaps—he turned over and pulled the heavy bedspread over his body. He stretched out under its weight, reached over to plug his phone in to charge, and turned off the blacklight. Now the only light in the room came filtering in through his closed blinds, but he found himself unable to fall back asleep. He tossed and turned in his bed for what might have been a minute or an hour before giving up and turning on the lamp next to his bed. He opened Susan's copy of *Atlas Shrugged* with the intent to read for an hour or so before trying to sleep again, but within minutes the book slipped from his hands and he was asleep once more.

When at last he woke with the morning, he marveled at the difference in the way he viewed the upcoming day at school—the way he no longer dreaded with his entire being the prospect of being thrown in with near-strangers who regarded him as undesirable at best and horribly *other* at worst. He played an old grunge album as he got dressed, read *Atlas Shrugged* on the bus, and reflected on his recent happiness. He hated feeling like he shouldn't trust it, but he couldn't quite escape the nagging suspicion that no change of this degree could last forever.

And the nagging voice of which he was so wary proved itself right, for he had barely walked to his locker before he became aware that the universe had indeed turned on its head once more. Digging around in its depths for enough spare change to buy a drink, he was too preoccupied to fully notice the sudden silence that had fallen like a thick curtain over the hallway. It wasn't until he felt a hand on his shoulder—an angry, tight grip—that he came fully back into the moment.

He turned, and it was somebody he had seen around but didn't know by name. The guy was big, not as tall as Leonard but in excellent physical shape and more confident in his aggression. "What do you want?" Leonard asked sharply.

The other boy grinned, but there was nothing friendly in his expression. "I was just wondering about something, man, that's all. So…does your girlfriend know she's just a cover, or is she actually a guy?"

The thinly veiled accusation and the implications it carried with it caught Leonard so completely by surprise that he couldn't even formulate a response for a moment; when he did, it was only an indignant, shaky "*fuck you*."

His retort was greeted by an even wider smile and a halfhearted shove against his shoulder. The boy shook his head and said only, "Yeah, that's about what I thought." He and his friends walked off in a cascade of laughter.

Aghast at the sudden change in the atmosphere of the school, Leonard broke off his search for coins, slammed his locker closed, and leaned against its door with his eyes closed for a moment. He thought back to the day shortly after his evening with Wes, and he wondered with a plunging heart how something could have made the rounds so quickly and violently, disappeared for a couple of weeks, and then come back around with apparent renewed fervor. Hadn't one wave been enough? There had been scattered insults and comments for the following several days, but the whole question had seemed to drop off the map when he'd started dating Susan.

Leonard's eyes snapped open again. He hadn't really made that connection until now, hadn't thought to connect the dots between his meeting Susan and his peers' waning interest in his personal life, but it fit. Apparently, what little public affection they displayed at school was enough to turn people's attention elsewhere—until now.

*Why now?*

It was a question he had no answer to, and as he sat through homeroom and his first couple of classes, mostly oblivious to the classrooms in which he sat, he found himself less interested in figuring it out than in wanting to disappear. Never before had a pointed glance or an outburst of laughter nearby carried such reason for anxiety with it. His cheeks burned with it, and when at last he looked down at his notebook, he found only aimless doodles and snatches of poetry and lyrics. Everyone from Charles Bukowski to John Lennon was present in the margins of the pages before him. He found himself wishing, only somewhat humorously, that he were more familiar with

Sylvia Plath's works.

This thought, in turn, made him think of Susan, and he imagined with discomfort and shame how she might react to seeing him like this. He didn't remember ever trying to appear to be more together than he was; he had certainly made no secret of the depressed spirit he seemed to always carry with him, but somewhere along the line, he had unwittingly taken on the role of the rock—*her* rock. Until that moment, he hadn't realized he'd stepped into the role, but it left him feeling trapped and uncertain of how to proceed.

He didn't want to lie to Susan about his current state, but he didn't want her to see him so weak, either. After visiting her at the hospital, playing the small-town rock star in Glenn's basement, and braving her parents—particularly her father—he could suddenly see himself as she must see him: strong, resilient, reliable. The discrepancy between his current self-image and the image of him that Susan surely held suddenly made him feel uncomfortable and a bit depersonalized, adrift in dissociation, as if the tension between the two roles left him existing as neither.

*I can't be afraid of what's around every corner* and *be the strong boyfriend she sees me as*, he thought as he approached the gym's locker room. He felt in no way motivated to participate in phys ed this morning, but lunch came next, and at least then he would meet some friendly faces. Various insults and chuckles followed him from one class to the next, many of which weren't new to him but were nonetheless degrading and humiliating. He needed an outlet for the negativity he'd all but forgotten recently, and he thought that maybe this class could offer it. He imagined himself playing hard in the gymnasium, tackling people or body checking them to get some aggression out, and he felt his pulse quicken in response. He wanted nothing more than to disappear, but retaliating might be helpful, too.

He'd barely begun to change when somebody called his name, and he paused a moment, steeling himself, before he turned to respond. When he did, he saw a squat boy named Brent, somebody who had never participated in bullying before. Leonard felt himself relax a bit. Here, at least, there was little danger of confrontation.

"Hey, Brent," he said, and turned back to his gym locker.

"Hey, Leonard. Got a question for you."

Leonard gave a *go ahead* gesture as he shook out the shirt of his gym uniform.

"Is it true that you suck dick? Because that's what I heard."

Despite himself, Leonard laughed. It was a single hard, harsh expulsion of air, almost a bark of laughter, and it originated less from a place of anger than of disbelief. It was just so far from what he'd expected—or, perhaps, it was the perfectly logical next step in his day.

"No, man," he retorted, and he felt more anger at having to lie than at the question itself. "Sorry to disappoint you."

Leonard didn't mean to say that last, but when he replayed the scene in his mind later, he found himself unable to produce a sharper, more perfect response. Nothing else would have turned the attention away from himself so effectively—or, he was later forced to admit, have resulted in the events that followed.

Brent reddened and took a step back as the implication of Leonard's response dawned on him. "That's not what I fucking meant, freak. I heard you do. And I heard you fucking invited that guy over and you both got drunk and you *begged* for it," he said, his voice growing louder with each word, and then he added one more for good measure: "*Faggot.*"

Later, Leonard couldn't remember deciding to retaliate. His recent daydream of body checking people seemed abstract and far away when Brent asked his question. His mind, however, seemed to act independently of his body, instructing it to do what he would not have been able to do consciously, and when he lunged for Brent, it was already too late to do anything else. He watched as if from a great distance as Brent was thrown back against the opposite row of lockers, an almost comical look of surprise on his still-red face, and then everything seemed to happen very quickly.

Leonard had gone low when he sprang forward, and he was still bent at the waist as he made contact with Brent and they both fell into the lockers. For a moment, all of his weight was thrown against the shorter boy, effectively pinning him so he could not move. In just a moment, Brent had recovered sufficiently to bring his forearm up against Leonard's throat, leaving Leonard with no choice but to lean back to catch his breath. As he did so, Brent clocked him in the face with a right-handed swing that might have been avoided if Leonard wasn't so preoccupied with catching his breath. He felt something hot on his face and tasted blood a second later. With the realization came the pain, delayed until that moment, of the punch, and at that moment he abandoned any sort of principles and brought his knee up into Brent's crotch.

The blow had the desired effect, and as he folded in on himself Leonard backed up, sudden realization dawning on him—

—and in the next moment his head was being snapped back by a fist in his hair. He caught a glimpse of this new assailant, registering the face of the guy from that morning, before he was knocked to the ground and kicked in the side.

He rolled, all the fight leaving him as suddenly as it had come, and instinctively tried to curl into a ball as the next kick landed. Gone were any fantasies of acting out to relieve his indignation; gone too was the automatic response of his body that had begun the fight. All he wanted now was to be somewhere else, *anywhere* else, and with each kick his desperation grew, until at last he caught the ankle attached to the foot in an awkward grip and just *yanked.*

There was a startled cry as the other boy, whose name Leonard still did not know, lost his footing and crashed to the floor, landing half on top of Leonard himself. Some part of his body hit the changing bench on his way down, and Leonard wondered wildly whether he'd just somehow killed him. Could such a fall kill somebody? Maybe if the corner of the bench caught the head, he thought, but he didn't think that had happened, and in any case there wasn't any blood. Did that matter? He realized with a chill that left him immobilized that simply had no frame of reference for this kind of event.

Thoughts of suspension fled his mind; images of terrifying interrogations in a cold, dingy police station culled from countless television shows and movies took their place. He had no idea how such things really worked, but his mind was cranking out hopeless scenarios with alarm clarity with apparent disregard to his lack of knowledge.

Gradually, after what seemed like hours but realistically could not have been more than seconds (*Where's the teacher?*, he thought incoherently; *Aren't they supposed to break these things up?*), he grew aware of the other boy's hot breath against his arm. Whatever else might happen, at least nobody died, Leonard thought with a kind of distracted gratitude, and it was at that moment that Coach Jasper finally burst into the locker room, a crowd of students at his back, only to stop short and gape at the scene before: a short kid sitting hunched over on the changing bench and cupping his balls with both hands, face white and eyes slightly glazed over; a larger boy lying awkwardly on the floor of the room, dazed but apparently otherwise unhurt; and, finally, a tall boy all in black, long hair disheveled, face bleeding heavily, half under the second boy but struggling to kick him aside.

"What the holy *fuck* is happening here!" the coach shouted, and it did not sound like a question at all. To Leonard, it sounded more like a demand or even a prayer.

Mr. Manfred's office looked the same that it had the last time Leonard had been sent there (*Has it really only been a month?* he wondered as he walked in, Brent close behind him), except the man himself no longer looked exasperated. This time, he looked livid. He didn't even wait for them to sit down, just immediately began pacing in front of his desk, striding with angry purpose from the wall on his left to the windows on his right. He barely looked at them for a few moments.

Finally, back to Leonard and Brent, he put his hands on the edge of his desk, hung his head, and exhaled loudly. Somehow this seemed to promise heavier consequences than an immediate shouting match would have, and Leonard and Brent shared a glance despite themselves. Neither said anything until the principal was seated behind his desk.

"You're back," he said quietly, and pointed emphatically at Leonard. "And you"—here he pointed at Brent—"I've never seen you down here."

"No, sir—" Brent began, but Manfred cut him off

with a dismissive wave of his hand.

"The coach already told me what he saw. I don't even care who started it, but you know the rules. Zero tolerance." He gave Leonard a meaningful glance, and it didn't hit Leonard until later that it seemed to communicate more than just *keep your mouth shut when I'm talking*. Later that night, after the meeting was over and he had accepted his punishment, he would wonder whether that look didn't mean *keep your mouth shut about the pass I gave you last time*. Was that even possible? He didn't know, but before that day, he would have said no, absolutely not.

Brent shifted in his chair, clearly meaning to speak again, and this time Manfred let him.

"I was just messing around," he said, and Leonard could almost believe him. The sincerity and contrition in his voice seemed that real. "I didn't know that…" but here his words trailed off. "I'm sorry, man," he said after a moment of silence.

"Be that as it may," Manfred said, "you *know* there's no fighting on campus. You *both know* what happens next." He stood up again—a nice technique for giving him a more imposing presence, Leonard thought distantly—and crossed his arms over his chest. "Three days, out of school suspension. Both of you. You can call your parents to come pick you up in the outer office."

Leonard had known that this was likely to happen, but he froze inside anyway. Looking over, he saw that Brent had gone completely white, and Leonard expected him to faint, but Brent recovered himself by degrees. That reaction would have told him that Brent had never been sent to the principal's office, even without Manfred's comment just minutes ago.

Both boys stood to go, but Manfred called Leonard's name when Leonard was nearly at the door and asked him to hang back a moment. Leonard turned warily.

Manfred had circled the massive desk again and now leaned against it, arms once more crossed over his chest. He raised one hand in a beckoning motion and Leonard eased the door closed again and reluctantly crossed the room.

The older man looked him in the eye, visibly took a deep breath, and then broke his gaze. “Mrs. Kearns was in touch with me just recently. She’s worried about you.”

Whatever Leonard had expected to happen next, it wasn’t this. “She…” It wasn’t a complete sentence, but it was all he could muster for the moment.

“Yes. She’s noticed a lot of ups and downs this year, and I’m inclined to agree with her. Last time was…well, what it was. But I can’t let this go unpunished. You’ll take your three days, and you’ll come back with a fresh start. Am I right?”

The tone of his voice brooked no argument, and Leonard nodded. “Sure.”

“I mean it,” Manfred said. “Whatever’s going on…there are counselors. Get it together, okay?” He held out his hand, and Leonard looked at it for what seemed a long time before accepting it. The principal nodded and took his hand back. “Good. Now go call your parents.”

Out in the hall a minute later, Leonard leaned against the wall and closed his eyes. His face hurt where he’d been struck, and he could still taste blood in his mouth, but something in the principal’s demeanor affected him more than Brent’s fists. It wasn’t just the note of care he’d heard in the man’s words, exactly, but it was something like that.

It came to him as he dialed his mother’s number from the main office’s phone.

There seemed to be genuine worry on Manfred’s face.

*From the journals of Leonard Kellison:*

<u>Oct. 31:</u>

So it turns out that out of school suspension isn't actually too bad, as long as the circumstances are right. Mom is pissed, obviously, and she's worried that Roland will find out. If he does, things will go south fast, and it's possible that she's protecting me instead of herself in whatever calm-between-the-drunk-storms situation we seem to be in right now. It goes in peaks and valleys, and he's been…not complacent, but at least inactive. Yeah, great standard for family balance, I know. The bar's pretty low.

Anyway, I'm surprised that she doesn't want him to know, but maybe I shouldn't be. She's no woman warrior, but she's not a sadist. What kind of mother would actively wish for her son to be harmed?

I should have mentioned, Roland has been working all day, every day, for two weeks now, so it's easy to hide from him. From what I understand, his boss gave him an ultimatum, and he has to get his shit together or find another job.

Tuesday didn't count as an OSS day, unfortunately. Three full days, so I'll be back on Monday. How ironic that I get a little vacation just in time for Halloween. Tuesday I spent the whole day in my room after Mom picked me up from school. She had to go back to work, but I didn't feel like being downstairs. I caught up on some video games (that shooter where you're trapped in an alien base, and the RPG where you have to gather citizens and armies and resources from across the world to protect against an ancient evil, etc.), mostly. Susan wanted to sneak in for a bit after school yesterday, but there's no easy way to do that, and I'm not going to try to sneak out. She said she'll drop by sometime today.

I hope so. It's not even time for lunch, and I'm already going stir crazy. I guess OSS isn't so fucking great after all.

# Chapter Sixteen

Sometime after noon, Leonard paused the beginning of the next episode of a true crime series he'd been streaming for the past few hours and headed into the kitchen to make himself another drink. Nothing strong: a splash of rum in a glass of soda, not enough to get him drunk or even halfway there but enough to stop him from thinking about things too much.

His schoolwork sat in a neglected pile on the end of the coffee table; he'd have to get to it at some point, but he still had a few days to do what he needed to. Today, day two of his three-day suspension, carried no sense of urgency with it.

He carried a bag of chips back to the couch with him, took a sip of his drink, and settled in for another episode and another hour of idly playing games on his phone. He supposed he would look completely relaxed and at ease to anyone who might happen upon him there, but inwardly, he was aware that these attempts to enjoy his time away from school functioned mostly as a way to keep himself from thinking. Keeping himself company tended to drive him a little crazy at the best of times, and being suspended for fighting—regardless of the reasons, which he truly believed warranted the altercation—wasn't exactly a point of pride for him. He could play it off as a nice few days of alone time to play video games and blow off the world, but he was surprised to find that he was itching to rejoin his friends and keep busy again.

Shrugging off this line of thinking with a real effort, Leonard reached over to unpause the series he'd been watching when a knock sounded from the front door.

"Fuck off," he mumbled in the general direction of the door, but it came again a moment later, louder and longer than before.

"Yeah!" he shouted. He tossed the bag of chips onto the coffee table, set his drink down beside it, and crossed to the door. He didn't know who it could be—*probably another Jehovah's Witness*, he thought—but he hoped to send them on their way with little pause.

Once, when Glenn had been over, Leonard had dodged a Jehovah's Witness visit by claiming that his "brother" was actually interested in learning more. He'd called Glenn over, introduced him to the two young men, and ducked back into the living room to catch the end of the show they'd been watching. Glenn had been pissed afterwards, irritation at the joke apparently simmering for the half-hour he'd spent at the door, but it had faded into a comfortable joke between them since then.

*Nobody here now, though*, Leonard thought. With a sigh, he opened the door.

"Hi," Wes said uncertainly, his hand still up in preparation to knock once more. "Can we talk?" He took a step forward, as if he already knew that he would be welcomed in. Leonard looked at him for a long moment, waited for that surety to fade, and finally stepped aside.

"Why are you here?" he asked his old friend. He'd never heard that tone of biting disgust in his own voice when talking to Wes before.

"I skipped out on last period so I could get here early. I just had to—you know. I wanted to talk to you."

Wes crossed the room and shoved his hands in his pockets. Leonard regarded him coolly before resuming his place on the couch, but he didn't say anything. *No*, he decided, *this is Wes's show. Let him drown in this. Whatever* this *is.*

After a long silence, Wes seated himself on the floor before the couch. He leaned back against the edge of the coffee table.

"I know you're with someone now," Wes began. "And that's cool. But I wanted you to know that I never meant for anyone to find out. I didn't know anyone would hear us talking. You've got to believe that. We've been friends for a long time, and I want to keep being your friend, but people started talking, and it all got blown out of proportion. You know how people are. If it's two girls, it's hot and they get popular. But..." He gestured helplessly. "You know. The double standard."

Leonard wasn't seeing Wes before him as Wes spoke. He saw their long friendship instead: sleepovers, video games, concerts, amusement parks. Glenn and Jez were his closer friends, maybe; they understood his struggles and his darker moments. But Wes was his *longest* friend, the one who for a while had kept him grounded in normalcy. He'd sometimes turned to Wes for support before he'd been able to understand the chemical changes affecting his mood and his outlook. He'd go to Wes's house, and they'd watch movies or bullshit the night away and he'd come away feeling better, more grounded.

And now, this.

"You left me on my own," Leonard whispered, and his throat was dry. He choked on the words and took a long sip from his glass before speaking again. "You just fucking *left* me *on my own*! You didn't want to own up to your part in this, and now people are saying that I *begged* you! They think we got drunk and I made a move and you finally gave in! What the fuck is *wrong* with you?" Dimly, he was aware that his voice was growing louder and higher with each new accusation, a tension-fueled rant that would surely soon be followed by angry tears. He found that he didn't care.

"Leonard," Wes said, looking up from where he still sat cross-legged on the floor. "I was embarrassed! What do you want me to say? Can't you understand?" He was clearly struggling to keep his own voice even, but there was also real emotion there. Leonard hoped it was shame.

This last thought shamed him a bit, too, because he *did* understand. If he'd been able to foresee the shit storm that would await him at school, would he have acted differently? Would he have tried to get in front of it and change the story so he wouldn't be attacked so badly?

He wasn't sure, and that bothered him.

Wes plucked idly at a shoelace. After a pause, he tried to continue. He rose to his feet, slowly and deliberately, and took a step forward. He raised his arms in what might have been the prelude to an embrace: contrite, conciliatory. "I'm sorry, man. I hope you know I liked what—"

"No," Leonard interrupted, and he was suddenly conscious of his nails digging into his palms. He was angry again, and that felt better. He felt surer of himself that way. He wanted to hit Wes, and the heated focus of that desire, though largely unfamiliar, brought him somewhat back to himself. "No, it's too late, you asshole."

Leonard turned away. "You should go."

"Leonard, man." Wes's hand, warm but hesitant, came to rest on his shoulder, and Leonard rose quickly and pushed him toward the door.

"Fuck off!" The anger fueled and frightened him. It dulled the betrayal, but it also compromised the self-control he needed at the moment.

Wes's face changed in a moment. It shut down, became harder. Leonard waited to see if what he said next would be a cheap shot. "Is this because of your new girlfriend? It is, isn't it? Because she's pretty androgynous—"

"Shut *up*!"

"—and some guys at school are saying you're only with her because it's as close to a guy as you can get without actually being gay."

This last struck Leonard as so ridiculous, so flat-out divorced from rational thought, that it surprised him by forcing a harsh bark of laughter from himself. Worse still, and even more idiotic, was Wes's sudden shift from apologetic blustering to this new, forced bravado. Not knowing what he was going to do until he was actually doing it, Leonard pushed Wes bodily out the front door and into the afternoon light. Wes's look of disbelief satisfied Leonard more than he cared to admit.

"Don't come back."

Leonard had his hand on the door when he saw a new and familiar figure hiking up the sidewalk in his direction. It should have been surprising, seeing an unexpected but welcome visitor crossing paths with one much less welcome—"When a body meets a body coming through the rye," isn't that how the old poem went? He'd have to check later—but it seemed poetic. The two travelers crossed paths just beyond Leonard's mailbox, the boy slightly hunched inward within his heavy vest and the girl straight-backed and unfazed, and if Wes tried to avoid eye contact, Susan made a point of keeping her eyes on him until he'd passed.

The sun caught the deep blue of her hair and the studded shoulders of her leather jacket and Leonard, feeling half-crazed with wordless anger and primordial desire, thought detachedly of fireworks. No actual sparks sprang from the studs; her hair reflected no bright light; but seeing her so unexpectedly seemed celebratory, somehow, almost victorious. He had never seen this particular coat on her, and it made her look capable. Tough.

"What did Wes want?" Susan asked. Together, they watched Wes slam his car door and speed off down the road. His taillights flashed red for a second at the stop sign, and then the car disappeared in a sharp right turn.

When he was sure the car wouldn't return, Leonard turned and studied Susan's face for any sign of suspicion or displeasure. Finding none, he sighed and led her up to the house with one arm linked through hers.

"First he apologized, and then he got pissed and I kicked him out."

"Pissed over what?"

"I think he wanted me to accept his apology, but I'm still too angry at him to just let it go right now. But he didn't try to—you know—"

"Oh, shut up," she interrupted, and kissed him briefly before settling onto the couch. "Even if he did, I'm not worried."

"Yeah?"

"I've known guys who lie and cheat and take everyone for granted, and you're not one of them." She took a sip of the drink on the table, eyed it approvingly, and finished the glass. "Anyway, I took your bus home and got off at your stop. I hope you don't mind."

"I don't, but if anyone is here when my mom or fucking Roland gets home I'll be in even more trouble. I guess OSS isn't a reason to celebrate in this house."

"No? Who would've thought."

Nevertheless, he did not object when she leaned against him on the couch, and when she suggested they go upstairs, he didn't argue. At her suggestion, he grabbed the bottle of rum from the cupboard on their way up.

* * *

Some time later, after a particularly energetic round of half-undressed kissing and frantic hands, Leonard leaned out of his window to blow some smoke into the darkening sky.

"I have an idea," he announced, and he waited for Susan's gesture to continue as she joined him and plucked his cigarette from his fingers.

"Shoot." She attempted a smoke ring and cursed when she failed. "I'll never get the hang of that."

"It's Halloween, right? And I know I'm in a lot of trouble—with school and also my parents—but come on, this sucks. Glenn is having this get-together at his house, not with the band but just to hang out and make some bad lifestyle choices. Lots of alcohol, maybe some pot."

Susan laughed. "Do you even like pot?"

In truth, Leonard didn't personally enjoy the way a marijuana high made him feel; he preferred the altered consciousness of being heavily buzzed or lightly drunk (but never blackout drinking; that was uncomfortably close to memories of his childhood with his father, who seemed to prefer oblivion to any degree of functional consciousness). He wouldn't often turn down a hit, but it was the social aspect he liked: swapping ridiculous stories and theories and laughing together with his friends, or feeling safe, somehow, in the knowledge that he wasn't the only one desperately craving fast food fries. He said as much now.

"It's okay when everyone's laughing together, but I'd rather avoid the huge amounts some of Glenn's friends bring to parties. But either way, this week fucking sucks. I had to take shit from people in the halls, in the locker room, and I finally just lost it. And then I had to kick my oldest friend out of my house because he didn't want to understand how I might not be too thrilled with him right now." He searched for a hair tie as he talked, suddenly aggravated again and feeling crowded by his own sweat-damp hair clinging to the back of his neck. A cold breeze swept through the room, and he closed his eyes for a moment, relishing the feeling. "I need to get out for a few hours, that's all."

Susan found a tie on his dresser and cocked her fingers into a gun, setting it up like a rubber band. "So what's the plan, MacGyver? Want to make a rope ladder from bed sheets and shimmy our way to your van? You could put it in neutral and we could push it down the road a few houses. We'll have to leave a recording of you snoring in here, though." She dropped the hammer of her finger gun and the shot went wide.

Leonard laughed despite himself, imagining Susan's tiny frame struggling to move an automobile. "You'll push the van while I steer, right? That's the logical step there. But no, I'll just…appeal to my mom's humanity. Wait here."

Susan felt a bit like human contraband when Leonard first left the room. Knowing that she wasn't supposed to be there by his mother's decree generated a sense of nervous foreboding, particularly because she'd never spent more than a couple of minutes in her company, but after a few minutes, the anxiety faded and she allowed herself to relax.

She sprawled out across the bed and browsed her social networks on her phone for a few minutes (every couple of her friends' posts included Halloween-themed videos, songs, and pranks), caught up on her favorite comic collective's new uploads, and finally grew bored with the electronic input and opened an eclectic music playlist before setting her phone down beside her. A couple of mid-nineties Type O Negative songs opened the playlist, but after the first she skipped ahead until she found a song from Our Lady Peace's *Clumsy* album. Much of her nineties music came courtesy of her father, who had an entire bookshelf crammed with CDs and old records in his study (it was really just a spare bedroom, but he always joked how wealthy he felt when he talked about his *study*). The goth and metal music from that decade had been her own discovery, or sometimes those made by her friends, but she'd grown up listening to bands like Our Lady Peace.

From her prone position on the bed she could see the mismatched fishnet tapestry across much of the ceiling; it rippled faintly when a strong breeze blew in. What had Leonard told her when she'd asked about them? *When it covers my entire ceiling I'll get away from here.* Something like that—but really, it was the intent that mattered, not the specific words. Thinking of him leaving someday—leaving her—was a difficult concept to wrap her head around. The aftermath, anyway. She tried to imagine how he might tell her he was going to leave town, and couldn't. The very thought left her needing a cigarette, but she didn't think she should smoke in his bedroom without moving to the window, so she relented. The end of the cigarette felt dry and useless against her lip, so she slipped it back into the pack, crushing it slightly as she did so.

After a moment's consideration, she rose and crossed the room to the line of musical instruments against one wall. She recognized the bass from the times she'd seen the band play, and she plucked the E string with a smile. He got so intense when he played; even now, she could close her eyes and imagine him crooning or screaming into the microphone, hands moving quickly across the frets.

There was more to see—a stack of CDs, a couple of video game consoles and some games lined up beside them, shelves of notebooks, folders, and books that spanned everything from horror to musical theory—but she didn't want to snoop. Instead, she returned to the bed, sat up against the wall, and picked up the copy of *Atlas Shrugged* that she'd lent him. She liked the sight of it right there on the little table beside his bed, between the lamp and the clock. It suggested that her presence remained even after she'd left; it symbolized—what? Something about her own presence, or more accurately, about their relationship. She remembered reading something about astral bodies once, about the idea that somebody could be in two places at once—the mental and the physical divided, spanning great distances. The possibility had tugged at her attention at the time. She felt that she could better understand that desire now. Her book occupying his space seemed similarly significant, somehow.

Leonard returned as she was reviewing a random chapter from the book. He looked conflicted about something, but not disappointed or angry, which she took as a good sign.

"What's going on?" she asked. She'd imagined that she would be able to hear something of his conversation from upstairs, but with the door closed and the window open to the sounds of children celebrating Halloween night, she hadn't heard a thing.

"Roland still doesn't know I got suspended, and he overruled her—my mother—when she said I couldn't go anywhere. I'm pretty sure he just wants me out of the house, like anywhere other than in his general vicinity." He shrugged. "She wasn't going to argue with him. She never does. So, they still don't know you're here. Maybe you could leave through the window and meet me at my van in a minute?"

She stood and grabbed her school bag. "I didn't have an exit strategy, anyway," she admitted. "I was probably going to ask someone to come get me eventually."

He kissed her, and in response she moved to close the space between their bodies. This close, he couldn't understand how he'd ever thought he'd never feel the desire again that he'd once felt for Anna. It seemed wrong to him to think of his ex-girlfriend when his current one was pressed against him, but the response stirring within him was all for Susan.

Susan stepped away before he could respond to her nearness more physically. "See you soon," she whispered as she turned to the window.

Leonard grabbed what he thought he would need—keys, phone, lighter, hoodie—and turned off the bedroom light on his way out. He was halfway down the stairs when his mother appeared from out of view and stopped before the first riser, arms crossed and face angry. He descended the rest of the stairs much more slowly, saying nothing because he didn't know what to say.

She stepped closer. "Don't think we won't discuss this later," she hissed, and he understood that she was about to unload on him because she couldn't talk back to Roland. Even tonight, in a rare situation where their dysfunctional family dynamic had for once worked in his favor, he found himself despising his stepfather with a vehemence that made him feel sick.

"Mom, I've got to go," he shot back, trying to sidestep her. She whispered his name in that same angry hiss, and he turned back and gave her a quick hug. "I'm sorry," he said, and he meant it. He didn't think she deserved to be overruled by both of the men in her life on the same night.

It was still relatively early, but the days had been growing shorter lately, and evening was already beginning to fall. It was chilly out, but not yet truly cold, and he rolled up the sleeves of his Whitechapel hoodie. Susan was waiting on the opposite side of the van, shielded from view in case anyone glanced outside from the house, and Leonard thought that was a nice touch. This appreciation was immediately followed by suspicions about where such a clandestine instinct originated, however, and for a moment, he was distracted by mental images of Susan hiding somewhere to hurt herself, or perhaps to meet with somebody else (*this would have been in the past*, he told himself; *you know she's more honest than that*), and he felt a shadow cross over his face. He noticed the scars on his own wrist in his peripheral vision and pulled his sleeves back down. He didn't want to go down that particular rabbit hole tonight.

The moment passed as quickly as it had come, and soon they were headed south, toward Glenn's house. As he drove, they tried to guess what craziness would go down at the get-together—Leonard thought it would end in Jez passing out drunk, while Susan had her money on a fight breaking out—and they had barely turned into the neighborhood when they heard faint evidence of the party. Raucous laughter and incoherent shouts drifted toward them, underscored by the muffled thump of the heavy bassline of whatever music was queued up. The house itself was surprisingly unadorned for the holiday. A large bowl of candy stood on a crate at the end of the driveway, overshadowed by a large sign that read "TAKE 1! HAPPY HALLOWEEN!" The figure 1 had been crossed out, replaced by 2, and then 3, and finally "SOME."

Leonard regarded "take some" as an open invitation, and when he reached down to grab a couple of pieces, he noticed smaller text on the bottom of the sign: "Not you, Jacob."

"I wonder who Jacob is," Susan mused, rejecting the bag of M&Ms Leonard offered her and digging through the bowl for a Starburst instead.

"No idea. Let's ask Glenn when we see him."

Glenn's father answered the door when Leonard knocked. They exchanged pleasantries before he excused himself and returned to somewhere Leonard assumed was much quieter. That was one of the great things about Glenn's house: his parents were able to make their presence known at any party or get-together Glenn might throw, but not in an oppressive or uncool way. (Leonard had once heard Glenn's mother refer to a particularly out-of-control party as a "shindig," as in, "Someone is going to call the police to shut this shindig down if you don't rein it in.") In general, his mother would take out her hearing aid and read in the living room, and his father would disappear somewhere to do…something. As long as nothing got destroyed and the police didn't appear, they didn't seem to care very much. The most Leonard had gotten Glenn to admit to about this dynamic was that they'd rather he party at home than wind up "raising hell" at some poor stranger's house.

Glenn met them at the bottom of the stairs and pushed a bottle of beer into each of their hands before they could say hello. "You're here!" he shouted over the music. "Jez, cut that shit for a second! *Jez*! Dammit, hold on." He fumbled with his phone and turned on the flashlight function, waving it in the air until Jez, who was standing behind a folding card table functioning as a DJ station, noticed it and paused the music. In the sudden silence, Glenn stood on the first step of the staircase and resumed his yelling. "Guys, look who's here! Mr. WWE himself, kicking ass and taking suspension!"

A couple of sparse replies greeted this introduction, some "Woo"s and "Yeah"s, and Leonard, embarrassed, motioned for Jez to resume the music.

"Uh, thanks, man. I didn't think I'd be allowed out of the house, but Roland basically forced me out the door because, you know. He hates me." He took a sip of beer and the three of them made their way over to Jez's DJ booth.

"What's up, *fucker*?" Jez yelled, and extended a fist. Leonard bumped his own against it and leaned against the wall.

"Nothing." And then, on an impulse: "Got into it with Wes today. He stopped by—"

"*What?* That cock lunch actually came by?"

"—and, yeah, and he tried to apologize but then got

angry when I—"

"Dude, he got mad at *you*? For not giving him a *free pass*? Let's fuck him up!"

"—Yeah, he got angry when I didn't just say 'it's cool,' and I pushed him out of the house."

Jez paused. "Through a window?" he asked carefully.

"No. What? No, out the front door." He turned to say something to Susan, saw that she'd disappeared with Natalie, who seemed to be something of a regular fixture now at Glenn's gatherings, and turned back. "Why did you ask about a window?"

"I don't know, man, you're just a fucking beast lately. I heard you really fucked that guy up."

"It was pretty even, I guess. Hey, who's Jacob? I saw his name on the candy sign outside."

Jez froze, and Glenn turned on his heel and met Jez's frozen gaze. There was a disorienting moment of terrible silence as the current song ended, and then, perfectly in sync, the two boys screamed: "WHO'S JACOB?"

Everybody else responded in kind and stood at once, and one by one they dumped whatever they were drinking into a large glass stein Leonard hadn't noticed before.

Leonard looked to Jez for an explanation, preferably something better than mass hysteria, but Jez was laughing so hard that Glenn took over. "You gotta drink, man."

"Wait, what?"

"That's the joke! We don't even *know* anybody named Jacob. But you asked, so now you have to drink your answer. Let's see, Hank was drinking rum, I think Natalie had vodka, I had a rum and soda—that's not too bad; it's the same rum as Hank's and the soda will make it easier to drink—and I think there's also some bourbon and

Jäger in there. And possibly some wine. And maybe a bit of beer."

Leonard groaned. "Jesus, is that it?"

"Um…I forgot, Natalie had a screwdriver, so there's probably some OJ in there, too."

"Fuck *me*."

"Nope, but Jez might!"

Jez was still laughing, but not too hard to give a thumbs-up.

"Shit." But he accepted the stein anyway, held his breath (breathing in only through his mouth, because he worried the scent of all of the different alcohols dumped into the container would make him gag), and—before he could think better of it—downed as much as he could in two gulps.

The effect was immediate, both in the group assemble there and within himself. An explosion of laughter and cheering erupted from the interior of the basement, and when Leonard moved to put down the stein, the world slanted dangerously and he was sure that he would fall. He grabbed Glenn's arm for support and the two laughed with abandon. Even as Leonard's body worked to accommodate the massive alcohol content it had just forced it to accept, he promised himself that he would gauge the full effects of the drink before he had another. He'd had a miserable week, true, but he didn't want it to end in injury or a blackout.

"Come on," Glenn shouted over the music. "Sit down before you pass out!"

He led Leonard to the couch and threw him, roughly but not without a sense of kindness, on the far right side, next to Susan. Leonard scanned the room when he was safely ensconced against the cushion, immediately feeling better now that he didn't have to actually support himself against gravity and the empty space immediately surrounding his body.

Susan and Natalie shared the couch with him, and he'd already spoken to Glenn and Jez. Perched on the loveseat closer to the television sat Hank and Jason. Ariel sat on the floor before the couch, leaning back between Jason's legs and watching a muted Halloween movie while Jason rubbed her shoulders. The movie looked cheap and made for television. Leonard felt an indignant twinge that Ariel should once more turn up at the same gathering he was at, but he let it go with a conscious effort. More than anything, he decided, he wanted her to leave because it made him uncomfortable to share the room with both her and Susan.

Elsewhere in the room were a couple of Glenn's friends, some of whom Leonard recognized. The rest were strangers. A few of them were passing around a joint and playing cards in a rough circle on the floor. As he watched, one of them checked his phone and leaned in to report something to the others; a wild cheer followed, and moments later, the basement door opened and a boy and girl, whom Leonard recognized as a couple from school, descended awkwardly, their arms laden with pizza boxes and plastic bags of pretzels and potato chips. Glenn sprinted upstairs once they had descended and returned with a couple of six packs of soda.

"Heeyyyyy!" came the unanimous cry, and one of the card players added something about how fucking hungry he was.

Susan turned to Leonard and reported that, believe it or not, Glenn's father had paid for the snacks and sodas, but not the pizzas. "That's cool of him, isn't it?" she asked, and Natalie leaned across and echoed, "Isn't that cool?"

Leonard leaned forward to see her better and was immediately reminded of how much he'd had to drink just a short time ago. "It's great," he shouted back, and then, without first thinking to censor himself: "My dad wouldn't do that. He'd say he was going out for it and then disappear for ten years and blame it on my mom when he came back!"

Natalie and Susan exchanged a startled look and laughed awkwardly. In his current state, however, Leonard was completely unaware of the stilted nature of their laughter, and, encouraged, he plowed forward: "That worked out well, though. Unlike my dad, who never works."

"Okay, that's enough with the dad jokes for now." This came from Susan, and Leonard turned to her, surprised.

"Really? I thought it was pretty funny." But he could see in her face that he was alone in this opinion, and he straightened up and used the arm of the couch as leverage as he stood. That sickening feeling of vertigo returned, and he mumbled something about needing some air. His voice sounded thick to him. He found his way to the side door that led outside, grateful that he could avoid the stairs, and heard the door open again a minute later. Susan appeared, a bottle of water in hand.

"Is everything okay?" she asked. She handed him the water, but she did so from a distance, forcing him to reach out and close the second arm's length between them. He'd told her some of the specifics behind his general rule to avoid drinking too much, and some of the particulars reminded her uncomfortably of the drunken men and the dynamic they'd forced her to navigate in her own past. She had no problem with drinking and laughing, but this had gotten dark, and very fast. She maintained the physical distance between their bodies when he reached for the water, tensed to sprint around the house and to the front if necessary, but he only thanked her and took a few deep sips.

“What happened?” she asked again.

He dropped into a seated position on the small concrete square before the door and looked up at her. He suddenly looked very young, but his eyes—those looked old. Weary.

“This is why I don’t get drunk,” he said, working to meet her eyes. “I get dark and I try to counter that with jokes, but obviously it doesn’t work very well.” He looked away and barked a harsh laugh. “At least it doesn’t make me violent. That was—” he paused, considered, and continued—“that was *his* deal. And his dad’s.”

Susan didn’t need to ask whom *he* referred to. She suddenly felt very foolish, keeping her distance from the boy she’d all but given herself to. It might have been instinctive, a learned survival skill, but she felt guilty knowing that it was unnecessary. She crouched before him and pushed some hair out of his face. He tilted his face down a bit, and she kissed his forehead. She’d never played this role before, the caregiver or protector, and it felt awkward to her. The only person whose wellbeing she’d ever truly been committed to monitoring was her own, and she’d recently ended up in the hospital for nearly dying from self-inflicted wounds, so she felt that she couldn’t be very good for the role.

As it turned out, though, she didn’t need to be an active participant at all. He lay back slowly, hands behind his head, and looked at the stars in silence. After a moment, he spoke, and Susan thought it seemed eerily like a confession, or perhaps an apology.

*From the journals of Susan Ingram:*

<u>Nov. 01:</u>

Holy shit, it's been a crazy 24 hours. One thing's for sure, this was a Halloween I'll never forget. I learned a lot more about Leonard, and I think I came to understand myself a little better, too.

I'm not good at being the caretaker, for anyone at all. Or at cooking, or at least that's what I was paranoid about earlier. I'm good at deceiving my parents, though, and I have to wonder if that's okay, since lying to them will stop them from worrying or being angry. Please, just don't let it be self-serving. I don't want to be that kind of person.

I wonder how the good doctor will feel about all of this. Maybe she'll caution me against seeing him again, but is he really the bad influence? Or was it everyone at the party?

Or was it me?

# Chapter Seventeen

"The thing you have to understand is that most of the time I don't waste too much energy thinking about my dad," Leonard said, and Susan was struck by how much more coherent he suddenly seemed to be. She wondered if he'd rehearsed this in his head at some point, and decided it wouldn't surprise her.

"I mean, he's always there somehow, which is an oxymoron because he's *never* there, but him calling on my mom's birthday changed things somehow. I used to joke a lot about not having a dad, but it stopped being funny a long time ago." He lit a cigarette as he spoke, and his eyes seemed pained in the lighter's tiny flame. "Back when he used to come around, he would try to turn me against my mom. If he missed a weekend, it was her fault for not letting me see him. If he was late dropping me off, it was her fault for not giving him enough time with me to have fun. You know what I mean?"

She nodded, but he didn't seem to be looking for an answer.

"So he's a ghost in my life, and then out of nowhere, he calls my mom to say 'happy birthday.' And I immediately turn into a paranoid detective, trying to figure out what his angle is. What's his motive? Because I know he isn't capable of just being a well-wisher. So this gets out of control in my head, and of course, the first time I get really drunk I have to unleash it in public and weird everyone out. So."

When it became apparent that nothing more would be forthcoming, Susan turned to look at him. He studiously avoided meeting her gaze, flicking the ash from the end of his cigarette and pretending to study the red tip instead. The cherry, his friends called it. It occurred to her that he seemed ashamed, although whether of his history or his behavior that night she had no idea. She took the cigarette from him, allowing their fingers to briefly intertwine before releasing his hand and bringing the filter to her own lips. When she returned it to him, he seemed fascinated by the imprint her dark purple lipstick left on the paper.

"Let's get out of here," she said, her voice barely above a whisper. It seemed crass to her to break the silence that had fallen after his confession.

Leonard laughed ruefully. "I'm not driving anywhere," he said, and as the words left his lips he had a momentary flashback of one of his early therapy sessions, when he'd made an offhanded comment about jumping off of a bridge—this was before he'd learned to drive—and left his therapist alarmed and a bit angry at his irreverence. He wondered if he would have risked driving tonight if circumstances were different, and decided he'd have to ponder that at some later date.

"So? My house isn't far. We can walk."

"I can't see your parents like this."

She hesitated. "No one's home," she admitted. "My brother had a soccer game at another school, so they decided to make a mini-vacation out of it."

She hadn't been planning to share this information, knowing that the temptation that would arise from being alone with her boyfriend all night would likely be too great to resist, but now she found that she wasn't worried. Apprehensive, yes, but that was for a different set of reasons.

He left his van parked on the street and texted Glenn what he hoped was a coherent explanation, and then they turned in the direction of Susan's house and began to walk.

Trick-or-treating was technically over already, but they passed a good number of young children being walked down the streets by their parents or older siblings. Neither of them spoke much as they walked, but Leonard noticed that the children didn't pay much attention to them on a night when everybody was dressed for attention. He studied Susan's profile for a moment and smiled inwardly. He was still embarrassingly drunk, but he was also…what? If not at peace, then at least in less angst than he might have expected.

Susan's house was dark when they approached it, but the porch light was on and an empty candy bowl sat in front of a small scarecrow. She unlocked the front door and turned on the hallway light, then reappeared a second later to retrieve the bowl. Leonard followed her in and sat down heavily on the couch, and she handed him a bottle of water when she joined him a moment later. He took it gratefully and finished half of it in a few large, greedy swallows.

"It seems different at night," he observed, and he trusted her to pick up the subtext: *I've never been here with you alone at night, and I don't know what to do now.*

She grinned and tugged at his arm. "Come here, check this out."

He followed her into a large room at the back of the house; when she turned on a desk lamp, he saw that it was a study or an office. Several bookshelves displayed neatly lined volumes of all sizes, but most of them look serious and either historical or financial. The bottom row of the shelf on the end alone held popular fiction. Diplomas and certifications hung framed on the wall, and an expensive-looking recliner sat in one corner next to a standing lamp. Against the adjoining wall stood a desk of dark wood. Leonard knew without having to be told that this was Susan's father's study; it practically screamed *masculine territory.*

"Is it cool that we're in here?" he asked. He stood in the center of the room, careful not to touch anything.

"Yeah, it's fine," Susan replied. She picked up a letter opener from the desk and toyed with it. "I used to come in here all the time when I was a kid and my dad was working. Especially at night. He'd work late into the night, and I'd have a nightmare or something, or I would be sick, and I'd sit on the loveseat that used to be in here and just watch him work." She shrugged. "It felt safe. And it always smelled good, back before my mom made him quit his cigars. He was like the typical *über*-dad."

"I get that," Leonard said. "At least, in theory. It's like little kids who hide in their parents' bed during thunderstorms, right?"

"Yeah, especially little kids who watched *Poltergeist* way too young."

"*Oh* yeah. I never thought I would have a reason to be afraid of trees, but then I watched that damn movie. Then I came across sentient trees again in a story by Algernon Blackwood, 'The Man Whom the Trees Loved,' and it was right back to hating nature."

"How do you always do that?" Susan asked, replacing the letter opener and leaning against the edge of the desk.

"Do what?"

"You just have this ability to pull references out of your ass. I'm pretty sure you have a book title for any situation."

Leonard shrugged, crossing the room to take a closer look at the titles on the bookshelves. "Like I said, I have a friend at a bookstore who recommends weird stuff when I go in there. And I used to blow off everything to just sit and read." He paused. "My therapist said it was a way to escape."

"That's probably the first time you've brought her up on your own. Why is that?"

"I really don't know. I used to think that only

desperate people, or people in crisis, ever bothered with therapy, but I know now that isn't true. I still feel that way, though. Like I must be two steps away from jumping off a bridge because I have regular sessions."

"Are you?"

"What, about to jump off of a bridge?" He laughed. "No, not anymore. Some things really suck, but I'm not about to give life the satisfaction of disappearing."

"I'm glad."

Susan looked like she was about to say more, but instead she moved to a record player in the corner of the room and knelt to flip through the records resting in a milk crate under the player's table. She thought for a moment, backtracked a few titles, and finally withdrew a sleeve and tilted the record out of it. She moved the needle to an outer groove and sat in the recliner, closing her eyes and nodding to the music.

"Who are we listening to?" Leonard asked. She handed him the cardboard sleeve, and he studied the artistic rendering of a woman against a white background before turning it over and reading the track listing. It was Joni Mitchell's *Ladies of the Canyon.*

"My dad has a ton of music on vinyl somewhere, but he only keeps his favorites of the moment here with the record player. I always used to tease him that most of the music he keeps in here is by women: Joni Mitchell, Billie Holiday, Janis Joplin, stuff like that. I tried to get him into Lorde, but he didn't go for it."

"Hmmm." He handed the sleeve back to her. "This isn't as trippy as I thought it would be."

"Trippy, hippie, they're a little different." She sat up suddenly in her chair. "Want to see trippy? Like, *really* trippy?"

"Um, sure."

"Wait here."

Leonard listened to her fading footfalls as she disappeared into the hallway. He wasn't feeling the effects of the alcohol as strongly anymore, for which he was thankful. Part of him wished he had stayed at Glenn's party longer, but on the other hand, getting sick had led him to be sitting here, in this chair. That was an unexpected turn of events, but it wasn't necessary *bad*, he thought. His eyes lingered on the titles embossed on the spines of the neatly arranged books. *No, this isn't bad at all.*

Susan returned after he had taken a book from a lower shelf, a well-worn reprint of John Ruskin's *Sesame and Lilies*, and opened it randomly. Old notes in pencil were written in the margins, and he was trying to decipher them while he waited. He closed the book and gave her a look of exaggerated guilt. "Robbing your dad of his knowledge," he admitted.

"Seems like a victimless crime." Susan took the book from him and flipped through it. "This was my dad's, from college. I don't know why he kept it all these years; he never had much interest in outdated social commentary."

"Maybe he threw it out but it kept coming back to him." He grinned. "What did you bring? Something trippy?"

She replaced the book on its shelf and held up a small sealed bag. "My brother left them here last time he was home from college. I don't think he even remembers that he had them."

Leaning forward, Leonard saw that the bag contained what looked like a variety of dark, desiccated dates. "What are they?"

Susan handed him the bag. "Mushrooms. Happy Halloween."

"Really? I've never tried anything like this. Are they addictive?"

"Nah, they're not supposed to be. I've never done them, but I did a lot of reading online when I found out Matt was. I was worried about him. They seem to be pretty safe compared to something hardcore like heroin, though. As far as I know, Matt has never done anything harder than these, and he's fine."

He thought for a moment. "Do they interact with medication?"

"Apparently they can make it harder to feel the high, but that's all I've ever seen on the topic." She reached over, and he returned the bag. "So…want to?"

"I don't know. Maybe. Actually, fuck it, why not?"

She extended her hand, and he rose to meet her in the middle of the office. "Let's go upstairs," she said, "but we should raid the kitchen first. People say you're thirsty during the experience and starving afterwards."

Leonard found that she was right. For the next couple of hours, he found himself desperately thirsty, yet so distracted by everything around him that he kept forgetting to drink. The drugs themselves were dry and slightly acrid, and for a good twenty minutes or so he simply sat and waited for something to happen. It wasn't until he started moving that he realized things were already beyond his control.

The folds in the dark curtains seemed to ripple, every movement caused by the heated air flowing out of the vents expanding outward in uneven concentric circles. He reached for Susan, meaning to point at the curtains, but his hand didn't seem his own: it was too pale, the fingers too long, the black nail polish too cracked and uneven. More surprising was how far away Susan seemed as he reached for her. She seemed to be right beside him, but when he returned his attention from his hand to her presence, he saw that she was actually across the room.

She stood before Dagny's aquarium, holding the reptile in her hands and cooing to her quietly enough that Leonard couldn't quite make out the words. Her voice seemed liquid to him, like mercury, or like how he imagined a stream might sound when nothing manmade was around to overpower its song.

"Speaking of music, this is a great album," he called over to Susan, and the sudden shout of his voice made him laugh. It was like destroying a symphony with the sound of a building being demolished, and this struck him as funny, too. Even the dim sense of alarm he felt at being powerless to control his laughter amused him.

Susan joined him and placed the ball python in his hands. "We weren't talking about music at all!" she exclaimed, and then she, too, began to laugh.

"We weren't? But this album is so great. Who is it again?"

"Some band called Om! This is 'Gethsemane.' They're like metal but not superbly heavy. They're almost spiritual, and I like how relaxing they are when I need to unwind or stop thinking. Their songs are usually pretty long, too, so you can just get lost in it. You know?"

He nodded. "Completely." That one word seemed to encompass everything he might have struggled to verbalize, and he suddenly felt so at peace, so *connected*, that he thought he might cry.

Susan pointed to the special that was playing, muted, on the television. "It also pairs really well with deep sea documentaries," she said with great sincerity, and they both laughed again. As they laughed, she moved to push her hair back behind her ears, and her arms seemed too impossibly long, too angular, to complete such a fluid movement. Suddenly she reminded him of an insect—

maybe a mantis—and he found himself oddly drawn to the image.

"Kiss me," he breathed, and she did. They shambled backward together until he felt the edge of the bed against his legs, and he collapsed back onto the quilt thrown over it, keeping his arms raised so Dagny wouldn't be hurt. Susan lay on her back beside him and reached for the reptile, who seemed to recognize her owner and moved smoothly back to her hands. For a moment, they each watched in silence as their hands were bound together by the reptile's muscular body—tail curled around Leonard's hand, upper body around Susan's—and then the moment passed and Dagny was all Susan's again.

In the past, lying across a bed with a woman who reciprocated his advances would have led almost inevitably to something more: more serious, more sexual, more dangerous, just *more*. This night, however, such a physical exertion and commitment seemed laughably out of the question. He'd worried that such a state of altered consciousness would be unpleasant or disorienting, but the truth was that he felt nothing negative in the experience. Everything was brighter, more enhanced and exaggerated, but not in a manner that concerned him. Instead, he found himself happy to just *be*—to be in Susan's house, sprawled next to her atop her bed, mesmerized by the repetitive music and soothed by the deep-sea exploration being chronicled on the television. He embraced the *being* and the simple *more*ness of his awareness.

That sense of exaggerated existence continued unabated for the next hour or more, until Halloween had expired and a nascent November had taken its place. At some point, Susan had returned Dagny to her enclosure, and since then she'd taken to wandering through the three rooms that comprised the second floor, examining things here and there with new eyes and laughing to herself now and then. Leonard joined her in the middle room to find her fastening a silver bracelet around her wrist. Tiny bell charms were attached to it, making high tinkling sounds as she moved her arm around. The sight seemed almost mystical to him, and he tried and failed to summon a line of poetry that matched how he felt. It didn't matter. He finished his bottle of water in a few swallows and tapped one of the bells in time to the beat of Om's music.

It was sometime after one in the morning when their awareness returned to normal, and Leonard found himself suffering from an acute feeling of being diminished in the wake of his high. He studied the blackout curtains and Susan's hair from his supine position on the bed, but they appeared ordinary once more. He mourned the absence of the strange magic he'd felt, but the feeling faded when he turned onto his side and saw Susan watching him from her perch atop the desk.

"What's up?" he asked.

She shook her head. "Tonight was fun. That's all; I'm glad I did this with you." She crossed the room and tossed something next to him on the bed; he glanced down and saw that it was a deck of playing cards. "I'm pretty wired. Let's play a game."

He shook the cards out of the deck. He'd expected them to be something horror-themed, but they were just plain, well-worn cards that could be bought at any store across the country. A smile crossed his lips: he may have been expecting novelty cards, but for some reason, this piece of normalcy was endearing.

"I only know a few games," he admitted, shuffling the cards on the soft surface of the bedspread. He attempted the bridge shuffle, but they fell from his hands in a random pile on the bed. Susan laughed and straightened the deck.

"Not poker or anything! Let's just split the deck and we'll play war-style, but the loser has to answer anything the winner asks. Like truth or dare, but without the dares, and we can play with just two people. What do you think?"

Leonard groaned, then laughed. "This is going to end badly! But sure, let's do it."

"A little mood music first, maybe?" Susan unlocked her phone and scrolled through her music app, settling at last on an old Cranberries album. She tilted her phone his way as the first song replaced Om's music, piping through the Bluetooth speakers set atop her dresser. "Do you know this one? *Everyone Else Is Doing It, So Why Can't We?*" she asked.

He shook his head. "Nope. Here, cut the deck and let's get personal."

She won the first hand, and she didn't waste any time with pleasantries with her first question: "What first drew you to the Goth look?"

He laughed. "*It's a way of life, not a look,*" he hissed, but he couldn't keep a straight face for more than a second or two. "No, I don't know. I mean, obviously I *know*, but it's hard to put into words. Things have been rough for a long time, and I just…embraced it. Like, it's not enough just to be enduring so much bullshit. Maybe I want people to know."

"So it's, what, more public? Masochistic? Because for me, I can't relate to most people at school, and this kind of externalizes that distance, I guess."

He considered this for a long moment before answering, and his previous joviality was gone when he replied. "It's definitely a way of externalizing. And if I don't externalize somehow, I internalize instead, and that's when I do get masochistic. Like, literal self-abuse. It's been a while, but still, anything that can keep me from thinking like that is necessary."

"That makes sense," she said, and glanced pointedly at her forearms. Leonard flashed back to his visit at the facility where she'd stayed, and wished he hadn't. To break that particular train of thought, he nodded to the cards. They each flipped the top card of their piles.

She had the higher card. "Me again! Okay, fuck those dark questions. Who would play you in the movie of your life?"

The change in mood caught Leonard off guard, and he searched for a realistic answer. To his own embarrassment, he'd actually considered this question before, but he'd never settled on a solid answer. Most people, he thought, would probably name somebody conventionally appealing, like Ryan Gosling or Brad Pitt—neither of whom particularly appealed to him, especially in terms of a realistic portrayal. He certainly didn't think of himself as having mass-market appeal. He admitted as much now, suggesting Danny DeVito instead.

Susan was aghast. "No! Really? But you're tall!"

"Yeah, but probably more recognizable for peculiarities than for anything conventional. Besides, I'm not buff or tan like the typical movie heroes." He dashed off a small salute with the water bottle. "No offense to Danny DeVito, of course."

"Oh, shut up."

Leonard won the next hand. Something had been bothering him since they'd left Glenn's party, and he struggled to find a way to voice it now. "I don't mean anything by this, but…" But that didn't sound right. "Never mind, that's too ominous. I just. Well. Are your parents okay with you staying here alone while they're gone?" They both understood that there was an unspoken question, as well: *Are you okay to be alone now, so soon after you were in the hospital?*

Susan looked down, suddenly finding it difficult to meet his eyes. Accepting her experience and supporting her through it was one thing, she felt, but acknowledging its impact—its consequences—with unflinching seriousness was another. For some reason, the former was less shameful to her than the latter. This, in turn, made her feel guilty, because she knew Leonard understood well enough that no judgment would be forthcoming.

"I'm supposed to be staying with Natalie, from the party," she said at last. "Either here or at her house, as long as we're together. But I texted her, and she knows I'm with you, and she'll cover for me." She smiled awkwardly. "Obviously, 'with you' means 'not alone.'"

"Yeah, I can understand that," he replied in what he hoped was an offhanded manner. "How about this. Let's do one more, and then we can crash. I think today's been overwhelming."

When she smiled this time, it seemed less forced, and he thought he detected relief in her face. "Sure. Hey, me again. Okay, big question, and be honest: do you want to see your dad?"

The question wasn't completely unexpected, given the events of the past couple of days, but it still left him reeling inwardly. Part of him felt like he should say yes, but another part was screaming no, and both answers used many of the same reasons. He'd suffered long years of confusion and conflicting feelings regarding the man who'd left so abruptly, and to hear the question asked so directly—from someone other than Dr. Wheeler, his therapist, at least—offered little clarification and no new insight into the issue. In fact, every time he tried to imagine what such a meeting would be like, the circumstances changed in his imagination, until he was invariably left confused and frustrated.

He told her as much as he tried to answer her question. "Sometimes," he explained, "I imagine him living in a rundown shack with nothing but empty beer cans and his regrets for company. But sometimes I also imagine him in a fancy house, totally happy and stable, and I don't know if that's better or worse. He could be happy to see me or resentful in either situation. The unknowns are horrible. But that random phone call made me even more fucking confused. So, maybe? He made contact, which is something new, at least."

It wasn't much of an answer, but she didn't push him for more. Instead, she kissed him, dropped the cards onto the table next to the bed, and pulled the blankets out from under their legs. He wanted to ask if he should take the couch, feeling that at least an unenthusiastic offer of separation would be proper, but he dismissed the idea as she dropped the covers back on top of them, curled up with her head on his chest, and pulled his arm down and around her.

*From the journals of Leonard Kellison:*

Nov. 02:

I've always read that the opposite of love is apathy, not hate, and your heart still has to work to feel hate. Unfortunately, after the past day or two, I almost wish my heart didn't work.

Not in an I want to die way, because that's too dramatic. But I wish I wouldn't feel the hurt anymore. Obviously, it's partly because of school, and what happened leading up to this point, and yeah, there's some regret there. I definitely have to cut Wes out of my life after everything that happened. And he might be friends with Jason, but Jason is dating Ariel now, and clearly that's a friendship that wasn't meant to be, too.

The more I talk about this, the more it sounds like we're an incestuous group of friends that can't exist outside of itself, and I don't know when that happened. Jez and Glenn will always be there, but after the blowout with Hank in the cafeteria, I don't trust him anymore. I don't want to lose any more friends.

I'm still processing my dad's phone call, and what I saw afterwards. I get the feeling that Susan has some family stuff going on, just based on some things that she's said, but at least her parents are both still there. I don't know if that's unfair to say, especially after she's been so supportive of me trying to figure everything out. I have a psych appointment coming up, so that's something. Maybe it'll help.

# Chapter Eighteen

The bright sun of the late morning filtered through the edges of the dark curtains in Susan's room, and Leonard regarded them with confusion as he woke slowly, by degrees, from an exhausted sleep preceded by alcohol and drug ingestion the likes of which he was unused to. At some point during the night they had shifted in the bed, so that now Leonard was on his side and Susan, her back to him, was curled up against the line of his body in a way that made him painfully aware of how little clothing separated his skin from hers. The sheets were partially kicked away so they rested at hip level, and he marveled at the smooth, pale length of her uncovered body.

She had slept only in a thin T-shirt and panties; he, only in his boxers. The shirt had ridden up in much the same way as the sheets had been kicked down, leaving everything from hip to sternum exposed. Her hair, thick and wavy and the deep blue of what he imagined the ocean must look like to deep-sea divers, splashed against the pillow and tickled his nose. He dipped his head an inch or two to breathe in her scent, pondering for a moment a poetic analogy that might exist between ocean divers and the depths of her personality that he was still learning to recognize. He again caught the faint scent of vanilla, and he stopped trying to think poetically and allowed himself to enjoy the moment as it was.

As he did so, part of an early conversation he'd had with Dr. Wheeler replayed itself in his mind.

Shortly after he and Anna had split up, Dr. Wheeler had tried to help him to re-envision his future. So much of what he'd believed that future to be had been contingent on that relationship, a dependency that the therapist had often tried to bring to his attention. At the time, he'd assumed she simply didn't understand the bond he'd felt with his first girlfriend; over the past year or so, however, he'd begun to suspect that she understood all too well, and had tried in her own way to protect him from the inevitable disappointment.

In his mind's eye, he saw himself trying in this particular session to describe how important it was to him to finally spend the night with Anna—not the possibility of sex, exactly, but the opportunity to wake up next to someone he loved, to kiss her good morning and feel the contentment that movies and pop culture always seemed to promise.

It was an idea that he'd fixated on; the curfews and time constraints imposed on them by their parents drove him crazy, and anything that could dispel that frustration seemed worth pursuing. He could recall Dr. Wheeler's words even now: "It's a blessing to be able to wake up next to someone you love, and it's not something that you should ever take for granted. Even ignoring that you're trusting somebody at your most vulnerable—while you sleep—the continuation of companionship without any interruption is unique and special." She'd then started in on one of his least favorite subjects: how he was trying to be too mature for his age, trying to force his way into adulthood and adult experiences before he was ready for their consequences. It was remarkably similar to his mother's refrain. "You're mature for your age, but you're still a young man," she'd tell him. "Emphasis on *young*."

Now, ignoring the stiffness in the arm that was under Susan's pillow, he felt himself somewhat less equipped than he'd realized to be an adult. For one thing, he didn't want to kiss her without brushing his teeth, but neither did he want to leave the bed to do so. He also wondered if there would be an awkward conversation when she awoke. Finally, he found it mildly frustrating that, in the midst of experiencing something he'd often imagined, he was replaying conversations with his therapist and indulging in anxiety instead of simply experiencing the moment itself.

That last thought did the trick. He settled back more fully into the bed as he felt himself relax again, and Susan turned as he did so.

"Good morning," she murmured, and stifled the yawn that immediately followed.

"Hey back. Um…so this was an unexpected Halloween."

"Mmm. So you mean you didn't plan to get suspended, break out of your house, get drunk and high, and fall asleep in my bed?"

Whatever exchange he'd been expecting this morning, this wasn't it, and her directness made him laugh. "You mean you didn't?"

They lounged in bed for another hour, until she excused herself for the bathroom. He reached for his phone on the floor in her absence and wasn't surprised to see nearly a dozen new messages waiting for his response.

> **Jez:** *How's your head feel today? Like this?*
> An animation of an erupting volcano followed his message.
> **Mom:** *We're going to have a talk when you get home.*
> **Glenn:** *Sorry if we fucked up your night, bro.*
> **Glenn:** *You missed Jez dancing in my mom's clothes. That'll teach her to leave things in the dryer.*
> **Jez:** *LYLALS! Love you like a lesbian sister.*
> **Mom:** *Are you okay? Where are you?*

**Mom:** *I talked to Glenn's mom and she said you're staying there tonight. Text me when you get up.*
**Mom:** *NO DRINKING!!!*
**Glenn:** *I told your mom we got you drunk and you had to crash here.*
**Glenn:** *J/k. About the drunk part. Did you get it in?*
**Glenn:** *Jez says only he can ask questions like that. Sorry for being rude. BTW, Jez wants to know if you got it in.*

Leonard wrote to Jez and Glenn first, telling them both in a group message that he was fine, it was a pretty good prank (although he had mixed feelings about that), and that he kind of liked mushrooms on his pizza. He knew they would catch his meaning.

Replying to his mother was trickier. He told her that, yes, he was safe, and he'd be coming home later that afternoon. After a moment's deliberation, he apologized: not for leaving, but for not letting her know earlier that he was okay.

Susan's parents had a fully stocked kitchen, but after the gauntlet he'd put his body through over the past fourteen hours, he wanted nothing more than dark coffee and a greasy breakfast. Together, they fried a couple of eggs and some bacon and sausage, added some toast to their plates, and sat at the dining room table to eat.

Susan eyed him over her plate as he sipped his coffee, clearly debating something in her head, until finally she set down her fork and cleared her throat.

"I'm sorry if I pushed last night. With, you know, the shrooms and the question game afterwards."

Leonard shook his head. "No, I needed that. I was too much in my own head. As for what you asked…I don't know. Maybe I should see him. I at least need to know why he called so randomly, when he had to know that it would cause chaos."

"I've actually been thinking about that. I'm no Nancy Drew, but maybe he was waiting for the right time to call and just said screw it. Or maybe he wasn't expecting anyone to be home, and he could just leave a message. If he wants to talk, he probably knows that you won't pick up your phone, if he even has the number, so maybe the house phone seemed safer."

He mulled this over for a few minutes. He tried to picture a reformed version of his father, and couldn't. What would that even look like? People could change—he believed that, if at least in theory—but could they change *enough*? Or for *long* enough? It seemed like a lot to expect, and he carried enough baggage already.

These thoughts led back to Dr. Wheeler. She'd long held that Leonard had the actual power in the dynamic between him and his father, and that his continued refusal to make any contact with him was his most effective method of self-protection. The same theory applied to ignoring any incoming calls, but those had been few enough over the years that his active maintaining of a safe distance relied on his refusal to look up any contact information. For years, this had held true. But now?

"What if I don't want to see him or talk to him? Would you also support me in that decision?"

She nodded emphatically, and the force behind her voice matched the set of her face. "Anything," she promised.

Lunchtime had come and gone by the time they stepped outside to return to Glenn's house to retrieve Leonard's car. The sky had darkened as the morning matured, broad clouds the dead color of slate now hiding the sunlight that had warmed Leonard as he lay in Susan's bed. It felt like an oppressive weight above them, as if the clouds were lowering by degrees until they would constrict the town and suffocate any optimism or happiness. Distantly, Leonard wondered if it would snow again today.

They said little as they walked, her hand gripping his and he taking strength from the contact. He'd been forced to put on yesterday's clothes, but today she wore a white shirt emblazoned with the iconic Cycles Gladiator image of a nude woman in profile, gripping the handles of a large bicycle while her fiery hair streamed out behind her. She had also slipped on a pair of oversized sunglasses that were probably unnecessary with the day's cloud coverage, but Leonard thought they made her look more glamorous than eccentric. Plain black leggings protected her legs from the cold, nothing but her lower legs visible from under the fake fur-lined coat she wore over the ensemble.

Nobody came to the door when Leonard knocked, so he sent Glenn another text, thanking him once again for covering for him, before he slid behind the wheel of his van.

"You'll have to direct me," he told Susan, and started the van to let it warm up.

His father's address had been almost comically easy to find. He wasn't listed in the phone book, a copy of which Susan's mother still kept in the kitchen, but a simple Internet search revealed only a handful of Kellisons in the general area, and only one with his father's name. It appeared that the online telephone book provided more information than the hard copy, leaving Leonard almost wishing that it were harder to find people in the modern digital era. A difficult search could at least be taken as a sign that he was pursuing a bad idea, but by that same logic, a simple search could also be taken as a sign.

Leonard understood double standards and disliked them, but he couldn't bring himself to impose them on imaginary rules he created for himself.

No, Martin Kellison lived fewer than twenty miles away, in the suburbs outside of the town proper, and for all Leonard knew, he could have been there for the past decade. All that had stood between them, other than bad blood and distrust, had been a simple Internet search.

The light had further leached from the day behind the heavy clouds when Leonard rolled to a stop across the street from the house at the address they'd found. He could easily see through the front windows and into the dining room by the bright lights shining within. The house itself was modest, small but tidy, unremarkable in every aspect but the significance it held for the van's driver and passenger. For some reason, this pissed him off. He hadn't necessarily expected to see the man living in squalor, but it seemed incongruous to him now that he should find him in a comfortable little house on a friendly-looking street. It struck him as unfair for reasons he couldn't quite verbalize.

As he watched from across the street, his father entered the room and took a seat at one end of the table, followed a moment later by a woman carrying a small child—a girl, from the way she was dressed. The woman picked up something orange sitting on the table and turned it upside down, and Leonard watched the girl sort through whatever had come out, select one, and tear at the wrapper.

With a sickening feeling of momentary vertigo, Leonard realized that he was watching his father with his new family, and the little girl was sifting through her Trick-or-Treating haul. It was at that moment that he realized he'd fully expected to see his father slouched on a porch swing outside of a shack, a beer in one hand and a dozen empties strewn around his feet. The possibility of seeing a happy man with a happy family had always been there, but

Leonard was now forced to accept that he'd never accepted it as anything more than an outside chance.

"Are you okay, Leonard?" Susan asked, and he just shook his head in response. He swallowed thickly.

"Totally not what I thought," he whispered, and Susan took his hand in both of hers and pressed her lips to it. He appreciated the gesture, and her refusal to offer empty platitudes, but otherwise he was at a loss.

"What do you want to do?" she asked softly.

With anger, regret, and an anxious sort of confusion, he silently flicked the turn signal and pulled away from the curb.

# III

*"'There are various kinds of forgiveness,' Mr. Kilroy replied. 'There is the forgiveness that washes its hands of the culprit and refuses to be further troubled on his behalf—the least estimable form of forgiveness; and there is that which proves itself sincere by the effort which is afterward made to help the penitent, that is the kind of forgiveness you should try to secure.'"*

—from Sarah Grand, *The Heavenly Twins*

*"I like it*
*Because it is bitter,*
*And because it is my heart."*

—from Stephen Crane, "In the Desert"

*From the journals of Leonard Kellison:*

Nov. 2 (continued):

It's weird sometimes to be regarded as an adult. It's also kind of scary, because I don't know how to navigate that kind of life. I mean, I don't exactly have a lot of strong male role models in my life.

It's even harder because in some parts of my life, I have no real power, and in others, I'm suddenly expected to "be an adult" and have all the answers. I have to go to school, which is basically an exercise in obeisance (I heard that word in a song somewhere), to the rest of my life, including therapy, where I'm supposed to know how to act and respond to everything around me, even when it's unfamiliar.

It's particularly weird to have adult conversations with my mom. I guess at some point, she realized that I'm an adult, or young adult, or whatever you want to call it—whatever comes after child, I guess—and decided I can handle "real talk." But again, I'm not a real adult there, either, because I don't have the freedom to do what I want.

I feel like I'm talking in circles, but fuck it, I'm not crossing any of this out. I think Dr. Wheeler would say that it's a necessary part of unraveling the things that are bothering me.

# Chapter Nineteen

Leonard drove around aimlessly for a bit, not knowing where to go but unwilling to return home just yet. He'd spent a couple of hours at Susan's, where they'd ordered takeout using the food money her parents had left for her. They'd talked a bit, watched a movie on Netflix, and then talked some more, but none of their conversations approached how he felt about their outing. Inwardly, Leonard appreciated that. Susan took her lead from him, and she seemed to respect that he wasn't ready yet to examine things out loud.

When he'd left, it was with a promise that they would talk about it soon, and he'd hugged her tightly and reassured her that she hadn't pushed him into the drive.

Mostly, though, he just wanted to be alone for a while. He had an appointment with Dr. Wheeler the following day, earlier than usual due to his suspension, and he knew that he would do enough talking and self-examination there to last him a week. Until then, silence—except for music; there would always be room for music, quiet or loud—seemed utterly necessary.

It was fully dark when he returned home, though it was not yet eight o'clock. The outside lights were on, illuminating his mother sitting huddled on the autumn-patterned chair she'd recently installed on the small porch; she raised a hand to shield her eyes as his headlights raked across her during his turn into the driveway. She stood as he got out of the van and locked it.

"Mom? What's wrong?" he asked, anxious now. She looked distressed, but whether it was from anger at his disappearance or something to do with Roland, he couldn't say. Was he in for major trouble? Was Roland drunk again?

Each scenario playing out in his head was worse than the last.

When he reached her, she just shook her head. "I'm fine, Leonard. I was just waiting for you to get home." A look passed over her face, and she sighed. "A call or a text would have been nice, you know."

"I know. Sorry. I'm okay, though. I was just..."

"With Glenn, I know. Was Susan there, too?"

"Yeah, but she didn't stay the night there." This was technically true, although he felt guilty about the deliberate misdirection. "Are you sure everything's okay? Why are you outside?"

His mother sighed again, and he was taken aback to see that she looked guilty, or maybe just embarrassed. She reached into the pocket of her oversized Lincoln Memorial High School sweatshirt and half-removed a pack of cigarettes. Still saying nothing, she returned the cigarettes to her pocket and then shook a cheap plastic lighter with her other hand.

"It's been a trying couple of days," she said at last.

She suddenly seemed very vulnerable to Leonard. He didn't know a lot about her life pre-marriage, but he knew enough to know that she'd had a tough go of it, and he felt guilty thinking that he'd contributed to her current level of stress. His recent conversation with Susan came back to him, about how he suspected his mother had traded her independence for a steady source of shelter and food for her son, and this made him feel worse. He remembered being very young, pre-Roland, and understanding that something was wrong, something that she was trying to hide, but not knowing what it might be.

"Let's go into the kitchen," she said at last, and turned toward the door.

"Mom—" But he had no idea what he was going to say, and he was grateful when she waved him off and held the door open. Following her through the living room and into the kitchen, he noticed that most of the lights were off inside the house: a sure sign that Roland was sleeping upstairs, and not to be disturbed.

Leonard took a seat at the kitchen island and was surprised when his mother reached into the fridge and returned a minute later with a beer in each hand. He knew she wasn't a big drinker, and she almost never drank in front of him. He supposed this was her way of keeping the alcoholism that surrounded them at arm's length, and he realized, perhaps for the first time, that he'd never before truly appreciated her efforts to distance herself from the dependency her husband seemed to live with.

She lowered herself onto the high-backed chair next to his and extended a bottle to him. "Go on, take it," she said, her voice and expression neutral enough that he had trouble reading her mood.

He accepted the bottle but made no move to open it.

"This feels like a trap," he said. "Look, I'm sorry I went out last night. I know being suspended..."

"Hush," she admonished him, and popped the cap off of her beer. She passed it to him and watched without comment as he opened his own. He played with it for a moment, halfheartedly trying to spin it like a coin on the countertop, and waited for her to take a sip before he drank from his own bottle.

"It's not a trap," she said. "But I feel like we haven't talked much lately, except for arguing, and that's not really talking. And I'm sure you had *nothing to drink* at Glenn's last night, but if you did, I hope it was minimal and you stayed safe inside." She paused to pick at the label on the bottle. "You're sixteen going on seventeen, but sometimes it feels like you're sixteen going on forty. I know you have a lot on your plate, and it probably feels overwhelming right now. But I've been thinking, and—

well—look, I understand why you got suspended. And I don't know all of the details of what happened, but I know you're not a guy who goes around starting fights. The principal told me how the fight started. What the other kid said."

"Mom. Listen."

"Leonard, I don't care. People can be horrible, and we can talk if you need to, but I love you *no matter what.* I don't understand why you do this—" and here she gestured vaguely at his clothing, hair, and nails—"but whatever. It's fine. I just need to know that you're safe."

He lifted his bottle to his lips and was surprised to see that it was nearly empty. Hearing his mother speak like this—his mother, who had generally fallen into the habit of keeping things light and indirect in order to avoid conflict—had shaken him. It made him want to both confess everything to her and keep everything from her; it was impossible to decide which was the better option. The truth, he realized, was that he wasn't used to opening up. Glenn and Dr. Wheeler probably knew him better than anyone else, and he knew that was because Glenn would never judge him and Dr. Wheeler's whole job was to hear the worst from him without batting an eye. At best, they provided objective feedback when he needed it most. At worst, he could terminate the conversation, just cut off the flow of information, without risking losing much.

He couldn't do the same thing with his mother, though; he knew that. Confessing too much now might not change how much she loved him, but it might change her impression of him, and he wouldn't be able to walk that back.

He finished his beer and set the bottle aside. His phone buzzed, and he glanced at it—a text message from Susan—before setting it facedown on the counter beside the beer.

"I'm okay," he said at last, and he saw something soften in her face. "Really. But why the beer? You've never let me have one before."

"You're almost an adult, and you're dealing with adult problems." She shrugged. "But it's just this once. *And* because I care. And I don't feel like I've been showing you lately that I'm proud of you. I know that your stepfather and I argue a lot, but we're both always doing things for you. He's helping to put aside money for your college, did you know that?"

The change in subject startled him, but he shook his head. "I didn't know," he said truthfully. "Are you telling me this because Dad called on your birthday?"

Now it was her turn to look confused. "No, Leonard, and I still don't know why he decided to call out of nowhere like that. I just wanted you to know. Roland may not agree with your lifestyle, or understand any of it, and I know he hasn't really tried to. But he's a hard worker. He just gets angry sometimes."

"Mom, he *hurts* you. And me, too."

It was the first time he'd acknowledged it in such naked terms, and he immediately wanted to take the words back. But he knew that he couldn't. They'd just turned a corner. It was the first time she'd spoken to him like this—as an adult, as equals—and there was no going back.

"He has impulse problems. I know the drinking makes it worse, but marriage is *work.* Families are *work.* I know he's horrible at showing affection, and I'm so sorry for..." She gestured helplessly. "Everything."

Leonard sat stunned. Too much information was being piled onto him too fast. He felt himself being overloaded. Dimly, he remembered a lesson in a psychology class from weeks ago, something about serotonin or dopamine not staying long enough in the synapses of the brain. He thought he remembered the teacher saying that this could cause judgment problems; it left no time to think. The person just reacted.

He also remembered something Roland had said weeks ago, when he'd warned Leonard to get his ass downstairs for dinner: *Eat dinner first or your mom will give me hell for it.* Was this Roland's way of co-parenting, of ceding ground to his wife? At a stretch, Leonard supposed to was conceivable, but Roland was such an asshole about things sometimes.

Suddenly exhausted, Leonard put his face in his hands for a moment. He'd learned and experienced too much in too short a time. He wanted nothing more than to leave the kitchen and be alone.

"I'm fine, really," he repeated. "But I'm exhausted."

His mother nodded, and he was relieved to see that there was no hurt in her eyes. He'd been worried that she'd feel brushed off, and that would be too much to bear after the conversation they'd just had.

"You look it," she said, and she rose and grabbed both bottles. "Go sleep." She transferred the bottles to one hand and hugged him awkwardly with her free arm.

A few minutes later, standing under a steaming shower, he braced himself against the tiles of the shower stall and began to cry.

Leonard made it downtown the next day with time to spare before his appointment with Dr. Wheeler, so he stopped at the small cafe a few blocks over to relax first. That, and to rehearse what he wanted to tell his therapist, and in what order. An hour sometimes seemed like a lot of time to fill up with conversation, but he knew that any of the topics currently on his mind—Susan; his suspension; his father—might take them right up until the end.

He ordered an Americano at the counter and grabbed a free table nearby, but he had his choice of seating that afternoon. Most of the tables were empty, everybody else apparently at work or school. The soft music coming through the speakers was unfamiliar to him, but it reminded him of the last time he'd been there. Then, he and Susan had ordered hot chocolates and watched the snow fall, but today he was alone, and the skies were clear, the day bright. His date with Susan hadn't been too long ago, but suddenly it seemed like an impossible number of events and days had separated that evening from this afternoon.

The barista announced his drink, and he retrieved it from the counter and paid for a bottle of water, as well. He knew from experience that talking in therapy was thirsty work.

He spent the next half hour sipping his drink and reading *Atlas Shrugged*, but his mind kept wandering until he finally closed the book and picked up his phone.

He texted Glenn: *Still coming over tonight with my homework? Feel free to say you don't have any for me.*

Glenn replied immediately: *Yeah man! It'll probably just be me. Jez is grounded again. Don't know why this time.*

Despite himself, Leonard smiled. Jez always seemed to be getting into trouble at home, although his infractions weren't always clear. It might even have been a case of Jez testing his parents, just seeing what he could get away with—and although he was often in trouble with his parents, Leonard believed that Jez had already gotten away with more in his life than Leonard ever would, no matter how long he lived. Jez truly enjoyed pushing boundaries and pressing people's buttons, while Leonard tended to play it safe when he could.

When his clock read a quarter to two, Leonard tossed his empty cup and drove over to his therapist's office, a small brick building set back from the road a bit. It was all street parking, but at this time of day it was easy to find a spot. He returned to his book in the reception area and rose when Dr. Wheeler strode out of her office and beckoned him in.

"So what are you reading today?" she asked by way of greeting. This was a common conversation opener between them, and it gave him time to organize his thoughts despite his earlier contemplation. It was an old ritual, and he appreciated her understanding.

He held up *Atlas Shrugged*, and she gave an approving nod, saying, "I read that in graduate school. It's quite the slog."

Leonard nodded in agreement. "I've done some reading online, and a lot of people say her philosophies make her kind of an asshole, but I haven't gotten far enough into the book to have an opinion yet."

"Be sure to report back, then. Meanwhile, how have you been?"

"Eh." He shrugged. She smiled pleasantly and waited for more.

One of the things Leonard appreciated about Dr. Wheeler was her willingness to wait. She pushed him in other ways, but she had learned quickly to interpret his silences and jokes. Early in their working relationship he had defaulted to dissimulation, attempting to minimize his feelings or deny them entirely, but that had never been an option with her, not really. She intuited too accurately, and too much, and as a result, he'd learned to trust her with details he hadn't told anyone else.

She sat across from him now and smiled encouragingly. He knew from their long history of sessions together that she would now do one of two things: wait patiently, or begin to prod a bit. She was always happy to catch up on small talk when there was time, usually at the end of a session, but she wouldn't let him off the hook right at the start.

Sure enough, in the next minute she tapped a finger against her lip thoughtfully and said, "Let's start with school. How is it lately?"

Leonard leaned back a bit on the sofa, grateful for the opening. "It's kind of a long story," he began."

"It's your story," she returned immediately—a favorite line of hers, and one he'd heard often from her in the past. "It can be long."

*Fuck it*, he said inwardly. The events of the past several days had been intense and, in some ways, paradigm shifting for him, and he knew he would regret not sharing everything later. Dr. Wheeler knew more about him than probably anyone else in the world, and in some ways she understood him—his actions, his motivations, even the way his chemically imbalanced brain pursued reasoning—even better than himself.

So he reviewed the recent series of events with her, beginning with his evening with Wes and concluding with the Halloween party and the subsequent discovery of his father's new life. He tried to be thorough in his account, but some of the details were hard to articulate, and he often found himself picking at a rough spot on the side of the sole of his boot. Through the story, Dr. Wheeler tried not to interrupt, allowing him to go at his own pace, jotting down the occasional keyword in the yellow legal pad she kept balanced on her knee but never letting her gaze waver from his presence.

"There's a lot here," she said after he'd concluded, "but I want to start at the end."

"With my mom?"

"Sure, that's part of it, but I specifically had in mind your reaction to all of this. You've had a very eventful life recently. How have you been handling it?"

Leonard thought hard. "I feel like I've mostly just been reacting," he answered at least. "It's been a lot, in a very short amount of time."

Dr. Wheeler smiled, and he knew he'd said something that confirmed her thoughts. "Exactly. You've been reacting to a lot of things that have happened to you, and it's interesting how those reactions have changes since we started meeting. Do you remember how you used to react to emotional moments?"

"Avoidance and…you know. Self-harm." It was still hard to admit to, even after the many conversations they'd had about it.

"And did you feel the urge to do that this time?"

"Yeah, I did, at one point. I didn't, though."

"And why not? What's changed?"

An unexpected wave of emotion crested within him, and he rubbed a hand over his face before he answered. Then: "I'm so afraid of backsliding. None of this has ever been easy, and being where I am right now isn't easy, either, but it's not a knee-jerk reaction anymore. I have to remind myself why I stopped doing it in the first place."

Again, the doctor smiled, but more warmly this time. "Exactly. You're reacting, but your reactions have changed. Remember, recovery isn't a straight line. We tend to talk about this more often in terms of substance addiction, but the idea is the same. At the start, before you're aware that you want or need to change a behavior, you're pre-contemplative. You're just acting, not ready to change anything. Then you become aware of why you might need to make a change—that's contemplative—and finally decide to actively change your circumstances.

That's preparation, which we always hope leads to action. But what can happen after you take action?"

"Relapse?"

"Right, you either relapse or you don't. If you relapse, you'll probably go back to the action stage, and then you'll have to maintain the changed behavior. But if you don't relapse, you're maintaining. This can be a life process. It can get easier or harder, but many addicts report that maintenance is continuous."

"Does it count as maintenance if the main reason I haven't hurt myself over this is because I've mostly been with my friends and Susan? I don't know how it would have gone if I'd been alone while this was all happening."

"Of course it counts! They all know that you have this action in your past, right? They're there because they care, and that's the most you can ask of a support network. It sounds like none of them will let you get to that point if you keep letting them in. In the meantime, in case you do ever find yourself alone and ready to hurt yourself, keep the TAP routine in mind. It works."

Leonard nodded. The first time she'd described TAP to him, it had sounded silly, and she'd acknowledged that it wasn't the most impressive name for it. Still, for those who had habitually cut themselves, the acronym was designed to either evoke the same bodily response as that type of self harm or to distract from the urge altogether: temperature (ice cubes against the wrists had worked for him in the past); activity (push-ups, for him); and play (intricate guitar pieces that required total attention had worked best).

The other activity Dr. Wheeler had introduced to him was mindfulness, and she reminded him of that now: "I have some homework for you this week. When you have some time tonight or tomorrow, set a timer for a minute or two and just focus on what's around you, on what you see and hear. Do a separate timer for each. In addition to TAP, this has been helpful in the past when you've needed to center yourself. Remember, the pain you're feeling might need to be felt, but acknowledging it and prolonging it are two different paths."

He nodded, and suddenly became aware that he he'd stopped picking at the scraped sole of his boot. "I'll do that."

"Good. You can report back next time." She smiled, and he felt the usual warmth of being acknowledged in therapy for doing something right. It was strange: he'd read and heard about the phenomenon of patients thinking they were in love with their therapists, but he'd always regarded Dr. Wheeler as a more maternal figure, probably because he'd always instinctively focused his romantic feelings elsewhere.

"Now," she continued, "tell me more about the fight that got you suspended, and about how you're navigating these ramifications of your actions in the present, with Susan."

*From the journals of Leonard Kellison:*

Nov. 12:

My suspension is almost over, but I don't think I can go back to school just yet. It's weird—I really thought I'd be ready to go back to normal, even if it's horrible and makes me want to drive off a bridge half of the time. I really thought I'd feel better with a routine, where I'd be out of the house and at least distracted for seven or eight hours a day.

Instead, I'm pretty sure I'm going to be so tightly wound that I might end up getting into another fight. I wish there were some way to stay home a while longer. Going back after Thanksgiving break would be better.

Dr. Wheeler asked me to try writing some questions—and only questions—about the whole thing with Dad. She said we'll try to tackle them together at our next session. According to her, asking the right questions is more useful sometimes than just beating your head against the limitations of your own walls over and over again.

So, first: why not us? Why wasn't out family good enough for him? Why did he end up starting a new family with someone else? Why did he call on Mom's birthday? What did he hope to accomplish? Does his new wife know that he called? I just don't get it. If you're going to ditch us, then ditch us. Stop contacting us, especially on a birthday or a holiday.

(He called a couple of years ago on Christmas day and tried to act like nothing had happened. Like it was totally normal.)

Am I supposed to forgive him? What would forgiving him do for my sense of reality? Isn't the whole "dad issues" thing a pretty defining feature of my formative years?

# Chapter Twenty

Glenn's basement was quieter tonight. It was the first time Leonard had been there since Halloween, and it had been so loud and crazy that night that it was easy to forget that the state of a room largely depends on who is present at any given time, and how much volume the people in the room bring to its space.

By Glenn's own count, upwards of forty people had swung by at some point or other for his Halloween party. Maybe a dozen had stayed the night, and of that crowd, only Jez and Hank had stayed behind to help clean up. The broken glass, empty beer bottles, and general party mess had taken two trash days to be fully collected, apparently.

But now, as Leonard watched Glenn roll a joint from his place on the torn loveseat adjacent to the couch, it was difficult to remember that he'd gotten so drunk in this very room that he'd had to leave. He told Glenn as much, but his friend just laughed and waved the idea away. "You sound like you're apologizing, man," he said with a snort. "And that's weird, because you don't have anything to apologize for."

Leonard thought about this for a moment. "No, I'm not trying to apologize, although it's pretty embarrassing that I got so drunk in front of everyone."

Glenn laughed so hard at this—or at the memory—that he dropped the joint. It hit his chest and rolled into the crack between the cushion and the back of the couch, where he carefully fished it back out and blew on it as if it were a piece of food. Leonard wondered absently whether the five-second rule applied to drugs.

"Now *that*, you should definitely be embarrassed about." Glenn laughed again and sifted through the piles of magazines and takeout cartons on the coffee table, in search of a lighter. "It was hilarious, though. Seriously, we all thought you were going to die or something." Defeated, he got up and started rifling through the pockets of the pile of clothes on the floor.

"Not that your death would be funny," he clarified. "What got you all in that headspace that night, anyway? You never told me."

It was true that they hadn't talked much about the party. After the initial rounds of "are you okay?" texts the following morning, most of their communication had been about the band, or their friends, or just trivial points of interest. Leonard reflected on their conversations over the past week or so and realized that he'd kept some of the major developments pretty private. He wondered if it were actually a matter of privacy, and then decided that he'd been so wrapped up in Susan's company that he hadn't felt like taking the time to explain everything.

The realization made him feel like a bad friend, and he decided to correct the situation now.

"Most of the alcohol was from that stupid fucking 'Who's Jacob?' game, remember?"

"I still can't believe you'd never heard of that game."

"No, I know, I'm stupid or whatever, but that's what got me so drunk. But I had a much better night at Susan's afterwards—" He ignored Glenn's hand gestures here. "—and I think I want to do mushrooms again, and Susan actually tracked down my dad."

Glenn was paying full attention now, standing frozen with the joint in one hand and a lighter in the other. "No shit?"

Leonard spread his hands. "It's true. He's really not even that far away."

"How much does she know about things?"

Leonard leaned back and threw his legs over the

arm of the loveseat. "I told her the history. She wanted to help me find out why he called on my mom's birthday last month." He paused. "I think. It happened kind of quickly. We drove over there, but dude, he has a whole new *family*. I didn't even get out of the van."

"Holy shit, man. Are you going to go back?"

Leonard didn't have an answer to this, but he was saved from trying to figure out what response felt the most true by a series of sudden loud crashes from the stairs.

Almost too fast to register, what looked like a green quilt and a series of disconnected limbs flew down the stairs to land in a tangled heap of fabric and body parts on the floor. There was a lot of shuffling around, and finally Jez disentangled himself from the fabric and stood shakily, arms raised in a *V*, and shouted, "Toboggan Olympics! That's a *gold* performance, baby!"

Leonard could now see that the fabric was a sleeping bag. Jez had ridden it down the stairs in a chaotic approximation of speeding down a slope on a toboggan—which, although dangerous, wasn't completely out of nowhere. Leonard could remember doing those kinds of things, albeit more cautiously, with his friends as older kids or younger teenagers. In one particularly daring episode, Jez had somehow stolen a lunch tray from the school cafeteria, and they'd taken turns sliding down the big hill next to the middle school's football field after a particularly heavy snowfall that winter. That particular escapade had ended in stitches after Glenn had careened off of a tree and into some maintenance vehicles parked in the lot at the bottom of the hill.

"You've got to come back to school," Glenn told Leonard now. "Jez is going to end up killing himself in some stunt double accident if he's left to his own devices."

Leonard reached for the joint and pointed it in Jez's general direction before he brought it to his lips. "Jez, quick: your three favorite devices. Go!"

Jez froze. "Um. Uh. Uh...egg beater, alarm clock, and crayons!"

"Crayons aren't devices, man!" Glenn tossed an inflatable beach ball at him, although Leonard hadn't seen one in the vicinity at all until now.

"Yeah they are! Devices do things! Crayons do things!"

The conversation devolved into a heated argument from there, with each of them examining the issue from different angles: utility, constituent parts, estimated life span. Although none of them cared very much either way, it was a return to normalcy that Leonard appreciated. The combination of the weed smoke and the company of his closest friends allowed him to forget his upcoming return to school, the question of what to do now that he'd found his father, and his concern that either his mother or his girlfriend had expectations surrounding either issue that they simply hadn't communicated to him yet. Not for the first time, he found himself wishing that he could freeze time. It might take him years to decide how to handle school or the relative proximity of his father, but both issues seemed far more pressing than that. He didn't have years.

Eventually, Leonard lost track of the conversation and found himself playing a trivia game on his phone when a text from Susan came in.

**Susan:** *Having fun with Glenn and Jez?*
**Leonard:** *We've been debating whether crayons are devices for the past half hour, so...*
**Susan:** ???
**Leonard:** *Yeah, don't ask.*

**Susan:** *Obviously they're devices! Do I need to moderate this discussion?*
**Leonard:** *I don't even know who's on which side anymore. It's not worth the confusion.*
**Leonard:** *So, listen...I don't think I'm ready to go back to school next week. Is everyone still talking about the fight? Or anything else? All I keep thinking of is coming back and having to deal with the same shit all over again, and it makes me want to drive off a cliff. SOS. Help.*
**Susan:** *School is school. People are assholes. But no, it's not like at the top of everyone's radar anymore. The other day Deanna Miller broke up with her boyfriend at lunch and now everyone knows that he was cheating on her, so that's kind consumed the gossip lately.*
**Susan:** *Can you actually come over tomorrow? Don't hold me to it, but I might actually have an idea. It might help.*

Susan knew that her older brother was currently on his way home to visit from college, and it was this knowledge that provided the beginning of the plan she had hinted at in her texts with Leonard. There was just one more week until Thanksgiving, and she knew her brother's university scheduled the holiday break to begin the day before Thanksgiving and last for a solid week. Her own school—hers and Leonard's—only gave them the holiday itself and the following day off from classes, but she thought she might be able to work with that.

When Matt pulled into the driveway later that afternoon he only had a duffel bag with him, which wasn't unusual for his visits. He fancied himself an adventurer and liked to pack light so he could come and go more easily.

She'd teased him more than once about the old Nissan that he drove; it didn't seem like the kind of transportation that any self-respecting adventurer would choose willingly. It was a small sedan, the red paint rusted or peeling or simply missing altogether in places. The previous year, he'd had to weld some metal over corroded areas near the bottom of the car just to get it to pass inspection.

On the plus side, he arrived alone, and upon seeing this Susan breathed a sigh of relief. Matt's roommate wasn't exactly her favorite person, and although they'd all grown up together, she hadn't spoken to him since he and Matt had left for college a couple of years ago. She certainly didn't want to reopen any lines of conversation now.

It was better this way. She still wasn't ready to face him, and she secretly believed that she would never be.

Matt, for his part, tried to stay "above the drama," as he put it. She both loved and despised him for this stance, but she couldn't imagine ever explaining to him why she was so adamant that he keep Thomas at a safe distance when she was around. He'd accepted this order without comment, but she knew he had questions. She just let him assume the worst and left it at that.

She watched him drag his duffel bag out from the passenger seat and immediately drop it in the driveway so he could check his phone. He leaned against the car and texted unhurriedly, and when it became obvious that he had other things to occupy his attention before even coming into the house, she abandoned the window and sprawled across her bed. Kidneythieves was playing on her phone, and she turned the volume down a bit so she'd be able to hear the front door when he came in.

She rolled her eyes as just seconds later she heard him slam the front door and yell, “Family! I’m home!”

Before she was even fully up from her bed she saw Riley tear down the hall from the direction of his room and take the stairs so quickly that he nearly fell down the last several steps. Matt was there at the last second to steady him before he could topple, and they high-fived before turning back to wait for Susan.

Not for the first time, she felt a deep wistfulness at the status Riley enjoyed in the family. As the youngest, he always got first consideration; he enjoyed the majority of their father’s attention on a daily basis; and nobody liked to tell him “no.” As a result, he was a confident, precocious kid, which were personality traits that Susan could never identify with.

But watching him now, fully ecstatic to be the center of their older brother’s attention, she couldn’t begrudge him his status of youngest child, either. She followed him downstairs and accepted the one-armed hug that Matt offered while he wrestled Riley to the ground with the other.

“Whoa, what’s up, Morticia?” he said by way of greeting, but there was no malice behind the words. It may have looked like they were from different worlds, but he had always been protective of her, and she knew that this part of his nature would never change.

“Not much, Ringo.” She reached out to mess with his hair. “Looks like you need a haircut.”

“Yeah, and it looks like you need to spend less time around graveyards,” he shot back with a grin. “Are Mom and Dad home?”

“Not right now, but they’ll be back soon. Listen, before we reunite to play the happy family, can I talk to you? I know you just got home; sorry to jump you right away.”

"Uh, sure. Everything okay?"

Before she could answer, Riley twisted out of Matt's grasp and pointed at her excitedly. In a dramatic stage whisper, he gasped, "Susan's got a *boyfriend* now."

"Shut up, Riley! God, I'm sure he doesn't care."

"I do seem to remember hearing something about that from Mom a little while ago," Matt said, and there was a mischievous grin on his face as he gave Susan his full attention. She shrugged but said nothing. This wasn't how she'd planned to broach the subject with him, and she found that she was frustrated to have to adapt.

"So who is this guy? Let me guess, he's a *rock star.* Am I right?" He waved his fingers in an attempt at jazz hands as he made his guess, and despite herself, Susan had to fight off a grin of her own.

"He's in a band, not that it matters. Vocals and bass."

"*Bass? A bass player?* Riley, what do we know about bass players? Let me tell you. They only want one thing."

At this point, his half of the conversation existed only to entertain Riley, and Susan wished that she could just have five minutes with her older brother without having to entertain her younger one. She tugged on Matt's arm impatiently, but he had to have the last word.

"They want *girls,*" he whispered conspiratorially, and Riley looked very seriously at Susan as if to confirm this.

"Well, this bass player isn't like that. You'll see when you meet him."

Matt groaned at this. "I have to meet him? What if he's really cool and I get intimidated by him? Can I just schedule a virtual meeting or something instead?"

"Just come *on,*" Susan whispered urgently, and this time he relented.

"Okay, okay, I'm sorry. Let's go. Riley, guard the house."

"We're not even leaving the house," Susan corrected, and led him back upstairs.

When they were safely sequestered in her room, she removed Dagny from her terrarium and let the snake curl around her fingers to keep her hands busy.

"Still got the snake, huh?" Matt asked, taking a seat at her desk. She sat on the bed and he turned the chair enough to face her comfortably.

"Still got the snake," she confirmed, and took an uneasy breath. "I want to ask you something, but first I should tell you about Leonard," she said. He spread his hands in an "I'm listening" gesture, and as Dagny twined between her hands and headed up one arm Susan told Matt a moderately edited version of what the past few months had been like.

She began at the beginning of the school year, when she'd had her first real conversation with Leonard at the pizza shop, and told Matt about how things had been during and after her institutional stay. She recounted how Leonard had visited her there and supported her afterwards, but left out the specific reason for the most recent bullying, saying only that it led to the principal suspending him from school after a particularly bad fight. It felt wrong to give too many details about his father and his home life, too, so she offered only the most necessary details.

Matt was left processing for a few moments after she was done, saying only, "that's some heavy shit."

"Yeah, it is. So I need you to do me a favor."

Matt looked up, alarmed. "I can't play sensei for the guy, Susan. I don't know the first thing about trauma counseling."

"Oh my God, get over yourself. He doesn't need a best friend. He just...needs to get away for a little bit."

"More than being suspended? I'm sorry, I didn't mean it like that," he backpedaled when he saw the look on her face.

"Just, can you please let him stay with you for a few days? Just this once. You can talk to Thomas first; I don't care; I know you're roommates. I just feel so bad for Leonard, and I'm afraid he's going to get in trouble again if he goes back right away because you know how this high school is. It's brutal."

"I don't know, Susan. We'll see."

"Please?"

"I mean, I don't even know the guy."

"You'll meet him when he picks me up this weekend. You can talk to him all you want. If you want."

Matt sighed, defeated. "We'll talk. I mean he and I will talk, and then *you* and I will talk."

He accepted her hug affably, and when she tried to thank him, he only said, "yeah, yeah."

Being home to visit didn't mean that Matt was going to stick around the whole time, and it wasn't long before he announced his plans to meet up for a drink with some old friends. With him out of the house for the night, everything reverted to being a normal night, and Susan found herself with nothing to do. Everyone, including Leonard, seemed to be busy, so she finally decided to get changed and grab something to eat.

The bus she caught at the stop down the road was mostly empty, and she averted her eyes from the people who were there as she walked down the narrow aisle until she reached the empty back third of the bus. Once seated, she pushed the hood of her sweatshirt back from her head and turned her attention to her phone.

She was aware of a young couple several rows away who shot her frequent glances and talked quietly, as if they were worried about her overhearing, but the heating system would have been too loud for her to hear anything even if she didn't have her earbuds in. They looked vaguely familiar, and she wondered where she'd seen them before. Not being able to place their faces made her uneasy.

One of them—the girl—laughed loudly at something her partner said, and after that Susan refused to give them the satisfaction of acknowledging them.

When the bus reached a stop just a block from Lino's Pizzeria she pulled the cord above her and got to her feet. She had to pass the couple again to get to the exit, but they said nothing this time, or nothing that she could hear. She pulled her hood back over her head and wrapped her coat more tightly around herself when she reached the sidewalk, more for an extra layer of defense than for protection against the weather.

It was cold, but only a few snowflakes fell from the sky as she walked. It reminded her of building snowmen with Riley when he was younger, and of competing to see who could catch the most snowflakes on their tongue. Riley would usually win, but she never tried very hard. It pleased her to see his excitement at knowing that he'd beaten his older sister.

Lino's, like the bus, was mostly empty when she entered. She stamped her feet and reached up to pause her music—which was on shuffle, but currently playing something by Snake River Conspiracy—before approaching the host's stand in the front of the building.

*Hostess*, she corrected herself, seeing for the first time the girl who was already reaching for menus. She was pretty, in a normal sort of way, and Susan wondered briefly what it would be look to be attractive by normal standards.

"How many?" the girl asked, and Susan shrugged.

"Just me."

"And are you waiting for anyone else?"

"It's just me," Susan repeated, and if the hostess had any reaction to seating a lonely Goth girl at eight on a Friday night, she hid it well. Susan was grateful for this. She was used to going out by herself—for meals; to the movies; to the mall—but not everyone was skilled at hiding assumptions or judgments, or, even worse, pity.

She followed the hostess to a booth near the front and tugged off her coat before sitting down. It was warm in the front of the restaurant, probably because the kitchen wasn't very far away, and a minute later she pulled off her Slipknot hoodie, as well. She piled both next to her on the bench seat and adjusted her hair and top (an old Nine Inch Nails tee over a red long-sleeve thermal shirt she'd thrown on to hide her scars) before turning her attention to the menu.

The server came by to take down her order of Caesar salad and a side of fries, and she dug her book out of her bag to pass the time while she waited. It was good, an older copy of Angela Carter's reimagined fairy tales that she'd borrowed from her mom's shelf. As usual, she tried to find a bit of herself in the book she was reading. It was an old habit that could be traced back to a teacher telling her that "not relating" to a reading assignment was no reason not to do it, because all literature came from human consciousness and as a result it had something to offer to everyone.

She barely remembered the teacher's name now, or what he looked like, but she'd found that inserting herself into stories, or finding something that resonated with her, forced her to pay attention to what she was reading. Reading *The Bloody Chamber* for the first time, she found that she could relate pretty well to the girl living in Bluebeard's castle. The concepts of personal property and respecting certain limitations made sense to her, but she knew that she would also eventually look into every shadowy corner if she were alone in a new house (or castle) shortly after marrying.

Go wherever you want to, but not in this one room? Please. It wouldn't take her long.

It wasn't just her own house, either. As a child, she had to know what was in every room before she could be comfortable at a sleepover. It wasn't so much a need to catalog everything as it was a general sense of vulnerability. She'd always needed an exit strategy: in case of fire, avoid using this window because it was painted shut. In case of stalker, cut through that alley because none of the houses had dogs in their yards.

In case of relationships...well, whatever guardrails were there were still solidly in place, but they were murky. This sense of questionable limitations, of boundaries that *looked* solid but might actually be quite permeable, concerned her. It wasn't a matter of an exit plan in this case, but she found that she was trusting the strength of her own boundaries less and less as she spent more time with Leonard. It was concerning, but it was also nice. Being with him felt so good that she almost didn't trust it not to be dangerous.

Of course, there probably was a danger of losing herself in him, or at least of placing so much of her happiness in him that their relationship could crumble under the pressure. *My own therapist told me that*, she reminded herself now. Fresh out of her in-house therapy stay (she refused to think of it as "being locked up"), she'd had to see the doctor several times a week to monitor her progress.

"Don't rely on Leonard for your happiness," Dr. Campbell had told her. "I know you're happy with him, but don't be happy *only* with him."

The implications there frightened her, but the warning hadn't truly made sense until tonight. Nothing had changed in their relationship, but she wouldn't have believed that she'd ever ask her brother to take in her boyfriend for a few days. It felt...not selfish, exactly, but entitled. Like she was taking advantage of Matt's kindness because Leonard was having a hard time.

Would this willingness to do things for him go too far?

Inevitably, she thought of their Halloween night together, and she felt herself blushing in the booth. Would their current limits stay their limits, or would he start wanting more? For that matter, didn't she already want more? Her logical brain said *no, wait*, but just the memory of him in her bed, lying under her but still clothed while she straddled him, drowned out any logic and left her with only desire.

She remembered his hands on her bare skin, and she shook her hair down to better cover her face and took a sip of water. Her therapist and her sense of logic might be waving warning signs in her face, but she'd never been so passive with her body before, or so open to someone else's hands on her skin. A painful period of time in her younger years had ensured that she would remain protective, watchful. Vigilant. Being with someone in the present who didn't simply take was changing her regard of intimacy.

Her reverie was interrupted by the arrival of her dinner, and she gratefully set down the Angela Carter book in favor of the large salad in front of her. She hadn't been able to focus on the book, anyway; not when Leonard was so heavily on her mind. It was easier to focus on her food. She smirked at the memory Matt telling her once that a friend going to college in Pittsburgh had called him in horror after learning that restaurants there loved putting French fries in everything: salads, sandwiches, anywhere that Susan had never thought to put them in her own meals.

Midway through her meal she became aware that she was being watched. The restaurant was still empty enough that it didn't take her long to figure out where the surveillance was coming from: a table near the back of the restaurant, two girls and a guy, about her age. It was the couple from the bus, she realized with a jolt, and she experienced a sudden terrifying certainty that they were stalking her. Would she end up dead in a ditch before the end of the night? Would they follow her home?

On the heels of these questions came what her doctor called "passive suicidal ideation," which was, quite appropriately not as active as the "normal" ideation. Rather than actively trying to jump in front of a bus, being at peace with the possibility that a bus might run a red light and hit you even though you had the right of way crossing the street—that was the example of passive ideation that Dr. Campbell had used. You don't specifically chase death, but if it finds you somehow, you might not be overly upset.

If these people did chase her down and murder her, or push her in front of a car, or whatever else they might have in mind, *it is what it is*, she told herself. She supposed that this was an improvement in her attitude.

Of course, the likelihood of any of that happening was next to zero, even if she did draw unwanted attention to herself through her extreme wardrobe (her mother's words) and dark makeup. A lot of things could make you targets in a lot of places, but this probably wasn't one of those things.

That knowledge didn't make her feel any less uneasy, though, and she felt herself shrinking into the booth a bit as she watched the girl from the bus approach her. Her boyfriend and the other girl remained at the table, trying not to look like they were watching.

"Hey, um, you go to Lincoln Memorial, right?"

Susan looked up guardedly. “Yeah.” It was probably overly terse as replies went, but it was all she could manage.

“Yeah, I do recognize you! You’re dating that gay guy, right? Or he’s maybe gay or something?”

“You don’t know what you’re talking about,” Susan hissed, suddenly very angry.

“But aren’t you worried? What if he leaves you for a guy he *really* likes?”

“*Get the fuck away from me.*” She barely recognized the voice as her own—she'd never been particularly quick to defend herself in a confrontation—but accusing Leonard this way seemed staggering in its audacity. She realized in that moment that there were some things she would fight for, after all, even if she herself wasn’t necessarily one of them.

The other girl shrugged and said something dismissive, and Susan watched her return to her table. The food in front of her suddenly seemed less appealing, and when she forced herself to eat a few fries, they had lost their taste.

*Is this what Leonard goes through every single day?* If it were, she thought she could understand his personality in an entirely new way.

Disgusted with the turn the night had taken, she left enough money on the table to cover the meal and tip, gathered up her belongings, and swept out of the restaurant in disgust.

Leonard stopped over the following evening and spent some time getting to know Matt, who, for his part, either wasn’t surprised that his sister’s boyfriend was an incarnation of the Goth aesthetic, or genuinely didn’t care. Leonard felt uneasy at the prospect of spending a couple of days with two people he didn't really know, particularly because he knew he wouldn't have any way to get home if he felt the need to—but he knew that Susan hadn't had to make the suggestion to Matt at all, and he appreciated the thoughtfulness she showed in doing so.

The conversation didn't really take off until Matt asked about music; it turned out that Thomas, his roommate, also played acoustic guitar. Matt listened with interest as Leonard described his band, his favorite cover songs to play, and their future plans (nothing solid yet, but they all felt a tacit agreement that they would play for as long as there was interest in their music).

They shared a similar interest over video games, although they preferred different consoles. Still, the conversation got easier as evening turned into night, and by the time Matt headed out to catch up with some friends, the idea of accepting his hospitality seemed less fraught with hypothetical problems.

"I hope you don't mind that I just kind of took over and tried to make plans for you," Susan said later. They were sitting on the porch swing on the back deck of Susan's house, although it was too cold to do so comfortably.

She shivered and nestled closer to Leonard, lighting a fresh cigarette from the end of his and making herself as small as possible.

He looked down at her and opened his coat, allowing her to slip her hands closer to the warmth of his skin. Her cheeks and nose were a bit red from the cold, and it reminded him, strangely enough, of the way her face flushed when they'd been kissing for a while and his hands began exploring her body. It was an unexpected connection, but it warmed him a bit more and ignited something in his chest, and lower.

"What?" she asked after a long silence, and he

realized that he'd been so transfixed that he hadn't answered her question.

"It's nothing," he answered, reaching over to brush some brightly colored hair back behind her ear. "I'm just thinking."

"Care to share?" She said it coyly, and he wondered if she'd guessed at his thoughts.

"I love you."

The words were out before he'd had a chance to examine them, and he sat rigidly in the silence that followed. He wanted to take them back, but as he played them back in his head, he found that he meant them, and he probably had for a while. There had been no switch to flip, no milestone that had tipped the scales; it simply *was*. He was actually aggravated with himself for not recognizing it sooner.

These thoughts probably took fewer than two seconds to form and be acknowledged, but it felt to him like much longer. He had to do something; he couldn't sit still, so he passed a hand over his face and cleared his throat. He was suddenly acutely aware of the intensity of the way she was looking at him.

"Susan?"

There were tears in her eyes: not falling, but floating suspended, catching the light and amplifying it so her eyes shimmered.

*"I love you, too,"* she replied at last, her voice barely louder than a whisper. "Tell me again. Please."

He did, and she kissed him, hard and desperately and without reservation or self-restraint. Her hands moved up to bury themselves in his hair, keeping him as close as possible, and the sudden pulling pressure forced a sound from his throat. She echoed it in her own, low and frenzied, and then suddenly she was pulling him by the hand, urging him up and back into the house.

"Where are—?" he started, but she shushed him and headed, quickly and lightly, for the stairs. The house was too quiet, making every tread of the stairs seem to shriek as they snuck up to her room. Her parents had gone to bed early, he remembered.

She didn't turn on any lights when they reached her bedroom, the only illumination the moonlight coming through the windows and the surreal red light from Dagny's heat lamp. She pulled him farther into the room, pulling at his coat and discarding it on the floor and then tugging at his shirt.

She'd known that he was fond of her, of course, and she'd also suspected that she was in love with him, but hearing him say the words out loud had ignited some primitive need that wouldn't let her ignore her it. Their clothes fell away into a tangled pile on the floor, and then they were embracing with nothing between them for the very first time, and he allowed her to tug him onto the bed with her.

They lay there for a short moment, temporarily stunned by the magnitude of the night, and when they kissed again it was gentler, slower. When she pulled him closer to settle over her, they both paused again, as if to catalog exactly what was happening, and he started to say something that might have been "are you sure?" at the same moment that she reached down to guide him.

Later, they would lie facing each other and study each other's bodies, gazing with the reverence unique to the overstimulation of young lovers. Later, they would talk about how this might change their relationship, and how they could approach it more responsibly with a bit of preparation.

Later, they would both regard this as one of the single most significant moments in their lives thus far, a watershed night that separated the *before* from the *after*.

For the moment, though, the world shrank, and all that existed was their breath, their physical contact, and the wonderment they felt at this new reciprocity of their affection for one another.

*From the journals of Leonard Kellison:*

<u>Nov. 16:</u>

I used to talk so much about getting away from everything, and I still know that I need to, even for a little while. I know it'll be good to get out of town and see where Susan's brother goes to college, just for a change of scenery—if nothing else, I can be depressed in a new location.

Mom was surprisingly willing to let me go. Maybe she feels bad for me, or maybe she sees that I feel bad about myself. She asked the basic "mom" questions (who, what, when, where), and made me promise to call if anything went wrong (whatever that means), and I guess she also talked to Susan's mom on the phone.

All I know is that it's happening, and I'll be glad to disappear for a few days. I don't know Matt very well, though, and I have no idea what his roommate will be like. Knowing my luck, they'll both be sick of me after the first day and have to drop me off early. It doesn't help that Susan doesn't seem to crazy about the other guy, the roommate, which is weird, because I thought they all grew up together. Maybe he's just an asshole, but I'll wait until I meet him.

Maybe when I get back, things will be clearer. Maybe I'll have a better idea of how to deal with this stuff with my dad. It sucks, but I almost wish I didn't know what I know now about him. That he has a whole other family. That he's happy, or seems to be. Did he have a change of heart, or a life-altering event, or some other revelation?

It just makes me angry. He already had a family, but he ruined that one.

Anyway, I need to get things together for the trip. I have no idea what to bring.

# Chapter Twenty-One

The university was larger than Leonard had expected, and navigating it by car seemed confusing enough that he had to tamp down his anxiety before it could take hold. Taking note of the numerous one-way streets and restricted parking lots, he was grateful that Matt was the one driving the car. Leonard counted four different dorm buildings and six student lots that required specific parking permits before they'd even gotten to the main street that bisected the campus, and he quickly gave up trying to memorize where anything was.

"We're close now," Matt said, cutting into his reverie. "Just a couple of blocks ahead." Leonard followed where he'd pointed and saw a series of three- and four-story brick apartment buildings on either side of the street beyond where campus ended and the small downtown area began. At least getting to campus would be easy, he reflected; he would just have to follow Main Street into its land.

Along the way, Matt had explained that most other universities in the state gave students the entire week off for Thanksgiving, but that Hamilton Valley, being a private university that still held tightly onto past traditions, still held two days of classes before turning students loose on Wednesday. Oddly enough, the break extended into the Monday and Tuesday of the week *after* the holiday, so HVU students technically still had a week off. In that sense, staggering the break by a couple of days seemed more obstinate than sentimental about traditions, but there were no signs of changing.

"Of course, it's a pretty big blow-off week for a lot of students here," Matt had laughed on the drive up.

"Really, colleges are in a no-win situation. Give students Wednesday off, and they'll blow off Tuesday. Give them the whole week off, and they'll skip classes the Friday beforehand. I'll still go to most of my classes because a lot of professors try to make it mandatory by giving quizzes and scheduling presentations during the last few days before break, but that's just me. It seems worthwhile. Plus, a lot of them will end class early anyway." He smirked. "We'll party all afternoon and night on Tuesday and then drive back home Wednesday morning."

Now, as they pulled into the parking lot of an apartment building that looked just like the buildings on either side of it, Leonard took mental stock of what he'd brought along. Aside from a few changes of clothes, he also had his journal (which, feeling somewhat embarrassed, he'd hidden at the bottom of his duffel bag), his laptop, and Susan's copy of *Atlas Shrugged.* He didn't know how much time he'd be spending alone in the apartment, but regardless, he rarely went anywhere without a book to read.

Matt kept the conversation going, jumping easily from one topic to the next, as they grabbed their belongings from the back seat and he led the way up two flights of stairs to the apartment he shared with Thomas. Whatever Leonard had expected an apartment building full of student tenants to look like, it wasn't this. He'd had some vague picture in his head of a run-down building badly in need of a paint job and a new roof, probably dim inside and littered with cigarette butts and condom wrappers, the scent of weed in the air and maybe spilled alcohol that stained the thin carpet in places.

On the contrary, this was a bright, clean

structure, if a bit institutional in its colors and style for Leonard's tastes. The stairs were free of any trash, and while Matt fumbled for his keys outside of apartment 318, he greeted a passing couple brightly by name. The apartment itself was small and tidy, too, Leonard saw as he stepped inside. A couple of *Game of Thrones* posters were hung in cheap frames along the hall, and in the living room on the right sat a beige couch, clean but clearly somewhat old, flanked by a plain kitchen chair and an expensive-looking gaming chair. The television was sleek and larger than Leonard's own, and a couple of game consoles were tucked away on the shelves below.

"Living room," Matt said, jerking a thumb in that direction; "kitchen is on the left, bathroom's down the hall on the same side, and then the bedrooms are at the end. Mine's the one on the right; you can throw your stuff in there if you want to."

Acoustic guitar music floated out from the other bedroom, clunky and not without obvious errors: Thomas, no doubt. Leonard hadn't realized either of them played the guitar.

"Cool, thanks," he replied, forced once more to compartmentalize the anxiety that he felt again. Getting away from home and all of the problems that surrounded him there had seemed like a good idea, but now that he was actually here, with no way of returning home on his own, the next three days seemed impossibly long and interminable.

*Two and a half,* he reminded himself. *We're leaving early on Wednesday.*

And then, barely missing a beat, he silently added, *That's still three nights.*

*It'll be fine.*

*You obviously don't belong here.*

*Just relax.*

*You're imposing.*

He realized that Matt had said something else, and he refocused his attention there now. "Sorry, what was that?"

"Just asked if you wanted anything to drink. Everything's fair game, man. We don't put our names on what we buy for ourselves, or anything weird like that."

"Sure, thanks. I'll just throw my shit down first, if that's cool."

*You're trying too hard.*

But if he was, Matt didn't seem to care, or even to notice. He pushed open the door to his room and Leonard dropped his bag beside the dresser, looking around as he did so. It was a small space, but it comfortably held a double bed, the dresser, a cheap desk, and a closet. A laptop sat closed on the desk, and a stack of textbooks was thrown haphazardly onto the shelf above; on the wall beside them a muscle car calendar was tacked. The bed was unmade and in the open closet sat a pile of laundry.

"I like it," Leonard said vaguely, and followed Matt back out to the kitchen. He accepted the can of soda Matt offered, and as they sat on the couch a loud crash caused them both to jump.

The crash was followed almost immediately by a cry of "*Fucking Neil Young!*" and the distinctive twang of a guitar being set down with some force. The other bedroom door opened, and Thomas came in and dropped into the gaming chair.

"Oh, hey, I didn't know you were already back," he said in greeting. He leaned over, arm extended "Thomas."

Leonard shook the hand and introduced himself, noting as he did so that Thomas hardly looked like somebody he would have pictured Matt being longtime friends with. Where Matt was neatly styled, dressed in khakis and a polo, Thomas wore loose jeans with holes in the knees and a plain black T-shirt; where Matt's hair was carefully parted, Thomas's was shaggy and falling in his eyes.

In the next moment, though, their easy friendship revealed itself, and Leonard revoked his snap judgment of the pair. "Thomas has been trying to master that song for a week, but he sucks too much to get it perfect."

"Neil Young is an asshole songwriter," Thomas shot back. "All those little fills and tricks, man. 'Old Man' is going to be the death of me, I swear. That giant crash wasn't even intentional. I just went to stretch my arms and I knocked a bunch of stuff over." He leaned back and crossed his arms behind his head. "But, uh, welcome. This'll be a fun week. I don't know about Matt, but I'm not doing any fucking homework before break. I've earned this break."

As if to illustrate this point, he turned on the TV and picked up a game controller that had been sitting next to the chair. Leonard watched, somewhat amazed, as Matt produced another controller from somewhere out of sight and joined the game. Most of his anxiety vanished as he watched them play a few rounds, laughing with them at their taunts and jokes as their characters sought to kill each other on-screen. This, at least, was something he was already familiar with. The game and the players were new, but he'd experienced this camaraderie and good-natured arguing over video games for years with Glenn, Jez, and the rest of their group.

He accepted Matt's controller after Matt's third consecutive loss and leaned forward on the couch. "No idea what I'm doing in this particular game, but get ready," he warned, and Thomas laughed.

"Humble, isn't he? Don't get too comfortable there; you're going down!"

"You're in the big leagues now, man," Matt added, punching him on the shoulder. "Now kill this asshole!"

The next morning, Leonard lay on the couch texting with Susan until he heard sounds of stirring from one of the bedrooms down the hall. The couch had been surprisingly comfortable to sleep on, and Matt and Thomas had been generous with the number of spare pillows and blankets, a fact for which Leonard was grateful—he hadn't planned ahead well enough to bring his own.

Near the end of the previous night's hours of Netflix and takeout, Thomas had offered to bring Leonard to his introductory art history seminar, which was held late the following morning. Curious, Leonard agreed; and now, as he changed quickly into a T-shirt and jeans in the living room, he found himself wondering what a college class would actually be like. Curiously, he wasn't overly anxious, but he ascribed this to the way Thomas had described the seminar room: huge, dark, and relaxed. He liked the thought of experiencing college, however briefly, from a relatively anonymous position.

Thomas shuffled down the hall in pajama bottoms and an oversized HVU hoodie, mumbled a greeting, and started banging around in the kitchen. Moments later the welcome smell of brewing coffee filled the apartment, and unable to resist, Leonard crossed the hall to join him in the kitchen. They took turns at the toaster and made small talk while they ate, and Leonard couldn't help but imagine himself as he might be in the future: a coffee-dependent college student living on his own, or at least with roommates and away from home, free to buy whatever he wanted for breakfast and to order takeout for dinner, his only concerns about whether there would be a pop quiz that day or how long it would take him to walk across campus from class to class.

It struck him that this was actually similar to his current life, only on a larger scale, but it was easy to parse out the main difference. In college, he would be away from home, free to live how he wanted without the apprehension of existing under the watchful eye of a disapproving stepfather.

It was an utterly enticing fantasy, and he couldn't help but flesh it out as he prepared to leave the apartment with Thomas. He imagined that he would spend his first year in a dorm, just to get a taste of college life, and then move off campus with a couple of friends. They would coordinate who would bring what—curtains, kitchen appliances, all of the little things that made living away from home possible—and come and go on their own schedules, passing each other during the weekdays in between classes but making plans to blow off homework and have fun on the weekends.

Of course, he had no way of knowing whether such a future would unfold in quite that way, but the important thing, as far as he was concerned, was that it was possible.

The day was unseasonably warm when they left the building, perhaps the last temperate day of the season, and Leonard was suddenly glad that he'd brought his leather jacket instead of the heavy trench coat he'd been wearing for the past several weeks. What snow was on the ground was melting, making the walk to the big humanities building on the north end of campus soggy and perilous anywhere but on the sidewalks. As a result, the long stretches of grass and carefully cultivated landscaping were emptier than he assumed they would normally be, and the sidewalks were crowded as students rushed to their next classes.

"Here we go," Thomas commented as they approached the humanities building. The lecture hall was as he'd described it, dim and vast, the tiered seats close together and curving in a semicircle around the podium and screen at the far end of the room. As they entered, Leonard noticed a small sign on the door that indicated the room's 300-student capacity.

Looking around while they waited for the professor to arrive, Leonard was surprised at how unimpressed the students seemed. To him, this was all exotic and exciting, but he supposed that everybody else was already used to the experience of sitting in such a large lecture hall, taking college courses, and living away from home. He wondered how long it would take him to be similarly accustomed to the college experience. Would he ever feel as jaded as they looked?

He was still thinking about this when the professor walked in, strode casually up to the front stage, and did something at the podium to dim the lights a bit more. Leonard watched with interest as he clipped something to his shirt: a microphone, it turned out.

"Well, I'm glad some of you made it in today!" he commented, and was met with muted laughter. "I'll check the sign-in later, but I think we're half empty."

As if on cue, everyone looked down at their phones or computers. Trying to blend in, Leonard did the same, while looking curiously over to Thomas, who sat beside him.

"Signing in," he explained in a whisper. "The bigger classes all do it this way."

"How big is the class normally?"

Thomas shrugged. "Around one-fifty? It's never full in here."

Leonard nodded and returned his attention to the figure at the front of the room. He'd had a vague expectation of a graying academic in tweed, but this professor was younger than that—definitely younger than Leonard's mother—and wore a striped button-down shirt tucked into dark jeans. Leonard thought he wouldn't have looked out of place at one of the hipster coffee shops they'd passed on their way into town the day before.

The next hour passed in a blur. Leonard had brought his journal along, just to have something to write in, but now he was glad he had. He didn't write down much of the lesson, but by the end of class he had copied several visuals from the slideshow in a series of brief sketches: a pyramid with a triangular gap near the top, which somehow distributed the weight of the stones more evenly; a couple of hieroglyphs that he found he'd neglected to label; and the most important images on a sarcophagus. He might never look at his notes after his college visit, but he was glad to have them. They functioned as a kind of proof that he'd been there.

He slipped his pen into his pocket and rose with Thomas, who would have to rush off in a minute or two to make it to his next class on time. Strangely, Leonard wasn't worried about having some time to himself. He put in his ear buds and listened to music for the next hour as he walked around campus, trying to get a feel for what it might be like to live there, one student among thousands who were all wrapped up in their own lives and problems.

Eventually, he found himself in one of the dining halls, where he grabbed an overpriced cheeseburger meal and paid in cash. Navigating to an empty table near the windows, he bumped into an upperclassman in a football jersey; an apology was already on his lips when the guy sidestepped out of his way and apologized, smiling with good-natured grace.

The exchange, while brief, stayed in the forefront of Leonard's mind as he ate. *Never in a million years would that have been a non-issue at my school,* he thought, remembering with a vague sense of indignity how many unpleasant encounters he'd experienced just this year. It made him long even more to move on from high school. At a college like this, he thought he could finally let his guard down a bit. Nobody had bothered him as he'd wandered the campus; barely anybody had even given him a second glance.

He had a couple of fries in one hand and *Atlas Shrugged* in the other when he became aware that someone *was* watching him. He turned the page and continued eating, but he still felt eyes on him. Trying to be casual, he glanced around the crowded dining hall, taking in the groups of students talking and laughing at tables and in line.

As Leonard scanned the crowd, his gaze landed on a full table closer to the registers. One of the girls seated there saw him looking, turned away momentarily, and then looked back; she smiled but reddened when she saw that she was caught. Something one of her friends said at the table made her laugh, and the moment was over. It was unexpected, but probably just one of those things (whatever "those things" means, Leonard thought distractedly), and he went back to his book.

The minutes passed, and Leonard was still reading when Matt texted him to ask where he was. He described the building and told him not to hurry, and he was finishing the last of his fries when he saw the same girl angling toward his table in a way that seemed too unerring to be completely unintentional. He watched her approach out of the corner of his eye, no longer reading, and only looked up when she was close.

"What are you reading?" she asked, and despite himself, Leonard found that he liked the way she'd skipped over any kind of introduction.

He closed the book and showered her the cover. "Probably the longest book in existence," he explained with what he hoped was a self-deprecating laugh.

"That's insane. Is it for a class?"

His laugh was more genuine this time. "Nope, I'm just *that* crazy. I actually don't go here. Sorry, do you want to sit?"

He regretted the words as soon as they were out of his mouth. She seemed nice enough, whoever she was, but he didn't want to give her the wrong impression, and he knew that Matt would be there soon. It seemed very ill advised to be found talking to a random girl when his girlfriend's brother was on the way.

On the other hand, he didn't want to be rude, and he doubted Matt would actually be suspicious over an innocent conversation. Surely, he thought, people made random connections and shared harmless small talk all the time in college.

"Thanks! I'm Bailey, by the way." She extended her hand with exaggerated formality, and he shook it once.

"Leonard."

"So, you don't go here? I didn't think I'd ever seen you before, and this school is big, but it's not *that* big." She blushed again, something that Leonard was beginning to assume she did often. "Not that I notice everyone. I mean, I'm not the registrar. But you're, you know..."

He picked up the thread where she trailed off. He knew what she meant but was too polite to say. "I stand out, I know."

It was true. He'd noticed a couple of guys with long hair during his trek across campus, but few of them wore earrings, and none of them, as far as he could tell, had painted nails. It was no wonder he stood out, and he'd grown used to that since he'd started in on this aesthetic, but this conversation was something he definitely wasn't used to.

He cleared his throat. "I'm actually here visiting a friend. He'll probably be here soon. I just figured I'd grab a burger while I waited."

Why was he speaking like he was being interrogated?

But if she noticed, she let it pass unremarked. "So you're reading a book that could be used as a doorstop, but it's not for a class. Where do you find the time to do that? What's your major? I'm in engineering, and the thought of doing anything more than I have to almost gives me a panic attack."

"Oh—I'm studying English." Technically, this wasn't a lie; it was the track he'd chosen for high school, and whenever he gave any thought to college, it was always to do something in the humanities. He figured he could give himself a pass for the misdirection.

"That explains the masochistic tendencies! Honestly, reading a book for fun when you probably have others to read that you'll actually be graded on is impressive, but wow."

They both laughed at that, but Leonard felt a sudden pang of guilt as he looked away and noticed Matt standing near the entrance to the dining hall and looking for him. He knew intellectually that he'd done nothing wrong, just shared a few kind words with a stranger, but the implications felt larger than the situation itself. He was suddenly acutely aware that he was laughing with a girl—an *attractive* girl, he amended silently, with her long, straight sandy-blonde hair and a university sweatshirt that somehow failed to hide her curves—while he waited for his girlfriend's brother to show up and whisk him back to the apartment. It didn't have to be an awkward situation, but he felt like it could easily become one.

Bailey frowned when she noticed his sudden change in attitude. "Shit," she said. "I didn't mean to make fun of your major. I *wish* I had the patience to read--"

"No, it's not that," he interrupted, and immediately wondered if he'd sounded too eager. "I just saw my friend," he finished lamely, waving brightly at

Matt and then beckoning him over.

Matt took a seat adjacent to Leonard and smirked knowingly. “Hey, Leonard! Who’s your friend?”

Leonard introduced Bailey, mentally kicking himself for assuming that Matt would be suspicious. It shouldn’t be that way, he knew, and besides, Matt had no reason to suspect anything of him.

Matt took over the conversation effortlessly, playing up the level of friendship he shared with Leonard and asking Bailey about any good parties going on in the final days before break. By the time she left, he’d secured a promise from her that she would show up at a party downtown from campus the following night.

“It’s the big brownstone with the bright red porch outside,” she explained as she gathered her things. “A couple of my friends live there, but they’re all throwing the party. I think there are six roommates total.”

“Oh, we’ll be there,” Matt reassured her, and gestured for Leonard to hang tight. He got into one of the food lines while Bailey headed for the exit. She smiled once more at Leonard as she passed him.

When Matt returned, he gave Leonard a mock-suspicious raised eyebrow. “So, what was that about?” he asked, draining the grease from his first piece of pizza.

Leonard laughed. “I don’t know, she just started talking to me while I was reading.”

“Well, that seems rude.”

“Nah, she could probably just tell that I don’t go here and wanted to know why I was being an imposter.”

Matt shrugged. “People tend to be nice here. Don’t let it go to your head, though. You don’t need cougars chasing you down; they'll eat you alive. Stick with Susan."

Immediately, Leonard could feel the heat begin to creep up his neck. He shook his head, trying to stop the flush from reaching his face, and found himself stumbling over his words in his hurry to defend himself. "No, definitely not—I mean, yes to Susan, obviously, but no to the cougars..."

He trailed off, and to his relief, Matt picked up the thread. "Relax, man, I was joking. I didn't think you were trying to meet college girls. That would be really shitty." He glanced down at the limp slice of pizza remaining on his plate. "Still not as shitty as this pizza, though. Come on, let's head back to the apartment."

*From the journals of Susan Ingram:*

Nov. 18:

The dreams have started again.

I thought they were gone for good, but evidently not. The last time I had them was probably last year, around the holidays. I saw him once, just in passing, and I guess it stirred everything up again.

It's stupid, but I keep thinking, of course this happens while Leonard is away. I wish I could see him. I feel safer when he's around, which is a major change when it comes to guys. I haven't exactly had the best track record. But he's so sincere, even if he's intense sometimes. When I first met him, I used to wonder what happened to make him so intense in the way he views the world. I know enough now to "get it," but it also makes me feel bad. Like maybe we're two damaged people, and together we make a whole person, even though that sounds creepy and codependent.

I wish he would come home. That dream really fucked up my day, and probably my week. I think maybe I should tell him about it. He should know.

# Chapter Twenty-Two

The dream is nothing at first: just an intersection of old memories, a random day at a camp her parents had first convinced her to attend when she was eight or nine. Just a random summer at the camp she'd attended happily for several years in a row.

It starts with faded colors and blurred edges, a seemingly random juxtaposition of sorts which leaves her confused and curious. Gradually she notices the date and time hovering somewhere in the sky, and she comes to realize that it is the timestamp on a video file. She remembers that day now, or at least her dreaming self does: it is Parent Visitation day, the one where her father had gotten into the inner tube with her, and complained about getting his butt wet in the shallow river because he added too much weight to the whole affair.

This isn't just a nameless day at camp; it's the middle of the summer of the last year she would attend.

Next she sees herself sitting in an unmoving tire swing, waiting for somebody to push her; her brother is still very young, and he is playing in the small sandbox next to the big metal snail that you can ride on, the kind with little footholds and a huge, thick metal spring beneath it so you can rock back and forth a little.

All this she remembers, and then suddenly it is night, and she is alone with her bunkmates. In the nonsensical way that dreams can go, the night ends almost as soon as it begins, and now she is sitting under a huge oak tree, bored because she opted not to play soccer with the rest of the group. She is watching the guys practice volleyball, and when the informal game is over one of them saunters over to her: J.T., the boy who had inspired a long, desperate crush that had never really gone away.

He saunters over to her, and his skin shines like bronze in the sun, and his eyes glitter beneath the chestnut hair that has grown shaggy over the past several weeks.

She is suddenly afraid, and somewhere in her mind, somewhere far away from where the dream is taking place, she tries to wake up, to avoid the memory, because she knows what is going to happen. She has relived it a thousand times now and she doesn't want to see it all again, to feel it again, but she cannot break away. Dimly, she recognizes that she feels like she deserves the unhappiness; she wonders if it is a penance for some long-forgotten sin.

J.T. is talking to her, but she cannot respond or even recall what he has just said. It is a hundred conversations; there are none before it and none after it. It is all of her bad memories rolled into one big speech, into the words of some entitled little shit who even at fourteen years old only wants to get laid, some self-confident bastard who will later inflict worlds of pain every time she sees him.

Then she realizes that there is no text labeling the day; there are no faded edges. This is not a VHS she has watched countless times before; this is the Bad Place, and she is in it for real.

Somewhere in the distance a radio is playing the new summer hit by a popular rap-rock band. J.T. asks her if she would like to take a walk with him, and she sees that his friend Steve is there, and Steve is nice enough, so she says sure, fine, whatever. She is actually a little flattered by the attention. Besides, she figures, she is at camp, and nothing can happen in public anyway, right?

It is optimistic thinking, too trusting, the kind of thinking that has not yet been revealed as dangerous to her—or, more accurately, to this dream version of her that is still a child of just eleven years.

But they take her onto a well-worn path through the woods, one with signs pointing to nowhere, one where no birds sing and no flowers grow. The sunlight is softened by the interlacing branches of the trees; the air is a bit heavy and not quite alive. They walk for what seems like hours; they walk and walk and walk.

They cross a ditch that used to be a stream bed, one that is now dried up because of the horribly dry summer, and she stops on the other side of it as she sees J.T. turn around. He pins her with his eyes. She tries to break his gaze, but for some reason he is mesmerizing. His friend--Steve--looks at him questioningly, and in response J.T. just shrugs. He turns back to Susan; he asks her if she likes him.

*It's a trick question!* her mind screams at her, but she can't change the past; what is done is done, and she is going to relive it no matter what, because she has been taken back to the Bad Place and she is going to be hurt again. He's never asked her this before, and the directness of the question stuns her. It's too fast, too abrupt, and when he repeats himself, it feels like she has cotton in her ears. Her sleeping brain struggles to wake up, but she can only watch herself look away and nod.

J.T. smiles, and the whole world seems to brighten with it. Susan is proud of herself, on some level, for admitting to her feelings. She feels more mature, and she wonders if this is how adults feel all the time: making brave decisions with quiet resolve, understanding that the bravery is in the ability to say *yes* or *no* no matter how hard it is.

J.T. says good-bye to Steve, and the words are so abrupt that Susan thinks she has missed some of the conversation.

But no: Steve looks just as confused as she feels. He says something to J.T., low, so she can't hear, but Steve just shrugs again and murmurs something in reply.

Still looking uncertain, Steve waves a good-bye that seems somehow forced, and Susan watches him go with conflicting feelings.

J.T. crosses to her side and they sit together in the grass, legs dangling over the ditch that used to be a river, and there they make small talk for a while. When he eventually leans in to kiss her, she is too stunned at the realization that she is having her first kiss—and with her crush!—to react. But he is patient, and he whispers instructions on how to be a good kisser, and gradually she relaxes.

Her panic doesn't manifest in full, gut-wrenching form until he begins whispering other instructions into her ear, and that panic won't recede for a very long time.

He'd made her lie down in the dry riverbed, and she remains there long after he leaves her with a final kiss on the top of her head. She realizes that she has no idea how to get back to camp, so she sets off the way that she came, and by some miracle she finds her way back.

Everybody is waiting for her; she looks to the sky and realizes that it is nearly dusk already. They ask her what happened and where she went but she cannot speak, and when she sees J.T. half in shadows, leaning against one of the supports on the porch of his bunkhouse and studiously avoiding looking at her, she finally begins to cry. Someone escorts her to the nurse's building, and if the nurse doesn't believe her story about wandering and getting lost, she says nothing about it.

Then she is curled into a ball on her bed, and there she stays for a while, until the memory fades like the film of some old camera. Everything slowly becomes black, and so it remains black until she can wake herself up, black and empty herself, and full of a sort of voided pain which she fears she will always live with.

The early morning sunlight peeking around the edges of Susan's dark curtains did little to improve her mood after the bad night of sleep she'd just had, and she groaned when she saw that her alarm was set to go off in ten minutes. She felt irrationally irritated by the prospect of going to school when Thanksgiving was so close, especially because she knew several surrounding schools were already on break. That fact, coupled with the knowledge that Leonard had the whole week off and was probably still asleep on her brother's couch at that very moment, made her feel even worse.

Falling back asleep seemed like an impossible task, so she forced herself to sit up in bed and reluctantly turned off the alarm on her phone. Two text messages were awaiting her when she unlocked her phone, both from Leonard. The first was a picture of Matt and Leonard sitting together on the couch, Matt's arm hooked around Leonard's neck and both holding gaming controllers in their hands. Both were open-mouthed, probably in mid-scream. She recognized the set of Leonard's face when he was screaming in front of a microphone, anyway.

The sight of them so clearly getting along made her run hot and cold at the same time, and she forced herself to examine the feelings further. Obviously, she was relieved that the visit was going well, but at the same time, it seemed unfair that she should have to watch things from afar.

But no: that wasn't all, or at least not completely. She scoured the background of the picture, feeling both selfish and neurotic for doing so, but nobody else was in the shot. She wondered where Thomas was, or whether he'd been the one to take the picture. He'd been one of Matt's best friends for as long as she could remember, but she balked at the thought of Thomas and Leonard becoming close friends, too. Admitting this to herself made her feel guilty—after all, Leonard didn't know anything about him, or about the dynamics that had accompanied such a long friendship—but the guilt was somewhat buried under the relief she felt that Leonard would be returning home the following day.

*One more day, that's all. One more day, and one more night.*

The message accompanying the picture was time-stamped two hours later, slightly after midnight, and it was a sweet goodnight message that made her smile to read.

Thinking about going to school a moment later soured her mood, however, and she was still in bed, browsing her social media apps on her phone, when her mom poked her head in and urged her to get ready before it was too late to catch the bus.

Susan sighed. "Do I really have to go to school today? Seriously, it's insulting. Nobody's going to go over anything important, and half of my teachers already told us that we'd just be playing review games instead of learning."

This was, in fact, true, and her mom seemed to read the truth on her face, because Susan could almost see her resolve failing.

"I don't know, Susan. You can't get in the habit of missing more classes. Aren't you still catching up from. Um, last time?"

The pause was subtle, but Susan caught it. She felt another pang of guilt, this time for getting herself hauled off on suicide watch and creating a situation that her parents couldn't even directly address. They were still walking on eggshells around her—not as severely, but still in certain situations.

"I actually turned in the last of the make-up work yesterday. I really won't be missing anything! Please?"

The last of the parental resolve crumbled away, and she accepted the coming hug happily. "Fine, but don't stay in bed all day. I have a half day at work, so I'll be home around lunchtime."

Susan smiled brightly, but she sagged back against the pillows as soon as she was alone again. No matter how many times she dreamed of that last summer at camp, she always awoke feeling drained and anxious. What had once been a fun place to spend part of every summer had been irreparably tainted, and while that day had been the first time she'd experienced abuse at J.T's hands, it hadn't been the last. Over the following year and a half, she'd found herself alone with him on half a dozen more occasions, and each time was a close variation of the time before. It was a series of escalating events that left her increasingly depressed and humiliated, and it had finally ended on Christmas eve when she was twelve.

None of the other times ever made it into her dreams, though; it was always the first one, always at summer camp. Sometimes she would look down at some point to find her hands red, stained with J.T.'s blood, but that hadn't come until later, when he would visit her alone for the last time.

And she hated to remember that holiday night even more than the night at summer camp, even if it should symbolize some form of escape, a concrete end to something horrible.

All of this she reflected on now as she lay in bed with the covers up to her chin again. It was too much to remember, too powerful to relive, and she forced herself to think of something else by clicking on a playlist on her phone. As the first song began she turned onto her side and ran a hand over the pillow that Leonard had used on Halloween night. She pulled it closer and hugged it, imagining that she could still smell him on the pillowcase, but of course that was impossible. Several weeks had already passed since that night, and it wasn't even the same pillowcase.

The memory of that night—the alcohol, the drugs, the first time falling asleep next to someone she felt completely safe with—threatened to overwhelm her, and she forced herself to breathe deeply. *I'll see him soon enough,* she thought. *Everything will be fine.* I'll *be fine.*

Just to be safe, she eased into the four-seven-eight breathing method she'd learned in therapy, focusing all of her attention on the breath entering and leaving her body.

*Empty the lungs.*

*Breathe in through the nose for four seconds.*

*Hold for seven seconds.*

*Breathe out forcefully for eight seconds.*

In the beginning, she'd had to halve the time, going two-three and a half—four—but unless she was on the verge of a serious panic attack, she rarely had to shorten the exercise anymore. She put everything into her breathing, feeling self-conscious for practicing her mindfulness even now, alone in her room, but gradually, the lump in her throat faded. Once that happened, she could feel the rest of her body begin to relax, too.

"This isn't going to be my whole day," she said aloud, and wished she meant it. The truth was, affirmations only seemed to work if you believe in them, and she wasn't at all sure anymore that staying home from school had been a wise choice.

It was still bright outside when Leonard and the others left the apartment to find the party, but the sun was starting to sink low on the horizon, and parts of the sky had a foreboding reddish-purple tinge that he probably would have liked more if it didn't remind him of a bruise.

This association, he reflected as they traversed the blocks leading away from campus, was probably due to the nerves that accompanied him as he walked. Outwardly, he was following Matt's and Thomas's conversation and even supplying some jokes that made them laugh, but he was acutely aware that he didn't have a real frame of reference for what to expect at the party. He'd seen countless depictions of college parties in television shows and movies, of course—from *Rules of Attraction* and *American Pie 2* to *Animal House* and even *Dawson's Creek*—but he suspected that many of those were sensationalized for successful on-screen scenes. He'd even tried asking his hosts what he might expect, but they'd just laughed and told him it would be fun.

Needless to say, this hadn't reassured him very much.

After that assurance, the subject had changed to party-appropriate apparel, and Leonard realized that he'd only brought minimal, uncreative changes of clothes. He certainly couldn't find anything in his bag worthy of a college party, and when he voiced his concern, Matt pulled an HVU hoodie from his closet and tossed it across the room.

"It's clean," he told Leonard, "and you'll fit right in. We're not bringing coats, by the way. Too much hassle at the end of the night, and sometimes they get *misplaced* at parties."

"Stolen," Thomas translated. "But also sometimes ransacked. Things go missing."

Now, as they passed a couple of impressively large student housing developments, Leonard was glad that he didn't have to worry about his trench coat. The walk was already warming him, and although anxiety left his fingers cold, he found that he actually liked feeling as if he fit in. It felt like a disguise, and while it wasn't one that he particularly wanted to wear forever, it gave him a different perspective on what the inscrutable, more *regular* people around him got up to.

Bailey's description of the house turned out to be perfect. Most of the student housing closer to campus was obviously student housing from the outside: massive apartment buildings; parking signs with specific instructions for visitors; flags and pennants proclaiming HVU pride in many of the windows. As they'd walked the last couple of blocks, however, the giant apartment buildings gave way to houses and duplexes, and although some had the same collegiate feel to them, others were clearly permanently leased or owned by locals. These had less of a college ambience to them. Leonard wouldn't have been able to explain how or why; maybe it was the lack of HVU bumper stickers on the cars, or the general better state of upkeep of the houses.

The house they stood in front of now, though, was definitely a college rental. The red porch was occupied by perhaps a dozen students, some drinking from the ubiquitous red plastic cups in their hands but others just leaning against the railing and talking. Many of them were smoking, and through the open front door Leonard could see that nobody inside had a cigarette in their hand. This small detail struck him as absurdly polite, and he laughed inwardly at the out-of-place courtesy that he hadn't expected.

"Seems pretty low-key," Thomas observed as they climbed the steps.

"It's still early," Matt reminded him, and they both laughed.

They were on the porch and heading into the house when a big guy in a T-shirt filled the doorway. He crossed his arms, and Leonard found himself astounded at the size of his biceps.

"Password," he demanded, and Leonard could feel himself freezing in place.

"Fuck you," Matt retorted.

The four of them stared at each other in silence for a long moment, and Leonard was ready to just turn around and leave when the guy in the doorway extended his arms and laughed uproariously. "Glad you made it, man," he said, and Matt walked into the bear hug and slapped him on the back. "Sorry, new guy, just having fun."

It took Leonard a moment to realize that he was being addressed, and he did his best to laugh and shrug it off. Thomas nudged him forward a step and winked.

"This is Leonard, just up for a few days," he explained. "He's cool."

"Yeah, so don't scare the shit out of him, Dave," Matt chimed in with a laugh.

"My bad, new guy Leonard. Come on in."

All of this happened in what seemed like a second to Leonard, but as he unpacked it, feeling somehow a step behind, he realized that he'd just been described as cool, and by someone he would probably have been intimidated by if they hadn't known each other. Again, he had to shake off the feeling that he was wearing a disguise, but now he suspected that he actually *was* wearing it well.

The thought that he was fooling everyone made him feel guilty, but he quashed the feeling as soon as it rose. *This is a party,* he reminded himself. *So party.*

With that in mind, he followed the others into the house and tried to open himself to the experience. Some of the stereotypes he'd expected to see were indeed on full display—a beer pong table against one wall; people playing drinking games around a coffee table; loud music pouring out from another room somewhere—but he found himself mildly surprised that there were no kegs or beer helmets or wasted girls dancing on tabletops to be seen.

They each accepted a beer from the fridge, none of them commenting on Leonard's underage status, and then stood together next to the couch while they tried to decide where to go. They made small talk while they looked around, and after a minute or two Matt urged them toward the coffee table when shouts of "new game! New game!" erupted from the group that had been playing the drinking game earlier.

A few people from that circle groaned and got up to leave, which Matt took as an invitation to join the new game. Leonard joined him on the couch, which most definitely did not match the one that they'd just arrived from, and watched as one of the players shuffled a deck of cards. Several of the cards were bent or torn, and they all looked vaguely sticky, but this didn't seem to faze anyone seated around the table.

"What are we playing?" Thomas asked, taking a seat on the floor between Leonard's side of the couch and a beaten-up recliner a few feet away. He was holding a second can of beer, although his first was still mostly full. He set both very carefully in front of him, against one leg of the coffee table.

"Kings!" came the shuffler's reply, and a few people around the table raised their drinks and amplified the shout. "Standard rules: two is *you*, three *me*, four *floor*, same as always."

Leonard hadn't recognized the game at first, but he found himself enjoying an unexpected sense of accomplishment at knowing about the game. "You" meant that whoever drew the card had to choose someone to drink; "me" meant that the drawer had to drink; "floor" meant that the last person to slap the floor had to drink. He ran through the rest of the rules in his head—five, guys; six, chicks—and found with some surprise that he remembered most of them. The last time he'd played the game had been at Jez's birthday party two years ago, and he vaguely remembered fully embarrassing himself at "Never Have I Ever" (Jacks) but doing well at "rhymes" (nines).

The game ran easily enough. Aside from himself and his friends, there were five other people arranged on folding chairs and pillows, and nobody second-guessed Leonard's presence at the party. A particularly chatty girl who was already pretty well intoxicated seemed to like picking on him, making him drink or choosing him as her "mate" (eights) when she had the chance, and one of the guys teased her each time she used her turn to make Leonard drink.

It felt good to belong, even if he didn't really. He'd grown so used to being defensive around people, even if he didn't perceive an actual threat, that at first he felt extremely exposed by lowering some of his walls. As the game went on and the alcohol did its work, though, he found himself leaning into the camaraderie of the game and giving as much shit as he took. That friendly mocking tone had quickly become the mood of the game, in fact, and it was strange to be teased without immediately feeling hurt or retaliatory.

In one particularly bold moment, he put a finger down at "never have I ever kissed another guy (or, for the girls, another girl)," and he was shocked when several others lowered fingers, too.

"Frigging parties, right? That's how it happened to me, too," someone commented, and everyone laughed. And that was the end of it.

Afterwards, feeling more confident in his ability to blend in, Leonard strayed from Matt's company and started exploring the other rooms. Thomas had disappeared with a girl already, a short girl with half of her head shaved and several visible tattoos. According to Matt, she and Thomas had a love-hate thing going, and they regularly hooked up at parties but weren't on friendly terms anytime else. Leonard wondered what that would be like, and decided that it didn't appeal to him. To have that kind of arrangement, they would have to be pretending that they *did* like each other at parties, or *didn't* like each other anywhere else, and pretending was exhausting.

He tried to explain some of his thinking to Matt, who did a see-saw movement with his hand. "Sure, but it's a sure thing when they're both at the same party, so I guess it kind of evens out."

Now, looking for a bathroom upstairs, the idea of a "sure thing" still seemed unappealing to him if it came at the price of arguing everywhere else.

He left the bathroom—a shabby affair, poorly cleaned and concerningly dark with half of the light bulbs out—and wandered back down the hall, studying the pictures hanging on the wall. Apparently, the house extended farther back than it had appeared to from the street, because a lot of pictures hung between more doorways than he had expected.

Several of the pictures were magazine pullouts taped to the wall—cars, girls, musicians—but at least one of them was an actual framed art print that he vaguely remembered seeing before, and still more were *Calvin & Hobbes* cartoons seemingly torn from a book.

He stepped closer to the art print to allow someone to pass behind him, but the person stopped just past him and a voice said, "I thought you didn't go here."

Startled, he turned to find Bailey eyeing him with a raised eyebrow. She stood with most of her weight on one foot so her hip cocked out, her arms crossed over her chest.

"I don't," he replied, momentarily confused. "Remember, you told us about this party?"

"No shit," she said with a grin. She stepped forward and plucked at his borrowed hoodie. "Did you steal this from some freshman?" She seemed surer of herself than she had in the dining hall, more confident, and Leonard wondered if she'd had as much to drink already as he had. He hadn't seen her at the party until now.

"Oh. No, I borrowed it from Matt." He turned back to the painting on the wall. "Do you recognize this? I know I've seen it before; I just can't place it."

Bailey moved to stand beside him and leaned in to examine the artwork. She stood unexpectedly close to him to do so, and he couldn't help but notice how she smelled up close. Under the alcohol and something that might have been weed smoke, she exuded an attractive scent that was too muted to be perfume. Some kind of oil, maybe.

He found himself watching her out of the corner of his eye when she snapped her fingers and grinned. "Got it! It's called *The Accolade.* See how she's knighting him or something? I wanted to call it *The Knighting* but I knew that wasn't right. It's fancier than that." She pulled him by the arm, adding, "There's an even cooler one down the hall here. Did you see the landscape there?"

Leonard had not, and he grasped for a way to explain that, although he appreciated art of all sorts, he couldn't imagine a landscape being "cool."

She laughed at that. "The guys who rent this house have all kinds of cool ideas. One of their girlfriends or something finds shitty art at thrift stores and adds things to them to make them better. Here, look at this."

He turned obediently, and took a long moment to study the art hanging before him. At first glance, it was a typical landscape: trees captured mid-sway in an invisible breeze; a farmhouse in the middle distance; a bright blue sky above. Mountains rose in the far background of the scene. Behind them, though, the sky darkened from blue to a deep purple, and the silhouette of some lumbering creature seemed to be rising from behind the peaks. A closer look revealed a suggestion of horns or tentacles, and when he looked with renewed interest for other additions, he could see something creeping out from behind the barn.

"Okay, that's actually awesome," he admitted. "It would just be a piece of hotel room art otherwise."

Bailey laughed again. "Told you! Here, let's see what else we can find."

Before he could protest she was retreating down the hall, trying doorknobs until she found a room that wasn't locked. She beckoned to him, but he found himself reluctant to follow her. Despite his current state of inebriation, he had the idea in his head that, one way or another, to do so would end the night badly.

Downstairs, the party was getting louder, and he could hear shouts of encouragement and insults as the competition around whatever game was being played got more serious. The second floor was entirely empty, and he felt both an invitation and a warning in the relative silence there.

"We should get back down," he told her by way of apology, but she shook her head and turned to enter the room.

"I'll just appreciate art all by myself, then," she replied.

He watched her disappear into the dark room, torn between keeping up the cool guy character and reuniting with Matt and Thomas, but in the end the new persona he found himself embodying won out. Strangers had called him *cool*. Older guys, college students, had welcomed him into the party and downed alcohol with him. Suddenly, the thought of retreating now, not as the cool guy but just as Leonard, felt unbearable.

The room wasn't as dark as it had seemed from the hallway when he entered. The glow of a laptop screensaver lit some of the area, and a desk lamp atop a dresser provided warmer light. Out of habit, he reached to close the door behind him, but at the last second he left it mostly open. It was a symbolic concession, but it made him feel a little better about being alone in a college house with a near stranger during a party.

As if sensing his thoughts, Bailey looked up from where she was sitting on the floor and offered an exaggerated shrug. "Most guys would have closed the door behind them," she commented.

*This is like a movie*, Leonard thought, and the realization forced him to consider his response more closely. "Do you think I'm most guys?" he asked carefully. It was meant to be an earnest question, but it came out sounding flirtatious, much more confident than he felt.

She studied his face for a couple of seconds before answering.

"I think you're a decent person," she said at last.

"What if I'm a bad person?"

The words were out of his mouth before he could consider them, and he regretted them almost immediately. He tried again. "What I mean is, how can you be sure? Doesn't everyone say not to go off with strangers alone?"

She shrugged off the implications of the question. "I've been in worse situations, and trust me, I could kick your ass if I needed to." She smirked as she said it, but Leonard found that he did believe her. "Anyway, we're just hanging out. I *hope* you didn't think following me in here was an invitation or something."

"No, not at all." He paused. "This isn't some movie; I know that." *And I'm still in high school, and I have a girlfriend, and I'm here with her older brother and his friend*, he added silently. He wanted to tell her all of this, but he found that he was afraid to—not because she might leave, but because he knew it would break the spell. He was having fun, pretending to be someone else, and he wanted to hang on to being that person for as long as he could.

"Don't you want a chair or something?" he added lamely, mostly because he couldn't think of what else to say.

"Nah, I like the floor. Besides, the only chair in here has clothes hanging on it, and I don't want to touch any of that."

He looked around and saw that it was true. The desk chair facing the laptop had several shirts and a pair of jeans draped over its back, and as he considered this, he realized that he had no idea whose room this actually was, or how its owner would react to finding two people talking in it. Everyone here seemed friendly enough, but he worried that it probably wasn't wise to linger away from the party for too long.

"Leonard. It's fine. Come sit with me." He turned back to her, and she reached an arm out toward him. "Please?"

He sighed. "Yeah, okay. Just for a little bit."

He sat facing her, cross-legged, and chatted about nothing in particular for a while. It was clear that she'd had more to drink than he had, and it struck him again that it would probably look bad if anyone were to walk in. When he voiced this concern, though, she just laughed and held out her hand.

"Okay, probably, yeah. Here, give me your phone for a second."

The fact that she was still slurring her words concerned him, but still he dug his phone out of his pocket and handed it to her. He knew that she was going to add her number to his contacts but figured that, at the very least, he could explain his situation later from a distance, or just block her altogether, if it came to that.

Everything about the night suddenly made him feel very tired, and he scooted back on the floor and lay down flat on his back for a moment. This repositioning reminded him that he, too, was well on the way to being drunk, and he closed his eyes and rubbed them with the palms of his hands.

"I just texted myself from this so I'd have your number, too. Do you want your phone back?" he heard her ask, and without opening his eyes he reached an arm out in her general direction.

When nothing happened, he groaned and sat up again, and when he opened his eyes Bailey was suddenly very close, face mere inches away. Her hair tickled his nose when he tried to look to the side.

"Hey," she murmured, voice much lower than it had been.

"Uh, hi," he whispered back. He tried very hard to ignore the implications of the situation, or the fact that he could practically smell whatever remained of the lip gloss on her lips. "What's up?"

"Just saying hi," she replied, whispering now as well, and before he could think of a response she was kissing him, one hand tangled in his hair and the other planted on the floor between them to brace herself. He could feel her tongue pressing against his lips, the taste of beer and the sickly-sweet licorice of some cheap party liquor invading his mouth. Despite his best half-drunk efforts, he felt himself giving in by degrees, and it was only when she pushed him back to the floor and tried to straddle him that he fully came back to his senses.

"I can't," he said around her mouth. She made an ambiguous noise in response and moved to kiss him again, and this time he pushed himself back on the floor so he could be heard. For the first time, he realized that she was no longer wearing her shirt, and he found himself unable to keep his eyes completely level with her face. She was incredibly attractive to him, and he knew that even without the alcohol he would be hard pressed to look away. In his disorientation, he could almost hear Jez, or maybe Glenn, making a joke about the "spank bank."

With great effort he closed his eyes. It was the only way he trusted himself at the moment. "I really can't, I'm sorry," he repeated, louder this time, unsure of what exactly he was apologizing for even as he said the words.

She just looked at him, the surprise and indignity of rejection plain on her face. He hoped she wasn't able to read his face as clearly, or she would be able to recognize the wistfulness he struggled to ignore. He knew that he would return to this moment later to examine that feeling, but there were more pressing matters right now.

"I'm sorry," he said again, and in some ways, he was.

"You seemed okay a minute ago. What happened?"

If they were playing out a scene in a movie, as he'd felt earlier, then they were clearly following different scripts. He'd expected her to yell, or insult him, or storm out, and her tempered reaction confused him. For reasons he couldn't explain, he was somewhat unsettled by it.

"Is it a girlfriend?" Bailey asked, and he nodded. It felt pathetic to him that he'd had to make her say it, but he conjured the imagine of Susan in his mind, and he felt an overpowering rush of guilt and pride in response.

"Shit." Bailey stood and retrieved her shirt from where she had left it on the bed. "And here I thought you were just too much of a gentleman to make the first move."

Leonard stayed where he was on the floor and looked up at her. "I'm trying to be," he told her, and he found that this was true.

She straightened her clothing and gave him a sad smile. She crossed the small room to the door, and before she left she said, "I think you are."

Before he could ask whether she meant she thought he was trying or thought he was a gentleman, she left.

Moments later he heard someone in the hallway laughing and clapping, and he felt his stomach drop and his body go cold.

"Who do you have in there?" a voice asked, and he heard Bailey tell whoever was out there that it was nobody, just let it go.

"Wow, he must be ugly! Why can't we meet him?" The guy's voice rose in volume as his enthusiasm grew, and now Leonard could tell that he was clearly very drunk.

With a sigh, Leonard got to his feet and moved to the door. Farther down the hall, he could hear Bailey talking with the loud guy, and to his relief they were moving away. He stood next to the door for another long moment, trying to gauge whether anyone was still nearby, and walked out of the room.

Matt was at the top of the stairs talking to Bailey and the drunk guy, and he gave Leonard a wave when their gazes locked. Even from down the hall, Leonard could see the recognition dawn on his face, and then—before he could even begin to formulate an excuse—Matt was walking toward him.

"Tell me you weren't just in a stranger's bedroom with Bailey," he said as soon as he was sure Leonard could hear him over the music drifting up from downstairs.

Too weary to even try to lie, Leonard stuffed his hands in the hoodie's pockets and gave a defeated shrug. "Yeah, I was, but not for long, and it wasn't what you think—"

"Well that's good, because I *think* she obviously liked you and was all too happy to get you alone. And if you weren't dating my sister, I'd be all for it, but what the *fuck*, man?"

Matt was keeping his voice even, for which Leonard was thankful, but it was clear that Matt was a little drunk, himself. Not so drunk that he wouldn't remember this tomorrow—Leonard knew he wasn't that lucky—but a drunk discussion was better than sober yelling.

They watched as Bailey gave a small, embarrassed wave, and then mimed texting before turning to leave.

Matt sighed heavily. "Does she even know that you're in high school?"

"No, it, uh, didn't come up. We were talking here in the hall, and then we were talking in there, and she was—I think she wanted to sleep with me, but I stopped it. I promise, man, I wouldn't do that to Susan."

Matt considered him for a long moment and then nodded. "I'm not saying a fucking word to Susan, because I don't think she could deal with it right now. But you've got to be better, okay? Don't even put yourself in that kind of situation. I'm serious."

"Yeah. Of course." The shame that Leonard felt was difficult to describe; it was almost more of a feeling of disappointment, but in himself, not in anyone else. It was both familiar and detestable.

"Cool." An awkward silence fell over them; it was only broken when Matt said, "Okay, let's go home. I have to pack tonight since I'll be staying almost a week when we get back tomorrow."

He clapped Leonard on the back, and with more relief than he cared to admit to, Leonard followed him to the front door and they began the walk back to Matt's apartment.

*From the journals of Leonard Kellison:*

Nov. 19:

It was helpful in a lot of ways to get out of town for a few days, but it's also difficult to figure out whether it was ultimately a positive or negative experience. I guess it depends on the consequences? I feel shitty saying this, but even though I didn't initiate anything with Bailey, I know I'm still complicit in it. I should have stopped things immediately. I shouldn't have gone into that room at all. I should have stuck with Matt and Thomas the whole night instead.

If this is what college is going to be like, I don't think I want to do it. It seems messy. If Susan had been there, maybe we would have been alone together in that room instead. But that makes it sound like I went in there with Bailey just because Susan wasn't there, which also isn't true.

Anyway, in a strange way, it's kind of good to be home. At least here, there are fewer unknowns. It's familiar. And hey, maybe it's just the whole "better the devil you know" thing, but I'm more comfortable when I know what to expect. Maybe it's my star sign or whatever. All I know is that I feel like an "old soul" adult and a scared kid at the same time. What do I do with that?

# Chapter Twenty-Three

Leonard had worried that the drive back home would be awkward, given the events of the party the previous night, but thankfully, it was uneventful. Matt, for his part, didn't seem willing to discuss the party at all, other than to fill Leonard in on what he'd missed when he disappeared.

"So Thomas ran off with that weird girl, or I guess it's just their relationship that's weird, because who am I to judge, right? Here name is Selene, by the way. I think she's a psych major, which is a major red flag to begin with because I've dated psych majors before, and all they want to do is analyze you to death.

"Anyway, they weren't gone for long, but next thing I know, she's running out of the room just swearing at Thomas, and he's chasing after her, tripping over his jeans because they're not all the way back on yet, and halfway to the front door she turns around and shoves him. He gives this cartoon *yelp* and falls backwards and lands on the coffee table, right on top of the card game that's going on, and people's snacks and beer just go flying. Whoever has to clean that up is going to be pissed."

They both laughed at the image, and Leonard desperately wished that he'd been there instead of alone upstairs with a half-undressed college girl.

"What were they fighting about?" he asked, both to keep the conversation going and to banish the guilt he was feeling.

"Man, I still don't know, but they fight *all the time*. I don't know why they keep going back to each other; they never actually dated, but they break up a hell of a lot. I assume he made some joke that she didn't take well, or called her by someone else's name—which he's done before, but it depends on how drunk he gets—but who knows."

"How long have you known him?" Leonard knew that Matt and Thomas had been friends for a long time, well before going to college together, but the idea of having a college roommate and a best friend in the same person appealed to him in a brotherly way. He hadn't grown up with any brothers or sisters, and although Glenn and Jez were as close to siblings as he could imagine anyone being, he assumed that actually living with somebody—sharing space, and responsibilities, and existence in general—must be even more meaningful. He'd considered the difference between dating a girl and living with her, certainly—with Anna, anyway, although he'd been a few years younger then, and probably much too idealistic—but cohabitating with a close friend, an almost-brother, was fascinating in a totally different way.

"Since we were nine or ten, probably," Matt was saying now. "We started hanging out in school, and I guess that never stopped." He laughed.

"That's cool," Leonard replied automatically, but he was distracted by his thoughts now, and the rest of the trip consisted mostly of small talk.

Returning home was both bittersweet and a bit surreal. Matt dropped him off first, and when Leonard entered the house he looked around as if seeing it for the first time. He tried to view his surroundings as a stranger might: the living room brightly lit by the afternoon light falling in through the windows; the kitchen somewhat darker, but clean and organized; the bathroom a little outdated but clearly well maintained.

Nobody was home yet, so he took his time settling in. He'd felt this slight disorientation upon returning home ever since he was a child, almost as if he were surprised that everything was still in its place. Almost as if it took a moment for his new surroundings to become real again.

He didn't realize just how tired he was until he stretched out on the couch, but the thought of Roland coming home and finding him that way was unsettling enough that he grabbed his bag and headed upstairs instead. There was never any guarantee for how Roland's mood might be on any given day, and if he came home angry about something, Leonard didn't want to be an easy target for his ire.

Sleep came swiftly and unrelentingly, and he barely had time to text Susan first. The couch at Matt's had been comfortable, but even if it had been a bed, it wouldn't have been as comfortable as Leonard's own bed. *There's something personal about a bed*, he thought, and it was the last coherent thought he had before succumbing to his dreams.

It was already beginning to get dark outside when he woke up. He had a moment of disorientation before remembering that he was back home, and when he checked his phone, he wasn't entirely surprised to see that the buzzing he'd been hearing in his dreams was actually his phone alerting him to several new text messages.

In his dream, he'd been alone in a dark movie theater with Bailey. The movie was in another language, not just one he didn't speak but one of which he'd never even heard an approximation. It was gibberish, and as the plot progressed, he grew angry that he couldn't understand what was going on. It seemed important, but he couldn't follow it.

Finally, Bailey forced his attention away from the screen by kissing him, and as they took off their clothes, piece by piece and then all at once, he became aware of a dub track over the movie's original audio. It was in Matt's voice, and it was by turns encouraging and admonishing:

*About time you got her pants off, man. My sister is going to be so pissed when she finds out. Whoa, where did you learn that move?*

It was both absurd and uncomfortable, and he'd awoken when Matt's confusing commentary took on the tone of buzzing bees and eventually resolved into the buzzing of his phone.

He groaned and sat up, rubbing the sleep out of his eyes as he did so. He found his glasses on the table next to the bed but didn't remember taking them off. The memory of the dream followed him as he stood under the water in the shower, turned as hot as he could stand it in an attempt to burn away the secret pleasure he felt at the sight of Bailey's body. Dream or not, she was attractive, and he was aggravated at the lust that the dream had generated. It wasn't even a very symbolic dream, he thought: it was just his subconscious's attempt to complete the scenario that he hadn't followed through at the party.

More importantly, though, he would be seeing Susan within the hour, and he didn't want the ghost of Bailey lingering between them. He already felt guilty enough as it was, but he told himself that the sooner he could reconnect with Susan, the sooner the party would be forgotten.

He got dressed without giving much thought to his outfit and headed downstairs, where his mother was cutting up vegetables in the kitchen.

"There you are," she said when he entered the room, her chopping barely slowing as her gaze left the cutting board. "You were passed out earlier so I let you sleep. How was college?"

*How was college* seemed like a strange way to ask about his trip, and he wondered if she would be asking him the same question in the same manner in a couple of years. He tried to conjure the image of himself in the dark lecture hall again, only a few years older, and found that he couldn't. It had seemed so momentous at the moment, crashing Thomas's art history course, and picturing himself as a college student had been so easy. He wondered if he were just overtired, or if the uncomfortable experience at the party had soured the whole concept of college for him.

But his mother was waiting for an answer, so he forced himself back into the moment. "It was cool," he said, taking a seat at the kitchen counter. "Susan's brother took me around campus, and his roommate let me crash his art history seminar. It was dark," he added quickly, seeing the look on her face, "and it was a big lecture hall. I doubt he noticed."

"They weren't doing drugs, were they?" she asked, very pointedly not looking at him as she posed the question.

"Of course not!" he answered honestly. He didn't count alcohol as a drug, but he wasn't going to voice the distinction to her.

"I just had to ask," she returned, looking at him now. "There's no handbook for this, you know. I don't know if letting you go was the right thing. You were just so adamant that going back to school right away was the *wrong* thing, and..." she trailed off, gesturing vaguely with the knife in her hand.

"I know, Mom," he said, his voice small. Too much was left unsaid in the silence that hung after "and," and it was easy for Leonard to fill in the blanks.

*...and I'm afraid that school has been so vicious that going back too soon would land you in trouble again.*

*...and I'm afraid that it would get so bad that you would hurt yourself.*

*...and accidents happen, and I can't stand the thought of losing you.*

*This is another of those adult-to-adult*

*conversations*, he thought, and he wondered if they would ever start feeling less awkward. He didn't think he was ready for this new dynamic, not when it meant that he would see more of his mother's vulnerable moments.

Unsure of what else to say, desperate to get out of the conversation but unable to do so gracefully, Leonard said, "It helped a lot, just to get away. It'll be fine after break."

"Okay, that's good," she replied, and although he didn't hear her, after he left to visit Susan she repeated it: "That's good."

The weather had gotten colder since the sunlight faded, and Leonard thought that he could taste snow in the air. While he drove, he thought about how strange it felt that tomorrow was Thanksgiving. Not for the first time, he felt that the past few months had both crawled and hurtled by, pleasing and harrowing by turns, the good followed by the bad. It seemed disingenuous to say that time was flying, but it was certainly moving at a good pace.

*Time flies when you're having fun,* he thought, *but it also flies when you're so depressed that you sleep 12 hours a day.* It amounted to the same thing, really—one less day on the earth. If it was a good day, that particular good day was gone forever. If it was a bad day, you might feel like it had been wasted, drained of potential, but it was also gone forever.

The evening gave no sign of whatever it thought of Leonard's evaluation, but neither did it curse him with an admonishment in the form of snow or freezing rain. It was cold in his van, though, and the heat didn't really kick in with any enthusiasm until he was nearly to Susan's neighborhood. His fingers were frigid despite the gloves he'd pulled on, and he remembered wistfully how Anna would sometimes warm his gloves with her hair dryer before they had to leave the house in the winter during which they had dated. She would turn up the heat and blow the hot air inside the gloves while he would sit back, feeling somewhat embarrassed, but also pleased by her concern for his well-being.

It was one of those small things that would pop up occasionally in his mind, summoned by whatever semi-related event was going on in his day. Thinking back, he remembered how often he would be reminded of her in those early days after their breakup, and how certain he'd been that this would never change. *He was never the same after she dumped him*, people would say. *It's such a shame. Talk about true love.*

Of course, like so many other things, he'd been wrong about this. He'd dated again, and enjoyed several romantic partners, and while this had put some much-needed distance between his past and his present, it had also landed him in trouble more than once.

*Enter Bailey.*

Yes, he thought: Bailey was the most recent, most egregious last of judgment, and it bothered him all the more because he felt so drawn to Susan. He'd spent the night of the party wondering what was wrong with him, trying to get comfortable on a couch that wasn't his, but feeling equally uncomfortable in his own skin.

Susan met him at the door with an enthusiastic kiss and a quick pat on his ass before pulling him inside. He followed her into the living room, where Matt and her parents were sitting in various easy chairs and watching an old sitcom on their overly large television. It was what he would have called a *widescreen TV* at one point, but that didn't really cover it. It was so large that it curved in at the sides, and it dwarfed any TV in his own house.

Leonard's parents greeted him with a familiarity that hadn't been present before, and he had a moment to wonder whether Matt had given them a positive review of the weekend that had warmed them to him before he got pulled into a conversation about the upcoming holiday.

"What are you doing for Thanksgiving, Leonard? Len? Or, uh, Lenny?" Susan's father asked, and she buried her head in her hands and admonished him for trying to be a buddy. *I'm sorry,* she mouthed to him from behind her hands, and rolled her eyes dramatically.

Leonard leaned forward on the couch and cleared his throat. Parents had never been his strong suit, and he was afraid of committing some grave error from which he would never recover.

"Leonard's fine. We usually just have a small dinner—nothing special. Then I'll probably have to catch up on homework before classes start again." He didn't know how much Susan had told them of his academic status, but he was afraid of volunteering too much information about his suspension.

"That sounds good! It sounds just fine," her dad responded.

Before Leonard could reply, Matt pushed himself up from his recliner next to the couch, muttering something about needing a beer.

"You want one?" he asked Leonard, and Leonard immediately froze in indecision.

"I think not," Susan's dad cut in, at the same time that her mom said, "No, no, and you shouldn't be drinking, either. You'll set a bad example."

Matt laughed a little too loudly at this. "I think Susan will be fine. She's already the person other parents warn their kids about talking to at the mall."

Susan shot him the finger in response.

The conversation felt easier from there, as if some invisible boundary had been crossed. Another episode of the show started on the TV, eventually overtaking casual conversation as everyone provided their own commentary of the plot. At one point, Susan's father excused himself and returned minutes later with his own beer. He toasted with Matt before he took his first sip, a casual tip of the can that elicited a quiet *clink;* as Leonard watched, he wondered what it would be like to share such a familiar, absentminded rapport with his own father.

He pushed the thought away and focused instead on the warmth of Susan's body as she leaned against him on the couch.

Eventually, her parents headed off to bed, leaving Leonard alone with just Susan and her brother. He liked Matt well enough, but he couldn't help but wish that he would find something else to do. Unfortunately, Matt had gone back for a second beer, and then a third, and he seemed too comfortable sinking into the recliner to consider relocating.

"I've got to monitor you crazy kids," he mumbled when he finally noticed Susan giving him pointed glances and aggravated gestures.

"No. You don't." She was annoyed, and Leonard found himself strangely attracted to the steel in her voice.

"But...no, but I should."

Leonard's phone buzzed in his pocket. He unlocked it without thinking and felt ice run down his spine when he saw the notification:

*New message from Bailey:* ***Thoughts?***

The message itself was innocuous enough, but it was accompanied by a picture of Bailey wearing a low-cut shirt made even lower by the finger that was hooked in the neckline and dipping it down even lower. The picture was taken from above, granting him a clear view of her entire cleavage as well as her red-painted lips. She'd made direct eye contact with the lens as she took the picture.

He felt Susan stiffen beside him. "What the *fuck?*" she demanded, not bothering to keep her voice low.

Leonard dropped the phone onto the couch, not knowing how to explain but knowing that there was no use in trying to hide the picture. She'd already seen it.

"No, listen, it's not what you think," he said, stumbling over his words, trying to make her listen. The room felt both too cold and too hot. "It's just—"

"Just what?" She was nearly shouting now, and he could see tears beginning to form in her eyes. Seeing this nearly instantaneous reaction filled him with remorse, and he wondered distantly how he'd ever thought he would manage to keep this particular mistake from her.

"I only just met her. It was totally by chance. Listen, she put her number in my phone, and I meant to block it afterwards, but I forgot..." He trailed off, gesturing helplessly.

"After *what? How* do you forget something like that?"

"He was drunk!" Matt sang from his chair, and immediately slapped a hand over his mouth in a comically exaggerated show of horror.

Susan whirled on him, fully standing up from the couch now. "You were there? And you just let him...?"

"Nope. Not getting involved in this." He pushed himself up from his chair and left the room, calling over his shoulder, "But nothing happened!"

Leonard stood up, too, and tried to touch Susan's arm—whether to get her attention or try to pull her into a hug, he wasn't sure. He only felt that he needed that contact, and he was horrified when she jerked away from him.

"You don't have to explain the rest," she said, and the tears overflowed now. "Just go. You should go."

"But, Susan—I didn't—"

"*I trusted you,* Leonard. I can't talk to you right now."

He tried, over and over again, to get her to relent, to listen to him, but he knew that the conversation was over. She turned her back on him, hugging herself tightly, and he could see her shoulders trembling as she continued to cry.

Wordlessly, he took his keys from his pocket, hoping that she would change her mind at the last moment, but she remained where she was.

"I love you," he said softly, because he didn't know what else to say, and he couldn't just leave without a word.

He heard the sharp intake of breath at his words, and, defeated, he slipped his phone back into his pocket and shrugged into his coat before leaving the house.

*From the journals of Leonard Kellison:*

<u>Nov. 20:</u>

Everything feels so dismal right now. I've been reading a lot of Bukowski in my free time, and obviously that's a bad idea when you're depressed. But I think if anyone could relate to my state of mind right now, it would be him. I went back through my favorite books of his (all poetry, even though I do like the novels, too), and re-read my favorite poems. I'm glad they're cheap copies, because I've dog-eared the hell out of them.

Anyway, I must have been really in the groove, because when I sat down to write, what I think is a pretty decent poem came out. It's totally negative, so it's not something I'll show my mom right now, because she's already worried about me. But maybe someday.

"Gnawing Through Periphery"

It's time to start
counting your blessings
when the bloated rats of your thoughts
keep you up at night;
when you feel
squadrons of angry mites
trekking from your
lips to your lungs;
when the calm of your headlights

reflecting off of mounds of
dirty snow makes you
want to cry.

You sit up, turn on the light,
give thanks when you discover
the house is on fire
because, really, it's an escape
conveniently placed to
lead you out of your life.

Maybe you are drawn to
those imaginary flames;
maybe the ice has melted
in the last of yesterday's drinks,
and, half-insane, you are
reminded of trivialities:
rosaries on bedroom
doorknobs and in rearview mirrors,
the rain finding entry through
a forgotten window,
everything wet and destroyed.

For all you know it is the apocalypse,
and all that matters
is that you have enough
hot chocolate mix
for one more mug.

You can
watch the bombs fall,
kill the bloated rats in your head

and finally get some
sleep.

# Chapter Twenty-Four

Matt drove Susan to the coffee shop on his way to meet his friends for the lingering Black Friday sales. Their plan, he explained on the way to The Better Bean, was to compare the blowout prices to the Cyber Monday prices and stick to the cheapest options.

Normally, she would have protested his offer, but she found herself loathing the thought of taking the bus again. Some superstitious voice in the back of her mind whispered that she would be taunted again, asked impossible questions by insufferable strangers, and the idea was simply too much to deal with.

"Thanks for the ride," she said when he pulled into the small parking lot. "Natalie said her mom would drop me off later."

"Sure, Sue." He knew that she hated it when he called her Sue, but she appreciated the effort to instill some normalcy into a holiday that had gone horribly awry. He reached over to touch her arm before she could leave the car. "Are you okay?"

She looked away. "That's kind of a dumb question," she murmured.

"Okay, then will you *be* okay?"

"I don't know. Sure. Maybe, but not right now."

Matt nodded, considering this answer. He paused, then told her what she most wanted to believe. "Leonard was in a shitty situation and it looked bad, and yes, it's his fault for being there in the first place. But based on what I know about him, and what I saw, I really don't think they did anything. She obviously tried, but..." He spread his hands helplessly. "He really cares about you."

The tears sprang back into Susan eyes, and she turned quickly and got out of the car. She turned back for a moment before closing the door, shrugged sadly, and left him with a halfhearted "thank you" before turning and walking to the café door.

Matt sat alone in the car for a minute longer, watching her through the large front windows as she found her friend inside. He was angry, and sad, too. It might not have amounted to much, but he felt guilty for whatever part he had played in the drama, and as a result he was upset with Leonard for putting him in this position.

Inside The Better Bean, Susan gave Natalie a hug and sat across from her at the table.

"How are you?" Natalie asked, and Susan felt a flare of anger. She wished everyone would stop asking her that.

But it subsided as quickly as it had presented itself, and she slumped down in her seat.

"I'm okay," she answered, aware of how noncommittal she sounded but unable to muster the strength to search for something more. "Have you been waiting long?"

"No, just a few minutes. See, my latte is still steaming." She tilted her mug a bit so Susan could see better.

"That's good." Now that Susan was here, she didn't know what to say, and she excused herself to place her order to buy more time and gather her thoughts. She was angry at Leonard, and she felt like a fool, but somehow she couldn't bring herself to unleash those feelings when he wasn't there to defend himself. She was angry about that, too.

She ordered a hot chocolate (shot of mint, no whipped cream) from the staffer at the register, dumped her change in the tip jar, and returned to the table, where Natalie was carefully testing the temperature of her latte. They sat mostly in silence until Susan's drink arrived, making small talk but beginning to circle around to Leonard.

"Do you want to talk about it?" Natalie finally asked.

Susan tried to hide behind her own mug for a moment, carefully considering several responses, but what came out of her mouth was "we slept together."

She could see Natalie's eyes widen even as she tried to avoid looking at her.

"I'm sorry, *what?"* Natalie's voice was louder than she would have liked, and she ducked her head and lowered her volume a bit. "When did this happen? Why didn't you tell me?"

Susan wanted to backpedal, or just to leave the café altogether, but she knew that the only way out was through. She took a deep breath and recounted that night, beginning with the cigarette outside and ending with how suddenly alone she'd felt when he had to leave a little later, but being careful to leave out any specific details. She'd never talked much about this side of herself, and as far as she knew, Natalie had never slept with anyone. As a result, she didn't know how much she should say.

"Susan, that sounds...well, really nice. It seems like he was careful, anyway. Patient."

"He was. I didn't feel pressured at all, which I really appreciated." She paused. "That was something new."

"Right," Natalie agreed. She didn't know everything about Susan's past, but she knew enough to recognize the allusion to less pleasant experiences. Then a new thought occurred to her, and she blushed a little. She took another sip of her latte to divert attention from her cheeks.

"What?" Susan asked.

"No, it's nothing. Sorry."

"No, what? I want to know."

"Was it *good?*"

Susan considered the question. *Was* it good? It was unrushed, and the act had unfolded in a manner she'd never experienced before. She'd certainly thought about it, fantasized about it, more than once since it had happened. On the other hand, because the experience was so new, she had no real point of reference. What haunted her dreams were memories of more forceful encounters, and this was nothing like that.

"Yeah, it was," she said at last. "Unless you mean, did I...?"

"I don't think girls do nearly as often as guys think," Natalie commented in a stage whisper, and immediately collapsed into giggles. Despite herself, Susan laughed, too. It felt good to do something other than cry.

"But..." Susan found it difficult to finish her question. "But does that mean that it was bad?"

"Based a little on my extremely limited experience, and a lot on the awkward conversations my mom insists on having over and over again, guys and girls view 'bad' sex differently. For a guy, it might be a boring girlfriend in the sack or just not finishing. For girls, at least according to my mom, it's more about not having a choice, or being hurt, or getting abandoned afterwards, or..." She waved a hand. "Whatever else fits into that category. I don't know. I'm just saying, if you enjoyed it, it was probably good."

"That makes sense. Uh, tell your mom I said thanks."

She wasn't trying to be funny, but Natalie choked on her latte nonetheless. "I most certainly will *not* be thanking my mom for those details. *Shit*." She wiped her chin with her napkin. "You owe me a muffin for that. Chocolate chip."

"We'll split it." Susan grabbed a few more dollar bills from her wallet and headed back to the counter. When she returned a few minutes later, muffin in hand, Natalie was texting someone.

"Is that your mom?"

"Oh, shut up." Natalie reached across the table and split the muffin unevenly down the middle. She pushed one half across the table on top of the bag it came in and set her half down on a napkin.

"But yes, if you must know, it was my mother," she continued. As Susan expected, Natalie tore a piece off of the bottom of the muffin and stuck it into her mouth. Natalie had always loved the tops of muffins, but she made herself eat the rest first. Seeing the continuation of such an ordinary habit while she currently felt that her life was coming apart at the seams was surprisingly calming.

They lingered at their table for another hour or so, taking intermittent breaks for more drinks and snacks, and in that time the conversation meandered from Leonard to Natalie's own love life ("still nothing to report," she said, a bit wistfully), and then to winter break plans and finally to small talk about new music and movies. By the time Natalie's mother arrived to take them back to Natalie's house for the night, Susan was beginning to feel a bit farther away from the ledge she'd felt herself on earlier in the day. She didn't want to admit it to Natalie, but she'd texted her to make plans in part so she wouldn't have to be alone, which translated into an environment where she would be able to hurt herself again.

*I'm trying,* she thought, and it felt more like a prayer than a statement. *I'm trying, but I don't trust myself.*

While Susan was drinking her mint chocolate and splitting a fresh muffin with her oldest friend, Leonard found himself sitting in his room alone and alternating between playing video games and attempting to write a new song.

He too was trying to distract himself from the possibility of self-harm, although he had no way of knowing it. Susan hadn't responded to any of his texts since this morning, and he was too afraid to call her. He thought he was better at communicating his thoughts in written form, where he would be able to make sure every word was perfect for his intended meaning.

In fact, he didn't even know if she and Natalie were still at the coffee shop. He had visions of them going to one of Matt's endless series of parties, Natalie wandering off, Susan meeting some open-minded college guy who wouldn't mind her extreme makeup and multiple piercings and had no compunction about taking advantage of a younger girl in an obvious state of distress...

But he knew that he was doing himself no favors by indulging in what-ifs, and although the scenario progressed a little further in his mind each time before he could banish the thought, he consciously forced himself to focus on something else to avoid thinking about it.

He looked at his phone for the dozenth or fiftieth or hundredth time that night, and he sighed with frustration when there were no new notifications. He picked up his acoustic guitar from where he'd left it earlier, leaning against the side of the bed, and played a few chords. As he tried to puzzle out the rest of the new song he followed along with the lyrics he'd already written:

*How can something lead to nothing?*
*How can lies feel bad as bluffing?*
*How can nothing promise anything?*
*What's the point in sitting, lonely,*
*Thinking life is one chance only?*
*Why can angels point to where you sing?*

He skipped the chorus for now, not knowing where

to go with it, and came back in at the second verse:

*Never could I bring myself to*
*Practice lasting gratitude*
*Just because somebody said they cared.*
*Psychos wander down the alleys,*
*Back from death, beyond dark valleys;*
*No one's hiding just because they're scared.*

It wasn't great, but it had kept him occupied for long enough that he no longer felt like he might drown in himself, so he tried to believe that it was a win. *If nothing else*, he told himself, *at least I have a new song to fuck around with.*

It was nearly ten o'clock when he returned the guitar to its stand and pulled up an old comedy series on Netflix, but focusing on the show seemed impossible so he returned to video games instead. He was in the middle of fighting his way through a dungeon full of mutant rats and living skeletons when his phone buzzed; he snatched it up so quickly that the screen was still lit up with the new message alert: *1 new message: Bailey.*

A wave of frustration washed over with such power that he dropped the phone and pressed the palms of his hands into his eyes to stave away the oncoming headache. Suppressing emotions this way had always had this effect on him, manifesting in physical pain when he tried to avoid their emotional counterpart.

When he looked again, a second message had followed the first, and a third appeared as he read the first two.

**Bailey:** *Hey again, cute book guy ;)*
**Bailey:** *Already off to a bad start. Sorry, I shouldn't be flirting and apologizing at the*

*same time. This is hard.*

**Bailey:** *I shouldn't have asked you to go off alone with me at the party, I know that. I hope your friends didn't give you too much of a hard time over it, and I'm not totally sure, but I think I remember you saying that you were seeing somebody. Not something a drunk half-naked girl wants to hear at a party.*

**Bailey:** *But I know I probably put you in an awkward position, and I hope it didn't cause any lasting damage. And we probably shouldn't keep texting, because...girlfriend and all...but you seem like a good guy. Those are in short supply.*

Leonard didn't reply immediately. He read the messages several times, put his phone down, picked it back up, and eventually typed *I'm not seeing anyone anymore, so we may as well have just slept together. The end result would have been the same.*

But seconds later he deleted what he had written and tossed his phone onto the bed. He left Bailey's messages unanswered.

The following day dawned brightly and looked warm and inviting from Leonard's bedroom window, but it was frigid outside. He wondered, and not for the first time, how he'd ended up living somewhere where the colder months often got so cold that it hurt to breathe, and for the first time in a while, he found himself seriously considering the old idea of disappearing when he'd collected enough fishnets to cover his ceiling.

Thinking of this old plan made him think of Susan, though, and how he'd explained this to her on the first night they'd met. He wondered if she would have left with him, if things were different. Would they have found somewhere together? Would they have lasted? Or was it just an unrealistic romantic fantasy?

In his current mood, he believed that it was all bullshit, and he wished the day were darker to mirror his mood. (The previous year they'd had a discussion in English class about how the weather in *Jane Eyre* often matched Jane's mood, and that idea was clever enough that it stuck with him.) But freezing weather or no, he couldn't sit still. He had to go out and *do* something.

He drove around aimlessly for a bit until he got bored, the act of focusing on driving sapping the nervous energy from him, and pulled into a used bookstore on the other side of town.

The used bookstore in the Market Way Plaza had long been his favorite. He'd first visited the place with his mother in the sixth grade when he'd run out of horror novels to read; since then they'd remodeled, expanded to absorb the vacant store next door, and added a small café in the back. It looked different now, but it still had the aura of the smaller bookstore he remembered from middle school, and no amount of updating could banish the old-book smell that he always associated with long hours spent browsing and reading inside.

Built in old-fashioned red brick, The Bookkeeper, as it was called (the owner loved telling new customers that "bookkeeper" was the only word in the English language with three consecutive sets of repeating letters, which may or may not be true), sat two stories tall, between a thrift store and a pet store, in the far right corner of the plaza it called home. Its name was written in stylized, curling lettering on a sign which hung, day or night, rain or shine, above the heavy door of the place. Upon entering the store, one would hear the soft chime of the silver bells hanging from the interior side of the door, and that used-book smell of old pages and long-dried ink seemed to hang in the very air, an inescapable presence seeming to whisper of the past. There were very few windows on the ground floor, and dim light was cast down from the long fluorescents which hid behind frosted glass covers to take the glare away from the bright bulbs. The effect was somehow both intimate and mysterious.

Soft music drifted through the area from invisible speakers, and Leonard had been there often enough over the years to be able to make a reasonable guess of who was working the café based on what was playing. Megan the college student, who had worked there through high school but now only returned to her position over school breaks, preferred nineties alternative; Terrance the underground rapper usually chose censored trip-hop playlists. The café staff always chose the music, and Leonard was familiar enough with most of their playlists that new additions or drastic changes sometimes caught his attention even when he was deeply absorbed in a book.

Tricky was playing on the sound system as Leonard walked in, alerting him that Terrance was working the café today. He caught Leonard's eye and waved as Leonard wandered toward the back of the store, and Leonard changed direction to meet him at the counter.

"What's up, man?" Terrance asked, holding up a to-go coffee cup as a question. He was in his mid-twenties and at least six-two, and he wouldn't have looked out of place in any clothing ad or gym commercial: slim but muscular; confident movements; striking gray eyes reminiscent of storm clouds gathering over a restless sea. He was proud of his musical and fitness routines, too. He always kept a stack of business cards on the counter when he worked at the bookstore, and even today, with such unwelcoming weather outside, his shirt was tight and fitted.

"Eh, nothing much, how's the music?" Leonard replied. He nodded at the cup and asked for an Americano.

"Slow right now. Nobody's really hosting open mics until closer to the actual holiday season. I've got some new material, though. I've been teaching myself bass, so the live music will be different. I'm transitioning more into *funk.* You know, Childish Gambino shit."

"That's awesome, man. I'll have to check your site soon."

"Very kind. *Blessings upon you,"* Terrance intoned with mock reverence, tracing a symbol in the air with Leonard's coffee cup that may have been the cross or a crescent moon or anything else.

Leonard accepted the drink gratefully and went in search of an empty easy chair. He checked his phone when he sat down, but he still hadn't received anything from Susan.

Not for the first time that day, he felt frustration threatening to overtake him. He closed his eyes in the overstuffed chair and tried to picture what a hypothetical conversation with his therapist might sound like, but she was silent in his head. Dr. Wheeler, it seemed, had little to say about the matter.

His drink hadn't yet fully cooled when he became aware that somebody was saying his name. He blinked, pulling himself back from his reverie, and found Gordon, the owner of the bookstore, leaning over the back of the chair across from him and waving a hand in his face.

"Hey, Gordon," he greeted, smiling somewhat abashedly. "Sorry, I was zoned out."

"I could tell!" Gordon said. He stepped around the chair and took a seat, excusing his intrusion as he did so but making no move to leave him alone. "Want some company?"

"Sure," Leonard lied, checking his phone one last time before returning it to his pocket. "What's up?"

"Nothing, but something's clearly up with you. I have some time; want to talk about it?"

Leonard would probably have told just about anyone else to fuck off, he wasn't in the mood to talk, but Gordon was a bit of an anomaly in Leonard's life. Single and in his fifties, Gordon put most of his existence and attention into The Bookkeeper. It wasn't abnormal for him to develop friendships with his frequent customers, and he'd shown Leonard kindness since he'd first made Leonard some book recommendations years ago. He seemed to see a kindred spirit in the boy: self-conscious, unsure of himself, and escaping into other people's stories whenever he could, because stories tended to be more enjoyable than real life.

It was Gordon who recommended the old, obscure books to Leonard; it made Leonard feel guilty to refer to him only as his "friend at the bookstore," but he was always worried that the reality would sound strange or suspicious to most people.

Over the years, Leonard had confided a lot in him, because Gordon never judged, and never dropped his poker face when discussing uncomfortable topics.

He'd helped Leonard to plan ways to avoid Roland whenever he could; he'd offered personal anecdotes and advice to help Leonard get through his breakup with Anna.

Even as a preteen, Leonard had noticed the old scars on Gordon's forearms, and had known what they meant. He'd hidden his own from Gordon for a long time, but the first time he'd let them show, Gordon didn't hesitate to give him warnings and helpful advice to avoid hurting himself too seriously, or doing anything even worse.

Now, Leonard told Gordon about Susan, the party, and the aftermath of Bailey's texts. Gordon listened without judgment, interrupting only to ask a clarifying question or two, and remained silent for a full minute afterwards. Leonard was used to this; Gordon wasn't the type of person to ramble without thinking. He watched the older man push his glasses up on his nose and push his short hair off of his forehead—a leftover habit from when he'd had much longer hair, he'd explained once.

"Okay," he said at last, and Leonard leaned forward to hear him better. "Have you ever heard of Quintilian?" He sighed dramatically when Leonard shook his head, and went on, "I can't understand why they've devalued philosophy so much in schools. But Quintilian was a Roman teacher, and an author on rhetoric. He tells us in *The Orator's Education* that there are only three ways to correct an error: by adding, by removing, and by altering."

Leonard waited for more, but Gordon seemed to expect him to say something. "So...I should do something according to that, right?"

"What do *you* think?" Gordon shot back, and

there was an expectant gleam in his eye now. He may have dedicated his life to buying and selling books, but he was an academic at heart, and although he hadn't enjoyed teaching (which he once told Leonard he had done for a while in grad school), he did still enjoy imparting wisdom during teachable moments.

Leonard thought for a moment. "I can't add anything to the situation, because adding Bailey to my contact list was a disaster. I didn't even do that myself. And I've already promised Susan that I would remove her from my life."

"So that leaves altering," Gordon supplied for him.

"But what can I change? She doesn't want anything to do with me right now."

"Why not?"

"Because...she doesn't trust me. She feels betrayed. I basically cheated on her without even meaning to." The admission made him feel terrible, but he found that he needed to say the words.

"Well, I'm no expert in love, obviously. But I do know a little about human psychology, and I think that she *did* trust you, which is why she feels so betrayed now. What can you do to change the situation right now?"

Leonard finished his Americano and set the empty cup on the floor. "My therapist tells me that actions are louder than words. Should I do something?"

"You tell me." Gordon stood up and reached out with one hand. "That will be $150 for today's session. You can make the check out to Dr. Freud."

Leonard laughed despite himself. "I'd rather just buy a book from you while I'm here."

"That will be fine, young man."

Leonard thanked him, and they parted ways: Gordon, off to take care of something in the depths of the shelves of books; Leonard, to throw out his cup. Before he started browsing the shelves, though, he sent two texts.

> **Leonard:** *Can I see you, Susan? I just want to talk for a little. I feel horrible and I want to make things right.*
> **Leonard:** *Bailey, let's just forget about the whole thing. I may or may not have a girlfriend, I don't even know at this point, but I wanted to say that I'm not mad at you before we cut contact.*

Leonard sent the messages, stared unseeing at his phone for a few seconds, and then added Bailey's number to his block list.

*From the journals of Susan Ingram:*

Nov. 24:

My boyfriend hangs out with my brother at college and ends up nearly hooking up with some college girl who's way hotter than me, and definitely more experienced. I can't believe she sent him a selfie in just a bra, and acted like it was the most normal thing in the world. Is that what college is like? Is that what adulthood is like?? I'll never be like that. I'm not even saying that to pretend to be a better person than she is; I just know myself. Meet someone once or twice and start sending raunchy pictures? Sorry, but that's not me. I'm not even built the right way for that.

That's what kills me. I'm not only jealous of her for spending time with Leonard; I'm jealous because she obviously has more to offer than I do. I don't have curves like she does. I don't have the confidence that she does. I'm still surprised sometimes that Leonard wants to make out with me, forget dating me.

Break is almost over, and it was supposed to be a really good time. Now I can't wait to go back to school because it'll give me something to do other than just wanting to die.

That's a joke. Or, not really a joke, but an exaggeration, I guess? I haven't picked up a knife since I got out of the hospital. I did the rubber band thing, snapping them against my wrist. That's what I've been doing. It's better than the alternative.

I'm just so fucking <u>sad</u> all the time.

# Chapter Twenty-Five

It was the last night of break, and Susan had successfully avoided seeing Leonard ever since the night she'd seen Bailey's text and picture on his phone. In some ways, it actually felt like a wasted break to her; she hadn't had much fun, even staying over at Natalie's, and the appeal of school had returned after she'd looked forward to the break for so many weeks.

Before her hospitalization, she'd kind of looked forward to school; it was an escape from being at home. Even during the best of times at home—when everyone got along and she could forget some of the emotional baggage that dogged her everywhere she went—she often felt the specter of her old fears following her around from unseen shadows. Being at school was better, because at least she felt less alone there.

Less seen, but less alone. She might have struggled to articulate this point, but the feeling was there: the safety of disappearing into the crowds of students rushing to their next classes; the comfort of knowing that everyone else was doing exactly the same thing that she was.

Apart from her visit at Natalie's, she was feeling more and more isolated as the break wound down. Even Matt being at home didn't help much; he was often out with friends, and when he was home, he usually slept or watched TV. Without Leonard to talk to, she found that she didn't want to talk much at all, so she mostly left everyone alone, and grew frustrated when others wouldn't leave her alone in turn.

Today had been particularly stressful. Matt had stayed in for once, but he'd had Thomas over all afternoon, and that was dangerous ground for her. She was unable to relax when he was around; she was fixed in fight-or-flight mode, and it was exhausting. Every time she closed her eyes, she risked believing herself stranded again, unprotected, unable to get out from under him—then, in a literal sense; now, in the present, more figuratively.

She hadn't responded to any of Leonard's texts over break, either. When she first saw Thomas in her kitchen she wanted to text Leonard immediately, just for a sense of normalcy, but when she went to contact him she realized that she no longer felt the same security with him. *It'll pass in time*, she told herself; *it has to.*

But for now, she couldn't muster the strength to overcome her anxieties, so she suffered alone.

And now, sitting cross-legged on her bed with a fleece throw wrapped around her shoulders, she felt more dismal than ever. The nights were getting longer, the sun giving ground earlier each day, and it was already dark outside. The lights in her room made the night seem even more threatening, because she couldn't see past her own reflection in the windows.

Sometime after eight, Matt knocked on her door and cracked it open.

"I'm heading out with Thomas for a bit, so I wanted to say goodnight," he told her.

"Have fun," she said without looking up from browsing on her phone.

He hesitated a moment longer, and finally asked if she felt any better.

"Of course not," she replied, her frustration seeping into her voice and making it sound almost like a snarl. "I hate this whole fucking situation."

Matt smirked. "You said the really bad word."

"Do *not* make me laugh right now, Matt," she warned with a grimace.

But he wouldn't be deterred. "I'm telling Mom. She's probably going to take away your computer."

"You're such an asshole!"

But she smiled when she said it, and he felt both gratitude and annoyance at his uncanny ability to crack her attitude. He'd always been this way: a little callous, but never showing her any true malice or impatience.

He made a "who, me?" expression and turned to leave. "I love you," he called over his shoulder. And, a moment later: "Text him!"

The smile slowly diminished from her face, and she looked down at her phone once more and opened her messages. She hovered over Leonard's name for a few seconds, but then messaged Natalie instead:

> **Susan:** *It's getting so messy with Leonard and my brother being friends now. Matt just told me AGAIN to text him.*
> **Natalie:** *That's so gross. But at least it's not your mom telling you to text him. Imagine if SHE and Leonard had gotten close.*

This was followed with a vomiting emoji and a laughing face, and Susan sent back a "haha" message and opened her music app. After some scrolling, she chose a Massive Attack album and dropped her phone beside her on the bed, where it began playing music.

She lay back and closed her eyes against the world, trying to lose herself in the music like she used to do to ward off the urge to cut.

The first song hadn't even ended when a knock sounded at her door again. She groaned and reached out to turn down the volume on her music, shouting, "What'd you forget now, Matt?"

There was a moment of silence, and then a different voice sounded from the doorway: "Uh, it's me."

A chill ran down Susan's spine, setting off little alarm bells in every nerve ending, and she opened her eyes to see Thomas standing in her doorway, one hand still on the doorknob, the other on the doorjamb.

She tightened her grip on the fleece throw and pulled it more tightly around her, trying to shrink into its folds.

Leonard felt more anxious than he'd expected to about classes beginning again the next day. The past week—or month, really—had been such a fast-paced series of unexpected events that he'd found it difficult to keep up with what was on the horizon; it was the *here*, the *now*, that demanded all of his attention. From the beginning of his relationship with Susan, to the fight that had landed him in suspension, to the ups and downs of his college trip with Matt and the argument that had followed, he hadn't really had the time or mental bandwidth to deal with the reality of returning to classes.

In the hypothetical, he'd assumed he would be relatively well equipped to meet it head-on. The suspension and the time out of town were supposed to relax him and give him the opportunity to reset, but the reality just made him anxious. *I need more time,* he thought. *I'm not prepared right now.*

What he most needed was advice, but that was followed closely by the need to aggress. He needed to blow off some nervous energy, but he didn't own a gym membership and he hated cardio. He hated to admit it, but he wanted an argument.

He paced in his room throughout the late morning and early afternoon, and when he gave up and went downstairs he found his mother seated at a folding table and sorting the pieces to the puzzle he'd given her for her birthday. How long ago had that been? Not long, he knew, but it felt like years.

"Hi, Leonard," she greeted him, glancing up briefly from the mess of pieces in front of her. "I wanted to tackle this sooner, but the holiday was busy."

"That sounds good," he said, not knowing whether she were offering an apology or just sharing her plans.

"Are you up to anything today? Seeing Susan at all?"

The sound of Susan's name sent a pang into his chest. He hadn't told his mother about their argument yet, and it seemed impossible to broach the subject now. He shrugged muttered something that might have been "maybe."

"Well, if you're going out, text me if you'll be late for dinner."

The truth was, he didn't know what he would do today, or when. "Will Roland be here?" he asked instead.

"Probably. He's out right now, but he said he would call later." She turned her full attention back to the puzzle, seemingly unwilling to pursue the conversation further. Leonard knew why: "out" was code for "at the bar with friends." She probably suspected that he knew what it meant, but she'd never actually verbalized it to him. He figured they would talk about Roland's shortcomings and what effect they had on their family eventually, but not now.

He reached down and set aside a corner piece before moving into the kitchen to find something to microwave. While he ate, he scrolled through social media on his phone, but nothing really caught his attention. Something was distracting him—something other than

Susan and school—but he couldn't put his finger on it until he was rinsing his plate in the sink.

The puzzle made him think of his mom's birthday party, which naturally led to the unannounced phone call from his father.

He thought too about his trip with Susan to his father's new house, and how he'd watched from the street before driving away.

*Fuck it*, he thought. *If this is going to happen, I'm going to do it now, when I'm already ready for a fight.*

He changed upstairs and looked at himself for a long time in the mirror, trying to see himself as a stranger might, and then changed again. He settled on a plain black T-shirt with the red outline of a voodoo doll on it, a gift from one of his friends who had taken a screen-printing class over the summer, and his usual black jeans. Over this he threw on a leather jacket, and then he wished his mom good luck on the puzzle and headed outside.

He'd been too preoccupied with his thoughts to pay much attention to navigation last time, simply turning when Susan told him to, but he remembered the way to the suburb where his father resided without double-checking the address or even the GPS on his phone. His previous trip there was etched into his brain, and for some reason, this raised a sort of angry indignation within him.

By the time he parked at the curb two houses down, his hands were sweating and he found himself wishing for an aspirin. Now that he was here, he wished he'd made some kind of plan, or at least rehearsed what he wanted to say, but he refused to just leave again. That felt like admitting defeat, and the last thing he wanted to do today was feel any more defeated.

Instead, he forced himself to take a deep breath and blow it out slowly. Whatever awaited him inside, if worse came to worst, he figured he could just leave and go back to pretending that his father either didn't exist, or existed so far outside of his own world that he'd might as well have disappeared.

From his vantage point down the street, he could see that two vehicles sat in his father's driveway, a sedan and an SUV. From what he could remember from before his dad left, Leonard thought of his dad as a truck guy; there had even been a couple of parental arguments about whether he should trade his truck for a more family-friendly vehicle. For whatever reason, the current Mrs. Kellison seemed to have won out where the former Mrs. Kellison had failed.

Leonard pushed down his second thoughts about showing up unannounced and got out of his van. He locked it behind him and crossed to the sidewalk, where he slowly closed the distance between himself and his father.

*"What are you doing here?"* Susan hissed, instantly experiencing the fight-or-flight flood of endorphins that Thomas always inspired in her. She looked wildly around her room, looking for something that could be used as a weapon, but her mind failed to actually register anything her eyes were seeing.

Thomas didn't move from his spot in the doorway—didn't advance, but didn't retreat at her tone, either.

"I wanted to say hi," he said, and even in Susan's panicked state she thought she could see by his face that he knew how stupid it sounded.

She wanted to scream. She wished she could spit on him. But instead, she stayed where she was, every muscle tense, just staring at him.

"Listen," he continued after a moment, "I'm glad your boyfriend got to spend some time at Matt's and my place. He seemed cool." He paused. "But I don't think he's right for you."

"What the fuck does that mean?" Susan whispered through clenched teeth.

Thomas advanced a few steps and leaned against her desk. "Just what I said. He isn't good for you. I like him alright, but he's too high-strung. And Matt told me that you found out about the party."

"Get out." She'd found her volume again, and the words were flat but loud.

"Susan—"

"I mean it, Thomas. Get out."

He signed, and a look of genuine sadness crossed his face. "I miss you, Sue."

"*Do not* call me that." Then, louder: "Hey, Matt? Come here a sec."

"Matt's in the car. I told him I forget something."

"What do you *want,* Thomas?" Now that the immediate fight-or-flight reaction had faded, she found herself able to respond more forcefully, and she was growing angry as well as scared.

"I miss you," he said with a small shrug.

"You *miss* me? We were never even *together*, Thomas. You stalked me!"

Saying it out loud ignited a series of flashbacks behind Susan's eyes: alone at camp; alone in the backyard; alone in the house. Whispered entreaties and veiled threats and stolen touches. The slideshow of her remembered trauma inflicted her with a sense of vertigo, and she suddenly felt very sick.

"But you liked me in the beginning."

This was true enough, but she wouldn't give him the satisfaction of acknowledging it. She'd liked him in the way that any girl might have a crush on her older brother's cool, guitar-playing friend. She'd liked the feeling of maturity that washed over her when he would smile, or pat her on the shoulder before leaving at the end of a visit.

That feeling hadn't lasted very long, as other, more shameful feelings overtook them.

"I never liked, you, *J.T.,*" she whispered, and now there tears in her eyes. It hurt her to use the name she'd once known him by. "Get out."

The invocation of his previous preferred name seemed to hurt him, too. A series of expressions paraded in quick succession across his face—surprise, remorse, desire, anger—and then resolved into sadness.

From downstairs, she heard the front door open and a shouted question from Matt: "Hurry up, man!"

J.T.—Thomas—immediately retreated to her doorway. "I'm not him anymore, Susan. J.T. doesn't exist anymore."

Instead of replying directly, Susan shouted for her brother. "Matt, there's a rat in my room!" She looked directly at Thomas as she said it, and a moment later she could hear Matt cursing and moving further into the house, toward the stairs.

"What the fuck," Thomas murmured, and ducked into the hall and then the bathroom. The bathroom door clicked closed before Matt made it to her room.

The front door eased open, and Leonard stood opposite his father for the first time in over a decade. Only a glass door separated them.

"I'm sorry, I think you've got the wrong house," Martin Kellison told him, and took a step back to close the door again.

Leonard's first attempt at speech failed, but he managed to expel a few words before the door was closed.

"You don't recognize me, *Dad*?"

Martin started to say something, but then froze. He opened the door again and ran a hand over his dark beard. Leonard remembered the beard from his childhood, but little else was congruous with the father from his memories. Martin was a little heavier, for one, and his hair was shorter. He wore it buzzed short and unstyled now. In a distant sort of way, Leonard noticed that the man's wedding ring, now visible as he braced himself against the doorjamb, was black: carbon fiber, maybe, or titanium. The observation struck something painful in him, and it took him a moment to realize that he'd expected to see the same plain gold band he remembered from his childhood.

Martin cleared his throat. "Leonard." He coughed into his fist. "Yeah, I can see it now. Definitely. Um. Do you want to come in?" He stepped back and seemed to freeze in place, as if he were unsure what to do if Leonard said yes.

Leonard nodded and stepped into the house. It was warm inside, but not uncomfortably so, and the scent of an early dinner still lingered in the air. It smelled good, and Leonard wondered what they'd had. It didn't really matter, but it gave him something to focus on. Distractedly, he wondered whether anyone else might be home at that moment. Would he be forced to meet Martin's wife—his stepmother? Or the girl he'd seen after Halloween, whom he assumed to be his half-sister?

He hoped not. The reality of him being here was surreal enough on its own.

"Why don't you come in here, have a seat?" Martin asked, and Leonard followed him into the living room. They passed the dining room on their way there; Leonard could see that its windows faced the front yard, which meant it had to be the room he'd seen the entire family gathered in while the girl sorted through her Halloween candy.

The living room was cluttered here and there with toys and children's books, but it was comfortable. An acoustic guitar hung on the wall, a black Ibanez with layers of gray stretching across the body in ripples that reminded Leonard of creased jeans. He walked over to examine it more closely before he sat down, and he could feel his father's eyes on him as he looked.

"Do you play?" Martin asked.

"Yeah, but mostly electric. Uh, I'm in a band."

"Lead guitar?"

"No. Bass and vocals." His phone buzzed, but he ignored it. He couldn't afford to be distracted now.

The small talk was necessary, he could sense that, but it also irritated him. He wanted to get to it already, whatever *it* might be.

Martin seemed to pick up on the energy, too. He took a seat on the couch and rubbed a hand over his face, asking, "Why are you here, Leonard? I mean, don't get me wrong, obviously I'm glad—"

And that was all it took.

Leonard whirled on him, eyes wide, knowing how crazed he must look but not caring.

"You're *glad?*" He demanded. "You walk out, we have no idea what's going on, *I* have no idea what's going on, and I track you down and now you're *glad*?"

"Listen, I—"

"Don't say 'I get it.' Don't. I want to know why you fucked off, and I want to know why you called for Mom's birthday."

Martin was quiet, but he didn't look contrite. He looked like a man weathering the indignity of an attack he feels he doesn't deserve.

"Are you done?" he asked after a long silence.

"*No.* Why do you have a family now? What the fuck was wrong with the one you already *had*?"

This seemed to finally break through Martin's front, and he gestured for Leonard to sit. "*Sit down*," he said, quietly but forcefully. "And stop yelling and swearing. Caroline and the kid are lying down in there." He gestured vaguely deeper into the house.

"Unbelievable. So that's it? 'My new wife and new kid are asleep so my old kid needs to be calm?'"

Martin stabbed a finger at him. "*Yes*. This is my home. They're my family, and you don't get to just come in here and upset anyone. God, I get a knock on the door and it's you, looking like Dracula, and I still don't even know what you want."

"I want to know why. You. Called." All at once, the absurdity of his appearance here became clear, and Leonard knew that coming here was a mistake. He wanted to take it back, to just get up and leave and pretend he'd never driven to his father's house for answers, but it was too late now. It couldn't be reversed.

Resigned now, he sagged back in his seat and waited for whatever painful information he would receive.

Martin seemed to struggle with his words, though, and it felt like forever until he gave an answer. "Caroline knows about you and your mom. She knows everything. Calling was her idea, I think because she wants me to make peace with the two of you." His eyes were on the floor while he talked, or just over Leonard's shoulder, but now he looked directly at his son.

"I was messed up, Leonard. You must know that. But there are also things that you don't know and don't understand. I…couldn't hack it. For a lot of reasons. And ultimately, I didn't want to keep bringing that into your life, so I stayed away. I did a lot of work on myself. It wasn't until after that that I could even think of meeting anyone again. I was..." he gestured vaguely.

"What do you mean, there are things I don't understand? I understand perfectly. You were selfish," Leonard finished for him. "You couldn't take it, so you just left."

Martin sighed. "Maybe. I don't know. I know I was drinking too much. And I know I spent too much time away from home as it was."

"No shit." It was difficult for Leonard to accept Martin's words, however sincere they seemed to be. He was piecing everything together as the information was given to him, and the picture wasn't anything pretty. A selfish, overwhelmed, young father who wanted to be on his own again? It seemed so trite, but if that wasn't the truth, what was? And why would his father lie now?

Martin was watching him digest the information. He didn't say anything else, just sat across from him and looked guilty and indignant and, to Leonard's mind, pathetic.

"So, what, you get to start over, you get the whole 'happily ever after' scenario. And I'm stuck here hating my life and Mom remarries, and the guy is a garbage person that I can't even *stand*? And who can't stand me? Yeah, that's fair."

"I shouldn't have called. I know that now. Maybe at a different time, but not on your mom's birthday. But if you'll listen to me—"

*I shouldn't have* called. The words echoed in Leonard's head, leaving him feeling disoriented. *That* was his takeaway? It seemed absurd to Leonard, willfully ignorant and dismissive. Nothing about the years without contact, nothing in the way of an apology, just *it was the wrong time to call.*

"Forget it," Leonard said, rising from the chair and turning in the direction of the front door. "I don't want to hear any more. This was a mistake, too. You have a whole new family, so fuck the old one."

"Leonard, that's not fair."

"Whatever. You don't have to worry about me intruding anymore."

Martin started to say something else, but Leonard was already leaving the room. He didn't turn around or look over his shoulder into the living room, where his father was still sitting. He just wanted to be back in the safety of his van, where the world made sense and he knew what to do. The whole visit had been dismally unsatisfying, and he felt worse than ever knowing the truth of what his father's recent life had been like.

The thought he'd had over Halloween rose up again, filling his head so that it blocked his vision for a moment, growing so big that there was no way to ignore it: it would have been easier if Martin had turned out to be a drunk living under a bridge somewhere. At least then Leonard could definitively say, *that's a* you *problem. Nothing would have stopped your life from derailing.*

But knowing that he was better, and functioning, and enjoying a new loving family? That was too much. He couldn't shake the thought that there was something wrong with the home he and his mother had shared with him. The household had been wrong, or his mother had complained once too often, or he, Leonard, had been too demanding as a child. There had to be a more tangible reason than *I had to work on myself.*

Without that explanation to hold onto, Leonard was just part of a failed family.

Matt and Thomas were both gone, and the house was eerily quiet in their absence. Even Riley was uncharacteristically inconspicuous, watching television downstairs rather than hanging out around her room or playing loudly with his toys. She'd been holding her breath while Thomas was around, but now that he was gone, she allowed herself to breathe freely again, and the house seemed to relax around her somehow. Her room seemed less constricting now that she knew she was safe.

After Matt had declared her room free of rats, he'd rounded up his friend and headed out with a shouted "be back later!" Thomas had avoided looking in the direction of her room as he followed Matt downstairs.

As soon as the front door closed, Susan grabbed up her phone and started to text—*who?* Her first thought was Leonard, but she wasn't ready to be back on speaking terms with him yet, and she didn't think Natalie would understand her desperation or the gravity of the situation. She would be sympathetic, but Susan couldn't tell her the whole story. For that matter, she couldn't just tell Leonard, either. The thought made her feel like a damsel in distress, and she wanted to believe that she was stronger than that.

Dismissing the phone entirely, she tried to lose herself in a streaming TV series, but five minutes later she'd retrieved it and tapped out a message with nobody in the *To:* box. *Hard fucking night. I don't want to be alone right now. Are you busy?* She paused a moment, then added, *Even vidchat?*

Her list of contacts was relatively short, split pretty evenly between friends and family. Before she could think better of it, she chose Leonard's name and sent the text. As the ensuing anxiety chilled her spine, starting low and working its way up to her skull, she admitted internally how rattled she was.

In the movies, she'd hit send, and the three dots indicating an incoming message would begin immediately. She would have a response in seconds, and the question—*Will I even get a response?*—would be resolved. Instant gratification.

This wasn’t a movie, though, and she stared at her screen for what might have been a few seconds or solid minutes. Nothing came through: no dots, no messages, not even a “message read” that would let her know that Leonard was actively ignoring her. She found that she was angry at Leonard, although she’d told him not to contact her while she worked through things.

*Why do you have to be so considerate?*

*What could you possibly be busy doing?*

But he was obviously taking her at her word, and she knew she couldn’t force him to pick up. She tried sending him a message through the universe, urging him to pick up his phone, but still nothing happened.

Frustrated and lonely, she locked her bedroom door, turned off every light, and cried in the glow of her laptop screen as a new episode started.

*From the journals of Leonard Kellison:*

Nov. 25:

Remember Ariel? That whole "Susan is awesome but so is Ariel and I don't know what I should do" situation? Obviously she made that decision easy for me when she completely fucking rejected me based off of one fact from one event in my life, but yeah, that Ariel.

Well, she confused the hell out of me today when I saw her at school. I don't know if she's trying to be a friend now because she feels bad, or what, but it was weird.

I know I've said this before, but if it weren't for my best friends, like Glenn and Jez and maybe one or two others, I honestly don't know where I'd be today. We've been friends for so long that they have this kind of barometer for knowing when I'm depressed, or about to do something stupid, or just in need of a distraction.

So, here's what happened today…

# Chapter Twenty-Six

Monday morning broke cold and gray, and it was only with great reluctance that Leonard rolled out of bed and got ready for school. He'd already missed the bus by the time he was fully dressed and got some coffee into his system, but his mother didn't have time to take him in before her shift at work began, so he was forced to dig through his desk and all of his jeans pockets to scrape together the few dollars he would have to pay for a one-day parking pass at school. He had money in his bank account, but for some reason, the parking-pass system was cash only.

It was just as well, he decided as he pulled into an open spot in the school's student lot. He'd grown to loathe taking the bus, and he never knew what kind of mood the other students would be in. It was always one end of the spectrum or the other: he would be left alone, or somebody would give him shit the entire way there. He mentally ticked off the reasons he'd been tormented just over the past year: his hair; his coat; his nails; his grades ("how do you look like *that* and still get the grades? You don't *look* smart at all"); his home life; his friends; his romantic partners.

This last was a particular sticking point with him, and he felt it gnawing at him as he signed for his pass and headed off to homeroom. "Still no Susan?" his mother had asked the night before, followed up closely by a cautious "what did you do...?"

She hadn't meant it to be accusatory; he knew that, but it had still hurt, and not only because it was presumptuous. She didn't know everything about his personal life, but she knew enough. She'd seen enough partners come and go, some more casual than others; she'd commented before on the number of people he'd been intimate with. Once, earlier in his band days, she'd warned him not to become a "groupie hound."

"People in bands were so popular when I was in high school," she'd told him. "Plus girls like the bad boys."

*Joke's on you,* he thought now, recalling something he'd recently seen online. *Because I'm bad at everything.*

He'd laughed at the turnaround when he saw it online, but it seemed a little too piquant now, too direct.

"We're just figuring some things out," he told his mother before disappearing upstairs for the night. "It's nothing major."

Of course, it *was* major, and he knew she'd have more questions if she never saw Susan again. He knew she would probably assume on some level that it was his fault, too. It wasn't like she held him in low regard, he told himself; she was just a little too pragmatic sometimes. She saw a correlation and fed everything that went on into it.

His other major preoccupation this morning was the text he'd received from Susan the evening before.

*Hard fucking night.*

What had happened? And was it something else he'd done to hurt her, or was it totally unrelated? If it were his fault, would she even have texted him? Would she have texted him if it weren't?

*I don't want to be alone right now. Are you busy?*

Of course, he *had* been busy. He thought of himself admiring his dad's guitar, sitting on his dad's couch, yelling at his dad when he'd finally gotten some of the answers he'd needed for so long. He wondered now where Susan was, and if she still wanted to talk.

Evidently not. She hadn't responded to any of his texts afterwards; he'd sent questions, reassurances, and finally—to his embarrassment today—a few that were passive aggressive. She'd finally gotten in touch with him, but he'd ignored the buzzing of his phone because he was yelling at his father, and then she hadn't wanted to talk to him afterwards.

The window had closed, and he didn't know when it would open again.

To make matters worse, he'd already crossed paths with Susan once today, as he made his way to first period. The east stairway was backed up as usual, students pushing past one another to get to class on time, and as he began climbing the stairs he saw her rushing down from the opposite direction, eyes downcast, using her small frame to her advantage as she moved as quickly as possible. She looked up at the sound of her name—briefly, distractedly—and offered Leonard a tight smile and a halfhearted wave as she ducked out of the stairway and back into the halls of the school.

That smile should have been reassuring, but it only served him a twisting feeling in his insides. He sat impatiently through first period, then through second, and when his free period came around, he ducked into the library and found an empty table near the back. There, he slipped in his earbuds and put his entire playlist on shuffle before settling back to continue reading *Atlas Shrugged.*

It was difficult to concentrate, though, and he spent most of the period jotting down lyrics from the songs that came on and doodling stylized logos for the band names. It was better than brooding, even though the two activities would look the same to anyone watching.

On his way to American History he bumped into Jez in the hall. He was heading toward the cafeteria, which was mostly in the same direction as Leonard's class, so Leonard fell into step beside him. Jez immediately launched into how excited he was about putting some extra money he'd found toward a second piece of French bread pizza, gesticulating wildly enough as he demonstrated his expectations for the perfect cheese pull that he smacked a passing student in the face.

"Watch it!" the kid warned, pivoting on his heel to shoot Jez and Leonard a withering look.

Jez was characteristically undisturbed. "I'm watching, but I don't see anything I like!"

"What does that even mean?" the offended student retorted at the same time that Leonard said, "Wasn't that technically a self-own?"

But Jez had already lost interest in the interaction, and as they approached the open double doors leading to the cafeteria he pulled Leonard aside. The jovial personality was still there, but Leonard thought he also detected something else now, too.

"What's up?" he asked, peering into the hall behind Jez to see if he could catch a glimpse of Susan. It was her lunch period, too, he remembered, and although she'd made it clear that she wasn't ready to talk—or had been, but wasn't any longer—he thought that Jez's presence might act as a sort of neutralizer of the tension between them.

Jez made a show of patting him comfortingly on the arm: *there, there, slugger.*

"Nothing, man, I'm just checking in. Word travels fast, you know? Faster than my dad was when he grounded me for stealing the neighbors' cable, anyway."

"People still steal cable?"

Jez just shrugged. "*I* did."

"No, man, I think I'm good. Obviously this is depressing as fuck, but you know. It is what it is right now."

"Did you really score that college girl? Because I don't believe in the whole 'it isn't cheating if it's in a different zip code' thing, but if it's true, let me live through you for a while. Except, you know, without the consequences."

Leonard wondered again whether actually sleeping with Bailey would have resulted in a different outcome. Susan still would have seen the text, they still would have broken up—or whatever was going on—and he'd still be wallowing in his feelings in school today.

But no, he reminded himself, it could have been even worse. Who knew what she might have texted him afterwards?

"No," he told Jez now, "I never slept with her. I'm sure you can find some similar videos online if you're looking for porny stories, though."

"Joke's on you! I already did."

Whatever response Leonard might have made was cut off by the sound of the late bell. With a sinking feeling, he checked the time on his phone and cursed. Mr. Hammell, his American History teacher, liked to deter tardiness by making a public spectacle of anyone who walked in late. Last year Leonard had heard a story of a student being made to take Hammell's lesson notes and transcribe them on the board before he could sit down. Apparently the teacher had completely ignored the student while he wrote out the notes, just lecturing about Reconstruction as if everything were normal.

Jez watched him check the time and grinned knowingly. "Dude, just come eat," he urged.

"They wouldn't let me back in for my actual lunch then," he pointed out, but he was already following his friend into the cafeteria.

He lingered at Jez's usual table while Jez hurried into line, reasoning that the lunchroom workers would only refuse him service later if they gave him lunch now. While he waited, he let his gaze wander around the large room, which was already getting louder now that lunch had officially started.

As far as he knew, Susan always sat with Jez and the others who had lunch that period, but he still hadn't seen her when Jez returned with his overflowing tray.

"You're looking for Susan, aren't you, you dirty dog." It wasn't really a question, so Leonard just shrugged.

"You sound like a pirate," he muttered.

He forced himself to engage in the conversation as Glenn, Hank, and a few others joined them at the table, but his heart wasn't really in it. They all seemed to be making extra efforts to keep the conversation light; he appreciated the sentiment, but what he wanted most was to go home and sit in silence. The demands of being friendly, even with his own friends, seemed too heavy for him right now. Instead, he let himself fade into the background, relying on them to carry the conversation while he faded into the role of observer.

He'd just said goodbye to his friends and was turning to head to English class when Ariel stepped into the hall right in front of him. They'd barely spoken since her earlier rejection of him—*knowing your lips touched another man's*—and he wasn't sure where they stood now, so he just nodded and moved to pass her in the hall. Engaging her in any way seemed like a mistake, and remembering her words still pained him. They'd largely ignored each other on the bus rides to and from school.

But she fell into step beside him now as he headed to class, and when she asked how he was, he didn't know how to answer.

"Depends on who you ask," he said balefully, knowing it was a cryptic reply but not really caring. He just wanted to keep his defenses up and make it through the day, and if anyone was offended in the process, he figured he could deal with the fallout later.

"Is Susan...was it a bad breakup?" she asked, looking sideways at him and then away again.

The assumptions he sensed behind the question irritated him. *You don't get to ask that. Why do you care? We didn't officially break up. I doubt you even know the real story.*

He considered each response, but all he said was, "I don't even know if we're done. It's complicated." Even admitting that much to Ariel bothered him.

They were nearing English now ,and he wanted nothing more than to turn out of the day's lesson and stare at his notebook. He certainly didn't feel like baring his soul to someone whom he had once, however briefly, considered as a potential partner.

"Well, if you need a friend..." She let the rest trail off.

"Why?" he demanded. "Why do you care? You pretty much wrote me off months ago!"

"I didn't mean it that way, Leonard! I thought you might need a *friend.*" It was her turn to get defensive, and despite himself, he felt bad for what he'd said. He wondered if he'd misinterpreted her intentions, a question that grew as she stopped him outside of the classroom door and pulled him into a hug.

He resisted, but she held on for a few seconds more anyway. "I hope you're okay," she said into his shoulder, and the warmth of her breath sent tingles up to his ears and all the way down his spine. He didn't want to notice how different it was hugging her—different body, slightly taller, more curves pressing against him—but it was impossible not to.

His reverie was interrupted by the first bell, and he extricated himself from the hug and felt his face flush.

"I'll be okay," he told her, hoping that it would be enough of a gesture to act as a sort of truce, and ducked into the classroom. He made a concentrated effort to dig out his notebook and textbook, wondering if anyone was looking but unwilling to meet their glances if they were.

Susan was still too upset to function in class, so after second period she'd headed for the nurse's office and begged for the chance to lie down. She hadn't corrected Nurse Bingham's assumption that it was bad cramps; it made her feel warm to accept someone's sympathy, and in any case, the true cause really didn't matter. What mattered was that she needed to be away from people, especially when rumors of the breakup were spreading and changing faster than she could endure them.

The nurse sent a memo about Susan's absence to Susan's teacher and led her to a bed in the back room, pulling a privacy screen around her when she'd gotten comfortable. Susan accepted the two pain tablets and the plastic cup of water she was offered, and then she was left alone.

Nobody else was in the "sickbay," as students referred to the back room, that day, and she was grateful for the relative silence. The room was dim, and the screen around her bed made her feel like the fatally sick love interest in one of the old movies her mom liked to watch. She remembered one about a young man coming back from war to find the woman he loved sequestered in a tuberculosis ward, and she smiled a little at the comparison.

*No one ever died of a broken heart*, her mom had told her the other night; Susan knew that it was meant to be reassuring, but it sounded too dismissive of her current state to be comforting.

She put on her earbuds and lifted her phone, seeing again the unanswered text messages from Leonard before she navigated to her music app. Matt had called them desperate when she told him about the attempted contact, but she wasn't sure. She had negative associations with *desperate,* and it didn't feel right to apply that label in this case.

With a sigh, she reread the messages Leonard had sent in response to her text following J.T.'s unexpected presence in her room:

> *Did something happen?? I'm sorry I didn't see this earlier!*
> *Do you still want to talk?*
> *What can I do to show you that I stopped it before it got too far?*

And, finally, from this morning:

> *I guess I was too late, but I really hope you're okay.*

She knew she would have to talk to him eventually, even if it meant sharing every last detail with him: her painful history with T.J.; the fear and shame that had forced her to keep it a secret from the beginning; her sense of betrayal that Leonard had become friends with him over Thanksgiving break, even though he'd had no way of knowing her feelings on the matter.

Would she be able to tell him all of that? She thought she'd be able to when she texted Leonard, but now that some time had passed, she wasn't sure. The path forward felt unclear again; she didn't know how to navigate the conversation.

She was still pondering these questions at the end of the period. Nurse Bingham popped her head in and tried to persuade her to go to lunch, but the idea was just too daunting. She and Leonard had mutual friends, and they would probably be there, asking her questions that she didn't have the answers to.

"I have some snacks in my bag," she reassured the nurse. "I'll be okay."

After a long pause, the nurse shrugged and said, "it's your choice, honey, but food might help you feel better."

It was true: she did have some snacks in her bag, but nothing particularly satisfying. She sat up in bed, her back against the wall, and tried to enjoy the granola bar and apple that she'd grabbed on her way out the door that morning.

She felt a little more grounded when lunch was over. She thanked the nurse for her kindness on the way out and headed toward her next class, filled with a new resolve to talk to Leonard and try to find a way forward. Despite her fears and the general dread that had consumed her over the past several days, she still believed that he was telling the truth. Maybe that, combined with the context for last night's text and her subsequent silence, would be enough. She hoped so.

As if she'd somehow manifested him from her thoughts, she turned the corner and found him at the opposite end of the hall, standing next to a very pretty girl—what was her name? Ariel? Yes, that sounded right—outside of a classroom. He looked unhappy, maybe even angry, so she was surprised when the girl caught him up in a tight hug. The surprise on his face was readable even from her distance down the hall—and so was the surrendering, the sinking into her embrace, that followed a few seconds later.

*This is two strikes.*

She watched as he broke away, said something to her, and disappeared into the classroom.

*Two strikes. I can't believe this.*

She recalled his account of the way Ariel had rejected him, and wondered numbly why he would be hugging somebody who had dismissed him in such a way.

*Now what?*

And then, as the numbness broke under the impending anger and confusion, she ducked into a nearby bathroom before she could be seen and locked herself in the last stall to cry again.

*From the journals of Susan Ingram:*

Dec. 22

I had an appointment with Dr. Campbell the other day, and surprise, surprise, she had a lot of helpful things to say. It's like she's completely dialed in to what it's like to be a teenager, and especially a teenaged girl, which is helpful because she usually knows what's going on. Lately, I feel like I never know what's going on.

It would have been helpful to see her earlier, honestly, but I missed a week because of the holiday, and then she was on vacation for a couple of weeks. She gave Mom and Dad a million instructions to keep a close eye on me, monitor my mood, etc. etc., and so if I wanted to do something like hurt myself, I couldn't. Not that I even felt like doing that. I just want to lie around and dissociate. Seriously. It's better than whatever this is. (I'm gesturing vaguely, but you can't see it.)

Anyway, Dr. Campbell listened to everything that's happened, and she was able to offer some clarity. I think I've said this before, but every time I see her, I feel a little better for a while. Then it wears off, and reality crashes back in, and I'm back to hating everything. Surprisingly, that didn't happen the same way this time.

Thank God nobody's ever going to read this, because I need to get this out. It's like poison, holding it inside.

She asked me if I've ever considered that I might have an addiction to self-harm. It's a fair question, even though I've never really thought of it that way. But she said everyone has addictions, and they're not all major or harmful, but they're still around. She suggested that maybe I'm addicted to hurting myself because I'm trying to fill a gap somewhere else in my life. Like, maybe drug addicts do it to feel good for a while, because they don't feel good about their normal lives. And maybe sex addicts are trying to find affection or acceptance or validation (her words) to replace the affection they never got as kids. There was more to it, but you get the point.

So I had to think about it. I guess I'm trying to fill a void, I don't know. She asked if it gives me a feeling of control, and that's true. Like, I've been hurt a lot and I couldn't control any of it, but at least I'm in control with this one thing. I guess that makes sense.

She also asked a lot of questions about Leonard, which was even harder to untangle than the cutting thing. Do I think Leonard would intentionally hurt me? No, I don't. Like I said a while ago, he's pretty sincere. And I believe him when he says he stopped whatever might have happened at the party.

Do I think he made a stupid decision? Of course.

There was no reason for him to be there in the first place. Not the party, but that room, with that girl.

Do I worry that he's still talking to her? Yeah, it's scary, and I can't know for sure. Dr. Campbell is right—I have to choose to either believe him, or accept that I think he's lying. But I also don't have to do that right this second. It's already been weeks, but if it takes longer, that's fine, according to her.

Last question: is he similar to J.T.? No. Just no.

My homework this time is to decide whether I want to talk to Leonard before we go back to school. This limbo state, not talking but not really broken up, technically, can't last forever, and it's impossible to avoid him at school.

Can I separate the pain of this event from what happened back then with J.T.? Is it possible to move forward from something like that? He's fucked me up so badly, and he knows it. Dr. Campbell says that it will always hurt, but it won't always be <u>present.</u> It won't define me. I guess that's possible, but I don't know if I'm there yet.

I hope she's right, though.

# Chapter Twenty-Seven

Heavy snow began to fall the night before the last day of classes in the fall term. The previous week had offered a dizzying sequence of sunlight and dark clouds, back and forth over and over again, making it difficult to adjust to the shortening days as the first day of winter loomed closer. When the days were clear, it was easier to forget that sunset was arriving closer and closer every day; on the overcast days, however, the window of hope for sunlight felt unsettlingly limited.

Leonard felt himself withdrawing as he counted down the dwindling days remaining before winter break. He'd relented the previous weekend to go to Glenn's for band practice, but it felt flat to him, perfunctory, as if he were merely going through the motions. Glenn, insightful as always, persuaded him to stay over after practice that night. He tried to sound bored as he made the offer, but Leonard suspected Glenn actually wanted to keep an eye on him. The concern might have aggravated him at another time, but that night he found himself grateful for the company.

"Things will turn around," Glenn told him late that night, or maybe very early the following morning. He was half-watching an old Christmas special on the TV in the basement, some Claymation movie that Leonard had no desire to watch. That animation style had always bothered him for some reason. It was just creepy.

Leonard paused the game he was playing on his phone and set it down next to him on the couch. "I guess so," he muttered, trying to sound unconcerned.

Glenn knew him better than that, though, and he wouldn't let his friend get away with such an escape tactic.

"At least Susan acknowledged your existence the

other day, right? That's got to mean something."

It was true. He'd been finding it harder and harder to get up for school on time, and a couple of days ago he'd been forced to drive himself in again. After school, he'd been heading over to the student parking lot when he'd seen Susan standing under the awning, braced against the biting cold and looking miserable. He'd taken a chance and asked if she was okay, and offered her a ride home when she admitted that she'd missed the bus. She would have summoned a ride on her phone, she explained without looking at him, but her parents were both busy at work, and she was basically broke.

"I took her home," Leonard told Glenn again. "But we didn't talk until I pulled up to her house and she said 'thanks' and got out." He'd played the ride over and over again in his mind, but he couldn't find a missed opportunity for conversation. The possibility just wasn't there; it was evident in her body language, the way she huddled into herself in a way that had nothing to do with the bitter cold that his van's vents struggled to dispel.

Remembering the warring emotions he'd felt in the van—wanting the ride to both last longer and end as quickly as possible—he added, "She seemed angry that she had to accept the kindness of the ride."

Glenn snapped his fingers dramatically. "But it *was* a kindness, and at least she didn't have to freeze her balls off."

"I don't think she has balls."

"You know what I mean."

Leonard was thinking of that conversation tonight, watching the snow fall and begin to accumulate on the ground. He watched first from the dinner table and then from his bedroom window, and by the time his mother poked her head in to say goodnight, the school had already announced that tomorrow's classes and events were canceled.

"Happy early Christmas break," his mother told him before she closed his door again. Even through the closed door, he could hear the gentle *swish-swish* of her slippers on the hallway carpet as she moved away. She'd been buying them from an all-natural source for years, some kind of sheep or alpaca farm.

He looked down at his own feet and found a hole in his sock.

He snaked a finger into the hole and wriggled it absentmindedly, lost in thought while he watched the snow fall. It was late enough that the traffic lights in town would have switched to a steady blinking yellow signal at all but the busiest intersections. Most nights he couldn't see the glow of the signals, but he found that if he leaned all the way to the left and looked down toward the end of his street, he could just barely make out a soft yellow light reflecting off of the snow. The roads were empty, and the unbroken snow seemed inviting, like an opaque chrysalis into which he could climb and hibernate until spring.

Of course, sitting at the scarred wooden table that served as his desk and looking out at the snow from the warmth of his room, it was easy to forget that the snow only looked peaceful. He loved the way it muffled sound, but it wasn't something that offered physical comfort.

He remembered writing a short story in middle school, something about a man who falls out of his second-story window and breaks his legs during a massive snowstorm. He freezes to death right outside while his family sleeps. Now, as then, he wondered what it would feel like to freeze to death. He'd heard that the body actually started to feel unbearably warm, which seemed to him like cosmic irony. The thought of somebody tearing off heavy layers of clothes while they froze to death was both terrifying and funny—not "ha-ha" funny, but "what the fuck is wrong with the world" funny.

The story he'd written hadn't made much sense, and he'd never shared it with anybody, but the general surreal tone of the plot still resonated with him when it snowed.

Christmas was less than a week away, and while everyone else was probably celebrating the early end to the term, he was contemplating dying alone under the weight of a blizzard's worth of snow. That didn't feel right to him, even in his loneliness, even knowing that he felt alone because he'd made a conscious effort to distance himself from everyone for the past couple of weeks.

To make up for the sense that he was wasting the gift of more time away from school, he moved to his bed and picked up the video game controller on the table beside him. He was already sixty hours into an immersive role-playing game, saving the world by fighting off dragons and rebuilding the castle and town his character had been chosen to defend. The open-ended storyline appealed to him; the game allowed the player to choose a combat class, a riding mount, a house style, and even a love interest.

This last had been a difficult choice. The game offered more than dozen options, and he'd eventually chosen a pretty herbalist who turned out to be an exiled witch from another kingdom. He'd originally been drawn to the character model—flaming red hair; lots of curves; usually accompanied by a cat that later turned out to be her familiar, a sort of witch's animal assistant—but playing it tonight, he was distracted by the way she almost looked like Ariel if he squinted his eyes.

He sighed. He and Ariel had spoken a couple of times since the awkward hug outside of the English classroom, but it had been strained, and eventually it seemed easier to fall back into old habits and not try to converse at all. In the immediate aftermath of that day, he'd worried that Susan might have seen the hug and gotten the wrong idea, but she hadn't said anything about it, even during the strange drive to her house when he would have been a captive audience, so he thought maybe he was in the clear. It wasn't a mistake he intended to repeat, anyway.

As usual, once he started thinking of Susan he had trouble stopping. He paused the game and scrolled his social media for a few minutes, but there wasn't much to see on her profile. She'd made a few updates since Thanksgiving, the most recent of which were song lyrics about a man who kept screwing up.

He didn't recognize the lyrics, but he felt sure that she'd shared them with him in mind. A quick search told him that they were from an old Aimee Mann song, and he wondered if it were from an album in her father's collection. He wished he could comment or text her and ask about the song, but he was afraid that would be foolish.

Scrolling through social media was only depressing him. He would have liked to talk to Susan, even if it were just to say hello, but instead he turned back to his game with the intention of losing himself in the storyline for a few hours before going to bed. Meanwhile, the only comfort he could take was in the knowledge that he hadn't bothered to check Ariel's profile. It was cold comfort, but then, it was a cold night, and it was better than nothing.

Saturday, two days from now, would be Christmas Eve.

This in itself wouldn't ordinarily be an issue of anxiety for Susan, other than the familiar "I can't believe another year is gone" awareness, but then, this wasn't an ordinary holiday season for her. Aside from the fact that she might technically still be in a relationship—which would make it her first Christmas in one—her parents had, surprisingly, warmed to the idea of having Leonard over for some of the celebration.

They knew that she hadn't spoken to Leonard much lately, but she hadn't told them of the intimate hug she'd witnessed between him and Ariel. What angered her most was that she wasn't afraid of feeling foolish—she was most worried that her parents would view him differently. It annoyed her that she didn't want them to think badly of him.

As a result, her plan was to explain away his absence over the holidays by simply telling her parents that he had other plans. It seemed simple enough, and it probably would have worked, if not for what she learned of her brother's own plans for the holidays.

"We're going to a party at Nolan's house for Christmas Eve," he told her as he wolfed down a massive breakfast. He'd woken up hung over, and according to him, greasy food was the best cure. "Me, Thomas, and a few others. But we're going to pre-game here, while Mom and Dad are volunteering."

This last wasn't surprising. Every Christmas Eve, her parents would help wrap presents and serve food at the community center. It was an outing that Susan and her brothers hadn't been invited to for years because they wouldn't behave when they used to come along. The community center leaders seemed to have long memories, and the grudges they held were decidedly uncharitable for what was supposed to be a charity effort, but, as her dad would often say, "it is what it is."

What *did* stop her short was the idea that Thomas would be at her house in a couple of days, drinking, in her company without any adult supervision. The thought chilled and nauseated her, and she felt herself completely freeze for a long moment. For what might have been the hundredth time, she was reminded how much easier it would be to avoid Thomas if she told Matt what he'd done.

Matt would undoubtedly cut ties with him, and if the rest of their group found out why, they would probably follow suit.

But she also knew that once she told him, there would be no taking it back. *Victimhood* wasn't how she usually thought of the situation; *preyed upon* had only entered her consciousness after hearing the term in a podcast about serial killers. She didn't accept the labels, and she knew that everyone who knew would use them to describe her.

No, it was better to take herself out of the situation entirely, whenever she could. Her parents were usually only gone until six o'clock or so when they volunteered, but a lot could happen before then.

Natalie would be busy, she knew. She and her parents usually visited out-of-town relatives over the holidays.

With a sigh, she picked up her phone and texted Leonard.

Christmas Eve broke sunny and cold, but at least it hadn't snowed again. The roads were clear, which allowed Leonard much more freedom to devote his attention to his own anxiety as he drove to pick Susan up from her parents' house.

The text had surprised him, and he was nervous about seeing Susan. She'd promised to explain everything—the mysterious text, the subsequent disappearance, all of it—and although he was eager to reconnect, he simply had no idea what to expect. Nearly a month had passed already since their last real conversation, and that was more of an argument than anything else.

She answered the door immediately, as if she'd been watching for his arrival. She'd dyed her hair jet black since the last time he'd seen her, and the makeup she wore was equally dark. Her black coat was open to reveal the Type O Negative hoodie underneath. Only her bright purple nail polish and the silver buckles on her boots broke up all that darkness.

She greeted him politely, her tone not unkind but not exactly friendly, either, but refused his offer to carry her oversize bag. He wondered what was in there, but sensed it would be a mistake to ask. Instead, he turned to the weather and the songs playing on the radio, taking what encouragement he could from her perfunctory replies. This side of her was unfamiliar to him, though, and by the time he pulled into the driveway he'd grown overwhelmed by her refusal to engage. She'd promised to explain everything to him when they were together, but he was beginning to wonder whether it might not be better to leave the details alone. Whatever she'd experienced over the past month—not just with him, either—she'd obviously been greatly affected by it.

"Like I said, nobody's home this afternoon," he commented as he unlocked the door and stepped into the house. "We can hang out down here, though." He paused. "Neutral ground, and all that."

He saw from Susan's expression that she understood what he meant. Not too long ago, they would have headed upstairs for the privacy of his bedroom as soon as the house was empty. Every possible moment in which they could be alone was irresistible: moments where they could kiss, or explore each other in ways that clothing did not allow, or simply lie together on the bed, his warmth at her back igniting little fires within her as they spooned. She'd told him once that she loved how much taller he was, because being wrapped up in him made her feel safe.

That memory ached now, and he wondered if she would be able to feel safe in the same way with him again.

They sat at opposite ends of the couch, and she accepted *Atlas Shrugged* when he picked it up from the end table and passed it to her.

"Did you like it?" she asked. It was a simple question, but after Leonard answered he thought he could feel some of the tension dissipate from the room.

"I really did," he said. "Your little notes in the margins were fun, too."

It was true; she'd left little notes, questions, exclamation points, and dog-eared pages throughout the book. He resisted adding his own comments, but especially during the time they were apart, her words seemed to bridge the physical and emotional distance that had grown between them. He wondered briefly if returning the book was a mistake. If she left today with the intention of never speaking again, he might never again have such a link to her.

She flipped through the book as these thoughts distracted him, then set it aside. "Thanks for giving it a chance," she said, and for the first time, a little of her usual personality flickered in her eyes.

"Of course."

After a long silence, Susan confessed, "I don't know how to do this, exactly." She'd been twisting her rings around on her fingers, playing with them nervously, sometimes sliding them up to her fingertips and then back down.

Leonard cleared his throat. "I'm not sure what to do here, either, but clearly we both have some things to say. Maybe we should just see what happens when we start talking."

"Okay." She hesitated, then looked up from her hands. "How?"

"Well...what have you been up to since I—since around Thanksgiving?"

*Since I got back from college and you saw Bailey's picture* is what he'd started to say. It felt shitty to dance around the words, but it seemed risky to approach the event head-on.

Susan sighed, but there was no exasperation in it. She'd planned this visit with a determination to exorcise everything—her experiences, her fears—but now that she was sitting across from him, the weight of such a confessionary conversation seemed almost overwhelming. The feeling of vulnerability that came with that weight frightened her.

"I don't want to talk about this, but you should know," she said, and then she started talking.

The story came out in a rush, and she was aware as she related her experiences that it was probably jumbled and difficult to follow at points. But she recounted everything to him: her time at camp; her repeated victimization at T.J.'s hands; her fear when she'd learned that Leonard and T.J., now Thomas, had become friends over Thanksgiving break; even how he'd propositioned her just days ago. She barely looked at Leonard as she spoke, her eyes jumping between different points in the room, and when she was finished, she felt a confusing sort of pride at having explained everything without crying more than a few stray tears.

Silenced stretched between them afterwards, as Leonard digested what she'd told him and tried to formulate a response that could communicate what he was feeling. He mulled it over, fitting the pieces into place, until at last a sort of understanding bloomed in his mind.

"I know I hurt you over the party," he said haltingly. "Was it worse because I was getting to be friends with—with *him*—and then him being around made everything more complicated?"

"*Yes,*" she whispered, and it was almost a hiss. She'd only just recently begun to come to this understanding herself, but once it entered her thoughts, she knew that Leonard needed to know all of the connections. "Yes," she repeated, louder this time, and then: "He's so fucked up, and it seemed like he was changing you, too, just by being around him. Then I texted you that night, when he came after me again, and you didn't respond, and I thought, *of course. Why would he, at this point? He knows who's out there now.*"

"I wasn't doing anything like that. I haven't. I went to visit my dad."

"Did you really?" she gasped, and the emotion invested in those words surprised them both.

"Yeah. It was disappointing. I pressed him for answers, and he got angry and I left." He exhaled slowly. "He has a whole new family, and it was his wife's idea to get in touch that day, to make amends or something. I really don't know. But fuck it, at least now I know. That door's closed now. If he wants to be a good father, he can be that for his new family."

"Do you mean that?" she asked softly.

He considered this. "I think so. I don't know, but I can't deal with that right now. It's just a big shitshow that I never should have tried to revisit."

"I'm sorry," she said, and she meant it.

"Me, too. For everything."

And at that moment, Susan's defenses dissolved, and she moved over and sank against his chest, pulling one of his arms around her shoulders. "I want to feel safe with you again," she murmured into his chest.

"I want that, too," he confessed, staring at the ceiling as he spoke. "But I don't know how to do that."

"Why were you hugging Ariel at school?"

She'd planned to ask this question at the beginning of their conversation; it had seemed important even that morning. Asking it now, out of nowhere, threatened to break whatever tentative truce they'd arrived at, but she still needed to know. She knew that if she didn't ask it now, she might never feel able to. It was the last major sticking point in Leonard's actions, though, and ignoring it would put the truce at a false start.

She was oddly relieved when he shrugged. It was such a genuine reaction: no deception or hesitation attached to it. "I think she's a hugger. She wanted to know what was going on lately, and she thought I needed a hug because I looked depressed. Which, obviously, I was, but I don't think a hug from her was going to solve anything."

"She was so shitty to you, though."

"Maybe she feels bad about that. I don't know—I hope she does. It definitely killed any interest in her. It confirmed early on that there's no chance of a connection there."

"Is that final?"

"Yes, definitely."

She shifted enough to look up into his face, and what she saw there was enough to convince her that he was being truthful. For the first time in what felt like forever, she felt the doubt and shame that gripped her begin to unclench. She believed him.

He experienced his own changes as she held his gaze. *I've come very close to losing everything*, he thought, *and it was a harsh lesson. I can't make that mistake again.* He felt no certainty that he would never do anything again to compromise their relationship, no universal affirmation of his determination, but he was resolved to try, and he thought that trying might be the best thing—the most honest thing—that he could do.

It was snowing outside now, the flakes fat and heavy, the kind of snowfall that his mother used to call "world muffling." It made him think of Christmas as a child: the smell of gingerbread in the house; the way he would track fallen pine needles across the living room floor as he played; the excitement and terror of waking to find definitive proof in the number of presents laid out for him of whether he had been well behaved that year.

Anything had seemed possible then, and it struck him now that becoming an adult meant that the reality of what was possible shrank year by year, the number of possibilities losing size and magic until it was simply a matter of following the singular path that you'd chosen for yourself, or been assigned by somebody else.

It seemed unfair but unsurprising.

The only thing to do, he supposed, was to commit yourself to a path when it presented itself.

He relaxed into the silence, took in his surroundings—the freezing snow outside, the warmth of Susan's body against his own—and mused that, whatever might happen next, this particular path was enough.

# Epilogue

Late on New Year's Eve, Leonard's phone buzzed to alert him that he had a new email. Half asleep, he squinted into the dimness of his bedroom and grasped blindly with his free hand until he found his phone. His other arm was pinned beneath Susan, who was already asleep next to him, the slim line of her body curled against his. Even facing away from him, he could hear the deep evenness of her breathing.

He carefully extricated his arm from beneath her pillow and raised his phone to his face, squinting in the sudden brightness of its screen. The clock on his home screen read 11:21p.m.

The email had no subject line, but he sucked in his breath when he registered his father's name.

*Leonard: I don't know if I'm doing the right thing by writing—*

He sat up straighter, accidentally waking Susan as he did so. She mumbled a question, but he was too focused on his phone to respond.

*Leonard:*

*I don't know if I'm doing the right thing by writing. Your email is listed on your social media. It might not be a good idea to get in touch, but I've been thinking about your visit, and I think some clarification is necessary. I doubt your mother would agree, but now I know that there are still some things you should probably know.*

*Yes, my wife, Caroline, did encourage me to call on your mom's birthday. She wanted me to put the past to bed, for our family's sake. But it's not what you think.*

*I was hoping to talk to you, too, but I was afraid. Then you came to my house, and I knew the door was open.*

*I know that I was never a great father, but I swear I tried. I had good intentions. But…God, Leonard, I don't know how to say this. Your real father is out there, but it's not me. I'd like to try to be, if we can patch things up, but your biological father is someone else your mom was with. I can't tell you more; it's not my story to tell.*

*When you were born, I was still so in love with your mom that I was determined to make it work. I stuck around as long as I could, but the pressure—you'll understand someday, but I hope it's not under the same circumstances.*

*So I drank, and I sabotaged my relationships, and the family started falling apart and I left. I couldn't handle it.*

*And now I'm dropping this bomb on you, and I know that if you didn't talk to me before, you sure won't now. I'm sorry for that. But please don't ruin your relationship with your mother. She's a good person—better than I am; I can say that for sure. It was an impossible situation.*

*I don't know how to end this, and I'm sorry for that, too.*

*—Martin*

Leonard read the email once, twice, and then once more, just to be sure he understood it correctly. Several parts of the message infuriated him, but more than that, he felt confused. Everything in the email, if it could be believed, left him unmoored. What was the purpose of the message? *I'm not your family. I want to be your family. Your mom had an affair, but she's a better person than I am.* None of it made any sense, and he couldn't wrap his head around it.

Of course, one new thing was clear: everything he had taken to be truth was wrong.

Susan propped herself up next to him, and he handed her his phone wordlessly. She read it carefully, murmuring "wow" and "oh my God" a couple of times, and she closed its screen before handing it back to him.

"Are you okay?" she asked, pushing some hair off his forehead and behind his ear.

"I'm pretty angry, actually," he admitted. "I never expected to rekindle a relationship with the man, but I would have at least liked to..." He shrugged, gestured helplessly. "I thought I could understand things better if I got to talk to him. Which, I guess now I do. But now nothing makes any fucking sense anymore."

"Did you ever suspect?" There was no judgment in her voice, but he felt stupid nonetheless, like there had surely been signs that he'd missed. How could there not be?

He shook his head.

"I thought he was a deadbeat dad. Now I find out he's…what? Just a deadbeat? And now I find out that the only reason he called at all that day was to get to me. To tell me all of this and ruin my life. But I still don't get why! He'd already disappeared. Why come back just to cut the final ties? You know what, fuck him. *Fuck* him."

"You're right. Fuck him," she agreed, and in some bizarre way, the exchange was so strongly reminiscent of her response to Ariel's rejection of him, on that night so many months ago, that a laugh escaped him.

"Seriously, what's the point of caring? With all of this going on, that asshole called me *Dracula*." He laughed again, and Susan allowed a cautious smile to escape, but she showed no surprise when the laughter turned bitter and devolved into a torrent of tears.

She held him while he cried, pressing her cheek against the top of his head and stroking his back. She murmured reassurances, and when his sobs stopped shaking his shoulders, she handed him some tissues.

"You know that whole 'new year, new me' thing?" she asked quietly.

Leonard sat up to face her and nodded. "Yeah."

"Well, happy fucking new year."

"No way."

"Check."

He twisted his neck and saw that the clock beside his bed read 11:59p.m.

"I don't think this is something that can just be left in the past," he muttered, but there was no anger in his words. He just sounded tired now.

"No, I wouldn't even suggest that. But you don't have to face this alone. We'll do it together."

Susan reached out and turned his face toward hers. She still wore the dramatic makeup she'd put on for their dinner date earlier that evening, and it both enhanced the brightness in her eyes and emphasized her pale skin. She hadn't reapplied her lipstick after dinner, but in the dimness of the room, her lips still looked deep with color.

Leonard sighed, willing himself not to cry again. They kissed, and he turned to lie on his back. He lay against Susan's chest, and he closed his eyes when he felt her arms around him again.

"Happy fucking new year," he echoed, looking up at the fishnets covering half of his ceiling. He wondered if they still represented an escape to him—*When the ceiling is complete covered, I'll disappear*—and could find no easy answer. Everything was overpowered by the warring emotions stirred by the affection of Susan's closeness and the magnitude of Martin's confession.

He knew he had to learn more; it was simply too momentous to be ignored.

But for now, for tonight, he didn't think he could

face the future. He'd been looking backwards for so long, stewing in the past, and having to look ahead seemed strangely threatening.

No, he decided. For the moment, the best place to be was the present.

The future held new, staggering challenges, and they would have to be addressed soon, but that was a problem for tomorrow.

# About the Author

Nicholas Beishline lives in central Pennsylvania, where he teaches English at a major university and drinks enough coffee that the local coffeeshops recognize his name and order. When he isn't teaching or writing, he can be found out and about with his wife and son, or inside with their many animals. He can be found on Instagram at @nickbeishlinewrites, which includes links to more of his writing. *No Evidence But Himself* is his first novel.

CPSIA information can be obtained
at www.ICGtesting.com
Printed in the USA
BVHW070848020622
638704BV00003B/4